EVIDENCE OF A FOLKTALE

EVIDENCE OF A FOLKTALE

NICOLE SCARANO

Evidence of a Folktale: Autopsy of a Fairytale Book 5

Copyright © 2025 by Nicole Scarano

All rights reserved.

No part of this book may be reproduced in any form or by any electronic or mechanical means, including information storage and retrieval systems, without written permission from the author, except for the use of brief quotations in a book review.

Paperback ISBN: 978-1-964112-06-0
Hardcover ISBN: 978-1-964112-07-7

Cover by Fay Lane
Character Art Mary Begletsova (@marybegletsova)
Crime Scene Sketches by A.M. Davis (@amdavis_author)
Interior Formatting by Nicole Scarano Formatting & Design

*No generative AI was used in the writing or design of this book, and this book may not be used to train AI models.

Contents

Author's Note	xi
Criminology of a Character Recap	1
Chapter 1	5
Chapter 2	27
Chapter 3	43
Chapter 4	51
Chapter 5	65
Chapter 6	83
Chapter 7	107
Chapter 8	127
Chapter 9	139
Chapter 10	157
Chapter 11	171
Chapter 12	189
Chapter 13	199
Chapter 14	211
Chapter 15	227
Chapter 16	249
Chapter 17	265
Chapter 18	283
Chapter 19	305
Chapter 20	313
Chapter 21	327
Chapter 22	347
Chapter 23	373
Chapter 24	389
Chapter 25	401
Chapter 26	423
Also by Nicole Scarano	429
About the Author	431

For China. I wrote Cerberus so that you would forever be with me

Author's Note

This is a darker crime series, so some of the crimes will be violent and weird. Rest assured, I don't write about SA, but this isn't a cozy mystery. There is romance of course, but it will be a sexy PG13 (think Vampire Diaries, Grey's Anatomy, etc.) - I also want to point out that while I did do research into crime scene investigation, I will be speeding up some of the processes. I also set this story in a fictional town (Bajka means Fairytale/Fable/Story in Polish) so that I can take liberties with some of the procedures and police structures. Plus with the fairytale elements, I wanted the freedom to bend the rules of nature.

Criminology of a Character Recap

After Isobel 'Bel' Emerson's hospitalization after the Darling kidnapping case, Sheriff Griffin gives her two weeks off. Bel and the reclusive millionaire Eamon Stone are finally dating, and Dr. Frank Victors (Bel's plastic surgeon) invites them to a private island owned by Dr. Jake L. Hyde for a charity event. Dr. Charles and Anne Blaubart (who they met at Wendy Darling's wedding) are also at the resort. Anne is hostile towards Bel, and she constantly folds blue gum wrappers into origami butterflies.

Halfway through their first romantic vacation, Bel meets two men she's convinced are somehow the same person. This suspicion, along with a news report confirming the man she saw was a mafia leader, leads Bel & Eamon to uncover a black market surgery deep in the jungle that specializes in altering criminals' faces. FBI Agent Jameson Barry takes over the investigation after Jake L. Hyde goes missing (who's later found to be an alias. He never existed), but before they leave the island, Bel notices one of Anne's butterflies in the illegal surgery.

The origami inspires her and her partner Olivia Gold to look into Anne's past to learn why a surgeon's wife would be in a black market doctor's office, and Eamon meets Bel's family for Thanksgiving (The Darlings are there too!). A body being found in a farmhouse wall cuts her investigation & holiday short, though. The victim's been dead for years, and they discover it's the farmhouse's owner, yet he's still paying his bills and 'living' in the house. Bel realizes the property is a front. She assumes drugs, but the police uncover an underground freezer where a serial killer froze over 40 women to death, giving them each a handful of matches to burn before they died while he watched from the cameras.

As they investigate the horrifying case, a college student with ladybug earrings goes missing. They don't believe she's a

Matchstick Girl, but when Bel and Griffin go to interview the suspect Jax Frost (a cameraman at their local news station who's also an award-winning photographer), they find a ladybug earring outside his backdoor. Having probable cause, they enter the house. The attic is sealed with a massive lock, but before they can break it, Jax Frost walks in and shoots with an automatic rifle. He wounds Griffin, but the sheriff kills him in the shootout. Bel then checks the attic, where she rescues the college student. They also uncover proof that Jax Frost is the Matchstick Girl Killer.

With the case closed, Bel and Olivia collect evidence from his victims. They find a blue gum wrapper origami butterfly in one of the frozen girl's hands, and Bel is convinced that somehow Anne, the black market surgery, and the Matchstick killings are connected. Eamon is on a business trip, so she leaves her dog Cerberus with her friend Violet and drives to the victim's family. They tell her their daughter had an older college friend named Annalise who also went missing. Annalise was known for chewing gum and folding the blue wrappers into origami butterflies.

Bel wonders if The Matchstick Girl Killer kidnapped Annalise too, but she surgically altered her face to become Anne Blaubart when she escaped but her friend didn't. Dr. Victors consults and tells her that's impossible. Annalise & Anne's eyes are too different to be changed by surgery, so Bel comes up with a new theory. What if Anne used her husband's connections to become Jake L. Hyde to help women like Annalise escape their pasts? She suspects the black market surgery started with pure intentions but became a criminal destination when Anne needed money. Bel drives to Charles Blaubart's office. She pretends to need a surgical consultation for her neck scars as an excuse to invite him and his wife to dinner, but she sees a photo on the wall that scares her. It's Dr. Blaubart and Jax Frost, with Annalise in the background. Bel realizes the men were friends, and that was the last time Annalise was seen. Bel flees the office afraid.

Eamon is still on his business trip when he overhears the news. There was a fatal car accident in Bajka. Bel is dead.

He rushes home distraught. He sees Bel's body in the morgue but realizes her scent is wrong. The dead woman is a Jane Doe surgically made to look identical to Bel. This means Bel is still alive, so he searches for Ewan Orso, the bear shifter dating Olivia. Eamon agreed to let Ewan live under his protection if he told Olivia he was a shifter, but he didn't. Eamon tells her the truth instead (much to her horror), and that Bel's alive. The trio searches for Bel with the police but can't find her.

Bel wakes up in a basement surgery with Charles Blaubart over her and Anne unconscious beside her. He confesses he's Jake L. Hyde, and the black market surgery was his. He was failing medical school, so he made a deal with a devil. The deal gave him a black magic scalpel that can perform the impossible. But magic comes at a price. It killed his wife, Anne, and he spent years trying to surgically recreate her in other women. Annalise is his most recent victim. Blaubart had an arrangement with Jax Frost. He helped him find girls to murder, and Frost would let the ones Blaubart wanted go so they'd be afraid enough to let him operate and turn them into his dead wife. Unfortunately, Charles became unhappy with every new bride, so he murdered them and started over. Annalise is wife number 7. He plans to kill her and put her in the preservation tanks with all his other deceased wives though, so he can transform Bel into Anne number 8 with his scalpel. Bel fights him off and rescues Anne, who's really Annalise. The women run down a snowy mountain to escape. They almost don't survive, but hours later, they encounter a road and are rescued.

Blaubart escapes the FBI, though, so while Bel is in the hospital, Eamon locates him and brings him to justice. He finally returns to Bel's side and tells her they need to talk...

Chapter One

"WE NEED TO TALK."

Eamon's words echoed throughout the hospital room, their dread bouncing off the sanitized walls, and Bel pushed herself to a seat. Dr. Charles Blaubart, a well-respected plastic surgeon, had made a deal with a devil over a decade ago, but the black magic used to bring him wealth had claimed his beloved wife as the sacrifice. The surgeon had spent years trying to recreate her in the bodies of living women he conned into loving him, and as fate would have it, he'd set his violent sights on Detective Isobel Emerson for his eighth bride. Faking her death for the world to mourn, Charles had dragged her deep into the mountains to carve apart with his cursed scalpel until her face was no longer her own, but that of a dead woman's. Only he miscalculated Bel's will to live, to survive even when faced with the impossible. She'd escaped his hell of a surgery to flee down the mountainside, surviving despite the desperation and falling snow, which was why she was currently confined to the hospital instead of preparing for the holidays at home.

"What's wrong?" she repeated, aching for Eamon to touch

her, to reach out his hand and grip her fingers as he rejoiced in her survival, but his fists remained firmly in his lap.

"The hospital isn't the place," he answered.

"No, it's not," she agreed. "But you brought it up, and if you believe it's worth a conversation, there's no point putting it off. If something's bothering you, just tell me because I can't bear any more turmoil. I survived a monster and a mountain because I knew you were waiting for me. You were the only thing pushing me to fight when I bit Blaubart's neck to escape, when I ran coatless through those frozen woods. All I wanted was to make it home to you, so if something's wrong, please tell me. I'd rather know now than worry about you while trying to heal."

"I'm killing you," he said, his words so abrupt that she leaned back as if seeing more of him would explain his meaning. "You're in the hospital yet again, and I'm the one that put you here," he continued before she could speak.

"What are you talking about?" Bel pinched her eyebrows at the towering man sinking into the chair before her. Escaping a serial killer was what had landed her in this bed. Her millionaire had played no part in it.

"I'm the reason you're here. I'm responsible for all your hospital visits over the past year. I'm why so much death and violence have entered your life. You've been lucky so far, but luck always runs out. How long before I get you killed?"

"Eamon, what has gotten into—?"

"I put those scars on your throat," he cut her off. "I almost killed you with my own hands. And if that wasn't sin enough, I moved to Bajka, luring Alcina after me. She almost killed you, and if your dog hadn't interrupted her magic, I might have bled you dry on the forest floor."

"You wouldn't have." Bel leaned forward to emphasize her words. "You could never kill me."

"But I came close." He jerked to a stand, his chair skidding backward, and she hated herself for flinching at his force. "Then Abel kidnapped you because he was jealous of me. I brought you onto the Darling case, where one lunatic almost blew you up and another shot at you. I introduced you to Charles Blaubart, who dragged you into the mountains with every intention of carving up your face until you were no longer my Isobel. Every time I do something, you suffer the consequences. When the news broke of your accident, there were hours when I thought you were dead. I cannot describe the relief I felt when I realized the body on the table wasn't yours, but it was a brutal wake-up call because one day it will be yours. One day, you won't escape. I'll eventually get you killed, and I won't do that. I won't let you die. I love you too much to bury you."

"What are you saying?" Bel balled her hands into a fist, the injuries on her palms so painful that it stalled her tears of panic. "What are you saying, Eamon?"

"I think you're safer without me."

"No." The word was a bullet from her mouth.

"Isobel…"

"No, I'm not."

"Isobel." Eamon grabbed her fists, unfurling them to ease her discomfort. "Seeing you in this hospital bed is a pain so ugly that I'm not strong enough to bear, and I love you enough to put you first. I won't be the reason you die."

"I'm not going to die."

"I know. Because I won't be selfish. I'm the problem, and if I remove myself from your life, you'll be safe."

"Stop."

"I can't be selfish, Isobel. I can't stay and let one evil after the next befall you until you end up in the morgue."

"So, you've just decided then?" she spat, unsure if she should slap him or dissolve into tears. Imagining their reunion was the only thing that drove her to brave that endless snow, but with the stroke of a few words, he'd butchered her reason for surviving. "You're leaving me?"

"No, I'm talking to you," he said, lacing his fingers through hers. "I would never just leave you. I couldn't hurt you like that, but I need you to understand why I feel this way, because if I get you killed, I'll never forgive myself."

"Stop saying that."

"But it's true, and you know it. Your problems began when I entered your life."

"But you swore to never leave me."

"I also swore to protect you, yet here you lie." He released her hands as if he was unsure what to do with his body. "Do you think I want this? Do you think I want to leave you? I would rather die, but if leaving saves your life, I'm willing to suffer. I would rather love you from afar than love you dead in the dirt. My old self would never put your safety above his desires, but I refuse to return to the monster I once was. You've changed me, and I'm putting you first. If we didn't at least have this conversation, you'd wake up one day and realize I'd brought so much suffering into your life, yet refused to do anything to stop it. You would resent me."

"No, I wouldn't."

"Yes, you would. You're smart. You have self-respect, and you'd eventually look back and see that I never took action to resolve the harm I knowingly caused you. You would hate me for never putting you first. What's more, I'd hate myself. I've seen wicked men love women before. Those girls often paid the price for loving men too selfish to save them from themselves. I won't let that be you."

"Eamon…" she trailed off as the tears came because she wanted to fight him. She wanted to scream and rage and beat him with her fists, but did he have a point? Would she hate him if he never grew self-aware enough to at least admit his concerns? She didn't blame him for her almost deaths, but if he blamed himself yet never acknowledged his guilt, would she grow to resent him?

"I don't want this," his voice broke, and Bel swore tears threatened his eyes. Eamon never cried. She didn't know he could, yet his black irises glistened as he stared down at her.

"I want to keep my mouth shut and pretend I'm not to blame. I want to ignore that I'm hurting you, but I hate myself for even considering that. This is new for me, willingly accepting pain to save someone else. But for you, I'd burn the world, myself included. And if saving you means leaving so you can live a long and beautiful life, I'll do whatever's necessary to keep you out of the grave."

"Please stop," she begged.

"Isobel..."

"Stop saying goodbye."

"I'm not saying goodbye," he argued. "I'm discussing this with you, but I need to express my feelings first. You are the love of my life. Please see that I only want your safety."

"I know that, Eamon. I've always known that."

"So promise me you'll think about what I've said, okay? Really think about it because what would your family say if they knew I was to blame for your near deaths? What would Griffin say if he knew I was the reason monsters kept coming for you, yet I never removed myself from the equation? What about your father? What would he say if he learned I was the one who ruined your throat yet stayed despite the constant threat to your life?"

"You what?" a horrified voice interrupted, and both Bel and Eamon's eyes snapped to their intruder.

"Dad—" Bel started, her mind scrambling for an explanation for what he just heard. How long had he been standing there? How much of their discussion had he witnessed?

"What did you say?" Her father ignored her as he stepped for

Eamon, his finger pointing accusingly at Bel's neck. "Did you do that to my daughter?"

"Dad—"

"Yes." Eamon's shoulders sagged with defeat. "I'm the one who left her disfigured."

"That's not the whole story!" Bel shoved the blankets off her legs and stumbled off the bed.

"Get out," Reese growled.

"Dad, stop." Bel feared she might choke on her panic.

"Get out!" her father roared, and with an expression of unbridled pain, Eamon stepped for the door. "I don't want you near my daughter again."

"I am sorry," Eamon said. "More than you'll ever know." He grabbed the handle, and Bel launched herself at him. But before she could cross the tiled floor, Reese caught her waist.

"Eamon!" she shouted as he crossed the threshold. "Eamon, look at me."

He obeyed, and this time, there was no mistaking his tears.

"This conversation isn't over," she growled at him. "Don't you dare leave me."

Eamon stared at her without a word.

"You'll be home when I get released, right?" she asked, refusing to let him walk out of her life so easily.

"Bel." Her father dragged her back.

"Swear it!" she demanded, fighting her dad's hold with every ounce of strength left in her aching body. "Do it, Eamon. I order you to do it. Swear to me that you'll be there when I get home."

"I'll be there." Eamon addressed his promise to her father, a battle of wills passing between the men as if he were warning Reese that no matter what he wanted, Bel owned him, and her word was law. "I'll be there."

Evidence of a Folktale

"WHERE'S EAMON?" Briar, Bel's oldest sister, asked as she plopped onto the couch beside her. "After Thanksgiving, I figured he'd be at all our family holidays going forward."

"He had to work," Bel lied. It was Christmas Eve, and she hadn't heard from or seen Eamon since her father kicked him out of the hospital. Upon her discharge, Reese had insisted she spend the holiday with him. She'd rented a vehicle since hers was in pieces, but Griffin refused to let her return to the station until after the New Year, so here she sat at her dad's house, Eamon's words festering inside her. For all she knew, he'd packed up his mansion and vanished into the world to change his name yet again so she'd never find him.

"No wonder you look so miserable. I would be too if I had to spend Christmas without Flynn." Briar patted Bel's thigh as they watched her husband help Reese put the kids' gifts under the tree. Briar, Flynn, and their two toddler boys were sleeping over for Christmas Eve, but their four other sisters, along with their husbands and children, were coming in the morning, and the living room was overflowing with presents. Normally, the colorful wrapping paper filled Bel with joy, but her father had barely spoken to her since the hospital, and the other half of her soul was ignoring her. There was nothing joyous about this holiday.

"All right, that's all the gifts," Flynn said, oblivious to Bel's misery. In his defense, their sons were finally old enough to understand Christmas, and his head was in the clouds as he prepared for that morning's magic. "You ready for bed?" He extended a hand to his wife.

"I should be," Briar said. "It's after midnight, but I'm so excited. I can't wait to see the boys' faces."

"Well, this Santa is tired," Flynn said. "Night, Bel."

"Night guys." Bel watched her sister climb the stairs with jealous tears in her eyes. Eamon should be here to carry her to bed. This wasn't how their first Christmas as a couple was supposed to play out.

Her vibrating phone interrupted her self-pity, and her heart stumbled at the name on the notification.

EAMON

Merry Christmas.

Two words. A single phrase. That's all he wrote, but after days of nothing, she knew. He'd kept his promise. He hadn't left her, not yet at least, and she burst into tears as she typed a response...

And then deleted it. A text was too small to contain the scope of her emotions, so she shoved her phone into her pocket and climbed the stairs to knock on Briar's bedroom door.

"Bel?" Flynn pinched his eyebrows in question as he answered the door. "Are you okay?"

"Yes... sorry." Back in her father's house, habit made Bel forget that she couldn't just barge into her sisters' rooms anymore. "I can talk to Briar tomorrow."

"Actually, I forgot to eat the cookies the kids left for Santa," Flynn said. "They'll be bummed if they wake up to whole cookies. I should go take a few bites." He smiled graciously at his sister-in-law and left the room to give the siblings privacy.

"I feel bad for kicking him out," Bel said.

"Don't be." Briar patted the mattress beside her. "With two young boys, we're always too tired to stay up late, but with family here to help, he can afford to stay up for a beer to watch a show that isn't animated. He'll have a blast."

"Okay." Bel climbed onto the mattress and collapsed onto her stomach like she used to when she was little.

"I can't remember the last time you crawled into my bed." Briar rubbed her back before pulling the blankets over them. "You okay?"

"No," Bel said. She'd been young when their mother had

passed, and Briar had stepped into the maternal role for her. She hadn't needed mothering in recent years, but she was suddenly twelve again and in need of her big sister.

"Is it Eamon?"

"Yes."

"He isn't working, is he?"

"No."

"What happened? Did you two break up?"

"No," Bel said. "I don't think so. I hope not. We were fighting... well, having a conversation I didn't like, and Dad interrupted at the wrong moment. He heard something that's true, but he doesn't understand the context, so he kicked Eamon out of the hospital. We haven't talked since, and I'm afraid it ruined us."

"Conversations, no matter how difficult, don't end healthy relationships," Briar said. "I saw you two at Thanksgiving. You seem to have a strong connection, so I doubt one fight will ruin things. Can I ask what the conversation was about?"

"Eamon blames himself for my problems this past year, and he stupidly believes I'll be safer if he leaves."

"Oh..." Briar blinked as she realized she might've put her foot in her mouth. "Why does he assume that?"

"Abel kidnapped me because he was jealous of my attraction to Eamon," Bel said, omitting the story of her scars. She already had one family member ready to murder her boyfriend. She didn't need another. She also didn't care to explain to her sister that Eamon's immortality demanded he consume human blood.

"Then he dragged me into the Darling kidnappings only for me to almost get blown up," she continued.

"Blown up!" Briar shouted before clapping a hand over her mouth to keep from waking her sons in the next room. "Blown up?" she whispered. "Oh my god, Bel."

"Right..." Bel's cheeks turned pink. She'd forgotten who she was speaking to for a moment. She usually hid the fatal stories from her motherly older sister. "I guess I should call more."

"You think?" Briar looked on the verge of tears. "Blown up, Bel? You were almost blown up?"

"The kidnapper placed explosives around the property," she explained. "He hoped to raise the death toll when Wendy and ultimately the police started searching for John and Michael. I nearly died when the IEDs were triggered, but Eamon saved me."

"Oh my god, Isobel." Briar used her full name as she rested a hand on her back. "Oh my god. I recognize your line of work is dangerous, but blown up? I'm going to be sick."

"That's why I don't tell you everything," Bel said.

"But you should. I'm your sister. I should know these things. Maybe don't tell the others, but I raised you, Bel. You can talk to me."

"I know. That's what I'm doing right now."

"I realize I'm busy with the boys, but you were my honorary kid first. You can always come to me."

"But I don't want to scare you."

"News flash, baby sis. I'm always scared. I was afraid when Dad was on the force, and now I worry about you. It's part of loving a cop."

"I think that's happening to Eamon," Bel said. "He blames himself for everything, including taking me to the island where I met Charles Blaubart. He thinks Charles targeting me was his fault."

"I don't know the whole story. Clearly." Briar gave her sister a pointed look. "But how could he have known that surgeon was a lunatic? And as for that Abel guy? That wasn't Eamon's fault, either. Falling in love doesn't warrant a kidnapping, so unless I'm missing something, he isn't guilty in either situation. He didn't hand you over to those men. He took you on vacation. Plus, didn't Dr. Victors invite you?"

Bel nodded.

"So someone you both trusted invited you to the island and

introduced you to Charles. Eamon isn't to blame for that. And as for the Darling case. I guess he involved you, but you're a cop. Kidnappings are kinda your job."

"They are," Bel said. "Just not when I'm the victim, and that's what haunts him... and almost watching me explode."

"Oh god, please." Briar shut her eyes. "Don't say that."

"Sorry."

"It's okay. I just can't handle picturing my baby sister like that."

"I don't like picturing myself like that. I really thought I was going to die."

"But Eamon saved you?"

"He's saved me more times than you realize."

"How?"

Bel froze, trying to work out a plausible answer that didn't involve her boyfriend's flesh being flayed from his ribcage.

"Never mind." Briar waved her hand dismissively. "Enough bomb talk. It's Christmas." She shifted against her pillows so she could run her fingers through her sister's hair as she returned her focus to Bel's relationship. "It seems Eamon isn't to blame. Of course, I could be missing something, but is he at fault? You don't have to tell me. Just think about it for yourself. Will you wake up one day and hate him for jeopardizing your safety, or will you wake up next to the love of your life?"

"He asked me the same thing."

"And only you can answer that, but this story might help. We never told you because it happened before you were born. Then, once you were old enough to understand, you wanted to be a detective, so Dad didn't want to scare you. But you know that scar on his leg?" Briar asked.

"The one he's always had?"

"Yeah, above the knee. That's from a gunshot."

"A gunshot?" Bel jerked off the pillow. "Dad was shot?"

Her sister nodded.

"Dad was shot, and you never told me?"

"He didn't want you to be afraid," Briar said. "Plus, it wasn't serious."

"All gunshots are serious. Griffin was shot while shielding me during our last case. I was almost shot during the Darling case. They are always—"

"You were shot at?" Briar blurted. "Oh my god, Bel, is there anything else you'd like to spring on me?"

"No... I don't think so."

"Good lord. Seriously, Isobel Emerson, start calling more. You are my sister, yet I didn't know you were almost shot and killed. Good god."

"Eamon saved me from that, too."

"Of course he did." Briar smiled. "The more you talk about him, the more I think this story will help."

"Okay."

"A month before Rose and Luna were born, Mom wanted to go on a babymoon," Briar said. "Dad worked weekends, so he switched shifts with a night officer so he could take Mom on their mini vacation. That night, dispatch received a domestic disturbance call. Dad assumed it was just a couple fighting, but when they arrived, they found the father threatening his family with a gun. The man opened fire on his son, but Dad jumped in and saved him. The boy lived, but a bullet grazed Dad's thigh.

"He went to the hospital, which canceled their trip, and Mom blamed herself. If she hadn't wanted to go, he wouldn't have switched shifts, and he wouldn't have gotten shot. Her guilt damaged their marriage, but she couldn't forgive herself. She believed Dad's scar was on her shoulders until Dad received a card delivered to the precinct. The little boy he'd saved drew it to thank him, so Dad took it home to Mom. He told her she needed to forgive herself because while he got hurt, he also saved a kid. A child wasn't murdered by his own parent because of him.

Evidence of a Folktale

"That card changed mom. She still worried, but she came to terms with Dad always being in danger. He defended the innocent, and she could live with the guilt if it meant that kids got the chance to see the future. His job was cruel. It eats at you when you see the things he saw, so he needed home to be his safe place. He needed Mom to be his refuge, and when she passed, we took up that mantle. Until her death, Mom protected Dad's mental health. She loved and supported him no matter what work threw at him. It's why they were so good together. In a world that was consistently dangerous for him, she was his sanctuary." Briar reached across the mattress and captured Bel's hand.

"It sounds like Eamon is experiencing what Mom went through," she continued. "Now, if he's to blame, that's a different story and you should leave him, but if he's going through the same guilt Mom dealt with, he needs to decide. Can he live with it and be your safe place, or is it too much for him? And if it's too much, he isn't the right man for you, anyway."

"He is the right man for me," Bel insisted.

"Then let him express his guilt and fear, and then tell him Dad's story," Briar said. "Because, like Dad, you almost got... well, you know... yet you rescued two kids. You also saved that surgeon's wife when you carried her down that mountain. As much as I hate it, you risk your life every day to help people because it's your calling, and Eamon needs to accept that. Like I said, if you're afraid you'll wake up ten years from now and hate him for putting you in harm's way, you absolutely need to leave. Please don't stay with a man who doesn't prioritize your safety... which doesn't sound like Eamon, though. Honestly, I think this conversation was good for you two."

"You do?"

"Yeah. It proves he's self-aware enough to realize that if he's the problem, he should remove himself. A selfish man would stay, regardless of the consequences. The fact that he's willing to walk away to save you proves he adores you. But should he actually leave? Only you can answer that."

"I won't resent him in ten years," Bel said. "I will hate him if he leaves me, though."

"Then tell him that." Briar rubbed her back, and Bel shut her eyes. How many times had her older sister rubbed her back when she didn't feel good as a kid?

"And I don't know what Dad overheard, but talk to him. We all love you too much for this fighting."

"I love you guys too."

"You're an amazing person," Briar said. "I like to take credit for that."

"You should." Bel sank further into the pillows. "I'm sorry you had to raise me, though. That's a lot for a teenager."

"I'm not." Briar settled beside her and wrapped her in her arms. "You were and always will be my baby sister. It was an honor to raise you. Plus, I can claim responsibility for all your heroics since I'm the one who taught you goodness."

"There it is." Bel smirked. "Thank you. For talking. For everything." She kissed her sister's cheek.

"Always, Isobel… just start calling more, okay?"

"Okay… I should give you your bed back. Flynn will miss you."

"Flynn will be fine." Briar hugged her closer. "He and Dad probably grabbed Cerberus for a boys' night, so you stay here."

"Yeah?" Bel shut her eyes, barely able to form words as sleep overtook her.

"Yeah." Briar kissed her cheek.

"I love you," Bel said, or at least she thought she said it. She was too tired to focus.

"I love you too, little sis. Merry Christmas."

Evidence of a Folktale

"WHY ARE YOUR BAGS PACKED?" Reese asked as he entered the kitchen the following morning.

"Because I'm going home," Bel answered from where she sat at the table with a pot of freshly brewed coffee, Cerberus lying at her feet to warm her toes. Briar's words had lit a fire inside her, and she wouldn't rest until she metaphorically slapped Eamon upside the head. She might physically slap him as well if the conversation called for it. He'd had his turn to voice his fears. It was her turn to speak.

"But it's Christmas," her father argued.

"And I belong with him today," she said.

"Isobel." Reese used her full name, which was never a good sign. "Did I fail you as a father? Did I not love you enough?"

"Of course you loved me."

"Then why are you returning to an abuser? By his own admission, that man almost killed you. You're forever marked by him, yet you want to go back so he can hurt you again."

"Eamon isn't an abuser, and he won't hurt me."

"Don't make excuses for him. You're better than that."

"I know," Bel said. "I deserve the world. You, Mom, and Briar taught me that."

"So why reduce yourself to a man's punching bag?" Her father's shoulders sagged, the pain of what he suspected she'd endured eating him alive, and Bel ached for the people in her life. She wasn't the only one who paid the price for hunting down the world's monsters. Everyone she loved suffered alongside her.

"I've always known I wouldn't love someone unless he loved me the way you cared for Mom," she said, her voice softening. "For me, that's Eamon."

"Isobel—"

"Dad, please sit," she interrupted because she couldn't leave this house until her father understood, but every second she spent apart from Eamon was another second that the hole in her heart

19

burned wider. "Because it's true. Eamon left these scars on my neck, but you don't know the whole story. The truth... you can't judge until you learn it, but before I tell you, I need to ask you a question because what I have to say will change everything."

"What are you talking about?" Reese sank to the chair across from her.

"The truth was thrust upon me, and I can never unlearn it, but you have a choice I didn't," she said. "I don't have to tell you everything. I can tell you just enough so you understand, but if I confess the entire truth, it'll irrevocably alter how you see the world."

"Of course I want to know."

"Don't answer now," Bel said. "Griffin knows some of what's going on, and he's made it very clear he wants to learn nothing more. I'll give you the same option, and I need you to think about how much you want me to divulge. I'll tell you some because you need to understand Eamon isn't the villain. He's saved my life more times than I can count. He used his own body as a shield for mine when the bullets started flying. That man would die for me. He's killed for me, and I've been dying to tell you the truth, but the extent of what I share is your decision. You deserve the choice I never got."

"What do you mean, he's killed for you?" Reese pinched his eyebrows at his daughter.

"Remember my first case in Bajka?" she asked. "The woman who built people into furniture? She was living next door and came after me in the woods."

"I recall."

"Eamon stopped her. Cerberus helped, though." Bel reached below the table and scratched her pitbull's head. "But it was mostly Eamon. She was... like him, and she wouldn't stop coming for me. He killed her to save my life. He also killed the kidnapper in the Darling case. You visited me in the hospital. You saw how he beat me up. The official report says I fought

Peter Pann off, and he broke his neck in a fall. That isn't the truth."

"Eamon broke it?"

"He did. I was on the ground, and I couldn't move. I was going to die, but Eamon came for me. He always comes for me." She paused, wondering if she should continue because her father looked seconds away from passing out. "You might think these deaths make him violent, but they don't… not when you know the truth." She decided to barrel onward. She'd started this. Her father deserved she finish it.

"What did you mean *'like him'*?" Reese asked, circling back to her earlier comment. "You said your neighbor was like him. Was the kidnapper in the Darling case the same?"

"In a way," Bel answered. "You were at the morgue when Eamon figured out Blaubart hadn't killed me with that staged car crash. Haven't you wondered how he knew I was alive when my own father confirmed I was dead on the table?"

"Yeah…" Her dad paused. "Griffin believed him immediately, and I worried they'd both lost their minds… You said the sheriff knows?"

"Some, yes."

"I guess I assumed that…" He took a deep breath. "I assumed Eamon realized it wasn't you because you two are intimate, and he noticed a discrepancy on your skin that I wouldn't recognize."

"It wasn't that, and you know it."

Reese sagged in his seat, and Bel could practically see the gears in his brain fighting to process his swirling thoughts.

"He's always made me nervous," he finally said. "I liked Eamon, but something about him terrifies me. A bone-deep, ancient kind of fear… there's a reason for that, isn't there?"

"Yes."

"And I'm not going to like it?"

"I don't know. I don't mind, but it took time for me to come to terms with it. It's why I'm giving you options."

"Is he human?" her father asked, but Bel just stared at him. Seemed he was figuring it out on his own.

Reese cursed and ran a hand over his salt-and-pepper hair. "That makes me more nervous for your safety."

"It shouldn't." Bell stood up and crossed the kitchen to pull him into a hug. "If there's one person powerful enough to protect me, it's him. These scars resulted from something else. Something neither of us could control. Something he shouldn't have been able to fight, yet he did. Eamon fell for me the moment he met me, and he's been fighting to keep me alive ever since. But there are things in this world beyond our understanding. Terrifying things, but despite his brutality, he isn't one of them. He's beautiful, and I don't belong here today without him."

"You swear to me he isn't hurting you?" Reese said. "You aren't returning to a man who puts his hands on you?"

"I would shoot him between the eyes if he ever tried, and he knows it," Bel laughed.

"I suppose you would. I worry about you, that's all. I want you safe and happy."

"And Eamon is my happiness. When you decide how much of the truth you want, you'll see that," Bel said. "And if it makes you feel any better, I didn't jump into a relationship with him until he proved himself. The first moment I realized he would rather die than hurt me was during the Darling case when he shielded me with his own body. There was blood everywhere, Dad. His blood, not mine. I forgave him for my scars that day, because while he didn't die, he'd been prepared to. He didn't even think. He just stepped between me and the threat, and he paid the price. It's hard not to love someone who would die in your stead."

"How come you never told me that?" Reese asked, his tone doing little to hide his offense.

Evidence of a Folktale

"Because if I told you, I'd have to admit the truth about him, and I wasn't sure you were ready. He didn't protect me like a normal person would. He didn't throw me to the ground to cover me from the flying debris. When I say shield, Dad, I mean shield. If you'd seen it, if you knew what happened to him so he could save my life, you would forever be in his debt."

"You're scaring me, baby girl."

"I'm sorry." She kissed his cheek as she finally pulled away. "It's why I won't tell you anymore. Mull it over, and decide how much of the truth you're willing to learn. It's a lot, though, so take your time."

"You mean there's more?" he asked. "More to him than finding out he was a human shield for you."

"A lot more. Some he hasn't even shared with me yet."

Reese cursed as he leaned back in his chair, his face drained and limbs limp. "You really love him, don't you?"

"I do…" Bel laughed, the emotion bubbling in her chest. She loved Eamon Stone, and this was the first time she'd admitted it to herself.

"And you're safe with him?"

"In every sense of the word."

"And you can't be convinced to spend Christmas with your old man?" He looked up at her with a hopeful expression.

"No, Dad." Bel cupped his cheek. "I love you. I always will, but I don't belong here. I need to fix my relationship. Let me know what you decide. Eamon won't care. He'll let me tell you whatever I want."

"Okay…" Reese trailed off. "I love you. So much, and I may be just a human parent, but if that man ever hurts you."

"I'll call in the big guns," Bel laughed.

"I don't care what he is or how rich he is or how tall he is. I will come for you."

"I know, Dad. He does too. Trust me, he does too, because he knows where I get my personality from." She kissed his head one last time before calling Cerberus to the front door. "For such a terrifying man, I'm pretty sure Eamon is afraid of two people, and you, my dearest father, are one of them."

BEL DIDN'T BOTHER KNOCKING before she unlocked the Reale Estate's impressive front door and barged in, dropping her luggage on the foyer floor with a loud thwack. Cerberus raced through her legs and disappeared down the hall in search of the home's owner, and Bel barely shut the door behind her when an alarmed Eamon burst into the room. His hearing had clued him in to a car's arrival, but by his expression, he hadn't expected her to walk into his mansion this Christmas afternoon.

"Isobel?" he started.

"I've had a lot of time to think," she interrupted. "And I've decided that no, you don't get to make me love you and then leave."

"Isobel—"

"You had your chance to talk. This is mine," she cut him off again as she stepped further into the foyer. "I love you, Eamon Stone. Do you hear me? I love you, and you swore to me you'd never leave. I intend to hold you to that promise. I understand your fear. I understand why you feel responsible, but you aren't, Eamon. You fell in love. You took me on vacation, and those aren't sins. They are signs you care, and I cannot fault you for that. I appreciate your willingness to put me first, to sacrifice so I don't have to. It makes me love you more, but you don't get to leave when things get difficult."

"I'm not leaving you because things are difficult," he interrupted.

"If you'd purposely thrown me in harm's way, that would be a different story, but you couldn't predict those tragedies would happen. You aren't to blame. I'm a cop, and the unfortunate truth of my job is that every officer leaves the house in the morning not knowing if we'll make it home. You didn't feed me to the wolves. Those monsters took me, so I don't blame you for what's happened. I forgave you for scarring me. I forgive you for taking me on vacation and accidentally introducing me to a serial killer, but I will never forgive you if you walk out on me."

"Isobel, it's not that simple."

"Yes, it is because we're not that kind of couple. You don't get to decide for me. You don't get to leave because it's what you think is right. We're either in this together, or we aren't who I thought we were."

"You were dead!" Eamon shouted so loudly that Bel flinched, and she unconsciously stepped backward as the custom chandelier shook above their heads. "You died, Isobel!" He pounded a fist against the wall, causing the plaster to splinter below his skin, and then, with an agony she'd never witnessed from him, he sank to the floor as if his heart had given out.

Autopsy Report

CERBERUS

PROD.NO.
SCENE TAKE SOUND
DIRECTOR
CAMERAMAN EXT. INT.

CINEMA TICKET
ADMIT ONE
9891102

CINEMA TICKET
ADMIT ONE
9891102

Chapter Two

"Do you think I want this?" Eamon shouted from his crumpled position on the foyer floor. "Do you think I want to leave you? You are the love of my life, Isobel. Look at this house. Do you see the furniture and décor? Haven't you noticed that it's all stuff you like? My entire home is a love letter to you. This isn't my house. It's ours. You belong here with me, and I want you every day for as long as you live. I hate the thought of leaving. I cannot stomach the idea of never seeing you again, but you were dead. You left me first. You died, and for those unending hours, I'd lost you." He slammed his head back against the wall, the life bleeding from his eyes. "Obviously, it was a mistake, but you ceased to exist, and I can't suffer that again. I cannot bury you. I won't do it. If you die, I die."

"Eamon..." Bel trailed off, a different brand of fear taking root in her gut at the shattered man before her.

"I won't bury you," he repeated. "Don't make me do that. Please don't make me..." his voice broke. "You were dead, and now that I got you back, I refuse to lose you again. I would rather live across the world than put you in the ground so young. You have so much life left to live, and I won't be the reason it's cut short. I won't be the reason your family has to attend your funeral."

"Eamon." Tears flooded her eyes until his outline blurred. "I'm so sorry. I was so caught up by everything that I never stopped to consider what my faked death did to you."

"And you shouldn't have to. What you suffered was far worse."

"It doesn't change the fact that you lost me." She crossed the foyer and sank to the ground, straddling his lap until she sat chest to chest with him. "For those first hours, you did lose me. I was dead for you, and I can't imagine the pain you went through. If I ever lost you, I wouldn't survive."

"Don't say that."

"It's true." She caught his face and forced him to look at her. "I can't lose you either. It's why you can't leave me. I need you... more than you realize. You won't bury me, but I won't live without you. Don't make me."

"But I'm not safe." Eamon gripped her hips as if he feared she'd stand up and vanish into the ether. "Look at all I've done to you."

"Eamon, you're a powerful man, but you aren't responsible for everything. You aren't God." She kissed his lips gently before continuing. "And have you ever stopped to look at things from another angle? You scarred me, yes, but that was because Alcina cursed you. She needed a sacrifice to complete her spell, and if she'd succeeded, her black magic would've owned you. Imagine the horrors you would've inflicted on this world if I hadn't been the sacrifice. I was the one who made you resist. I was the reason you fought back. When you think about it, I saved you."

"Isobel." He pulled his face from her hands.

"It's the truth." She wrapped her arms around his neck, refusing to let him escape the conversation. "I saved you from becoming a monster. I gave you a reason to fight, and you're a free man because of it. My scars are proof I survived. They're proof you did the impossible when you defied Alcina, and I hate hearing that you think you disfigured me. You always make me feel beautiful. Don't undo that."

"I'm sorry for what I said at the hospital." His grip tightened on her hips, but she didn't move, letting him cling to her. "I didn't mean that you were deformed. I just meant I hurt you."

"I know." Bel ran her fingers over his chiseled jaw. "You love me, scars and all. You love them because they remind you we're worth fighting for."

"We are." Eamon's head collapsed against her chest, all the resistance leaving his muscles, and Bel tightened her hold on his neck.

"And you blame yourself for Abel, but your only fault was getting my attention. Abel was unstable, and he fixated on me. If I hadn't fallen for you, I would've dated someone else, and he still would've come after me. The only difference is that another boyfriend couldn't have saved me. I escaped his basement ten minutes before you arrived. Ten minutes, Eamon. If I'd just waited, you would've broken down that locked door with your bare hands. You were why I never gave up hope when I was with him. I knew you were coming for me."

"But I'm why you moved to Bajka," he argued. "If I hadn't attacked you in New York, you would've never met him."

"And he would've kidnapped another girl," Bel said. "He wasn't stable. My presence made him snap, but I'm not special. Another woman would've eventually triggered him, and she might not have had the strength to escape. Am I glad he took me? Of course not. But you didn't cause it. Abel was a broken man, and he was going to kill whether he met us or not. Then there's the Darling Case," she continued, the words a flood from her mouth now that she'd started. "Wendy hid the truth about her brothers until it was too late to un-involve me. We didn't have all the information, and while we lost lives, we saved two children.

Kids, Eamon. We saved kids. The FBI tried to help them, but they didn't decipher the clues." Bel jabbed a finger into her chest. "I did. I found those boys, and you helped rescue them. We did that, and you cannot blame yourself for a madman's actions when we're the reason that family is alive. They were at my dad's for Thanksgiving, playing with my nieces and nephews and my dog because of us. I never want to step on an IED again, but I also refuse to watch a ten-year-old drown. And even if you didn't introduce me to the Darlings, the police would've eventually gotten involved. Think about how that IED blast would have ended if you weren't there."

"Don't say that."

"It's the truth. I would've been called in to investigate a kidnapping, but without you, I'd be in pieces."

"Isobel." He gripped her biceps as if it would silence her.

"So, don't you see all the good being with me does?"

"But I couldn't save you from Blaubart," he argued. "That man was planning to cut apart your face and turn you into another woman."

"But taking me on vacation didn't make him kidnap me. Charles' obsession with me was largely my fault. I'm like a dog with a bone, and you know it. Once I have the scent, I can't let it go. I wouldn't stop digging into his wife, and I made a mistake. I ventured into the lion's den alone, and he took advantage. You had no responsibility in what happened. I am more to blame than you, but in the end, I saved Annalise. Fleeing that mountain was traumatizing, but she survived because of me. She didn't die because of you."

Eamon tilted his head in a question.

"Don't you see?" Bel cupped his jaw again and forced him to meet her gaze. "You make me a better cop. I'm braver because of you. It's been terrifying, and yes, I've landed in the hospital, but Griffin was shot in a case that had nothing to do with you. I was in that shootout too. I could've died in that hall-

Evidence of a Folktale

way. My job is dangerous with or without you, but I'm ten times the officer I used to be because you guard my back. I know you're always coming for me, so if you leave, I won't be any safer. I'll eventually end up in another hallway with another gunman, only I won't have you to shield me. You'll no longer be there to stop the bullets, and I need you to feel brave, to be fearless."

"You're a little too fearless." Eamon smiled up at her, and a weight fell from her shoulders at the sight. "I can't lose you."

"So I'll stop being reckless."

Eamon burst out laughing. "I don't think you have it in you."

"Fair. So, we'll make a plan then," she said. "Half the time, I get in trouble because I think I'm doing something harmless. From now on, I won't make any moves without alerting you or another officer. If I want to interview a doctor because I suspect his wife, I'll wait for you. If I recognize a madman's clue, I'll let you go first."

"I get that you're trying to prove your point, but Isobel, if this is what you want, you need to be serious about calling me. I cannot help you if I can't find you."

"But I am serious. I don't particularly want to run down a snowy mountain without a coat while being shot at again. I want us to work, and if our relationship means I'll sometimes go toe-to-toe with the world's most dangerous creatures, I swear to you this Christmas afternoon on this floor that I'll change my approach. If Griffin, Olivia, a deputy, or my father aren't with me, I'll make sure you're informed of my every move."

"I should embed a tracker in you," Eamon teased as he lifted her wrist to his lips.

"Hard no, but you can track my phone."

"Already do that."

"I'm aware." She leaned forward and kissed his forehead.

"But it isn't always enough. I can't help you if you disappear without a word."

"I've learned my lesson. Trust me. Mankind isn't the top of the food chain, so I'll let you take charge."

"I don't want to take charge," Eamon said. "I just want to keep you alive."

"I want to stay alive too." She leaned back and extended her hand to him. "So, do we have a deal? Do we work on our communication skills so the Blaubarts, Abels, and IEDs don't happen again? I'm willing to do whatever it takes because you can't leave me."

"Like let me embed a tracker under your skin?" he asked.

She playfully tapped the side of his head before extending her hand again. "Except that. I'm not a dog that you microchip."

"Careful," Eamon said. "Cerberus can hear you."

Bel rolled her eyes. "Do we have a deal?"

"Only if you promise me something."

"Okay."

"If you ever feel I'm to blame, tell me. If I ever make you feel unsafe, make me leave."

"That's not going to happen."

"Isobel, I'm serious. I've seen what happens to the women loved by selfish men. They always suffer the consequences. That won't be you."

"Yes, I promise." Her face sobered. "If I'm ever threatened by your actions, I'll tell you, but until that day comes, you aren't allowed to walk out on me."

"I didn't bring this up to hurt you," Eamon said, still not taking her hand. "I didn't suggest leaving to control or insult you."

"I know that... now. I wanted to hate you for this, but I talked to Briar. I guess my mom experienced similar emotions when my dad was shot. She felt guilty because she'd been the one to request that he switch shifts, but in the end, she realized Dad didn't need her guilt. He needed her support. He needed a safe space, and she gave that to him... I need a safe space to come home to, Eamon, and I pray that's you. My sister helped me realize that your willingness to leave was proof of just how much in my corner you are."

"Because I am in your corner," he said. "I don't want to leave you. I don't even want to sleep without you. It's been so long since I had you in my bed that your scent has faded, and I'm losing my mind. But I'm trying to do the right thing."

"You did the right thing. You put me first." She waved her hand between them to remind him she was waiting. "And I love you for it. But for god's sake, Eamon, do we have a deal, or are you going to leave me hanging?"

"Say it again."

"Say what?" she asked.

"You know."

Bel lowered her hand and wrapped it around his neck. "I love you, Eamon Stone."

"Again," he whispered as their lips brushed together.

"I love you."

"Then we have a deal." Eamon kissed her, his arms pulling her so tight that she couldn't breathe, but she didn't care. She sighed against his mouth, her fingers winding through his hair as she pulled him close. His hands on her waist bruised her skin. Her nails dragging against his head stung his scalp, and their kiss turned desperate as they sealed their deal on the foyer floor. The tile was cold, but Eamon was warm, and as her sweater joined her jeans in a heap, their heartstrings drew them another stitch closer. Their fear and anger and reconciliation mixed with their love. It was raw and messy, filled with tears and moans and bruised knees. It was beautiful and honest, filled with their promise to each other. It was endless and breathless and sweaty, and when Bel's shaking body collapsed on his heaving one, she felt the truth in his grip on her bare hips. He wasn't going anywhere. She was his home, and he'd designed his house to be hers.

"I'm glad you came to talk," he finally said through his gasps for breath. "I got in my car at least once a day to visit you, but then I remembered your dad's face at the hospital, and I chickened out."

"I knew it," she smirked.

"Knew what?" he asked.

"That my dad is the only person Eamon Stone is afraid of."

"And you. I'm definitely afraid of you." He slapped her ass playfully, and she slid her glistening body up his chest to kiss him.

"Good. If you're afraid of me, you won't leave."

"You do know if I'd left, I probably would've made it as far as the next town before I turned back."

"Absolutely no discipline. How embarrassing." She shook her head in mock disapproval.

"Thank you for forcing me to talk this through so I didn't ruin us. You're right. We aren't that couple, and I'm sorry I acted like it. I've never loved anyone the way I love you, so my emotions get the better of my rational brain sometimes."

"In your defense, you saw my dead body. If I walked into the morgue, and Lina pulled back the sheet to reveal your face, I would… I don't actually want to picture that. How did you figure out it wasn't me?"

Eamon dragged her seductively over every inch of him as he buried his nose in her hair. "Your scent. It was all wrong. Your blood too. The taste was foul."

"You tasted what you thought was my corpse's blood?" She jerked off his chest to glare at him.

"I had to be sure."

"Gross." She gave him an exaggerated gag. "But thank you for figuring it out. And thank you for not leaving behind my back while I was at my dad's."

"I'm not that stupid. I'm sorry my words came across as a final decision and not communication, but I'm not at my best

Evidence of a Folktale

when you're in a hospital bed. You told me once if I ever stepped out of line, you'd pin my hide to the wall, so I knew if I abandoned you, you'd hunt me down to do just that."

"I'd never do something that crazy." She deadpanned, and he pinched his eyebrows at her until she laughed, curling her body tighter against him as her drying sweat chilled her bare skin.

"I would never disrespect you by just leaving." Eamon rose to a seat and pulled her into his lap to keep her warm. "You may be the first person I've loved, but I've had friendships. I've seen the importance of communication, so if I ever do up and abandon you, I hope you hunt me down and put me in my place."

"Another deal, then."

"This one I'll shake on," he teased as he gripped her hand, pumping it playfully as she beamed at him. "So, I didn't ruin us, right?" he asked.

"A single mishandled conversation won't ruin us." Bel pulled free of his grip and cupped his face, pulling him down so she could speak against his mouth. "If it did, then we shouldn't be together, but I think we're strong enough to handle a disagreement."

"After hearing what you survived to escape that mountain, I believe you're strong enough for anything." Eamon kissed her, long and slow and deep, and Bel wrapped her arms around his neck, seconds away from repeating what had just happened on his foyer floor.

Until a wet nose poked her in the back.

"Oh god!" She jerked in Eamon's lap before bursting into laughter. Cerberus stood behind her with expectation in his eyes, and Eamon rubbed his head before pulling Bel to a stand.

"Guess he's done giving us our privacy," he chuckled.

"At least he let us finish our conversation before he reminded us it's dinnertime." Bel grabbed Eamon's sweater off the floor and slipped it on.

"I missed seeing you in my clothes." Eamon leaned down

and kissed her, slipping on his boxer briefs without bothering to put his pants back on.

"I missed wearing them. I missed everything about you."

"I'm glad. I needed you to help me escape my head, but how did you convince your dad to let you come?" he asked as the trio entered the kitchen.

"I'm almost thirty-five, that's how," she teased, and he rolled his eyes as he dug the dog food out of the pantry. "I told him I'd tell him the truth."

"You what?" Eamon froze.

"Is that a bad thing? I assumed you'd be okay with it."

"I am." He resumed scooping Cerberus' dinner into his bowl. "I just didn't think you wanted your father to know."

"He heard you confess to scarring me. I had no choice, but I haven't shared any specifics. I just promised him the truth when he decides how much he wants to know. He's already suspicious because of your and Griffin's behavior at the morgue."

"Yeah, he was freaked out about that." Eamon gripped her hips and hoisted her onto the counter by the stove, fisting his sweater in his fingers and yanking it up to her neck so he could plant a kiss on her chest. "You have no idea how amazing it feels to see your skin whole." He ran a palm down her bare belly to her thighs before dropping his shirt back in place. "Before I caught the victim's scent, I thought it was you on that slab… your lower half was severely mutilated. Blaubart must've done that to hide any differences the body double had, but at the time I wasn't thinking rationally. I just saw the love of my life ripped apart."

"I'm sorry you went through that." Bel shuddered, trying not to imagine herself dead in the morgue with her flesh peeling off her bones.

"I never want to live through that again." He pulled open the refrigerator door, not meeting her gaze as he selected ingredients.

"I didn't expect you home until after Christmas, so I didn't shop for anything special."

"I already had my Christmas dinner." She scanned his mostly bare body from head to toe with exaggerated appreciation, and he rolled his eyes before capturing her in a kiss.

"I'm still going to feed you. How hungry are you?"

"I fled Dad's before breakfast, so I've had car snacks and that's it."

"Isobel." Eamon lovingly glared at her.

"This is why you can't leave me." She shrugged. "Someone has to make sure I eat."

"Thank goodness I enjoy doing it."

"Why do you love to cook when you need blood to survive?"

He shrugged, the kitchen silent for a moment before he answered. "I guess I survived on only blood for so long that when I started eating, I realized how amazing well-prepared food was. Plus, I like watching you eat. It's cute how you light up around a proper meal when you're too busy to cook."

"I love you," Bel blurted, unable to keep the words in. Now that she'd spoken them, they wanted to spill out endlessly.

"You need to stop that." Eamon leaned over the sink, every muscle in his massive frame tensing. "I'm trying to make you a nice dinner, but if you don't stop saying that, I'm going to take you upstairs and lock you in my room." He shifted to stand between her thighs. "You drove all this way to be with me for Christmas. I don't want to send you to bed starving."

"I love you." Bel shot forward and planted a quick peck on his lips. "But if you want me to make it through dinner, find your pants. I haven't been home in a while, and I forgot how handsome you are."

"I like it when you call this home."

"Calm down." She patted his chest. "I meant Bajka. Besides, you just raised the question of leaving for my safety. Are you really back to asking me to live with you that fast?"

"You promised to stick closer to me so I can protect you." Eamon winked before returning to the cutting board. "Living here would solve that problem."

"Oh my god, you're hopeless." Bel jumped off the counter and scanned the wine rack before selecting a bottle, patting Cerberus's head as she passed his kitchen dog bed. "But did you mean it when you said you're designing this house for me?"

"Yes. Didn't you notice that?"

"Maybe... but why? It's your home."

"It's my house," He corrected. "You're my home."

"Then how could you contemplate leaving me?" All couples argued. It was how they emerged from the conversation that defined their relationship, and Bel had no doubts that this would strengthen their bond, but it was impossible to undo days of anxiety in a single hour.

"Because home is always home no matter how far you travel, but if your house burns to the ground, you have nothing to return to," he answered without looking at her. "I want to always have something to return to."

Bel set the wine bottle down and settled behind Eamon, wrapping her arms around his waist as he sauteed the vegetables. "Do you want help with dinner?" she asked, because how was she supposed to respond to such a heartbreaking answer?

"I'm sorry." He placed the knife on the counter and leaned all his weight into his hands. "Are you sure I haven't ruined us? I don't want my leaving to be the only thing you think when you see me."

"I was pretty depressed when you left me at my dad's," she answered honestly, her lips tracing his spine as she spoke. "It'll take time to get over it, but that's relationships. Do you know how many times my dad or sisters said something that pissed me off? Six girls in one house led to a lot of fights. Sometimes we'd be so mad that we wouldn't speak to each other for days, but I love them more than anything. Actions are what matter, and

Evidence of a Folktale

you're a man of your word. I know that if you promise to stay, you'll fight tooth and nail to keep it."

"I will. I'm not going anywhere, and this time I mean it. Unless you order me away, you're stuck with me."

"And your constant requests to move in with you."

"See, I always knew you were the smartest of us."

"So, where did a man who never loved anyone learn the importance of communication?" Bel released his waist and returned her focus to the expensive bottle of wine.

"I've had friends. This is actually the part of my past that you'll like."

"Tell me?" She poured them both a glass before hopping back onto the counter beside the stove. The counter was her unofficial spot when Eamon cooked, and like a moth to the flame, his hand found her thigh.

"It was World War Two," he started. "By that point in history, I'd grown a conscience, and war was the perfect position for me. No one would miss the blood of dead soldiers, and I could let my inner monster out. Only I started caring about the men in my unit. For the first time in my life, I cared about humans, but they kept dying on me. I couldn't take it, so I stopped hiding who I was. I kept all of them alive, and when the war ended, I remained in contact with one of them. He was different from the others. He never acknowledged the fact that every time we saw each other, he was another year older, while I forever looked the same. It changed something inside me, and I found myself unconsciously emulating him. He taught me about love and family, and on his deathbed, I promised to watch over his descendants. They assume the money comes from a trust, but I discreetly check up on them in person from time to time."

"That's beautiful." Bel wiped a tear from her eye, ignoring the reality that she, too, would forever grow older while he looked the same.

"Glad you think so. Remember this when I tell you the rest of my story because you won't think I'm beautiful then."

"I don't scare easily."

"Thank goodness for that." He leaned sideways to steal a kiss. "Now go grab some plates so we can eat." He hoisted her off the counter. "It's been weeks since I've seen you, so I want you properly fed because once I take you to my bed, you aren't allowed to leave it."

The morning sunlight peaked through the curtains, and Bel burrowed further below the blankets. The hours their bare bodies had spent beneath the sheets had left her deliciously sore and peaceful until she registered the chill at her back.

"Eamon?" she twisted on the mattress, but his pillow was cold. He'd been absent for a while. "Eamon?" she called, knowing his hearing would catch her voice no matter where he stood in his mansion, but when the home remained silent, Bel knew. He was gone.

Autopsy Report

CERBERUS

PROD.NO.
SCENE
TAKE
SOUND
DIRECTOR
CAMERAMAN
EXT.
INT.

CINEMA TICKET 9891102 ADMIT ONE
CINEMA TICKET 9891102 ADMIT ONE

Chapter Three

Bel jogged down the stairs, Cerberus hard on her heels for his breakfast. No text message. No note. Just an empty house, and she warned herself not to freak out as she fed her dog. Eamon hadn't left her in the middle of the night. He wouldn't do that. *He wouldn't, he wouldn't, he wouldn't.*

Cerberus' ears twitched, and with a grunt, he abandoned his bowl. But after a few steps, he twisted to gaze longingly at his remaining breakfast and returned to inhale the last bites. He swallowed them whole with greedy snorts, and when the final piece vanished into his mouth, he bolted for the front door with a bark. His deep voice echoed off the foyer's high ceiling, a warning to whoever drove up the gravel drive that this house was protected, and Bel peaked out the window to watch an unfamiliar SUV skid to a halt. She couldn't see the driver through the tinted windows from her angle, and she wondered if she should leash her dog. Strangers always balked at Cerberus' beefy appearance and cropped ears, but men with guns weren't afraid of pitbulls with fangs, and she didn't want to risk his safety when confronting this stranger. No one in town owned a car that nice, meaning one of

Eamon's contacts had probably decided to bother him only hours after the holiday's end. Seemed not even his clients knew he'd disappeared.

Bel opened the door, a blast of icy air slapping her in the face, and Cerberus bolted outside before she could catch him. If her first-thing-in-the-morning visitor was a colleague of Eamon's, her dog wasn't in danger, and based on the vehicle's price, the nature of this intrusion was indeed business.

"Oh good, you're up," the driver said as he jumped out of the SUV, and Cerberus leaped into his arms as he rounded the car. "I was rushing to get back before you woke."

"Eamon?" Bel jogged down the front steps, mad at herself for worrying for even a second that he'd abandoned her in the middle of the night. "Back from where?"

"Getting your Christmas gift." He captured her in a hug, but before he could kiss her, Cerberus' head popped up between them, slobbering all over their faces as he greeted his two favorite people.

"Christmas gift?" she repeated, pushing the pit's messy tongue out of her eyes. "But I forgot to get you one. Between the hospital and being at my dad's, I didn't have time to shop."

"You told me you loved me." Eamon shoved past the pup's exuberance and planted a kiss on her lips, dog slobber and all. "That was a better gift than anything I could buy you."

"I still should've thought of something."

"Next year." He set the pitbull down, and Cerberus ran off down the drive to do his business. "And I forgot to get Baby Beast a present, so I'm slacking. You've done a much better job this Christmas than me."

"He'll forgive you." Bel wrapped her arms around his neck, trying to play it cool. She didn't want him to notice she'd woken in a panic. She was embarrassed enough by her reaction as it was. He'd given her his word. They were in this together, and he'd merely left to buy her a gift. "So, what did you get me?"

Evidence of a Folktale

She smiled at him, and he tossed his head over his shoulder as he hugged her waist.

"Wait..." Bel gently shoved him away as she realized what he meant. "The SUV?"

"I returned your rental." Eamon crossed his arms over his chest. "It was a cheap ride, and you need something safer.

"You got me a car?" Bel gawked at the gorgeous vehicle... the very expensive, gorgeous vehicle.

"Blaubart totaled your car when he used the body double to fake your death," he said. "It's winter, and with snow coming, you need reliable transportation. You also need something big enough to cart Cerberus between our houses, since you won't live with me. He'll like the SUV better than your coupe."

"You got me a car?" she repeated.

"I know it's not romantic like heels or jewelry, but you need a safe vehicle. I don't want you driving around in some piece of trash because some lunatic totaled your car. SUVs are pricy, so this seemed like a perfect gift."

"Yes, they are pricy, Eamon." She glared at him. "We talked about this. I'm uncomfortable with excessive gifts. An occasional dress is one thing, but this costs far more than an outfit. I can't accept this... especially this model. I appreciate the thought, but the rental was enough until I figured it out."

"See, that's where I got you." Eamon smirked, his expression entirely too pleased with himself. "You can accept it because it wasn't expensive. In fact, it cost me nothing."

"Nothing?" She gawked at the luxury SUV. "What do you mean?"

"It's one of my cars," he said. "I drove to the garage to pull it out of storage because I know you. A brand-new car would make you uncomfortable, but if you take this, you'll actually be saving me money since I won't have to pay to park it anymore."

"Oh, you're good." Bel laughed.

"I'm aware." He handed her the keys and nodded for her to

45

check it out. "I worked with a client a few years ago who lived upstate in the dead of winter," he said as she climbed into the driver's seat. "I wanted something reliable in the snow, so I bought this, but I had no use for it when I returned to the city. It's been in the garage ever since."

"It gets cold here in Bajka. Won't you need it?"

"I have my car, my old work truck, and the new truck," he said as he settled into the passenger seat. "Trucks are best for renovations, and they handle snow well, so I don't need this. I was considering selling it, but I'd rather you have it. I feel safer knowing you're driving something reliable. So, in reality, you accepting this gift is for my benefit."

"Oh, you're really good." Bel slipped the key into the ignition, grinning as the engine purred to life.

"Good enough to convince you to accept this?" Eamon leaned over the center console.

"I have to test drive it first, obviously," she teased. "Cerberus! Come on, buddy. Wanna go for a ride?"

The pitbull came charging, and she helped him into the backseat before slipping into the front. She wasted no time throwing the vehicle into drive, and with a smile at Eamon, she slammed on the gas. The SUV launched forward, and for the next ten minutes, Bel sped through the expansive Reale Estate.

"You can really handle a car." Eamon beamed when they finally skidded to a halt a few miles from the mansion. "It's unreasonably sexy. Why do I always drive when we're together?"

"Driving a squad car in New York City taught me a thing or two." She shifted the gear stick to park and leaned against the headrest with electricity running through her veins. "You're still a better driver than me, but I can handle a car. Especially one this nice." She ran her fingers over the steering wheel. "Do me a favor. Never tell me how much this costs. I love it, but I'd never be able to afford something this beautiful."

Evidence of a Folktale

"So I'll just buy myself another when this breaks down."

"Eamon…"

"Isobel…" He furrowed his brow at her. "This SUV should last you years. By the time you need a replacement, we won't be having these conversations because what's mine will be yours."

"What's yours is mine?" Bel's smile fell. "I panicked this morning when you weren't in bed. I knew you wouldn't do something so cruel, but I couldn't help it. It made me nervous," she admitted. "I'm not saying this to make you feel guilty… I guess I just wanted you to know."

"I'm sorry." Eamon reached across the console and gripped her thigh. "The idea struck well after midnight, but I didn't want to wake you, so I snuck out. I was rushing to return before you woke up so I could surprise you."

"It's a lovely surprise, and it's a gift I really need." She slid her palm over his knuckles. "It's just when you say what's yours is mine, I want to look forward to that. I don't want to worry about you abandoning me."

"I would never abandon you," Eamon said. "But seeing you dead did something to me. I'll never forget the image. I'll never forget that pain, so I didn't suggest leaving to scare you or make you feel inadequate. Something broke inside me when I saw your death on the news. It'll take time for that wound to heal. Even now, seeing you alive, feeling your warmth below my palms, hearing your heart beat and your lungs breathe, all I can see are your vacant eyes staring up at me from the slab in the morgue. I have to force myself to believe you didn't die in that car accident. It's partially why I left in the middle of the night. I couldn't sleep. I just kept watching you to make sure your chest was moving."

"Blaubart told me you found out about my faked death on the news." Bel wiped the tears from her eyes. Every time Eamon opened his mouth, she understood more and more why he'd mentioned leaving. Was that why they'd spent hours tangled in the sheets last night? Had he wanted to feel her gasping for breath against him so that he knew she was alive? Had he been too afraid to sleep for fear that she'd stop breathing beside him?

"He made that Jane Doe look just like you," Eamon whispered.

"Thinking about that makes me sick." She peeled his hand off her leg and pressed it against her chest so he could feel her heartbeat. "I'm still here, though. It will take a lot more than a madman to steal me from you."

"Promise?"

"I love you, remember?" She lifted his fingers to her lips and kissed them before returning them to her heart.

"I could never forget." He leaned across the console and pulled her into a kiss, lingering against her until she was gasping for breath.

"Thank you," she whispered against his mouth.

"For what?"

"For the car, for being honest." She kissed him again before leaning back in her seat. "For letting me be honest. I was so mad at you for contemplating leaving... but then I hear what you went through, and I understand. Most men would bottle up their emotions and just leave. They'd assume they were doing it for my own good, and I'd be left angry and alone with unanswered questions. But hearing the story from your perspective? I probably would've done the same thing in your shoes."

"The past month has been hell for both of us," Eamon said. "There are many things I wish I could do differently."

"But we're still here, and we're still together. I think we're going to be okay. We're the couple that makes it to what's yours is mine, aren't we?"

"Detective Isobel Stone." Eamon smiled.

"Okay, slow down," she laughed, swatting his chest. "We're not there yet."

"Right… gotta convince you to move in with me first." He winked.

"Exactly. I'm just saying we'll be okay. If we can survive this, we can survive any fight."

"We better. Cerberus likes this car," Eamon said as he glanced at the pitbull who'd fixated on a squirrel outside his window. "He'll be upset if he doesn't get to con goodies out of me."

"That's low." Bel captured Eamon's face in her hands and kissed him. "Using my dog against me."

"It's a guaranteed win."

"You, sir, are good." She settled back into her seat and shifted the gear stick. "I love you… now can you help me really drive this car? It's so nice, and most of Bajka is residential. I won't get many chances to test her."

Eamon leaned closer and brushed a seductive kiss over her scars. "I thought you'd never ask."

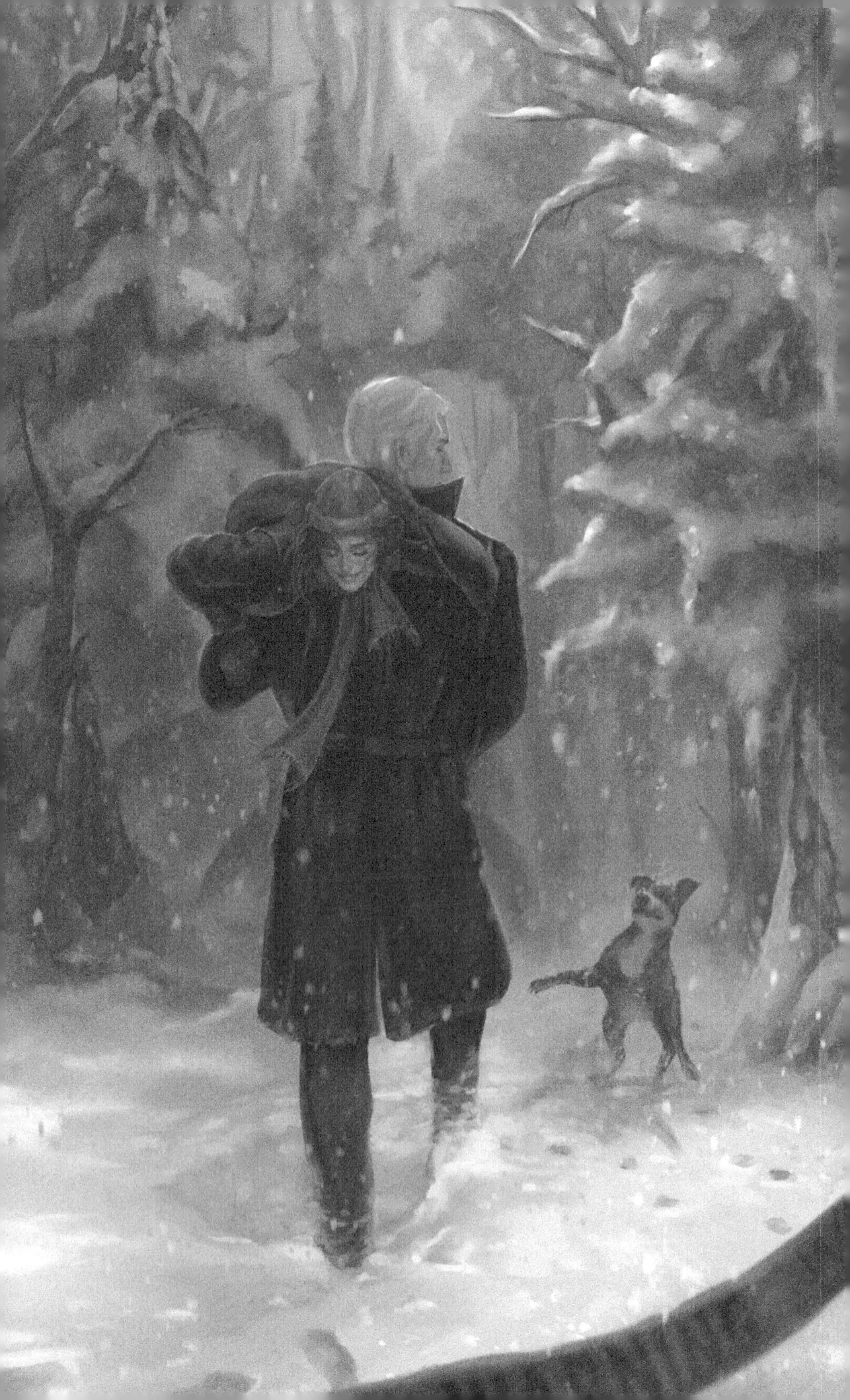

Chapter Four

"Let me start this morning's briefing by saying, Happy New Year!" Griffin said as the station gathered fully staffed for the first time since before Christmas. "I hope everyone had an amazing holiday, and I'd like to take this moment to put Detective Emerson on the spot." He extended a hand to Bel, and she rolled her eyes before joining him at the front of the room, the officers cheering her on except for her partner Olivia Gold, who stood arms crossed and sullen at the rear of the crowd.

"This is Emerson's first day on the job since her resurrection," Griffin continued, wrapping an arm around her shoulders. "She gave us a horrifying scare, so I think I speak for everyone when I say we're so thankful to have you back."

"I'm happy to be back," Bel said to the soundtrack of applause. "And to be alive."

"Here, here!" A deputy cheered, and it stung that Olivia didn't so much as smile.

"We all love you," Griffin continued, and Bel could tell his use of *'We'* really meant *'I'*. "But if I know you at all, you'll jump in headfirst, so I'd like to ask everyone to keep an eye on our detective here and stop her from working too hard on her first day. Give us at least a few boring days before you take on the forces of evil."

"I'll try," she laughed as her boss captured her in a suffocating hug.

"Don't do that to me ever again," Griffin whispered in her ear. "I won't survive seeing you in the morgue. I feel guilty admitting it, but I'm glad the victim we found wasn't you." He pulled back and gripped her biceps, forcing her to meet his gaze. "I don't care what time of day it is or how ridiculous your hunch is. I don't even care if it's not police related. You need help? Call me, and I'll be there. I'm not watching an autopsy on you again."

"I see you and Eamon exchanged notes." She cupped his cheek with a smile. "I promise. If he doesn't answer, you're the next person I'll call to help me with my wild goose chases."

"Thank god that man figured out it wasn't you. And thank God he found Blaubart in Venezuela. I disliked the guy for a long time, but now I get his appeal."

"You don't say?" Bel teased. "You hid it so well."

"Oh, be quiet. You were convinced he was a serial killer at first too." Griffin rubbed her back before returning his attention to the officers. "Okay, now for the big news," he continued as she found her seat. "I'm sure you've all heard of the wildly popular TV show Aesop's Files?" He paused as the crowd murmured their acknowledgment. "Well, our town has recently caught the eyes of the show's location scouts. Upcoming episodes take place in a beautiful small town during winter, and they've decided Bajka is the perfect location. The filming permits and contracts have been signed, so I'm thrilled to announce that we'll be home to Aesop's Files for the next month or so."

Bel clapped as the room exploded in excitement. She didn't watch the famous show. Its plot was a campy version of her entirely too real life, so she always changed the channel when an episode came on. But she was well aware of the chokehold the

Evidence of a Folktale

paranormal crime series—and its sex-on-legs lead actor—had on its viewers.

"Now, before everyone gets too excited, there's a catch." Griffin raised his hands to settle the chatter. "I don't need to remind you how popular this show and its actors are, and while it's unconventional, the production studio seems very keen to exploit that fact for as much financial gain as possible. Because Bajka is a smaller town, it's easier to protect, so the studio has announced they'll be hosting... what do they call those cons? Comic something? Whatever. They plan to host those style events during their month here. Signings, meet-and-greets, breakfasts, photo ops, Q&A panels, the works. It's unusual, but they see Bajka as the perfect excuse to blend filming and fan interactions.

"I'm personally not thrilled with this arrangement. Obsessed fans gathered for an extended period as the cast and crew shoot could spell chaos, but the mayor has agreed to the proposal because it'll be incredible for Bajka's economy. Almost all the hotels and rentals have been booked, so it'll be amazing for our businesses and a headache for us. Our town will double in size, so unlimited overtime has already been approved. I won't lie. It'll be a lot of work, but it's a once-in-a-lifetime event. How many police officers get to say they worked the Aesop's Files protection detail?"

"Is the show bringing their own security?" Bel asked. "This scale seems beyond our station's capabilities."

"Yes. The actors have bodyguards and drivers, but due to the sheer number of fans expected to flood Bajka, their security isn't enough," Griffin answered. "Plus, police presence will help inspire order. Emerson and Gold, I realize you're both detectives, but for the conventions and fan events, it might be best if you wore uniforms. I want everyone to see we are present and serious. We don't need any funny business while the show's in our town."

The officers murmured their agreement, an undercurrent of excitement thrumming through the bodies, but Bel wasn't fooled by the promise of famous visitors. These actors would be a month-long headache, but at least there'd be overtime. She'd missed a lot of work on account of being declared dead, and her paychecks were looking thin.

"I'll have more information and schedules for you over the next few days, but I wanted to warn you to enjoy your quiet evenings and spend time with your families because when the show gets to town, we'll all stop sleeping for a month. On the bright side, you can bribe your loved ones into forgiving you by introducing them to their favorite actors. I know my wife is not so secretly excited about meeting Beau Draven."

"I don't think we want to bribe our girls with Beau Draven meet-and-greets," a deputy laughed, and the surrounding men groaned in agreement.

"I guess this is a good time to be single," Officer Rollo said. He was Bajka's newest hire, a man whose attractiveness rivaled the show's star, but the last Bel heard, he was well on his way to being taken by her friend Violet, but she'd been preoccupied with her own relationship issues. Perhaps their spark had fizzled out.

"Well, you know what they say," Griffin said. "Never meet your idols. Maybe Beau Draven isn't as charming in real life as he is on screen."

"Yeah, right!" A deputy blurted as he wiped his laughter tears from his eyes. "We're in trouble."

"Alas, we probably are." Griffin joined the joke. "But it'll at least buy us some favor when we miss weeks of family dinners. And on that note, let's get to work. Draven and Aesop's Files will take up enough of our time. Let's not let it ruin today."

The room surged with conversation as the officers dispersed, and Bel bolted from her chair, eyes scanning the bodies for her partner. She hadn't seen Olivia since the hospital, but her friend

Evidence of a Folktale

had barely stayed at her bedside long enough to confirm proof of life. She hadn't answered any of Bel's texts, either, not that Bel had sent many. The days with her father had been consumed by Eamon's absence, and the days after Christmas had been filled with difficult conversations and rekindled intimacy... in every room of the mansion. She'd had little time to consider Olivia's distance. She assumed it was due to the holidays, but now she wasn't so sure that's why her texts remained unanswered.

Spotting blonde hair, Bel pushed through the gathered bodies, but by the time she reached Olivia's location, her partner had fled the briefing room, her legs carrying her swiftly toward her desk.

"Hey!" Bel breathed a sigh of relief when she caught up, but as she leaned in for a hug, Olivia blocked her movements by yanking her coat off her chair.

"Hi." One word. Bel had returned from the dead, and all Olivia had was one word.

"Was your holiday nice?" Bel stepped back, at a loss for what to do with her outstretched arms.

"It was." Two words. This time, Olivia only had two words.

"Did you spend it with your family?"

"I did."

"Sounds fun." Everything inside Bel's chest ached. Olivia and Violet Lennon were her greatest friends in this town, and while she understood that her presumed death had wreaked havoc on those who loved her, she couldn't fathom why her partner was using her coat like a shield. "I'm dying for a latte," she continued, desperate for a way to connect. "Want to stop by The Espresso Shot before we settle in?"

"Sorry..." Olivia paused as if trying to come up with an excuse. "I have stuff to take care of. You go get a coffee. David will be happy to see you."

And with that, she left an aching and confused Bel in her wake.

"Guess what?" Bel called as she unlocked Eamon's front door and kicked off her shoes. The sound of thudding feet answered her greeting, and within seconds, Cerberus was barreling recklessly down the grand staircase.

"Hiya, Baby Beast." She caught him as he leaped off the steps and pulled his squirming body into a hug.

"What?" Eamon shouted from upstairs, and Bel climbed toward his voice, seventy pounds of excitement giving her a burning thigh workout by the time she reached the upper level.

"Where?" she called as she approached the yet-to-be-renovated hallways. Unlike him, her hearing couldn't pinpoint his exact location, and she rarely ventured into this section of the mansion. It had come a long way since the night she'd broken in, but the fear the darkness inspired when she thought Eamon would kill her all those months ago kept her far from these damaged rooms… and that her foot might fall through the floorboards. Eamon had focused his renovations on the main living areas first, so the half they lived in was so stylish and expensive that she often forgot that most of the Reale Estate was still crumbling.

"Here!" he shouted, and Bel put Cerberus down. He took off running, and she followed him until she found the shirtless and grimy Eamon ripping up damaged floorboards.

"Wow. Looks awful." She smiled at how his muscles rippled below his skin with his every movement, and she marveled at how the perfectly smooth and powerful back hunched before her had once been blown to pieces.

"You say the nicest things." He dropped the rotting wood and charged for her. Bel shrieked as she tried to escape, but he was

Evidence of a Folktale

too fast and caught her in his filth-streaked arms before she could take two steps.

"Gross!" She shoved his sweaty chest, but he simply leaned forward and planted an exaggerated kiss on her lips. "You've ruined my sweater," she grumbled against his mouth.

"That's what you get for making fun of me slaving away up here." He kissed her again, and this time, Bel surrendered to the embrace. Filthy or not, a shirtless Eamon was glorious to behold.

"I'll buy you a new one if the stains don't come out," he said as he finally released her.

"Fine, but what if I'd loved this sweater?" she challenged.

"You don't."

"How do you know?"

"Because you've been staying with me since Christmas, yet never wore it. Your sisters packed your clothes when you were in the hospital, so you only have what they gave you, and instead of going home to repack, you did laundry here... even though that sweater was clean in your luggage the whole time."

"Okay, fine. Why do you have to be so observant?" She swatted his chest. "You and my dad are a pair. Other guys don't notice things, but you two are always watching me. I can't get away with anything."

"I'm always watching you." He pitched his voice low and menacing, and even though he was joking, her skin flushed with a prick of fear at how quickly he could flip the switch and uncaged the beast.

"Creeper." She stole a kiss before sidestepping him to study the gutted room. "Looks like you're taking the walls out too. What will this become?"

"Not sure yet. I'm just going with whatever comes to me at the moment."

"Am I allowed to make requests?" she asked.

"Do you want to?"

"You said you were restoring this house with me in mind."

57

"I am." He came up behind her and wrapped his arms around her chest. "What would you like?"

"An office," she said. "For when I sleep over."

"Of course." He kissed her cheek, seeing right through her request.

"I work on sensitive cases, and while I'm terrible at keeping things from you, it would be smart to have a designated area separate from my living space. I don't have that at the cabin, so if I bring home a case, it's just death on my dinner table and my counters and my mattress. It would be nice to have a room to leave it behind in."

"Done," Eamon said. "But not here."

"Why not?" she asked.

"Because it's too far from my office, and if you're going to work here, I require the ability to roll my chair across the hall to visit you."

"Okay, not here, but yes? I can have an office?"

"You could have mine if you wanted it. Take the whole house for all I care. I actually have safety nets in place in case anything happens to me. You get everything."

"Seriously?" She gawked at him.

"Close your mouth." His fingers pushed her jaw closed. "All it does is give you my estate and wealth if I die. One day, we'll add you to the paperwork while I'm still alive, but for now, it's just in the event of my death. And we both know I'm not the dying type."

"You better not be." She leaned her head against his chest because he was right. She didn't love this sweater.

"You're stuck with me, unfortunately. You made that very clear." He kissed her cheek before releasing her to return to his work. "So, what am I guessing?" he asked, referring to her earlier question when she'd barged through his front door.

"Oh, right... I'm already dirty. Should I help?"

Evidence of a Folktale

"Sure, but put gloves on. I need all these floorboards ripped out."

"My first time helping you. This feels significant."

"If you're good, I'll have to put you to work more often."

"Careful, buddy," she teased. "Don't get excited about the free labor just yet. I'm about to be busy."

"Really?" His face fell. "What happened?"

"Nothing bad," she said. "It might be annoying, but it's also cool. Are you familiar with the show Aesop's Files?"

"Um… no, wait… is it that popular paranormal crime drama? The one where the detectives deal with werewolves, witches, vampires, and so on."

"Just like me," Bel laughed, and Eamon glared at her. "Okay, kind of like me." She nudged him with her shoulder as she gripped a floorboard. "In an exaggerated, completely unrealistic, and ridiculously fake way. I've seen a few episodes, but now that I know evil exists, I can't watch it. It's so… silly. To me, at least. I have scars from the teeth of a man hundreds of years old. I've looked death in the eyes. That show's an insult to the darkness that corrupts below the surface, BUT… people are obsessed with it. I guess it's fun if you don't know magic exists."

"Or is it fun because Beau Draven stars in it?" Eamon winked at her before ripping a floorboard out with such a display of strength that Bel couldn't wait for their shower later.

"So, you don't remember the show, but you know he's in it?" she teased.

"Yeah, yeah." He rolled his eyes. "So, what's going on?"

"They'll be shooting here for the next month." She recounted that morning's meeting, and by the time she was done, Eamon was visibly annoyed that the town he hid behind was about to swarm with attention.

"Having the show shoot here is cool, but I'm wary of the fan events," she said in closing. "Too many variables can go wrong.

The overtime will be good, though. I blew through all my vacation days and then some, so I could use the money."

"If you need money, I'll give it to you. Don't stress yourself out your first month back."

"I don't think I have a choice—uff." She pulled too hard on a floorboard and crashed to her backside. "Film shoots don't normally include fan conventions. They're usually separate events, but that's how this studio operates, so unfortunately, Bajka will be a madhouse. I doubt I could bow out even if I wanted to. At least you live in a secluded mansion. No one should bother you out here."

"I'm not worried about me." He helped her off the floor, and she rubbed her stinging tailbone to ease the discomfort. "I'll be grumpy, but what's new? I was just hoping for your sake that life would calm down."

"Maybe it'll be fun." She shrugged, trying to remain positive because she'd hoped for the same. "We get to meet the actors and watch them film. I've never seen a set before."

"I hope it is." He rubbed her back. "And I'm serious. If you ever need the money, you can ask me instead of running yourself ragged. There's a difference between using me for my wealth and needing help."

"I know, and as much as I groan about you giving me things, if this OT wasn't mandatory, I'd take you up on it. It's winter. It's cold and dark, and I don't particularly want to work late or weekends."

"I don't want you to either. I need to get over it, but I'm still nervous about letting you out of my sight. At least Olivia will be there to keep an eye on you."

"About that." Bel shifted to her knees to meet Eamon's gaze. "I tried to talk to her today. She's been ignoring my texts, but I figured it was the holidays, and maybe she felt weird interrupting us. But she practically crawled out of her skin when she saw me. I get my faked death messed people up, but I didn't think finding out I was alive would make her so uncomfortable."

Eamon cursed, yanking a rotting board too hard, and its splinters flew everywhere. "That's probably my fault."

"Your fault? How?"

"I told her the truth about me."

"You did? That's surprising, but why would that make her avoid me?"

"Because..." Eamon met her gaze. "She didn't know about Ewan."

"What do you mean?" Bel asked. Ewan Orso was a bear shifter and Olivia's boyfriend, and while alpha predators never lived peacefully when forced to coexist, Eamon and Ewan were the exception because of their detectives. "I thought you two made a deal? He tells her the truth, and you don't kill him for living in your territory."

"We did make that deal," Eamon said. "But he didn't hold up his end of the bargain. After I realized it wasn't your body in the morgue, I barged in on them, demanding the bear's help. I assumed Olivia knew, and I wasn't in the proper headspace to be diplomatic. I told her the truth since Ewan hadn't, but I wasn't kind. I feel bad. I do, but the conversation occurred an hour after I learned you were alive. It was not my finest moment, and she freaked out. She was ready to pull a gun on me, so I did the only thing I could think of to prove my words. I cut myself so she could watch me heal."

"Oh god." It was Bel's turn to curse. "Why didn't you tell me?"

"I was a little preoccupied." He captured her hand and pulled it onto his lap. "I'm sorry. I know she's one of your best friends, but it wasn't on purpose. I assumed she knew about Ewan, so learning about me wouldn't be a surprise. Unfortunately, I traumatized her, and it seems she's still angry about our deception."

"But I just came back from the dead. Why would she be

upset with me? I get Ewan. He lied… although that makes sense now. If he'd told her the truth, I suspect she would've tried to hint at it to me."

"She asked if you knew what I was. Maybe she's hurt that you didn't trust her enough to tell her."

"But that wasn't my truth to reveal."

"It wasn't." Eamon brushed a hand over her hair. "But she loves you, and you hid a secret that changed everything. Then you almost died. I wouldn't worry about her. She probably just needs time to process everything."

Autopsy Report

CERBERUS

PROD.NO. | TAKE | SOUND
SCENE | |
DIRECTOR
CAMERAMAN | EXT. | INT.

CINEMA TICKET — ADMIT ONE — 9891102
CINEMA TICKET — ADMIT ONE — 9891102

Chapter Five

"Well, this is cool," a menacingly deep voice whispered in her ear before massive hands slid around her hips and yanked her against a wall of solid muscle.

"Give out nine parking tickets to belligerent fans and then get back to me if you still think this is cool," Bel said, tilting her gaze to peek up at Eamon through her eyelashes.

"You're having a blast." He kissed her forehead before releasing her waist. "Other than the parking tickets, how's it been?"

"For starters, Beau Draven is even better looking in person," she teased, knocking him with her hip.

"Better looking than me?"

"Oh, for sure," Bel said. "He was also very flirty with me when we were introduced. So I might have to leave you for him."

"Dang it." Eamon sighed with the drama of an old Hollywood actor. "Wait…" His voice sobered. "How flirty?"

"Oh my god," Bel laughed. "Telling you he's more attractive than you doesn't faze you, but him flirting does?"

"Because the first is obviously a lie. Have you seen me?" He gestured to his body with mischief in his death-black eyes, which even clothed looked borderline illegal. "But I don't want him making you feel uncomfortable. You've been through enough."

"Eamon?" She stared up at him.

"What?"

"I love you."

He smiled a grin just for her, and suddenly, giving out nine parking tickets didn't seem so terrible.

"It was harmless," she continued. "He's full of himself, but in a charming way. I think Mr. Draven is used to women fawning over him, so when I was professional, he didn't know how to respond."

Following Griffin's announcement, Bajka had surged to life as its residents prepared to host a film crew and hundreds of avid fans. A bitter winter settled over the town as the cast and crew of Aesop's Files finally arrived. Before the chaos of filming got underway, the actors had conducted a meet-and-greet with the Police Department and her loved ones. Eamon had declined the invitation to attend the signing. Fraternizing with celebrities didn't aid in his life's quest to go mostly unnoticed, therefore he'd missed the way the starring actor had flirted with Bel throughout the afternoon.

"Sure, that's why he was flirting with you." Eamon kissed her temple, and she elbowed him in the ribs. "So…" He smirked at her response. "What scene are they shooting?"

They were filming outside, and the harsh wind was miserable for everyone involved. After the police meet-and-greet, the cast and crew settled into their lodgings, and within days, Bajka was more film studio than town. The first fan event wasn't scheduled to start until the weekend, but eager spectators had already started arriving, hence the need for Bel to write nine parking tickets all before lunch.

"That's Beau Draven." She pointed to the almost too-manicured man standing in the picturesque main square. The police were present to maintain the perimeter, but at this distance, Bel couldn't hear the dialogue. Eamon undoubtedly could, but she saw right through his curiosity. He didn't care about the scene. He missed her.

"His character is the lead detective in Aesop's Files," she continued. "And that's Taron Monroe. She's the newest detective on the show after she replaced Beau's first acting partner. She's the future love interest, and they solve campy paranormal murders, but that's the extent of my knowledge. I have no idea what they are shooting, but they're walking down the street holding coffee, so I guess the scene involves them discussing their case with barely veiled attraction coloring their banter."

"Speaking from experience, I see," Eamon said.

Bel shrugged as if she didn't know what he was talking about. "This show is weird for me because it's a mockery of my entire life. These detectives and these creatures. They're silly... they have no idea how dangerous it is to come face to face with evil."

"Yes, but before films and shows, there were stories shared around the fire. Humans have been weaving tales inspired by people like me since the dawn of time, and while some accounts are too accurate for comfort, most are so far-fetched it's insulting."

"I hadn't thought of that." Bel twisted so she could shove her freezing hands into Eamon's protective fist. His skin was cooler to the touch than most human's, but compared to this blustery wind, he was a furnace. "If this show weirded me out, I can't imagine how it's been for you."

"I'm not that bothered by it, actually," he said. "The more stories mankind creates, the further from the truth they drift, and the safer my reality becomes. How many times have my reactions to certain situations surprised you?"

"Like you not needing to be invited inside," she teased. "That would be a nice one, though. Would've kept you from breaking and entering."

"I know your father raised you better than that," Eamon said. "Stop with all the lying."

"I have to protest your illegal behavior. What kind of cop would I be if I didn't?"

"Still the best of us." He leaned down and captured her frozen lips in a kiss.

"I'm on duty," she whispered against his mouth.

"Everyone's looking at the on-screen couple," he reasoned as he deepened the kiss.

"You keep kissing me like this, and they won't be." She nipped his lip before shoving him away.

"Cut!" the director shouted.

"Check the gate!" the assistant director said.

"I recognize that phrase," Bel said. "They're done shooting. I hope that means lunch soon. I am freezing and need a scalding hot coffee. Want to grab one with me?"

"I can't. It's why I stopped by to say hi," Eamon said. "I have a videoconference with a client that won't be quick. You might as well stay at your place tonight."

"Okay."

"And Check the Gate means they're ready to move on from a shot because it was a signal to the cameramen to double-check the camera and film. I'm no expert, so don't ask me what the gate is, but they call that out because if dust or something gets into it, it'll ruin the take. If they finished filming without checking it, all their work could be lost. Equipment has evolved over the years, but the phrase is still used."

"Look at you." Bel smiled at him. "You hate being filmed or photographed, so how do you know that?"

"I become someone new every few lifetimes, and I spent time in Hollywood before cell phones made it impossible to fly under the radar."

Evidence of a Folktale

"Have you ever worked as a cop?" she asked. "Because I'd be embarrassed if you'd been one and were just playing dumb to make me feel smart."

"Actually, I've never been a police officer," Eamon said.

"Oh, thank god," she laughed. "But why not?"

"Me? A cop?"

"You're right, that is ridiculous." Bel collapsed against his chest, shaking despite her thick coat.

"All right, that's lunch!" a voice shouted, and she exhaled into Eamon's pitch-black overcoat. Hopefully, there weren't too many outdoor shoots. She wasn't an actress making the big bucks, and overtime was no longer appealing now that her fingers and toes ached.

"Good luck with your meeting." She hugged Eamon tighter, secretly wishing the overtime wasn't mandatory. The air was so bitter that she was willing to take him up on his offer to help her financially. "I need to get something hot to drink before I freak out. This weather reminds me too much of running down that mountain."

Eamon stiffened in her arms, and she grimaced. She didn't want him worrying, but it was true. She'd never felt cold like she had when she fled Dr. Blaubart, and it was one reason she'd spent every night since her return at Eamon's mansion. She loved the man, and their days together helped them work through their issues, but a small part of her stayed because she was afraid of the chill. Sleeping between him and Cerberus left her sweaty, and while most people hated waking up damp, it was the only thing stopping her from panicking as she rose to consciousness. Keeping this set perimeter was the first time she'd been truly cold since the mountain, and panic was trying its best to consume her.

"I'm okay." She peeled herself off him. "I just need to get inside and find a hot drink."

"You sure I can't take you home?" Eamon tugged her hat

further down her ears. "I'll talk to Griffin. He'll understand, and if he doesn't, it's not like he can stop me from taking you."

"I've missed so much work, though, and it isn't fair to ask the other officers to pick up the slack for me again."

"I don't care about everyone else. Do you need to come home?"

"I care about them. And get back on the horse, right?"

"That phrase means to face your fears, not push yourself to the breaking point."

"I know." She scanned the crowd, duty warring with trauma inside her.

"If you get too cold, call me," Eamon said, realizing she was too stubborn to leave. "I'll bring you soup, tea, a feather quilt, your dog to hug, whatever you need."

"What about your clients?"

"I'll put them on hold."

"I'm not going to interrupt your meeting."

"You better interrupt my meeting if you need something." He glared at her. "Swear it. It's the only way I'll go home. Picturing you running down that mountain by yourself makes me physically ill."

"Okay, I swear it." She crossed her heart with her gloved hand.

"Thank you." Eamon kissed her quickly since the crowd was no longer focused on the actors' scene. "I love you, Isobel. Go get your coffee." He shoved cash into her hands. "Order as much as you need."

"I will." She didn't bother arguing and tucked the bills into her coat pocket. "I'll talk to you later."

"Bye, Detective." Eamon turned and slipped into the crowd, vanishing so effortlessly that Bel hadn't even realized he'd stepped out of sight. The moment he moved out of earshot, she released the anxious breath she'd been fighting to hold inside. Turning on her heels, she power walked through the raw wind to

The Espresso Shot and shoved her way through the crowded cafe.

"David, can I use the employee bathroom?" she asked the shop owner as she passed the register.

"Of course, Detective." David tossed his head over his shoulder, barely looking at her as he served the horde of customers, and Bel fled for the back. The minute she locked herself inside, she tore off her gloves, turned on the hot water, and sobbed an ugly cry as her fingers shoved into the heat.

She'd held it together in front of Eamon. He was always so worried about her, and they'd been working through their trauma from her kidnapping. She didn't want her meltdown to inspire him to mention leaving again. He promised he wouldn't unless she demanded it, but she didn't want to pile on the guilt. She didn't want to remind him he hadn't saved her or that the cold reminded her of those hours when she would've lost her fingers if not for gripping Blaubart's wife the entire way down the mountain.

"Detective?" A knock at the door startled her, and she turned the water off, snatching paper towels from the dispenser to dry her puffy face.

"Is everything okay?" the voice came again. David Kaffe's wife Emily had been one of Alcina's victims in Bel's first case in Bajka. He and his daughters had taken over running The Espresso Shot in honor of their beloved Emily, so if anyone would understand Bel's struggle, it was David.

"I'm fine. Just freezing." She opened the door, and he smiled at her, his fatherly intuition seeing through her lies.

"Come on. The kitchen feels like the thermostat is set to hell because everyone's ordering food. I'll get you a coffee and soup, and if you stand back there for a few minutes, you'll boil. Do you want tomato or chicken noodle?"

"Tomato."

"Perfect." He patted her shoulder, and Bel wanted to cry all over again at his kindness.

Five minutes later, she stood in the sweltering kitchen with David's oldest daughter, a cup of steaming soup, and a slice of toasted bread. The staff liked her, so they had no problem letting her thaw out in their workspace, and when she finished the food, David handed her the largest coffee cup they had.

"What do I owe you?" she asked when she finally emerged from the kitchen, sweating as if she had indeed been boiled, and she felt fantastic.

"Nothing," David said. "You always look out for my family. It's our turn."

"Thank you." She hugged him. "I needed that."

"I always have soup and coffee, so stop by any time." He returned the embrace. "I don't care that there are actors in our town. You're our real MVP."

"Because I spend a fortune here?"

"Exactly." David laughed. "See you soon, Detective."

"Bye." Bel waved and shoved some of Eamon's bills into the tip jar as she spotted her partner leaving with her lunch clutched in her hands. "Olivia!" She weaved through the crowded shop to catch her friend. They still weren't talking, and she was ready to explode. "Olivia, wait up."

"Oh, hi." Gold paused with an awkward glance at the exit.

"It's so cold," Bel said, opting for a safe conversation topic. "Hopefully, there aren't many outdoor shoots."

"Yeah." Olivia opened the door and stepped onto the sidewalk just as a group of fans lunged through the entrance. A flash of fur surged into the women's line of sight, and Olivia screamed, her alarm earning her a snicker from the masked fan.

"Olivia." Bel reached for her as the werewolf-masked teens charged at the pastry display. It was clear by their outfits that they were cosplaying a character from Aesop's Files, but by

Olivia's reaction, it seemed she'd assumed a real-life monster had come to rip her throat out.

"What?" Olivia cursed, the obscenities odd spoken in her southern accent as she fled The Espresso Shot.

"It's just kids in a costume," Bel said, chasing after her.

"Really?" Olivia pinned her with a glare. "Just an outfit? Just some kids? How do you know that? How can you ever know that?"

And without letting Bel answer, she charged off down the street.

BEL SAT on the bench in the little garden Eamon had designed for her. He and Ewan had mangled the trees behind her cabin when the bear shifter first moved to town, so Eamon had cleared out the damage and replaced it with a stretch of beautiful landscape. Bel loved to drink her morning coffee or make calls on the bench while Cerberus roamed the yard, and since he was busy stretching his legs after being home alone for hours, Bel pulled her phone out of her pocket. The day had been long and frigid, and as if standing outside to guard actors hadn't been enough, she now sat in her backyard with Cerberus while he expelled his pent-up energy. Eamon had bought the dog an oversized ball that couldn't fit in his mouth, so he was currently shoving it around the yellowed grass, adorably trying to bite it in vain. At least in her garden, she could sit wrapped in a giant fuzzy blanket without anyone judging her.

BEL

> I know you can't talk, which is good, actually. I prefer texting this when you can't respond right away.

Bel texted Eamon, Cerberus barking a joyous soundtrack for

her messages. It felt easier to discuss the difficult things with a seventy-pound black pitbull growling like a hellhound in the background, and she needed to be honest with her boyfriend. Hiding her emotions because she was afraid he'd bring up leaving again wasn't healthy. If they were going to make a future together, ignoring the painful parts of their lives wasn't an option.

> I downplayed how much standing out in the cold bothered me earlier. I didn't want to freak you out before your meeting, but I should've told you. David caught me crying in The Espresso Shot bathroom, and he was awesome. Gave me soup and hid me in his kitchen to warm up, but he isn't you. I would've felt better if it were you.

She shoved her phone into her pocket, relieved that she'd admitted the truth, but dreading the moment he read it. He'd find a way to excuse her from work, and she was afraid she'd let him. And if he bailed her out, would she ever go back? She loved this job. She didn't want to give it up, but after the frigid day she'd endured, it would take little to convince her to quit.

"Hey! Stop that or you'll need a bath!" she shouted as Cerberus forgot his ball in favor of rolling in the dirt. "I'm serious!" She stood up and chased after him. "Get up or you're going right in the shower, Mister." She reached down and playfully swatted his haunches, but Cerberus jumped to his feet before her fingers barely touched him and took off running. A car door slammed, and Bel jerked up to find Olivia ignoring the dog's exuberant greeting as she charged for his mom.

"Did you know?" she blurted. "Did you know what Eamon was? What Ewan was?"

"Olivia," Bel started.

"Did you know?" she demanded.

"Yes." Bel's shoulders sagged. "Yes, I did."

"How could you know and not tell me?"

"Come on." Bel turned toward her front door. "Let's go inside and talk."

"No. I don't want to go inside and talk. I want you to tell me why you let me date a monster."

"Because I thought he told you." Bel whirled on her. "Those were Eamon's conditions. Now, get inside. I'm tired of the cold. I'm not having this conversation out here." She turned on her heels without waiting for a response and ushered Cerberus into her cabin. She tossed her blanket onto the couch and grabbed the teapot as Olivia thankfully entered the house and shut the chill outside behind them.

"Tea?" Bel asked.

"I'm not staying," Olivia said.

"Suit yourself." Bel filled the kettle with a single serving of water and set it on the stove to boil.

"So why didn't you tell me?"

"I already told you why."

"Yes, because you thought Ewan told me," Olivia said. "How could you think that? How could you believe I learned my boyfriend confessed he was a murderer and a monster, and I just went about life like it was nothing? If I'd known the truth, don't you think I would've freaked out or that my behavior would've changed drastically?"

"He isn't a murderer," Bel interrupted. "That hiker the bear attacked was a hunter targeting his pack. He would've killed Ewan's entire family if your boyfriend hadn't stopped him."

"Oh my god, and now you're justifying murderers!" Olivia shrieked. "First you lie to me, and now you act like Ewan's crimes are nothing."

"Because they mean nothing to us." Bel seized the teapot a little too forcefully and poured the scalding water into a mug, but the fragrant scent of peppermint couldn't calm her nerves. "Human rules don't apply to ancient beings, and even if they did, it wasn't murder. It was self-defense. You should've seen the weapons that hunter was traveling with. Eamon hid them before we officially booked the evidence, but that man had a custom rifle built to hunt down and exterminate people like Ewan."

"So you really have known this entire time?" Olivia stepped away from her, and Bel's heart twisted in her chest. How had it come to this? How had her best friend grown so disgusted with her?

"Yes…" She sagged against the kitchen counter. At least the tea mug was hot in her palms. "I learned about Eamon the hard way, and I figured out what Ewan was after we arrested him. He was supposed to move on from Bajka after we released him from custody when Abel took you, but then he kidnapped me too. Eamon wanted help searching for me, so he enlisted the bear. They struck a deal, which is apparently rare for their kind. Eamon lets Ewan stay in town under one condition. He had to tell you the truth."

"Well, he clearly didn't, because your freak of a boyfriend barged into my apartment and slit his wrist to prove a point. How could you date someone like him? How could you let yourself be with something so—"

"Careful," Bel warned. "I love you… so much, but he means the world to me. The things we've gone through together. The things he's done to keep me alive. You can hate him all you want, but not in my presence."

"If you love me, why didn't you tell me?" Olivia shouted so loud that Cerberus ran from the kitchen to hide under the bed. "We are friends. Women don't let their friends fall in love with monsters."

"Because he isn't a monster!" Bel shouted back. "Ewan's a good man who loves you. He's an idiot, that's for sure. He should've never disobeyed Eamon, but he adores you. He'd never hurt you."

"But I can't love a man who isn't honest, and I can't love a friend who doesn't have my back."

"Olivia, I always have your back." Bel set her mug down, desperate to pull her partner into a hug, but Olivia stepped further away from her.

"Then you should've told me."

"They weren't my secrets to tell! Eamon doesn't want word spreading, and Ewan was the one who owed you the truth, not me."

"Well, if I'd learned Eamon was some beast, I would've warned you," Olivia spat. "You owed me that much."

"I couldn't—" the trill of Bel's cell phone cut her off, and her first instinct was to ignore it. She assumed it was Eamon calling her back, but then she saw Griffin's name on the screen.

"Hello," she answered, trying to keep her voice from wavering.

"Emerson, I hate to ask, but can you help with this outdoor night shoot?" he said. "Fans got wind of it, and the crowd is getting unruly. Unfortunately, some of our deputies are a little too star-struck by Taron Monroe, but she won't affect you. I'll give you tomorrow off in exchange, but I need you."

"Um…" she glanced up at Olivia, her heart breaking. "Sure. I'll be there soon." She hung up the phone and met her partner's gaze. "I'm sorry, I have to go. Griffin needs me."

"It's fine." Olivia's words were clipped as she backed up toward the door.

"Olivia, please. Can we talk about this later?"

"There's nothing to talk about. You lied to me for months. You knew that a bear capable of killing a human being was sleeping in my bed, and you kept silent. I don't need to hear anymore."

"Olivia, stop…"

But Gold ignored her and left the cabin, slamming the door behind her. Bel burst into tears as the slam echoed off the walls.

Her relationship with her father was strained. She'd almost lost Eamon. She was losing Olivia, and now she had to venture back out into the cold. She thought filming would be a fun experience, but she hadn't expected to be stuck outside in the dead of winter so her mind could endlessly repeat her run down that mountain.

"You're okay," a whiskey-smooth voice soothed as massive arms scooped her off the floor, and Bel flinched. She hadn't heard anyone enter her home. "It's just me," Eamon said.

"I thought you had your meeting," she said as she hugged his neck.

"I told you I'd make them wait if you needed me, and I felt that text required an in-person response… seems I was right." He stood to his full height, cradling her in his embrace. "Come hang out at my place while I work so you don't have to be alone. You can sit beside me and shove your cold toes under my legs." He kissed her forehead as he aimed for the door. "Come, Cerberus. Car ride."

"I can't," Bel said. "I have to go back to work."

"Really?" He paused before the front door.

"Griffin's giving me tomorrow off, but I have to work the night shoot. The crowd is getting out of hand, and I guess Miss Monroe is distracting some officers. Griffin asked if I could cover the shift."

"But it's guaranteed you'll have tomorrow off?" Eamon asked.

"Yes."

"Good. I'll take Cerberus home with me now then. Come to my place when you're done, and I'll keep the fire going all day tomorrow for you."

"Ugh, don't mention your fireplace. I'm already dreading leaving my house," Bel groaned as she slid down his body until her feet landed on the hardwood. "Thanks for stopping by. You have no idea how badly I needed you."

"You were crying on the kitchen floor. I think I do know." He

Evidence of a Folktale

cupped her face and forced her to meet his gaze. "Thank you for telling me how you felt, but don't hide it from me again. I can take it. I swore to you we would communicate and make this work. I meant every word."

"If it makes you feel better, it was Olivia and the cold that had me on the floor, not our conversations. I think I've lost my friend."

"What happened?"

"She hates me for lying." Bel grabbed her coat and slipped into her boots. "I'll tell you more later, but I have to go."

"Okay." Eamon snapped Cerberus' leash on his collar as he readied to take him home with him, his entire body fighting the urge to argue with her. "If you get too cold, or if you just want company, text me, and I'll come warm you up."

"We should just have you run the security." Bel raised onto her toes and kissed him. "No one would dare approach the sets."

"I'd do it if it kept you out of this weather."

"I wish… I'll be okay." She squeezed his hand as they separated to go to their respective cars. "And Eamon?"

"Yes, Detective?"

"I know I give you a hard time about breaking into my place, but do me a favor? Never stop."

BAJKA FELL into a routine over the next few days, and Bel found a rhythm even though Olivia ignored her. She was too busy to dwell on their rift, or at least that's what she told herself. Between the night shoots and the overtime, she barely had time to sleep, and Eamon's love of cooking came in handy. On the nights they didn't stay together, he left meals in her fridge, most of which she ate while running out the door.

The outdoor shoots were brutal, but the first fan event was thankfully a different experience. The show had rented the hotel's convention center and hosted a two-day meet-and-greet. Photo ops, signings, Q&A panels, merchandise tables. It was a madhouse, but Bel enjoyed herself. The event was indoors and heated, allowing her to focus on the charm of the convention and not the ice biting with ruthless fangs at her skin. Eamon had also purchased a ticket so he could move freely about the hotel. He kept his distance, but Bel thoroughly enjoyed looking up from her position guarding the signing tables to find his death-black eyes watching her. She enjoyed sneaking off to make out like teenagers even more.

The weekend was overwhelmingly hectic, but by the time Monday morning rolled around, Bel found she was happy to return to work. The lack of murders, the presence of famous actors, and Eamon sticking by her side did wonders for her love of the job. He'd been careful to support her without becoming overbearing or suggesting she quit, and as she poured coffee into her thermos, she remembered why she loved being a detective.

"I'll drive you," Eamon said as he jogged into his kitchen. "It snowed heavily last night, so the roads will be messy. Plus, today's shoot is on my property, so I might as well."

"Really?" Bel smothered Cerberus' meaty head in kisses as they said goodbye. "I didn't know we were shooting on your land."

"To be fair, half of Bajka is my land." Eamon snagged his keys and helped her carry her things out of the front door. "The filming scouts didn't realize this was my property when they selected that section of the woods. I had my lawyer work with the town to approve the permits, so the crew doesn't know they'll be on the Reale Estate, but because it's mine, I figured I should come along and watch the action."

"The action, or *The Action*?" She swung her hips seductively as she walked ahead of him.

"Dating a detective means I get away with nothing." He jogged to catch her, slapping her ass playfully before climbing into his truck. "In all seriousness, I'm curious how much has changed compared to the last time I was in Hollywood. I didn't care to linger around the crowds in town, though, so I haven't had a chance to examine the process or the equipment."

"I don't blame you," Bel said as he started the engine. "But watching them film is cool. I'm unfamiliar with the industry, so it's been an experience."

Eamon threaded his fingers through hers as the truck aimed down the snowy drive, and the two chatted as he pushed through the barely plowed roads that led into the mountains. It had been snowing on and off over the past few weeks, leaving the ground magical but bitter, but this snowfall had Bel thankful she'd been locked away in Eamon's mansion. White coated the land with her deadly beauty, and the only reason they made it to the location in such good time was because the icy trails seemed almost a game for him.

"I'm dreading the cold," she said as they parked. "The shots will be beautiful, but it'll hurt." She gripped the door's handle, but the moment the door cracked open to allow a sliver of fresh mountain air into the truck, Eamon's hand shot out and seized her wrist, refusing to let her leave the safety of the truck's cabin. Bel quirked her eyebrows at him, the force on her arm almost bruising, and she opened her mouth to ask why his black eyes had suddenly darkened when she understood. Eamon sat frozen in the driver's seat, fist gripping her wrist with a predatory hunger, and bile ran up her throat at the meaning.

Blood. Eamon Stone smelled blood.

Autopsy Report

CERBERUS

PROD.NO. TAKE SOUND
SCENE
DIRECTOR
CAMERAMAN EXT. INT.

CINEMA TICKET 9891102 ADMIT ONE
CINEMA TICKET 9891102 ADMIT ONE

Chapter Six

"Human?" Bel asked.

"Yes," Eamon answered.

"Fresh?"

"Yes."

"Close by?"

"Yes."

Bel cursed. "Is it possible that a crew member cut himself setting up the equipment?" she asked. Eamon didn't answer, but he didn't need to. She read the answer in his hunger. An accident hadn't spilled the blood he scented.

She cursed again. "Okay…" She avoided Eamon's gaze as she stepped out of the truck. She didn't want him to witness her falter.

They'd parked beside the other vehicles in the trail's pull-off, which meant they needed to travel the rest of the way on foot. She'd been looking forward to today's shoot. The scenes filmed in town depicted normal life, but the paranormal aspects of Aesop's Files often occurred in the woods. She'd been eager to observe how the show created its monsters, but now, she wanted to climb back in the truck and drive home because if he smelled that much blood, a body would follow.

"Everyone looks fine," Bel whispered as they approached the bustling location. The director was shouting orders. Deputies already stood watch to keep any rogue fans obsessed enough to brave this weather away, and cameramen were positioning their shots. No one was bleeding out in this endless expanse of white.

"It's not here." Eamon lifted his nose into the wind and inhaled. "It's close, but not here." He extended a hand, and when she took it, he pulled her through the deep snow into the trees.

"I hope a fan didn't do something stupid and get themselves killed," she said, dread creeping into her gut as they battled the fresh drifts. Everything within her pleaded with the powers that be that this was an accident. That this tragedy of spilled blood didn't herald a new darkness come to plague Bajka, but with every step, her anxiety mocked her. This deep in the woods after a heavy snowfall? This wasn't an accident.

"Wait..." Eamon pulled her to a stop and inhaled. "This way." He tugged her forward, and after two minutes, a pop of morbid color filled their vision.

"Oh my god." Bel picked up her pace. "That's a lot of blood."

"It's not all blood," Eamon said.

"What on earth?" Her words died on her tongue as they closed the distance. "Can you hear a heartbeat?"

"No."

"What in god's name happened here?" Her head spun at the sight, at the red in the snow, at the bloody feminine hand peeking out from below a crimson cloak. "Women don't just end up dead in the middle of the woods naked except for a red cloak by accident," she whispered.

"No, they don't," Eamon agreed, and Bel cursed as she fished out her phone.

"Griffin," she said when he answered, and by his stillness,

her tone already warned him of what she was going to say. "There's a body."

"I'd hoped you'd found a prop that got blown off set by the storm," Griffin said as he and Bel hovered over the body bathed in crimson. He cursed, the harsh words echoing off the trees, and then he stared at Eamon's hulking form flanking them. A wordless conversation passed between the men, and Bel knew the sheriff had arrived at the same realization she had. Eamon had located the corpse, and if he'd found it, it was no prop.

"We need to keep this quiet," Griffin said. "We have hundreds of fans in town and a month-long filming schedule. If word gets out that we found a body in the woods..."

"It's going to get out," Bel said.

"I know, but if we control how the news is released, it'll cause less panic... there's no chance this was an accident, is there?"

"Naked except for this red cloak and left to bleed out from a chest or abdomen wound? No, someone killed her. See here?" Bel crouched beside the woman's legs. "I'm no medical examiner, but I've seen enough bodies to recognize lividity. She died in this position and hasn't been moved."

"A naked girl running through a snowstorm gets killed in the middle of nowhere?" Griffin stared at their surroundings. "What on earth happened out here?"

"Not the middle of nowhere," Eamon interrupted, speaking for the first time. "She died close to today's filming location... on my property."

"This is part of the Reale Estate?" Griffin asked. "Good god, Mr. Stone, is there ever a murder you aren't potentially involved in?"

"In this town, apparently not," Eamon said. "But as you can

see, this wasn't me. She bled out in the snow. If I'd done this, there'd be no blood."

The sheriff grunted in protest. "I don't want to know."

"He has an alibi." Bel stifled her laugh. "He was with me last night."

"His girlfriend would be a terrible alibi if it weren't you. If Eamon committed something this gruesome, you'd be the first person to have him pinned to the ground and handcuffed," Griffin said as deputies, techs, and the medical examiner arrived. They drove silently, absent lights and sirens, and then they walked to the location to keep the scene from attracting spectators.

"Sounds fun," Eamon said, and Bel couldn't stop the laugh this time. She knew he was pushing her boss, and as horrible as this death was, she loved his presence during a case. The darkness didn't weigh as heavily on her shoulders when the devil kept the demons at bay.

"Nope." Griffin glared at them, but Eamon just shrugged.

"Oh my god," Lina Thum whispered as she settled beside the body. She was Bajka's respected medical examiner, and Bel pitied the poor woman. The Matchstick Girls autopsies had been a depressingly daunting undertaking, and now, barely a few weeks later, another dead girl lay frozen for her to witness. "What happened to this poor girl?"

"We're hoping you can tell us," Bel said. "I noticed lividity, so she hasn't been moved. She's also covered in a light dusting of snow, which suggests she died as the storm was ending. Not sure what time that was, though. I was sleeping."

"I can call the weather channel and get an update," Griffin said.

"You're right about lividity," Lina said. "The position doesn't appear posed either. She fell face down like this."

"Which means she was probably on foot when she tripped since there are no tire tracks." Bel moved to the victim's legs.

Evidence of a Folktale

"Her feet don't look rough, though, so she didn't run far. Unfortunately, our shoes have destroyed the scene, but there weren't footprints when we arrived. I think placing the time of death at the end of the snowfall is correct. It was falling long enough to cover her tracks, but not long enough to bury her."

"Plus, bodies are warm immediately after death. Some of the snow would've melted off her at first," Lina said. "And it's a short walk from the parking spots, so her feet wouldn't have suffered much damage if she ran from down there…" She gazed back the way they'd come. "I didn't see blood, though, yet there's a ton below the body. So, she wasn't bleeding while she was running."

"This is probably where the killer caught up with her," Bel said. "Maybe she was trying to escape a car."

"But why risk the woods in a storm to kill this poor woman?" Griffin asked as a tech photographed the scene.

"She's naked and wearing a red cloak. It's a little theatrical," Bel said. "I don't watch Aesop's Files, but a red cloak fits its narrative. I wonder if fans drove close to today's shooting location to hook up, but things went too far. Maybe she felt uncomfortable and tried to escape, and her date killed her for it."

"Oh god," Lina said. "I hope not, but I'll check for signs of sexual assault during my autopsy."

The officers fell silent, and for long moments, no one spoke as they worked. Bel stared at the girl in red, her stomach roiling until she felt Eamon step closer to her. Murder was heinous enough, but to be assaulted beforehand? She gagged at the possibility.

"If everyone has what they need, I'd like to turn her over and see who we have," Lina said, finally breaking the mournful silence as she gripped the woman's limbs. "She's partially frozen, so it'll be difficult to confirm the presence of Rigor Mortis, but the snow is a solid indicator that she died last night— Oh my god." She yanked her hands away from the corpse, and the officers froze where they stood when the victim's abdomen came into view. Her pale skin had been eviscerated, slashed apart in a brutal display of violence, the cold perfectly preserving the horror in vibrant color.

"What did this to her?" Griffin stepped backward. "That... that looks almost animal."

"It does," Lina agreed, and Bel whirled on Eamon, her eyes asking for her voice. They'd found a bloody body in the woods once before. Was it happening again?

Eamon leaned forward and inhaled before returning his gaze to her. He nodded, then pinched his fingers together until only an inch of air separated them. It wasn't confirmation that someone like Ewan had murdered this woman, but it seemed it was possible.

"No ID," Lina said. "But I didn't expect to find any. We'll have to wait for the autopsy to learn more."

"Wait..." Bel lunged closer to the victim's face. She'd been too preoccupied with her flayed stomach to notice her features at first, but even frozen in death, she recognized this woman. "I've seen her on set a few times. I don't know her name, but I recognize her. She's Aesop's Files head writer."

Griffin cursed.

Lina cursed.

And then Bel cursed.

"You sure that's her?" Griffin asked.

"Yes," Bel said.

Griffin cursed again. "This isn't good."

"I don't think my hookup theory explains this."

"How do you mean?"

"A hookup turned violent between fans obsessed enough to brave the weather is plausible, but the writer? The episodes are her creations. Why would she risk something so dangerous when her job already requires her to be on location? I guess it's possible, but..." she trailed off.

"But what, Emerson?" Griffin asked, and every eye zeroed in on her.

"Naked save for a red hooded cloak and slashed apart as if attacked by an animal... or a creature. This feels an awful lot like the killings on the show."

"You think someone killed the writer in the same way she'd write an episode?" Lina asked.

"I don't know what I think," Bel said. "This just feels like an episode of Aesop's Files. Less than a mile away, they're shooting a murder scene, and what do we find? A real death in the woods. And to make it worse, we won't recover much evidence. The blood and the melting snow would've contaminated anything of importance."

"Good god, this is bad." Griffin looked as if he might sit down on the drifts and give up. "All right, everyone, I realize our odds aren't great, but let's find something. This just became a very high-profile case."

"Something like that?" Eamon asked, pointing to the snow beside the body. Bel followed his directions, squinting at the ground for long seconds before she noticed it. It blended in with its surroundings flawlessly, and if Eamon hadn't spotted it, they might have missed it entirely.

"It's a gift box." Bel directed the techs to photograph the tiny white square wrapped with a crimson bow, and when they were done, her gloved hands plucked it free of the scene. "It was on its side. I wonder if the killer placed it on the body, but the wind blew it off."

"The red's the same as the victim's hood." Griffin settled next to her to examine the object. "They're probably related, but that seems too small for a gift box. What's it hiding?"

Bel grabbed the ribbon and started to pull, but Eamon snatched it from her, his hands protected by stolen gloves she hadn't seen him slip on.

"I'll do it," he said.

"Mr. Stone, you're not a police officer," Griffin said. "You're here only as a witness."

"I'm here to ensure no one kills the woman I love… again." He glared at the sheriff, a battle of wills rearing its masculine head. "This is probably nothing, but in the event it's a trap, I'll open it, not Isobel."

"Let him," Lina said, the authority in her voice warning she was not to be argued with. "I never want the real Bel on my morgue table."

"Fine." Griffin waved his hand, and Eamon untied the bow and lifted the top. He sniffed the contents, much to the curiosity of the watching techs, and then returned it to Bel.

"It's safe," he said. "It's just paper."

"Paper?" Bel withdrew a folded note and flattened the sheet. "I don't get it. It's a jumble of letters." She tilted it so her boss could see. "Why leave a gift box on a body with only nonsense typed on it?"

"Why kill this poor woman and leave her naked with only a red hood?" Lina asked.

"To mimic the show," Griffin answered. "I hope we don't have a crazed fan on our hands. The last thing we need is someone targeting the cast and crew while they're in our town."

"Let's not get ahead of ourselves," Lina said. "We just closed a case with multiple victims. Let's not start racking up imaginary ones."

"Thum, are you good to get the body to the morgue?" Griffin asked.

"I am."

"Great. Emerson, can you finish up here? I don't want to pull Gold in yet. One homicide detective missing from patrol isn't suspicious, but two? I want to meet with the producers before word gets out and we have chaos on our hands."

"I'll be fine," Bel said.

"Meet me at the station when you're done. Hopefully, the

producers will have answers for us..." He glanced at Eamon with an expression that told everyone he didn't believe that for a second. "Too bad you aren't a cop."

"You scented something," Bel said when Griffin was finally out of earshot. "Are we dealing with a killer like Ewan?"

"I don't know," Eamon said. "The falling snow covered their tracks so scents are muddled. They killed outdoors where the elements degrade evidence. Hundreds of strangers have flooded Bajka, many of whom are supernatural to some extent, so I can't confirm if the killer is a shifter of sorts or if the victim merely came in contact with power before she died. Shifters in their human form are harder for me to—"

"Hold on, rewind a bit." Bel pressed a gloved palm against his chest. "Many are supernatural to some extent? What do you mean?"

"Don't worry." Eamon rubbed her hand, cementing it against his body despite their dwindling audience. "Conventions and fandoms always attract the less powerful. It's a way for them to express who they are without hiding."

"Because everyone assumes it's just a costume or sleight of hand."

"Exactly. Alpha predators avoid attention. We stick to the shadows, but lesser witches and shifters flock to events like this. Our town is teeming with them. It's another reason I'm not a fan of these conventions. If I can sense them, they can definitely sense me. Should help keep them in order, though."

"So this murder might be human, even if her wounds look claw-inflicted," Bel said. "A supernatural would be foolish to risk your wrath."

"No lesser power would kill in a town ruled by someone like me without acquiring my approval first," Eamon agreed. "It would be their death sentence."

"Ewan did."

"That was a desperate act of self-defense. He had no choice if he wanted to survive."

"So, the writer wasn't killed with claws?"

"She might have been. There are those like Ewan who act out of desperation and others who are crazed enough to disregard their own survival. But given the situation, I'm inclined to suspect another murder weapon."

"Why's that?"

"It was suggested that a fan is killing crew members in ways that mimic Aesop's Files," he said. "A show with props, special effects, custom weapons, and entire sets that recreate the violence of werewolves, vampires, and witches."

"And if you're going to kill to mimic a show…" Bel gripped the tips of Eamon's fingers with her gloved ones. "…you might as well mimic it in all its ways."

"CAN you think of any reason Gwen Rossa would've been in the woods last night?" Griffin had requested the show's producers—Alistair Rot and Evelyn Pierce—come down to the station and answer questions. The director Warren Rouge, who'd grown borderline aggressive when asked to halt shooting, had brought that same hostility into the conference room, which was why the producers were the only two participating in the conversation.

"Miss Rossa was a talented and dedicated writer," Evelyn Pierce said. She was a no-nonsense businesswoman whose reaction to this interview told Bel she was a *'time is money'* type, but of the three present, she at least appeared sympathetic to Gwen Rossa's fate. Her fellow producer and the director were disappointingly far less accommodating with their responses, though. Bel realized these three probably weren't friends with the victim, but head writers had close working relationships with their directors. It was odd that Warren Rouge was more concerned about losing the afternoon light than the episode's author. She'd also expected the producers to display outrage as they blamed Bajka for the death of their own, but the trio sitting on the opposite end of the conference table seemed solely interested in solving this issue with as little inconvenience to their lives as possible.

"She produced quality work," Pierce continued. "She was one reason Aesop's Files has such high ratings, but our knowledge of Miss Rossa ended at her writing. Her personal life was none of our business. We cannot say why she ventured into the woods last night, nor can we guess who she was with."

A conveniently diplomatic answer. They weren't getting anywhere with this trio.

"Unfortunately, we believe Miss Rossa's death wasn't an accident," Griffin said, switching gears. "We don't know if this attack was personal or a crime of opportunity, but it would be wise to halt shooting and postpone all fan events until the killer is in custody."

"I appreciate your concern, but we can't do that," Alistair Rot said. Unlike his fellow producer, Rot was almost callously uninterested in the murder. It bothered Bel that this man cared so little that a woman he worked with had been gutted like an animal, but maybe that's what happened when fame demanded you keep the proverbial wheel churning. Shows often employed multiple directors and producers, but the three present were Aesop's Files most prolific. Perhaps being at the top for so long destroyed one's ability to love anything other than success.

"We're on a tight schedule," Alistair continued. "Aesop's Files is expensive to film with an obsessive fan base that spans multiple countries. Tickets to our events have been sold out for months, and we cannot afford any delays."

"A woman is dead." Griffin leaned his elbow onto the table for effect, and Bel had to stifle a smile. He wasn't going to let these three off the hook so easily. "She was chased naked and alone through the snow, and she died violently. I respect you have a job to do, but a woman lost her life. We don't know if the killer was targeting Miss Rossa or the show, so until we find the responsible party, I strongly urge you to reconsider. The safety of your cast and crew and your fans should be our priority."

"Sheriff, our writer was murdered in your town, not on our sets or even in our lodgings." Alistair leaned forward to mimic Griffin's pose, a silent battle for dominance waging between the men, and the unspoken standoff clearly illustrated why Griffin wished Eamon was an officer. One glare from him, and this obstinate trio would cave.

"In fact, her death occurred on private property, if I'm not mistaken," Rot continued, and Bel flinched. Were they planning to pin this on Eamon? "Miss Rossa's murder had nothing to do with Aesop's Files, therefore we have no reason to shut down production. We'll certainly dedicate these last episodes to her, but we aren't responsible for what our crew does after hours when not on set. Her unfortunate demise in your woods is not a reason for us to ruin our entire season."

Bel bristled, fighting the urge to reach across the table and slap the producer, and she could practically feel Griffin's body temperature rise beside her. She forced her gaze to remain forward, though, because if she saw her anger reflected in her boss' eyes, they'd both say something that would land them in trouble.

"Did Miss Rossa have any enemies? Someone who'd want to hurt her?" she asked, changing the subject.

"Enemies?" Evelyn repeated. "I can't speak to her personal life, but we were unaware of any professional grievances."

"What about obsessed fans?" Bel pushed.

"We all have those," Warren said, finally breaking his sullen silence. "It's part of the business. Most of the time, it's flattering or funny, sometimes it's annoying, and occasionally it's dangerous, but it comes with the territory."

"Did Gwen have any that were dangerous?"

Evidence of a Folktale

"I don't think so," the director said.

"So, no dangerously obsessed fans? Was she dating anyone? Did a fan find out and seek revenge because he couldn't have her?" Bel asked. She was well acquainted with how possible that scenario was. She'd lived it.

"I don't know if she was dating," Warren said. "She was married to the show. We all are."

"Is there someone I could talk to about fan communications?" she pressed. "Maybe there's a letter or an email that'll point us in the right direction?"

"Well..." Alistair Rot glanced at Warren, and Bel couldn't tell if the wordless conversation between the producer and director was wariness or a conspiracy to lie. "One fan stands out. He's extremely... passionate when the show doesn't adhere to the storylines that he believes it should. He sends the writers essays on the issues along with scripts that rewrite his problematic episodes. It's been a thorn in our side for months. I don't know his name, but Gwen's writing assistant has access to her email. We can get it from her."

"Please do," Bel said, thankful they were finally getting somewhere.

"If there's nothing else, we need to get back to work." Evelyn stood with an air of finality. "We have to meet with the writers to discuss how to move forward with the season in Miss Rossa's absence, and we've now lost an entire afternoon of filming that'll need to be rescheduled. We also need to contact our lawyers to help us navigate her loss and contract."

"Thank you for coming." Griffin stood and shook their hands, Bel following suit even though neither gesture of appreciation was sincere.

"Thank you, Sheriff. Detective." Evelyn Pierce nodded her goodbye and exited the conference room, Alistair Rot and Warren Rouge in tow, and when they vanished from sight, Griffin collapsed back into his seat.

"And just like that, I am no longer star-struck," he said. "Gwen Rossa was ripped apart and left to freeze, and those three acted like they were seconds away from billing us for the inconvenience... as much grief as I give your Mr. Stone, I will say this about him. He's god-awful rich, terrifying, aggressive, and stubborn, but he would never dismiss such a brutal attack as if it were no more important than a weather report."

"Don't let him hear you talk like that," Bel smirked. "He'll think you love him."

"Oh shush." He rolled his eyes in mock offense. "Now, for the worst part of our job. I have to deliver the death notice to the family. Keep an eye out for that email from Miss Rossa's assistant, and if you don't get it soon, let me know. After this meeting, I'm in the mood to nag those three."

"GRIFFIN?" Bel knocked on his office door an hour later. "Gwen Rossa's assistant emailed me the obsessed fan's name, and guess what?"

"He's in town for the events?"

"Ding, ding, ding." Bel strode to his deck and perched on the corner as she spoke. "She also sent over copies of his letters and rewrites, and saying he was upset about the show's trajectory is putting it lightly. Tony Royce is passionately angry about Willow Moon's departure from the show."

"Who?" Griffin asked.

"Beau Draven's original costar," Bel answered. "She played his detective's partner and future love interest in the first few seasons, but she left and was replaced with Taron Monroe. Most fans prefer Monroe's character. Reviews say she has more chemistry with Draven, but Mr. Royce is apparently a huge Willow Moon fan. He blames Gwen Rossa for her departure from

Aesop's Files. He believes she purposely wrote her out of the show, therefore ruining it."

"Did she write Miss Moon out of the show?"

"No," Bel said. "Rossa's assistant was generous enough to include an answer to that accusation in her email. The show's gaining popularity put Willow Moon firmly in the spotlight, and she was pregnant while shooting her last season. She hadn't announced the news, though, so fans ridiculed her for the sudden weight gain. Moon realized that her fame would lead to constant scrutiny and criticism for her and her family, and she didn't want that for her child. Her departure from the show was amicable, and according to Rossa's assistant, she became heavily involved in the independent film scene after marrying her child's father."

"So our victim had no control over Willow Moon's retirement, yet this Tony guy blames her? Seems stable."

"Exactly," Bel said. "He bought a ticket to this past weekend's meet-and-greet but had to be escorted out after he harassed Gwen Rossa about the scripts' direction."

"He harassed her this weekend, and she ended up dead Monday morning?" Griffin repeated.

"Certainly doesn't look good. I just called the local hotels and inns. He's staying in a budget motel right off the highway. According to the front desk, he hasn't checked out."

"That they know of."

"I'll head over and see for myself," Bel said. "Even if he fled, the motel believes he's still in his room. Hopefully, housekeeping hasn't cleaned yet, because a crime this bloody would leave evidence behind."

"Sounds good, but take Gold with you," Griffin said. "If Tony Royce killed Gwen Rossa, he's capable of unthinkable violence, and I don't want you alone with him."

"Therefore, ruining the romantic character arc by giving the audience a flat and unauthentic resolution to the questions posed in season one," Tony said, and Bel gasped for breath. The man's long-winded and run-on sentence analysis of the show's multi-season plot and literary failings convinced her that if she didn't breathe for him, all three of them would choke to death.

She and Olivia had driven out to the motel to confirm that Tony Royce was still checked in, but unlike their normal outings, her partner had opted to drive herself, refusing Bel the chance to discuss their situation. Arriving at the lackluster lodgings, they'd knocked on Tony's room, not expecting to find him, so it surprised them both when a five-foot-seven man opened the door with a bag of chips in his hands. He had no muscles to speak of, save maybe in his jaw from talking so rapidly, and Bel knew the minute he'd answered their knock that he wasn't the killer. People were often surprisingly capable of the unexpected... except for Tony Royce. She felt guilty for judging him by his cover, but it was as plain as the empty soda bottles strewn about the dressers and floor to keep the discarded episode drafts company that he hadn't chased a woman through the snow and slaughtered her. Bel could probably bench press him in her sleep, but in favor of doing their due diligence, they asked him the questions they would ask any other suspect... which had resulted in an exhausting analysis of Aesop's Files post-Willow Moon.

"So, you see, I had to talk to her this weekend," Tony said, completely unaware that both of Bajka's homicide detectives weren't here to listen to his writing lecture. "Miss Rossa is sending the show down a path she can't recover from, and I needed her to read my episodes. If I can just reason with her, she'll see I've fixed the rest of the seasons. That's what I was doing here." He gestured to the crumpled papers littering the room. "She turned me away at the meet-and-greet. My drafts weren't good enough, so I've been reworking them for hours." He snatched a full bottle of soda off the table, and Bel had to fight the urge to steal it from him. If he didn't stop drinking, he might give himself a heart attack. "I haven't slept," he continued. "I was up all night. My draft needs to be perfect so she realizes Willow must come back."

"You do know that Willow Moon left the show of her own free will?" Olivia said, finally finding a pause in his speech. "Gwen Rossa didn't write her out of Aesop's Files. Miss Moon had a baby."

"What?" Tony asked as if he didn't realize he had company.

"Did you leave the motel last night?" Bel changed the subject.

"No, but I left my room to find the vending machine. I needed caffeine to stay awake, but I never left the premises," he said, shaking the soda for emphasis. "It was snowing hard, and I wanted to finish my script before the next event. This time Gwen Rossa has to acknowledge I'm right."

"Mr. Royce." Bel softened her tone to counter the man's caffeine jitters. "Miss Rossa was killed last night."

"What?" Tony took a breath for what seemed like the first time since the detectives' arrival.

"Gwen Rossa was murdered last night," she repeated.

"What... Murdered?" The lanky man sank into the motel's provided office chair. "How?"

"That's what we're trying to figure out. You were one of the last people to have an issue with her."

"I had an issue with her writing, not her," Tony said. "Besides, I was here all night. I told you that."

"You did," Bel agreed. "And we'll confirm that with hotel security."

"Good, because I'd never kill her. I'm a writer. Not a killer... although, maybe the show will finally hire someone who can fix its problems."

Bel and Olivia exchanged raised eyebrows, and for a fraction of a second, they were back to normal. Just two detectives marveling at the oddities people verbalized when faced with murder.

"Did you notice anything odd at the meet-and-greet this weekend?" Bel asked. She doubted it since he was the one escorted from the property for harassment, but sometimes smoking guns came from the unlikeliest of shooters. "Did anyone strike you as dangerous?"

"No. All I saw were fans too brainwashed to realize that writing Willow Moon out of the show has destroyed it."

"Gwen Rossa didn't write Willow Moon out of Aesop's Files," Olivia repeated, her voice tinged with frustration. "The actress left of her own volition."

"Well, except for that one guy," Tony said, oblivious to Olivia's comments.

"What guy?" Bel leaned forward at his words. Now they were getting somewhere.

"That really tall man. Blond hair, scary. He must have been wearing contacts because he had black eyes. Not dark. Black… like the devil."

Bel bit her lip to stifle a laugh, but a glare from Olivia stole the humor from the room. A woman dead on an ancient being's property? In Olivia's mind, Eamon was already guilty.

"If you ask me, that guy killed her," Tony continued.

"We'll look into him," Bel said, not caring to discuss her love life with this man or her angry partner. "Thank you for your time." She stepped for the exit, hoping the movement would put an end to Mr. Royce's critiques. "We have your information; we'll be in touch if we have any more questions."

"Let me guess. Don't leave town?" he asked, as if eager to experience the famous cop phrase.

"Sure, but don't harass any more writers. Next time, you won't just be removed from the event. You'll have to deal with me." Bel shut the motel door behind them. "Well, he certainly didn't kill anyone. Drive people crazy? Absolutely, but there's no way he chased a woman through a storm or cut her apart."

"I agree," Olivia said.

"Hopefully, the autopsy will point us in the right direction. I'm going to talk to Rossa's assistant and retrace her steps the night before she died. If we can identify her movements, we might find out if she met anyone. Want to come?"

"Sounds like you got it under control." Olivia unlocked her car. "No need for both of us to go. I'll get started on the paperwork."

Volunteering to do paperwork? Her partner really must hate her.

"Yeah, okay..." Bel didn't know what else to say. "I'll call you if I find anything."

But she found nothing. Gwen Rossa and her assistant had gone their separate ways after the fan event, and she believed her boss was asleep in her hotel room until the producers told her someone had gutted her in the woods.

"Wow, it's cold out there," Eamon said as he and Cerberus dragged snow through Bel's front door. He'd volunteered to shovel her parking spot and walkways if she wanted to spend the night at her cabin, so she'd come home after her frustrating day. It was late and dark and frigid, but that she didn't have to clear her driveway was a small light at the end of the tunnel. She got to sit inside with fuzzy socks and steaming soup while Eamon and her dog did all the work.

"It must be brutal if you're cold," she said. "There's soup in the pot. It's canned, but it's hot."

"Thanks." Eamon tugged Cerberus' sweater off his stocky body and lifted him onto the couch beside his mom, wrapping him in a blanket to warm him up after his snowy playtime.

"What are you working on?" He kissed her cheek before moving to the stove, and his normally cool lips felt like solid ice against her skin.

"That paper you found at the scene," she answered. "I printed out a photo of it, but I can't make sense of it. A girl sliced apart and left naked in the woods save for a red cloak accompanied by a white gift box hiding a jumble of letters. Makes tons of sense."

"Can I see it?" He asked as he settled at the kitchen table to eat.

"Legally? Not really." Bel joined him, resisting his request because, at this point, insisting he couldn't do something was more flirting than denial.

"Well, I already saw it when I opened the box, so if anyone asks, I memorized it." He winked before planting a kiss on her lips. "Hand it over."

She slid the paper across the table and watched as his death-black eyes roamed the page.

```
Cngz hom keky eua ngbk
```

"It's definitely words," he said. "And small ones at that. My guess is it's a code."

"I figured as much, but that's as far as I got," Bel said.

"I think it's a Caesar Cipher."

"A what?"

"Julius Caesar used this for his private correspondence, hence its name," he explained. "It's where you take the letters of the alphabet and shift them forward by a predetermined number. To make it simple, if you use the number four, the letter A becomes the Letter E. You shift all your letters before sending the message, and then your recipient counts backward."

"Is there anything you don't know?" Bel bumped him with her shoulder. "Check the Gate. Caesar Cipher. What else do you have up your sleeve?"

Evidence of a Folktale

"When you've been alive as long as I have, purposes dampen the boredom," he said. "The years all blur together, and you can lose yourself to time. I always reinvent myself every few decades. Keeps me under the radar, but it also makes life interesting. I change everything about myself, and suddenly I'm at the bottom of my new chosen career, forced to start over thus keeping my mind sharp. This lifetime has been the least boring, though... in fact, I would prefer a little less anxiety." He reached below the table and squeezed her thigh. "I could use a break from stressing about what this human detective will do next."

"So Eamon Stone isn't even your real name. And this." She gestured to his chest. "He's a reinvention... just like the man who will come after me."

"There is no after you," he said, his tone suddenly serious. "There will never be an after you. There was a before. There's a during, but there is no after. You're it for me, the reason I survived for so long. And as far as I'm concerned, Eamon Stone is the real me because it's the name that belongs to you. He's the only version that matters."

"As unnerving as that is, I would love you no matter your name and no matter the lifetime," she whispered.

"I will love you in every lifetime." He put his spoon down and captured her face in his hands, pulling her close to kiss her with such hunger that when they broke apart, Bel was light-headed and flushed.

"Okay, back to the cipher." Eamon winked at her.

"Right, um... numbers," she blushed as she tried to reign in her very different train of thought. "How can we decode this without the number used to create it?"

"We're lucky. This is a short phrase with short words. Three or four-letter words always have one or two vowels, and identifying those will make decoding easier." Eamon pulled the paper closer and studied the coded message.

Cngz hom keky eua ngbk

"Okay, here." He grabbed the pen from Bel's grasp and pointed with its tip. "The letter G shows up a few times, as does the letter K. Those might be vowels based on where they are in the words, and if not, one of these letters is. Process of elimination. There are five vowels in the alphabet, so we'll test each one."

"I'm glad you're here." Bel leaned over the jumbled words. "This would've taken me forever. How did you notice this so quickly?"

"I had my own Roman Empire... as in it was the Ancient Roman Empire... although, if you were to ask what it is now, I'd say you in my tee shirts."

"A Roman Empire is something you think about all the time," she corrected.

"I know. For you, it's probably your dog, but for me, it's you in my shirts. I really do think about that all the time. The way your legs peak out. The way you look so small inside the fabric, yet so sure of yourself. All. The. Time. Detective."

"You're right, my Roman Empire is my dog," she teased in a dismissive tone.

"I knew it." Eamon rolled his eyes in mock defeat.

"So the Roman Empire? What was that like?"

"A lot of blood and a lot of death. How do you think it went?"

"You were a monster."

"Yes. And one who ate well," he said. "That's where I picked this up. It's easy for me to recognize the patterns even now. So, I believe K and G are vowels. The G is in the middle of two words, so it might be an A. The letter K appears at the end of one word and twice in another. That's maybe an E. Let's see. If G is A, and K is E, that's six spots. So, now, we just count each letter backward by six."

He fell silent as he deciphered the code, writing the new letters below the old, but when he was finally done, his eyebrows pinched at his handwriting.

"Well, subtracting six certainly creates real words, but that's not saying much," he said.

"What do you mean?" she asked.

"Here." He shoved the decoded message across the table, and as she read the five-word sentence, she understood what he meant. The phrase was no longer a jumble of letters, yet it was equally as confusing.

What Big Eyes You Have.

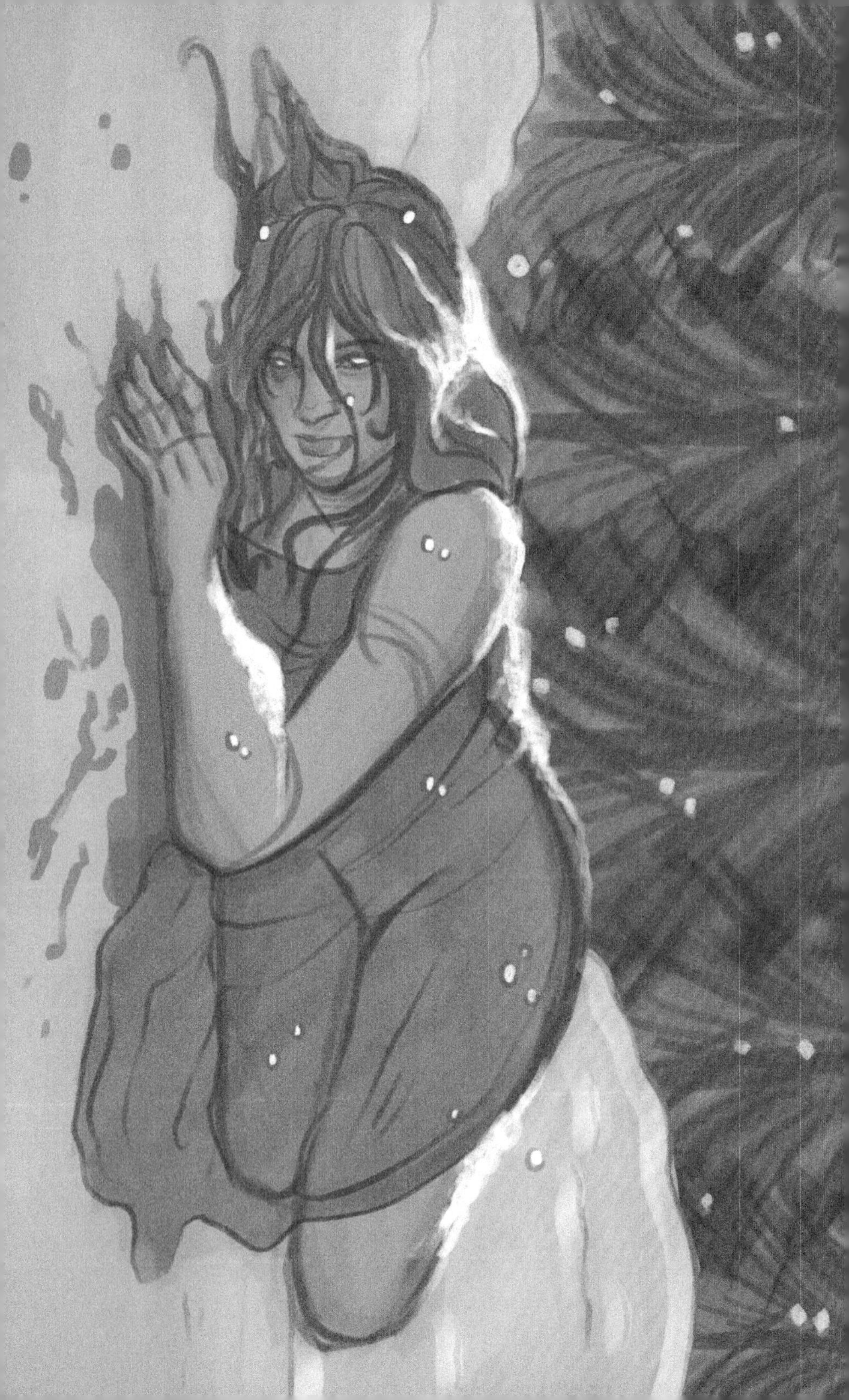

Chapter Seven

"I've never been so happy to see you walk through my doors," Lina Thum said as she wrapped her arms around Bel. "Don't ever end up on my table again."

"I don't intend to." Bel recovered from her surprise and returned the medical examiner's embrace. The women had never hugged before, so it took her a second to respond.

"Sorry I didn't welcome you back properly yesterday," Lina said. "I wasn't expecting to find a woman torn apart in the woods."

"None of us were." Bel released the M.E. and followed her into the back to prep for the morning's autopsy.

"Some welcome home, huh?"

"I'll say."

"If the exam becomes overwhelming for you, let me know," Lina said as they donned their protective gear. "I'll get Gold to come down instead."

"Olivia isn't coming?" Bel's stomach dropped.

"No, since you're here to collect the evidence, she said her time would be better served elsewhere. But again, if it's too much for you, I'll call her."

"I doubt this will be worse than seeing the victim bloody in the woods yesterday. I don't want to give up this job, so I shouldn't put things off. The longer I do, the harder it'll be to get back into the swing of things… besides, you were the one who saw my dead doppelgänger. It will be good for me to stay with you."

"I agree. Thank you," Lina said as the women entered the exam room. "I still can't figure out how that surgeon transformed another woman into you. If we ran your fingerprints and DNA, we would've eventually learned it wasn't you, but it was eerily exact. I don't understand."

"I don't know. I didn't see the body," Bel lied. She knew exactly how Dr. Blaubart had faked her death. With a scalpel cursed by black magic. A dangerous weapon that was now under Eamon's protection.

"I'm glad you didn't see it. You've been through enough." The women paused before the examination table. "Are you ready?"

"I hope so."

Lina began the exam, documenting her finds as she went, and Bel stood watch to collect the evidence. She tried to focus on the job and not the disfigured torso, forcing herself to be clinical in her approach. She could do this. She was a detective and a survivor. She'd been gifted a second chance when Gwen Rossa hadn't, and she refused to waste that.

"There are no defensive wounds on the body," Lina finally spoke. "She has some scrapes on her arms, but they aren't injuries associated with self-defense. They were probably from running through the trees."

"So she wasn't made to wear that cloak with force," Bel said. "She either disrobed willingly for the killer or took her clothes off under mental duress."

"There are no signs of sexual assault or activity of any kind. If she'd planned to hook up with someone, she died before they got very far. And this attack feels animalistic." Lina pointed to the torn abdomen. "A sharp, curved blade carved these wounds... like a claw, but I don't think any North American predators possess claws this specifically elongated. The animal would have to be massive."

Ewan flashed through Bel's memory before Eamon's words shoved to the forefront of her mind. "I have a theory," she said. "Aesop's Files is a paranormal police procedural. Monsters and crime scenes and over-the-top drama."

"I've heard, but I don't watch it," Lina said. "It has its fans, but it's too unrealistic for me. If I'm going to enjoy a show with vampires, witches, and werewolves in it, I need them to scare the living daylights out of me. I also believe that if supernatural beings existed, they wouldn't be quirky characters interacting with humans. They'd be predators, and we'd be the prey."

'Like Eamon,' Bel thought to herself. *'And Ewan, Alcina, The Tinker, Dr. Blaubart.'* They were all predators, and she'd been terrified of every single one of them.

"But your theory?" Lina prompted.

"Gwen Rossa was the Aesop's Files head writer," Bel explained. "And she dies in an overly dramatic way that's reminiscent of the show's deaths. Ripped apart in the woods while wearing only a red hood. It's like the killer's mimicking the show, paranormal aspects and all."

"Well, that's scary," Lina said.

"Is it possible that these lacerations were inflicted by prop claws?" Bel asked. "Did a fan want to live the show so badly that they created a weapon to reenact its murders?"

"Honestly? That makes a lot more sense than an animal killing this woman. I'll keep that in mind when I examine the wounds," Lina said. "Plus, that box with the ribbon. It was so... theatrical. You might be right. Someone could've followed the cast and crew here to recreate episodes with the very people that produced them. Is there a red hood case in one of the seasons?"

"I'd have to double-check," Bel said. "It pisses me off that the producers won't halt filming while we investigate. This is merely a theory, but if someone's recreating the show, a lot more people could die. The studio is willingly putting both its cast and crew and the fan in danger."

"Good lord, please no more bodies," Lina said. "Our town is overflowing. If we have a delusional killer on our hands, things will get messy quickly... not to mention the publicity. Can you imagine what will happen to Bajka when word gets out? Now add more than one crew member to the death toll?" She shuddered.

"Hopefully we find something during this exam that points us in the right direction. Most killers get sloppy."

"Not in this town," Lina laughed humorlessly. "We seem to attract the smart criminals... Oh, that box. Did you figure out what those letters meant?"

"Yes, I think so," Bel said. "Not that it makes sense."

"What do—what's that?" The M.E. leaned over Rossa's head, aiming the overhead light for a clearer view. "Come here. This is weird."

Bel joined her, and after snapping some photos, Lina pressed her gloved finger to the woman's eyeballs.

"Contact lenses," she said as she pulled the object from Gwen's eyes.

"What's weird about that?" Bel asked.

"There's something wrong with them. Hold on." She moved to the magnifying glass. "Yeah, look. There's a design on them. These aren't normal contacts."

"Design?" Bel joined her, and sure enough, the tiny lenses had what appeared to be a miniature landscape etched into them. "What big eyes you have," she whispered, Eamon's decoded message suddenly obvious.

"What?" Lina asked.

"The random letters in that gift box. It's a Caesar Cipher, and it spelled out, *'What big eyes you have.'* The killer was telling us to look in her eyes."

"I'll have a tech enlarge the image, but it looks like snowy trees. Do you think it's Rossa's murder site?"

"I can't tell, but I doubt it," Bel said. "These were manufactured in advance, so how could the killer know exactly where he would kill Gwen? Unless multiple perpetrators corralled her, he couldn't have predicted where she'd flee."

"Maybe it's meant as a vague representation," Lina said. "She died in the woods, and her eyes saw woods."

"Either way," Bel said, "this murder was premeditated."

"OH MY GOD, IT'S HER!" a voice shrieked as Bel stepped out of her car. "That's the detective!" A swarm of fans surged for her, and she launched into a jog, barely slipping inside the precinct before the cell phone mob accosted her.

"You all right?" Officer Rollo asked as he planted his body in front of the glass door, signaling with both his size and his uniform that no one was getting into the station.

"I'm fine, thanks. I take it word got out?" she asked.

"Unfortunately. It's all over the news and social media, and fans are holding vigils. I'm surprised you haven't heard."

"I don't have social media, and I was in the morgue all morning."

"Gotcha."

"Is Griffin here?" she asked.

"In his office," Rollo said.

"Thank you." She jogged up the stairs. "And good luck out there today," she called over her shoulder. They all needed it now. "Sheriff?" She knocked on his door, and when he beckoned her inside, she

111

gave him a rundown of the autopsy, starting with her decoding of the cipher and ending with the discovery of the contact lenses.

"We got a tech to enlarge the image, and I printed it out as well as uploaded a digital copy." She lay the shot of the snowy forest before her boss. "Whoever killed Gwen inserted the contacts into her eyes, and they act similarly to film negatives."

"These woods don't look like the crime scene," Griffin said. "The snow's in the foreground, with the trees in the background. Gwen Rossa was murdered in the middle of the forest."

"Lina wondered if it generically represented the scene. Girl found dead in the woods with woods in her eyes," Bel said. "Or it's an actual place."

"What kind of place?"

"Who knows?" Bel shrugged. "Where he hid victim number two?"

Griffin's gaze shot up from the photo to meet hers. "You don't think…?"

"I don't know," she said. "Maybe Lina is right, and they're symbolic. Maybe this location meant something to Gwen or the killer. Or maybe this clue points to where we'll find the next body."

"I certainly hope not. Half of the Reale Estate and all the state parks are forests. We could search for years, and never locate these exact trees."

"I hope not too," Bel said. "I was just thinking out loud since everything about this death is strange."

"Mmhmm," Griffin grunted. "These contacts are a custom job, though. Where would someone get something like this?"

"The costume department," Bel blurted, an idea suddenly coming to her. "Films often use contact lenses to change actors' eyes. Especially when the characters are supernatural creatures." She gave him a rundown of her theory about the killer mimicking the show, ending her explanation with how both custom contacts and weapons were something art departments were well versed in creating.

"You mentioned Rossa had no defensive wounds," Griffin said. "So, she most likely knew her attacker. If it were someone she worked with, she wouldn't have fought back until it was too late."

"If a crew member wanted to kill his coworkers, Bajka is the place to do it," Bel said. "Smaller town, sprawling nature, and a horde of fans to blame it on. It's much easier here amidst the chaos than in the city or on a closed set."

"Make the deaths theatrical, and suddenly, we're looking for a crazed fan, not a disgruntled employee. That's where my brain certainly went."

"Mine too."

"Come on." He stood and grabbed his keys. "The weather compromised the scene, so we have little else to go on. Let's speak to the producers about who had access to the set design. They might respond better if I'm there to question them."

"You sure?" Bel chased after him. "Olivia and I can go."

"I have Gold helping elsewhere," Griffin said, aiming for his truck, and Bel opened her mouth to ask if her partner had requested that they be separated, but her boss cut her off before she could speak.

"I hope you don't mind since you're friends, but we're stretched too thin to have you both running down every lead together. Plus..." he glanced at her as if deciding if he should admit the truth. "Don't yell at me, but I want to keep an eye on you."

Bel laughed as she slipped into the passenger seat. "Did you and Eamon meet and designate shifts?" she teased.

"No... but we should," her boss teased back. "Oddly enough, I'm generally wary of your boyfriend, but when it comes to your life, he's the only person besides myself, your dog, and your father that I trust with your safety. He's repeatedly proven that you come first… even before the law."

"Not everyone is perfect." Bel shrugged. "And he'll be glad that you want to follow me around. Christmas break was… tough for us. I scared him."

"Emerson, you scared us all. I was terrified when Abel kidnapped you and Gold, but seeing your body double on the slab? You were dead." Her boss twisted as if he were checking the road for traffic, and Bel played along, both of them knowing the movement was to hide the tears threatening his eyes. "It's why I want to work this case with you. I need proof you didn't die on my watch."

"Okay, now I really think you and Eamon got together for a chat."

"Maybe we should if it'll stop you from scaring us."

Thirty minutes and a few gentle police badge threats later, Bel and Griffin sat in Bajka's Bed-and-Breakfast dining room with the producers, Evelyn Pierce and Alistair Rot.

"Anyone on set could technically access our costumes and props," Miss Pierce said. "Our entire show revolves around creatures and murders. Custom works appear in every episode, so it isn't hard to steal prop weapons. We use different types based on the scene's requirements. Rubber for when actors need to wield them. Bladeless for fight scenes. They're just handles, and we digitally add blades in post-production. Then there are the real deals for close-ups. Those, along with some creature suits, could be deadly… although I can't think of any reason a crew member would want to murder Miss Rossa. Her scripts are well-received by the public. This show has created steady work for everyone involved, so killing her wouldn't be in anyone's best interest."

"So to confirm, almost anyone on set could access the custom weapons and costumes?" Griffin asked, and when Evelyn nodded, he continued. "Have you noticed any props go missing recently?"

"Props disappear all the time," Alistair Rot chimed in. "Actors and crew members love their souvenirs. And even if they weren't stealing them, a set is the best example of controlled chaos. There's a fine line between making art and meeting deadlines, and it's hard enough finishing a season, let alone keeping track of every item that may or may not have gone missing."

"Even if that missing item becomes a murder weapon?" Bel asked, and she could tell by the way Mr. Rot stiffened he disliked that she kept challenging him.

"We don't make murder weapons on purpose," Evelyn said.

"Technically you do," Bel said. "Your entire show revolves around murder."

"Fictional murders, Detective. Our crew makes props, not weapons. Now, if someone used a prop for a reason other than its intended use, I'm unaware, but I doubt it. We're all committed to making Aesop's Files a success."

"Regardless of your intentions, can we have the names of the art department's crew members?" Griffin asked. "We'll need to talk to them."

"Yes, of course. What email should I send the contacts to?" Evelyn glanced up expectantly as she sat with her phone poised at the ready, and Bel didn't miss the way every fiber of Alistair's body protested her willingness to help. She studied the producer as his colleague typed the art departments' names, and while he said nothing with his voice, his eyes spoke volumes. He didn't want them digging, which meant they were on the right track.

"Hello? Anyone in here?" Griffin called as he and Bel climbed into the production trailer.

"Hi, can I help you?" A woman emerged from behind one of

the many clothing racks vomiting color and fabric over every inch of available space. "Sheriff? Is something wrong?"

"I'm looking for the costume designer, Ellery Roja," he answered.

"That's me," she said.

"Miss Roja, I'm Sheriff Griffin, and this is Detective Emerson. Do you mind if we ask you a few questions?"

"I guess not." She scanned her surroundings. "As long as you don't mind if I work while we talk."

"Not at all," he said as they followed the woman to her sewing machine.

"Thanks. We have a decent-sized cast, and both Beau and Taron need multiples of the same outfit for their fight scenes. First is the clean version, then the dirty version of the same outfit as the struggle progresses, and a destroyed version for the end. Plus, many of our creatures are achieved with makeup, practical effects, and costuming—which I've won awards for—so I can't afford to take a break… ever."

"We won't take up too much of your time," Griffin said. "Do you recognize this?" He showed her a photo of Gwen Rossa's red cloak.

"Um… no," she said. "We haven't had a character wear a crimson hood."

"How long have you been the costume designer?" Bel asked. So much for their theory that the killer was mimicking a specific episode.

"Since season one," Ellery answered. "Back then, it was just me. Now I work with an entire team of seamstresses, leather cutters, metal workers, jewelry designers—you name it."

"Could your team members have created this without your knowledge?" Bel asked.

"I guess so, but not for the show. All episode designs come through me."

"But in their free time?" Bel asked.

Evidence of a Folktale

"Sure, but if you think someone on my team killed Gwen, you're mistaken," Ellery said. "We are artists. Not murderers."

"Still, where were you the night before last between midnight and sunrise?" Griffin asked.

"In my hotel room," she answered. "It was snowing... a lot. I wasn't going outside."

"Can your department make custom contact lenses?" Griffin asked. "And you said the creatures are created using practical effects. Would that include functional claws?"

"Um, have you seen this show?" The designer gawked at them as if they were aliens who'd never set foot on Earth.

"I take that as a yes," he said.

"It's half of what I do." She leaned over and snagged what looked like a shaggy carpet. "Here's an example." She handed Griffin the fur, and he twisted it so Bel could see the bear-like claws.

"What do you think?" he asked.

"I don't know." She fingered the sharp tips. "They seem too small."

"We make all sizes," Ellery said. "There are a lot of creatures on the show, and these are just the costumes. The prop department makes the weapons, and the special effects team oversees the practical effects. We have every version of a claw that you can imagine."

"Can anyone come by and take stuff?" Bel asked as she slipped her hand into the glove, her fingers transforming into a monster.

"We lock up at night, but sure," Ellery said. "Our production assistants run props and costumes for us. My team and I handle the important or expensive items, but the cast and the crew have access to everything else."

"So someone could've created that red cloak or a weapon without your knowledge, then removed it from set?" Bel pushed.

"Well, I can't speak to the prop department, but it's entirely possible. We're incredibly busy, Detective, and we sew costumes. It's not like we're creating bombs and leaving them unattended for anyone to snag. The special effect crews are the ones with explosives, but they maintain a much tighter control over their creations. I just make outfits and creatures."

Bel glanced at Griffin, and the hardness of his gaze told her he agreed. It wasn't the slam dunk they needed to identify a suspect, but it supported her theory that a cast or crew member could've used the show's designs to kill one of their own.

"Did you work with Gwen Rossa often?" Bel asked.

"No. I knew her, but we didn't work closely. She wrote the scripts and edited them with the directors, who then met with me to map out the character visions. The show rotates directors, but Warren Rouge has the most episode credits. I know him well, but Gwen and I rarely spent time in the same room."

"So, you wouldn't know if anyone hated her or wished her harm?" Bel asked.

"Unfortunately, no... why all the questions? The reporters are saying it was a crazed fan."

"We cannot comment about ongoing investigations," Griffin said.

"Ha," Ellery scoffed. "So weird hearing that outside of set. But I understand."

"Are there any problematic crew members?" Bel pressed. "Or someone who had a grievance with another cast or crew member?"

"No. Aesop's Files was almost canceled a few years ago, but after going viral, we became one of the most viewed shows. We're all thankful for this opportunity."

And there it was.

Bel figured Miss Roja didn't even realize she'd done it, but the second she said they were thankful for the opportunity, her demeanor changed. It was a subtle shift, a flash across her features, but Bel had been watching for it. Someone wasn't happy with the show's success, and Ellery Roja knew who it was.

"So, no disgruntled employees?" Bel stepped closer to the woman, forcing her neck to strain as she looked up. "Someone who didn't stick around long enough to see Aesop's Files' fame?"

"We've had people leave," she said. "Like Willow Moon."

"We heard Miss Moon's departure was amicable," Bel said.

"It was... I was just saying everyone from production assistants to directors has left."

"A show this size. It's unlikely that everyone departed on good terms. Someone must have been fired."

"Of course, people were fired," Ellery said.

Now they were getting somewhere.

"Were any of these fired employees disgruntled?"

"I don't know." The weird look passed over Roja's features again, and Griffin crossed his arms over his chest.

"Withholding information in a murder investigation could result in an obstruction of justice charge," he said, hovering authoritatively over the designer.

"There was one guy." Ellery caved. "But we all signed non-disclosures."

"Why?" Griffin asked. "The Bajka Police Department had to sign a non-disclosure agreement since we're outsiders, but is it normal to gag all your employees from talking about their colleagues?"

"The contracts are to protect from spoilers and leaks," she explained. "But anything that happens on set cannot be talked about outside of the show's production, and since this happened while filming, I am legally required to keep quiet."

"Convenient," Bel said. No one on this show liked to answer questions.

"I could lose my job if I speak about it." Ellery's eyes flicked around the trailer as if someone might pop out the minute she spoke and drag her away from her machine, but Bel remained silent. Sometimes silence was more effective than interrogations, since most people often couldn't bear the weight of a police officer's wordless stare.

"I can disclose what was released during the court case." It seemed Miss Roja was weaker than most. "A set designer named Orion Chayce worked for the show a few years ago, and he was in charge of rigging the practical effect. There was a malfunction one day during shooting, though, and it killed a lighting technician. The investigation proved the accident was due to negligence on Chayce's part, and he was charged with involuntary manslaughter. He served time for it and was fired, obviously."

"Obviously," Griffin repeated.

"Is he still in prison?" Bel asked.

"I think so?" It came out like a question. "I'm not sure. Now, if you don't mind, I need to get back to work. I have a lot to finish before tomorrow's shoot."

"Of course. Thank you for your time." Griffin gripped Bel's elbow and guided her out of the trailer.

"Was it just me, or was she lying about that technician's death?" he asked when they'd locked themselves inside his truck.

"Oh, she was lying through her teeth," Bel confirmed. "There's something about that story that she doesn't want us finding out."

"Or maybe she was warning us." Griffin started the engine and cranked the heat before grabbing Bel's hands and pressing them against the blowers. It seemed she wasn't the only one haunted by the memory of her bandaged fingers. "She can't tell us what happened, but she didn't have to bring him up, either. I'm sure dozens of employees have been fired over the years. She could've picked any of them, but she mentioned the only person she's not allowed to talk about. We're cops. She knows we'll figure it out."

"Which makes you wonder what really happened to that prop," Bel said. "If it required a non-disclosure agreement, was it an accident? I'm willing to bet it wasn't."

"LEARN ANYTHING?" Bel asked as she slipped inside Griffin's office with sandwiches in one hand and coffees in the other. Neither had eaten, so she'd volunteered to grab them a quick deli lunch while he looked into Orion Chayce's case.

"You're never going to believe it," he said as he accepted the food. "Thanks."

"No problem." Bel plopped onto the couch. As much as she missed Olivia, she enjoyed working with her boss. The safety he offered made it easier for her to slip back into the role of detective. "And don't tell me. Chayce is out on parole."

"He is, but that's not all." Griffin bit into his sandwich. "He never showed up for his last check-in with his parole officer, and no one's seen him since."

"He's missing?" Bel almost choked on her lunch.

"He's missing."

Bel cursed and set her food down on her boss' desk so she wouldn't accidentally suck another crumb down the wrong tube. "What if the malfunction that killed the tech wasn't an accident? It felt like Ellery Roja was lying when she mentioned Chayce, so what if he was just the scapegoat? He gets blamed for an accident he didn't cause and ends up serving time."

"And now he's out for revenge," Griffin finished for her.

"If he skipped parole, he could very well be in town," Bel said. "He has special effects experience. He could've easily created the custom weapon used to kill Gwen Rossa."

"But why her?" Griffin asked. "She's a writer. How could she be responsible for a prop malfunction?"

"I don't know. Maybe she ran into it and knocked a piece off, but didn't bother to fix it, so he blames her for the accident. Or maybe she was simply present when it happened, and Chayce associates her with the guilty parties."

"I don't like this." Griffin placed his half-eaten sandwich on the desk. "If Chayce skipped parole to get revenge on the people who sent him to prison, I doubt Gwen Rossa is his only target. He'll kill again, and our town is bursting at the seams with strangers. If he's here, he won't be easy to find."

"We're already stretched so thin," Bel said. "We don't have the numbers for a manhunt."

"I can talk to the producers again. With this new information, they might consider canceling or postponing the fan events... not that I have high hopes for that. Without concrete proof, all we have is a missing parolee and a theory."

"And they seemed adamant about keeping to the schedule," Bel said. "The whole thing is weird. Refusing to pause shooting when your show's writer is brutally murdered. Creating a madhouse by hosting events at the same times as a location shoot. It's unorthodox. Does a show this popular really need extra money?"

"Unfortunately, we've seen what wealth drives people to do," Griffin said. "A man married a woman just to murder her and her young brothers to gain their inheritance. Meet-and-greets are nothing compared to that."

"You're right. It's just—"

"A lot," he finished for her. "Are you sure you're okay? I can always call for help."

"I don't want another detective taking over my case," Bel said. "This is my town and my job. Blaubart took enough from me. He isn't stealing anything else."

"Okay. I had to check. I'll stick with you when I can, though."

"Thanks... but I don't want to be a burden."

"Isobel Emerson a burden?" Griffin rolled his eyes. "We'd

have a lot more cold cases if it weren't for you. Now eat your sandwich so we can brief everyone about Chayce. We need to find him before he finds his next target."

"Olivia!" Bel chased after her partner, catching up with her just as she exited the station.

After lunch, Griffin had called a meeting to discuss the Orion Chayce lead before leaving to reason with Aesop's Files producers. The officers returned to the chaos, and the rest of the day transformed into a madhouse of paperwork, endless patrols, evidence examinations, and volatile crowd control, all against the backdrop of eager reporters and nosy social media posters. It seemed everyone with a cell phone considered themselves a reporter investigating Gwen Rossa's murder, and Bel almost ducked out of instinct as she exited the precinct. She hated that her face had undoubtedly appeared on dozens of social media posts, and she wondered if Eamon had a contact that could scour the internet and erase her features from the fans' online hysteria.

"Are you hungry?" she asked when Olivia stopped walking. "We could grab takeout and work at my place, or yours."

"I have leftovers in my fridge," her partner said. "But I'll email you if I find anything."

"Olivia." Bel wrapped her arms around herself as she cut off Gold's escape. She should've grabbed a coat because it seemed they were doing this in the freezing parking lot. "I don't care what we eat, but we work together. We haven't had time to talk, but if we don't make time, we'll avoid each other forever. You're my best friend, and I—"

"No!" Olivia hissed. "Because if you were my best friend, you would've warned me I was sleeping with a monster."

"He's not—"

"He is." Olivia stepped closer so she wouldn't have to raise her voice and risk being caught on someone's cell phone camera. "You might think so because compared to whatever devil Eamon is, a bear is normal, but to me? I was in love with him, Bel. I told you I thought he was the one, and you just kept your mouth shut. You were going to let me marry a bear without warning me who I'd let into my life. You were going to let me end up with cubs for kids, and that's not something friends do. So no, I won't make time to talk. I'll work with you because I'm a professional, but I can't be friends with a liar."

"They weren't my secrets to tell," Bel argued.

"Maybe not Eamon's, but Ewan's? You owed me the truth about him. Have you seen it? Have you seen his bear?"

Bel nodded.

"How many times?"

She didn't answer.

"How many times?" Olivia's volume increased.

"Twice," she admitted. "Once before I knew what he was and again when he shifted in front of me."

"You've seen him shift? When?"

"Olivia…"

"When?"

"The Darling case. He helped us find the boys."

"The Darling case? You've known for that long?" Olivia walked away before whirling around and storming back. "The minute I mentioned I loved him, you should've warned me."

"I couldn't."

"What if he'd been cheating on me?" Olivia asked. "That technically would've been his secret to tell, but if you'd caught him in the act, would you have just stayed silent? Would you let me plan a wedding to a man who didn't care enough to stay faithful?"

"Of course I would've told you," Bel said. "But that's different."

"It's not! You knew something damning about my boyfriend,

and you kept it a secret. I would've never dated Ewan if I'd known the truth."

"He's a good man," Bel argued.

"He's a liar. Just like you."

"In case you haven't noticed, my life has been hell lately," Bel spat. "So, I'm sorry I didn't tell you about your boyfriend when my boyfriend ordered him to tell you. That was between you two."

"Why? Because your boyfriend said so?"

"Yes." Bel got in her partner's face, unsure if she was mad about Olivia's accusations or that she was losing her temper. "We aren't dealing with humans. Our laws don't apply to them, so to you, Eamon is just some wealthy prick, but in their world, he is a god. He's one of the most powerful creatures to walk this earth, and men like him kill men like Ewan for trespassing in their territory. But Eamon loves me, and I love you, so he made an exception. He ordered Ewan to tell you in exchange for staying in Bajka unharmed, so I'm sorry I said nothing in between the murders and my own kidnappings. It wasn't my job."

"I know your life has been awful," Olivia hissed. "I worked with Eamon to help find you because I'd never leave you to die, and I'd do it again, but there's a difference between not wanting you dead and not wanting to be your friend. I won't ever let you die, but I can't get past the lies, Bel. You and I had plenty of unchaotic moments together. You could've warned me what I was walking into, but you didn't. So, I'll work with you. I will always protect you, but we aren't friends anymore. Stop trying to talk to me. Unless you have case information, I don't want to hear it."

Autopsy Report

CERBERUS

Chapter Eight

"Isobel?" Eamon's voice drifted through the mansion, and seconds later, he appeared at the top of the grand staircase. "I thought you were staying at your place tonight." He jogged down the stairs to greet her as Cerberus made a beeline for his toy box in the living room. "Is everything okay?"

"No." Bel fell into his arms, bursting into tears as he caught her collapsing weight. "I'd hoped her anger would blow over, and we'd work through this, but I think I've lost my best friend."

"Olivia?" Eamon asked, holding her up with one arm to peel her coat off with the other. "She doesn't hate you. I just freaked her out."

"But you didn't hear the way she spoke to me." Bel stared up at him through her tear-soaked lashes. "I love her, and I thought keeping the truth to myself was best. I figured she would either attempt to broach the subject, or Ewan would confirm their conversation with you, so I stayed silent. But I don't think she'll ever forgive me, or Ewan, for that matter."

"Don't worry about him."

"Did I do the right thing?" She shoved free of his embrace

and kicked off her shoes as she paced deeper into the foyer. "Was I right hiding this from her?"

"It wasn't your responsibility," Eamon said, crossing his arms over his chest as his gaze tracked her erratic movements. "I gave Ewan an ultimatum. The only person responsible is him."

"But she blames me." Bel whirled on him. "He disobeyed you, but somehow, it's my fault. He's cost me my friend, and I feel guilty. She claimed my omission of the truth is the same as knowing Ewan was cheating and staying silent, and now I'm blaming myself too."

"Don't."

"But I am!" she shouted. Eamon didn't so much as bat an eye at her volume, and it wasn't lost on her that she was probably the only person in history to yell at him without consequence. "I hid something important from her, and I'm not the friend I thought I was. I kept your secret because I owe you that, but I don't owe Ewan, yet I chose him over Olivia."

"And how would that have worked out for you?" Eamon asked, his stoicism unbothered by her outburst. "What? Were you going to bring a bottle of wine to her house for a girl's night and randomly slip in a comment about her boyfriend being a shifter between sips? It would've landed you in a psych evaluation. It's why he needed to tell her. His shift can prove his words."

"I..." She fell silent. He was right. What was she supposed to do? Ask Olivia to pass the cheese and crackers and then blurt out that Ewan could transform into a bear of unnatural proportions?

"I think I need the truth... all of it," she said. "I want to know what you are so I can decide if these secrets are worth destroying friendships over." Her desire to learn his story had been warring with her fear of hearing his horrors for a while now, but it was time. If she was going to move forward with this man, she needed to understand who she slept beside. Olivia hadn't known,

Evidence of a Folktale

and it destroyed her relationship. Bel wouldn't allow that fate to befall her.

"I promised I'd tell you." Eamon finally uncrossed his arms as Cerberus jogged back into the foyer, an oversized rope hanging from his mouth. "But is this how you want to find out? Because you feel guilty for something that isn't your fault and you're trying to justify your convictions? I want to tell you. Trust me, I do, but not because Olivia's anger is making you doubt yourself."

"Her reaction is part of it, but I need to know," Bel said as Eamon grabbed the toy rope and gave it a tug, Cerberus growling in excitement as he played. Her dog loved him. She loved him. His entire mansion was a love letter to them in both its design and toy collection. She needed to hear the truth about the man she was willing to defend at all costs.

"I need to know." She crossed the floor and placed a palm on his chest. "It's time you tell me."

"All right." He sighed, releasing the rope as the pitbull forgot it to go look out the front window, and Bel swore she felt his heart stutter below her hand. "But this conversation calls for a drink... a strong one." He pulled her into his arms and kissed her with a fierceness that stuck her feet to the tiles. "One last kiss in case you change your mind about loving me," he said as he released her.

"Don't say that." She didn't want that to be true.

"Learning about Ewan caused Olivia to not only end their relationship, but yours as well," Eamon said. "And he's a relatively innocent shifter."

"And you're evil." She recited his favorite words of warning.

"It's why I was brought into this world." He started toward the kitchen. "You've always been forgiving, but I worry that not even your goodness can atone for my sins."

"I'll join you on the strong drink," Bel said, her stomach twisting into knots. Oblivious to her nerves, Cerberus barreled after Eamon, whacking him in the legs with his remembered toy rope as he shook his head with a growl, and her heart swelled at the adorable interaction. She couldn't hate her boyfriend, not when her beautiful dog wanted nothing more than to live with him. She'd noticed a difference in the animal's behavior over the past few weeks. He was subdued when they spent long periods without him. Cerberus had accepted Eamon as part of his pack, and if she learned the truth, would she be like Olivia and sever ties with him? The separation would break her pitbull's heart. She refused to imagine what it would do to hers.

"Make it a double," she said as Eamon poured the alcohol into two glasses. He was the whiskey drinker, but wine wouldn't cut it for this conversation.

"I love you." He handed her the amber liquid that reminded her so much of his voice and then took a seat across the kitchen island from her, the sudden divide silencing her from returning the sentiment.

"You drink human blood," she whispered when he remained silent, her fingers fighting the urge to touch the scars he'd gifted her. "You're a vampire."

"No," Eamon found his voice. "The vampires are dead. I saw to that. But I am the son of one."

"The son of one?" Bel asked. She didn't think vampires could birth children, but then again, her knowledge came from fantasy novels and television shows. She'd never met a vampire, and if Eamon was telling the truth, it seemed no one had in centuries.

"I'm what they call a Dhampir, a human/vampire hybrid," he explained. "A sin against nature."

"That's why you have a heartbeat and can walk through sunlight." Bel exhaled the tension suffocating her chest. She'd always suspected Eamon was a vampire of sorts, so to hear he was half-human was a relief. How terrifying could the truth be if he shared the DNA that ran through her body?

"It's why we were created," Eamon said. "To survive the sun. In the first ages of men, vampires ruled the night. Superstition and mysticism reigned, and humanity's primitive societies were no match for the demons that had crawled their way out of hell. Humans were nothing but blood bags to the first vampires, but mankind is surprisingly resilient. No matter the oppression, no matter their weakness, they always prevail, and eventually, they learned the vampires' vulnerability. Sunlight. It burned them alive. They weren't creatures of this world. They weren't meant to dwell on Earth. Hell was their home, and the sunshine reminded them they were trespassers. Humans used their newfound knowledge to their advantage, and despite the heavy price, they began to wipe the vampires from the face of the earth. The human race didn't care if the individuals perished as long as their sacrifice ensured the race's survival. Fathers died so their sons might live, and that was a concept my ancestors couldn't comprehend. Men hunted them like animals, and the death toll rose on both sides. Vampires turned humans with their venom in an attempt to bolster their ranks, but their efforts weren't enough. They were dying out. So they created us."

Eamon sipped the whiskey and leaned back in his chair as if the words about to leave his mouth were too heavy to bear sitting up straight. "The vampires discovered they could breed with humans, but we aren't like shifters, who are symbols of mankind's harmony with nature. Creatures like Ewan are both animal and human, a celebration of the life that walks this earth, but vampires clawed their way out of hell. To procreate with humans was a sin against nature, and invoking black magic was the only way their children survived. Dhampirs are a blasphemy, therefore they needed hate to create us... I meant what I told you at Thanksgiving. Love had no part in my making. It was all fear and anger."

Bel shoved the whiskey away, the alcohol churning in her stomach, and stared at the liquid instead of the man sitting across from her. He didn't have to spell it out. She understood his meaning, understood the nature of his birth, and she realized why he'd hesitated to tell her the truth. She wanted to reach out and capture his hand. To comfort him by taking him into her arms, but his tone warned this was only the beginning of his horrors.

"My father was one of the most powerful vampires to walk the earth," Eamon continued, even though she wouldn't look at him. "He forced my mother to stay alive to raise me. She hated him for it, but she hated me more. She raised me until I was old enough to survive on my own, and then she waited until he took me on a hunt. She killed herself, careful to leave her body where I'd find it. She bled out long before I returned because she wanted her scent to foul. All that blood I craved, yet I couldn't drink it. It was her last punishment before she abandoned me to my father's control.

"The vampires created us because they needed protection. Someone stronger than humans who could survive the sun. My father tortured me until I became the perfect soldier, and I spent decades spilling blood under his command.

"Eventually, I earned more fear than him, and that's when the vampires realized their mistake. They assumed they were still the alpha predators, but we weren't weaker versions of our fathers as they intended. We had the strength of the vampires, combined with mankind's resilience. Immortality, power, and invincibility united with the ability to day walk and survive without blood for extended periods if we ate food. We were the best of both worlds. Our fathers bred their replacements, and we were gods. Dhampirs can reproduce both with venom and childbirth as long as they inspire enough hate to invoke black magic. We grew in numbers while they dwindled, for we were superior beings."

"Did you..." Bel felt sick asking because that was one sin she couldn't forgive.

"Bear children?" he asked. "Never. My brothers did, but I fathered no sons nor turned no humans."

Evidence of a Folktale

"Oh god." Bel fell into her hands, the relief violent as she sobbed. She'd faced death before, yet fearing that the man she loved had possibly forced a woman to carry his child was unbearable. "You can continue," she finally whispered, the tightness in her chest dissipating slightly at his confirmation.

"Realizing the power had shifted, my father sought to eradicate our kind. He was the most powerful of the vampires, but I'd sensed the oncoming war. I gathered my brothers and sisters to my cause and set out to seize power. I slaughtered my father's men and then killed him, putting an end to the animal whose treachery is still written about today."

"Written about today?" Bel repeated before she could stop herself. The pain pouring from Eamon's mouth settled deep in her chest, and the despair settling over her begged to be satisfied.

"You know who I'm talking about," Eamon answered. "Everyone does."

"Dracula?" She met his gaze, her voice barely audible. Dracula was a myth. He was a story. He wasn't real, yet the anger in Eamon's death-black eyes was unmistakable.

"It's what the legends call him," he said. "A name created to instill fear through paper, but the man behind the inspiration was the devil who raised me."

"Vlad the Impaler is the ruler historians credit with Dracula's origins," Bel said.

"Vlad was one of my father's many personas," Eamon said. "But he wasn't the Impaler."

"But history—?"

"Got it wrong. He was never the Impaler. I was."

"What?" Bel hadn't heard him correctly. Her ears were lying.

"I was my father's enforcer. His right hand. His general. He was the devil, and he made me in his image. Historians link Vlad to the Impaler, but that honor belongs to me. I was the Impaler in his name. I'm the one history remembers for his brutality."

"Eamon..." Bel trailed off. This man. This beautiful man she loved. He was the one responsible for mounting thousands of still-living men onto spikes. The famous Impaler was a paragraph in the history books, a monster who didn't seem real to the modern mortal, but he was real, and he was sitting across from her.

"How many?" she whispered. "How many did you kill?"

"I don't know... I lost track," he answered. "Enough to send me to hell."

"Thousands?" she asked.

"More," he said. "I liked to kill. I was good at it, and I did it for sport."

Bel started to cry again. She couldn't help it. All she could see was her beautiful beast shoving living bodies onto spikes, and she pressed her palm against her mouth to keep from getting sick on the kitchen island.

"Is your father still alive?" she asked through her fingers.

"No," Eamon answered. "He realized his mistake in creating me. I was his downfall. A child born to serve became his god, and I led the vampires to the slaughter, saving my father for last. I wanted him to feel fear, and he did in the end. The vampire breed died with him, and I seized power, often killing my brethren to stay in control. I murdered so many that I don't think there are any left. I'm the only Dhampir to walk this earth that I'm aware of... which is why Alcina Magus tried to bind me to her with your death. My power is unmatched. I've been alive so long that I'm nearly invincible. Honestly, I'm not even sure I can die."

"A stake to the heart?" Bel asked. She didn't know why she asked, but with all the horrors laid out before her, her brain needed something trivial to latch onto.

"A stake to the heart would kill anything, supernaturals included," Eamon said. "The hard part would be penetrating my chest. Not even an IED could do that."

"The armor-piercing rounds," Bel said, referring to the

weapon guarding John Darling's death trap during his kidnapping case. Eamon had implied those would harm him, but was he just being cautious?

"If shot point blank, probably. You would have to aim for my brain or heart, though, and you'd have to be close," he confirmed, and Bel had the sneaking suspicion he was instructing her how to kill him.

"And you need human blood to survive?" she asked.

"Yes."

"Do you still hunt like you used to?"

"No."

"How do you drink, then?"

"Blood drives," Eamon said. "I work with a lot of collection and storage facilities. It's easy to launder the donations."

"So you don't slaughter people anymore to drink?"

"No... you were the last person I've tasted from the vein," he said. "After I met you, I stopped hunting completely. I haven't had fresh blood since."

"That's less than a year," Bel said.

"I know."

"And before me? When was the last time you killed someone? Not to protect me. Not to save your friends in World War II. Just to drink."

"Isobel..."

"When?" she demanded.

"Sometimes the devil in me is hard to suppress," Eamon said, avoiding her question. "I'm unnatural, and my father spent so long breeding violence into me that my nature occasionally rears its head. I struggled to fight it... until I met you. Seems the devil is afraid of something, after all, and it's losing you."

"Until it isn't. Until you can't suppress it anymore, and you let the Impaler free."

"That's always a possibility," Eamon said as he reached for the whiskey, but instead of pouring it into his glass, he drank straight from the bottle. "I warned you I was evil. I always will be. You soften my edges, and at times, you almost make me honorable, but I was born of hell and violence. Death is in my DNA. It won't ever truly leave. All I can promise is that I'll never harm you again... or the people you love. My darkness might rear its head, but because of you, I battle that part of me every day. I once lived for the hunt. I needed it. I craved it, loved it, belonged to it. But now? Now I want to be the person you see when you look at me... or at least the man you thought I was before tonight."

"I..." Bel stood up. She couldn't breathe. The weight of his confession was crushing her chest, forcing her lungs to collapse in on themselves. Eamon wasn't the monster he was painting himself out to be. He couldn't be. She loved him too much. Yet she saw it in his black eyes. He was death on Earth. The Beast of Bajka. He'd never lied to her. He'd warned from the beginning that he was evil, and she always suspected darkness shrouded his past. She just hadn't expected the terror of being confronted with one of history's most unsettling murderers.

"I... um," she stuttered as she stepped away from him, hating how his shoulders hunched in rejection, but before she could sift through her thoughts, Cerberus ran for the front door. He tapped his nose on his leash and then barked, signaling he needed to relieve himself, and Bel stared helplessly between the two men in her life.

"He..." she started. "I just..." She backed away from Eamon and grabbed her coat. The house was spinning. Or maybe she was. "I need to take him for a walk," she said as she snapped on the pitbull's leash and fled the mansion into the frigid night, leaving a crumbling Eamon in her wake.

Autopsy Report

CERBERUS

PROD.NO. | TAKE | SOUND
SCENE
DIRECTOR
CAMERAMAN | EXT. | INT.

CINEMA TICKET 9891102 ADMIT ONE

CINEMA TICKET 9891102 ADMIT ONE

Chapter Nine

Bel walked Cerberus until she lost track of time, the mansion's lights so far behind them she had to use her phone's flashlight to keep from tripping on her pitch-black dog. Her body was numb, but she wasn't sure if it was the frigid night air or the truth she'd fled. She knew who Eamon was. He'd never hid it from her. They'd met when he'd left her bleeding out on that lonely New York City street because of Alcina's curse, but to learn he was the monster behind one of the most infamous killers history remembered? She was a police officer. She upheld the law and hunted down murderers, and while she was aware of his destructive past, she hadn't expected the true scope of his brutality. Could she forgive that much bloodshed? And what did it say about her that she wanted to?

Bel sank to a seat atop a fallen tree trunk and watched Cerberus dig his way to some hidden treasure only he sensed. The freezing tears burned her cheeks, and she craved the warmth of her bed. She wanted to stop being cold, to stop being transported back to that nightmare of a mountain she'd thought she'd die on. She wanted to go home… only her cabin wasn't the home that came to mind.

Her tears fell harder as she curled her legs against her chest to brace against the wind. How could his mansion be home now? How could she ignore the magnitude of his crimes? Or that his true nature might rear its insatiable head again? She was a hypocrite. She'd argued with Olivia that Eamon and Ewan were men worthy of love, yet here she sat, hiding among the ice to avoid associating the man she loved with the murderer history remembered. Bel hated herself for being a coward, for being no better than Olivia as she fled from the truth. In reality, she was worse because while Ewan had lied to her partner for months, Eamon's honesty surfaced the moment her survival broke Alcina's curse. They'd met with his teeth around her throat, and Bel had instantly understood he belonged to the darkness. He hadn't even pursued a friendship with her until he confessed to scarring her. She'd entered their relationship with eyes wide open, and while he hadn't told her everything, he'd warned it was terrifying. She knew the devil was in her bed, yet she welcomed him anyway, so how could she run away now? And how could she justify staying? Could she give her heart to a man who killed infinitely more people than the most heinous serial killers to walk the earth? She'd thought the Matchstick Girl Killer was a monster unmatched, but compared to Eamon, his dozens of homicides were child's play.

Her phone rang, the trilling too loud in the empty darkness, and Bel almost fell off the tree trunk. "Hello?" she answered as she captured Cerberus' leash. The cold had grown unbearable, and she suspected the aggressive frost and not the horror of Eamon's birth was to blame for the new tears slipping down her cheeks.

"Hey... are you all right?" Briar asked through the connection.

"I'm walking Cerberus, and it's freezing," she lied.

"This weather is miserable," Briar said. "But it sounds like you're crying. Are you okay?"

Evidence of a Folktale

"I don't like the cold," Bel said. "It deposits me back on that mountain, and my brain keeps preparing to freeze to death."

"Oh, Isobel..." Her sister's voice broke. Now they were both crying. "That's actually why I called. I saw the news about that writer's murder, and I wanted to check on you. After our last conversation, I realized I haven't been doing a good job of that."

"You're busy with the kids. It's okay."

"No, it's not because I never knew my baby sister was almost blown up. I should know these things."

"Why? So I can stress out yet another person in my life?"

"Yes!" Briar practically shouted. "For all intents and purposes, I am your mother, so yes, I want you to stress me out. It's better than realizing I barely know you because you feel uncomfortable talking to me." She paused, clearly waiting for Bel to speak. "Would you like to talk about it?" she asked when the line remained silent.

Bel opened her mouth to answer because she wanted to talk. Only not about the snow. She'd been unpacking her mountain survival with her therapist, but her discussion with Eamon was something she wanted to share with her sister. She wanted to ask how a cop could forgive such a bloodthirsty killer. Or why she still loved him despite the images of him impaling ancient armies on spikes. Or why her brain had started associating his mansion with the word home?

"Eamon and I had a rough conversation," she blurted.

"Okay..." her sister dragged out the word. "You guys all right?"

"Yes... no... I don't know."

"Can you tell me what it was about, or is it personal?"

"Personal," Bel answered.

"Okay... was it a rough you two will grow from, or the kind you don't recover from?"

"He told me about his past, and his childhood was so different from ours. His family survived on hate, and it drove

141

him to become someone I could never love. It was painful to hear, and I never want to meet that version of him. The man I know uses his body as a human shield to save my life. The man I love bought almost the entire pet store for my dog. He isn't the heartless person he warned me he used to be, and I..." she trailed off.

"What do you mean, human shield?" Briar asked.

"He covered me during a shootout," Bel said, keeping it vague for her sister's sake, but her memory played out the real version. He'd used his own back to protect her from an IED. And he hadn't hesitated to take a bullet for her when Wendy Darling's lunatic husband tried to shoot her. How could the man who'd willingly been torn to shreds to save her be the Impaler?

"Oh my god, marry that man," Briar said. "Also, that's terrifying, and I'm sorry that happened to you, but he threw himself over you?"

"Yeah," Bel lied. Better to let her sister think Eamon pulled a movie stunt and lay on top of her than to learn the blast had peeled the flesh from his bones to expose his lungs.

"Wow, that's brave. I take everything I ever said about him being terrifying back. Thank goodness someone is watching over you."

Bel wiped her eyes. Her sister had a point. Eamon might be the devil's son, but he forever stood between her and death. The universe must have urged Briar to call because her words reminded Bel that Eamon had always been honest about his darkness. He was also a man of action, and he'd made a life-altering decision when he earned her affection. He'd chosen to be worthy of her love, and he'd proved he would go so far as to die or even leave to protect her.

"Okay, I'll try to move past you getting shot at so I can help, but it seems you're worried that whoever Eamon was before you met will resurface," Briar said. "It sounds like he opened up about something painful and was incredibly vulnerable, which is saying a lot. He trusts you with the worst parts of himself. I don't know the specifics, but from what I can see, it seems he genuinely wants to change. Why else would he confess the truth? By laying it out on the table, he's given you power over him since you now have the opportunity to leave or use his past against him. It also ensures he can't manipulate you. If you're familiar with his old personality traits, you'll recognize them if he reverts. It'll be harder for him to gaslight you. I think he truly cares about you, and sharing his history is his first step toward accountability... Bel, why are you crying again?"

"Because my partner and I aren't speaking, and I needed someone to talk to, and then you called, and I love you."

"Breathe, Isobel," Briar said.

"I just needed this," Bel said as the mansion finally came into view. "I've spent so long trying to protect you guys from my mess that I started alienating the only people who can help. I don't want to ruin things with Eamon, but I'm not good at romance like you are."

"You think I'm good?" Briar burst into laughter. "Oh, Isobel, you should've heard Flynn and my fights when we first moved in together. There were days I contemplated smothering him in his sleep."

"Really?" Bel paused in the driveway.

"Really," her sister confirmed. "But we love each other, so we worked through it. Our disagreements didn't break us. It made us stronger, and here we are, married with kids. Relationships start all warm and fuzzy, but then real life hits the fan, and it's a mess. Couples who survive aren't those who never fight. They are the couples that struggle and grow together. I admit, you and Eamon are going through growing pains earlier than most, but you've both been through hell. Kidnappings and murders force emotions and stress to explode, so you're facing hardships faster than most. But hard conversations are healthy. Never marry a man you can't argue with because one day you'll wake up and learn he gaslit you by faking everything. Couples that are too perfect are bombs waiting to detonate..." Briar cursed. "Sorry."

"It's all right." Bel smirked. Her sister stumbling into a cliche wasn't triggering. If anything, the jokes made her reality easier to bear.

"Okay. Well, you know what I mean. You don't want a partner who picks fights or demeans you, but you need someone willing to put in the work. Only you can recognize which Eamon is, but I think he's trying to strengthen your relationship."

"He isn't picking a fight," Bel said. "He's being honest... painfully so, but not in a mean way. He just doesn't hide things from me."

"That's a good thing, even if it's sometimes painful," Briar said. "He freaked me out when we first met. He is intimidating, but it's obvious that you're important to him."

"So, we aren't falling apart?" Bel started crying again. The past months had been fraught with terror and emotions, but these tears felt like a personal assault. Maybe she was getting her period, and her hormones were bullying her.

"I can't answer that for you," Briar said. "It's your relationship, not mine, but you're communicating, which is the healthy way to sustain a relationship. Have the hard conversations before you waste too much time because you'll either learn you dislike each other, or you'll realize you're soulmates. Romance books paint happily ever afters as stagnantly simple happiness, but relationships aren't fairytales. They're gardens you cultivate, and with gardens come both roses and weeds. Pulling weeds can be excruciating, but when those flowers bloom, the pain is worth it. If you don't pull the weeds now, your roses will choke to death."

"Don't let this go to your head, but you're insanely smart," Bel said as she and Cerberus pushed through Eamon's front door into the heated foyer.

"It's about time you realized that," Briar laughed. "I may not solve murders, but I am happily married. I'm overjoyed you finally need my romantic advice. Do me a favor, though. Don't wait until you're crying to call. I want you to be happy, and I think you truly love Eamon. I hope you two succeed."

"Me too." Bel smiled, realizing she meant it. Eamon's history had freaked her out, understandably so, but her sister was right. Hard conversations weren't the sign of the end. It was how they would survive this life together.

"Do you feel better?" Briar asked.

"Yeah."

"Good. And what did we learn?"

"Okay, okay, I'll call more."

"Mission accomplished. All right, I have to wrestle two little boys into their pajamas, so I'll say goodnight... Before I do, what's that banging?"

"Oh, that?" Bel laughed. "I tune it out, so I didn't even notice. It's Eamon with the renovations. He's rebuilding the entire mansion himself."

"Wow. Want to send him my way when he's done?"

"Sure.... He's designing the house for me, apparently," Bel said, the girlish urge to share something romantic unexpectedly bubbling out of her. "He's been paying attention to what I like and incorporating it."

"Oh, that's hot," Briar said. "See, that man loves you. Mark my words, he's planning to ask you to move in with him, and he wants you to feel comfortable."

"Been there, done that," Bel laughed as a child shrieked on her sister's side of the call. "He asks me to live with him once a month."

"Already? Isobel Emerson, you guys are fine—put that down right now... Because I said so—sorry, what was I saying? Right, communication is healthy. Don't date a man who never lets you see his truth. You'll end up married to a stranger you can't stand or one who's dangerous."

145

Bel's mind flashed to Olivia. Ewan had concealed a monumental truth from her, creating their relationship on a lie. Eamon hadn't done that. He wanted her to love him with eyes wide open, and that took courage. He'd put everything on the table, risking her hating it enough to leave.

"Yes... yes, Mommy's coming. Sorry, I need to go," Briar said. "Bath time is getting out of control without me."

"Thanks for calling," Bel said as she climbed the stairs toward the sounds of demolition.

"I'm always here for you, so pick up the phone and call me."

"Deal."

"Okay, love you."

"Bye." Bel hung up, her chest infinitely lighter, and she thanked whoever her guardian angel was for inspiring her sister to randomly call so late on a weeknight.

The crash of a sledgehammer crashed against a wall, jerking her to attention, and she followed the thunder through the peeling halls until she found the source of the rage. Eamon's back faced her, and while his heightened senses always heard her long before she entered a room, he seemed oblivious to her return. She read the tension in his muscles, the fear in the way they coiled, the agitation in his rigidity, and he was taking his frustration out on the crumbling wood of this forgotten level.

Bel crossed the floor and captured him in her arms, pressing her cheek against his sweat and dust-streaked back. He'd stripped his shirt off, his skin filthy from his exertion, but she didn't care. She cemented herself against his spine, her fingers digging into his chest as she pulled him closer, and his body sagged. All the tension bled from his muscles, and for a long moment, he stood hunched before her, his relief at her return so palpable that it seeped through his skin and settled in her chest.

Evidence of a Folktale

BEL AND EAMON stood side by side, brushing their teeth before the colossal bathroom mirror in the perfect image of domesticity. He wore only boxer briefs. She wore only his tee shirt, both of their hair damp from the shower as they brushed in unison. Back and forth. Back and forth. They were just a normal couple readying for bed, ordinary people hovering over their his-and-hers sinks, and then Bel destroyed the facade.

"Why me?" she asked as she broke eye contact with her reflection and twisted to face the towering wall of muscle beside her. "You admitted to softening over the years, especially after your friendship with the World War II soldiers, but by your own admission—or lack thereof—you didn't bury the monster until you met me. Why? And are you truly different, or will the beast rear his head when I'm no longer enough to inspire goodness?"

"You'll always be enough," Eamon said.

"So why me?" she repeated. "It's about what you tasted in my blood that night we met, isn't it?" When he didn't speak, she had her answer. "What did you taste? What about my blood made you change your entire life? And if you say we're some sort of fated mates, I will walk out of this house and never return because I refuse to be in a relationship where I have no say. I won't be with a man like you because fate preordained our joining. If I'm with you, then it needs to be because I chose to forgive your past. Because I love you enough to make this work."

"We aren't mates." Eamon put his toothbrush back in its holder. "There's no such thing. At least not for the sons of hell. Do I believe you're my soulmate? Absolutely, but in a very human way. A preordained path didn't force us together. I think fate had a hand in our meeting, but you're standing in my bathroom wearing my shirt because you chose me of your own free will."

"Oh, thank god." Bel sagged against the counter, rubbing her

147

chest as if it might slow the thundering of her heart. "So, some irresistible magic isn't demanding we love each other?"

"No," Eamon said. "It might make you feel worse to learn you picked a man like me instead of fate forcing us together, but nothing's controlling you. If you love me, it's because you want to. Some might find that unromantic, but I'm of the opposite opinion. I think the fact that you choose every day to stand by my side makes you the most beautiful person in the world."

"It doesn't make me feel worse," Bel said. "I'm relieved. I want to be here of my own free will."

"You are." He crossed his arms over his chest and leaned against the sink.

"So what did you taste?" she asked. "What about me made you love for the first time in centuries? What about me made you kill the half of you birthed by hell? Or is this just a reprieve?"

"I honestly don't know, Isobel," he said. "I'll never be a good man. I'll always be the worst of humanity, and I can't guarantee that the murderer won't rear his head again. All I know is that while I'm no hero, I can be the hero in your story because I like the man you see when you look at me. I want to be the reason your eyes light up and your lips smile. The devil my father bred into me left me hollow and angry. I can never purge hell from my veins, but for the first time, I feel alive, and that's because of you."

"Heroes sacrifice for the greater good." Bel stepped closer to him, the warmth of his presence kissing her skin despite the fraction of air separating them. "Villains burn the world to save the ones they love. Maybe it's okay that you're a bit of a villain."

"I would burn it all down for you." Eamon closed the distance, capturing her face as he towered possessively over her. "Myself included. That much you can count on. I can't promise that my true nature won't fight its way to the surface, but I can promise that I'd die before I hurt you ever again. And that I'll do my best to never re-inhabit the Impaler."

"Thank you for being honest." Bel slid her palms up his chest. "I realize that wasn't easy, and I'm sorry I freaked out. I was expecting the killing-people-to-drink-their-blood bit, but I wasn't expecting the rest."

"I know, and I'm sorry. I'm no better than Ewan."

"That's not true," Bel said, once again thankful that her eldest sister had impeccable timing with her words of wisdom. "And it's why I stand by my decision not to tell Olivia. You didn't trick me into dating you like Ewan tricked her. Unconventional relationships like ours are impossible without honesty, so if I'd told her, it would've meant nothing. Your teeth were on my throat the first moment we met, so I've always understood. You never pursued so much as a friendship with me until you confessed the truth about New York, and after witnessing Alcina's magic force you to attack me in the woods, I was very aware of the man I'd let into my life. Your honesty helped me see past your darkness." She rubbed his bare chest for emphasis. "My soul might be damned for saying this, but Impaler or not, you're the person who makes me feel the safest. You're who I want to be with."

"Do you mean that?" Eamon tugged her closer.

"Yes… if I can forgive you for scarring my throat, I can forgive you for something that happened hundreds of years before I was born. I won't pretend that I've magically flipped a switch and forgave all your sins tonight. It'll take me time to come to terms with both your past and process my emotions."

"But you aren't leaving me?"

"No." Bel caught his face in her hands. "You're not allowed to leave me. I am bound by that same oath."

"Then I don't care how long it takes for you to forgive me." Eamon's forehead collapsed against hers, and each time she exhaled, he inhaled, filling his lungs with the breath that had once filled hers.

"You're a good man below the darkness, Eamon Stone." Her

voice faltered as her throat tightened with emotion. History might condemn her for this belief, but she loved the Impaler. No matter the horror, she loved him, and with love came redemption. "It took a lot of courage to be honest with me, and you've been fighting for us since we met. You aren't afraid to have hard conversations, either. I admit they hurt, but we need to fight."

"I wouldn't classify any of our conversations as fights. Disagreements or arguments maybe, but I never want to truly fight with you."

"Semantics." Bel swatted his chest. "The point is, I don't want to wake up and realize you're a stranger because we weren't honest. This isn't a fairytale where the couple meets and lives happily ever after. We exist in reality, and if we want a healthy relationship, we need to confront difficulties head-on. It's why Ewan needed to tell Olivia himself. You can't love a lie, and thankfully, I don't. When I told you I loved you on Christmas, I knew who I was confessing that to. He's the same man standing in front of me."

"I love you." Eamon pulled her lips to his, kissing her as his hands trailed down to her thighs to hoist her up his body. He wrapped her legs around his waist, and for a breathless minute, he showed her how desperately he loved her.

"But if we're being honest, there's one more confession I need to make," he whispered against her mouth as he carried her to bed.

"I can't take any more confessions today."

"It's not like that." Eamon rubbed Cerberus' head before pulling the sheets around the trio. "It's about what I tasted in your blood. It's what made me save your life instead of killing you that night in the city. It was love."

"But you said we weren't fated mates."

"Not ours. Your parents."

"My parents?"

"Little is known about it," Eamon explained. "Mostly

Evidence of a Folktale

because people like you have an incredible power flowing through your veins. If you think hate is strong, you should see the strength of pure love. Unfortunately, most of what's known about the offspring of true love is rumors because beings like me spent our lives hunting them down. When a couple's love is unadulterated and pure, their children are born with the sweetest blood. It's believed to be the strongest magic known to mankind, but there's little proof. Witches hunted them down and slaughtered them as sacrifices. My kind sought them out to feed on them. Historically, humans like you don't survive long enough to prove the rumors. I've killed every child of love I'd encountered and drank them dry until you and now your sisters."

"Why me, though?" she asked, curling into the safety of his chest. "If you killed all the others, why did you let me live?"

"My friend from World War II," he answered. "He thawed something inside me. For the first time in my life, I cared, and then I met you. Through my drunken haze, I realized you were special. You were the product of a love so rare it birthed a sort of magic, and I couldn't kill you. I wanted to. Your blood is my drug of choice, but I couldn't go through with it. All I could think was no one had ever loved me, and I fantasized about what being loved would feel like. I craved your presence. It was intoxicating... Why are you crying?"

"I can't imagine living for centuries without someone loving me." Her tears tickled her nose as they dripped down her face, but before she could wipe them away, Eamon drew her head against his chest, his cool skin erasing the dampness.

"You're lucky in that respect. So many people love you."

"Well, you're not alone anymore because I love you... we're the couple that makes it, right?" She gazed up at him in the darkness, desperate for him to agree, to confirm that every ugly truth and painful moment they'd suffered would lead to triumph in the end.

"Yes, we make it." He pulled her into his arms, practically

suffocating her against his chest, and for the first time all night, Bel relaxed. "I'll make sure of it."

"It feels so good being warm," she whispered against him, her exhaustion shifting gears as her mind slowed, and she savored the way his skin twitched as her lips formed the words against him.

"I know, Detective." Eamon tucked the blankets tighter around them, his muscles tense at her meaning. "It's why you should live with me. I'll keep you warm every night."

Bel laughed, the stress from the past hours escaping her body with her voice, and she smiled at the realization that she never wanted him to stop asking her that question.

"You can't go more than five seconds without suggesting that, can you?" She yawned. Without anxiety fueling her erratic heartbeat, she could barely stay awake.

"I figure if I keep asking, the answer might eventually be yes."

"You keep telling yourself that," Bel teased, falling into hazy oblivion, so she missed his response. "And Eamon?" She regained consciousness for a moment. "Talk to Ewan and make him fix things with Olivia because I stand by my belief. These secrets aren't mine to tell. I love her, but I love you more, so my loyalty lies with you. I'm not responsible for Ewan's mistakes, so talk to him. I want my friend back."

"Based on the traffic, I take it the producers didn't listen to you and cancel the fan events?" Bel asked Griffin the next morning as she leaned against his office doorway.

"No, they didn't," her boss groaned. "It'll cost them too much money, and without proof that Orion Chayce is guilty or in town, they have no intentions of halting production."

Evidence of a Folktale

"I don't understand why they don't care," Bel said. "Their writer was murdered."

"On Eamon's land," Griffin said. "Not on set or in the bed-and-breakfast or at the hotel hosting the events. Her death unfortunately has no actual connection to the show. Until we can prove Chayce is here and guilty, we can't force them to be rational."

"I can't imagine money being more important than a woman's life."

"Don't ever let that change."

"I have no intentions of letting it."

"Good." Griffin stood from his desk. "And we'll just have to be vigilant. If Chayce is in town, we have to find him before he hurts someone else."

"Olivia and I should look into Gwen Rossa," Bel said. "If Chayce is here to exact revenge, there's a reason he started with her. Did she cause the accident and blame it on him? Was she merely a witness? If we find a connection, we might be able to predict his other targets... if there are any. It also might help us locate Chayce."

"Good idea," Griffin said. "I'll—"

"Detective Emerson?" Officer Rollo interrupted him. "A package was delivered for you. I put it on your desk."

"Thanks," Bel said. "Did you see who it's from?"

"No. There were no addresses on the box. Just your name and the station."

Bel raised her eyebrows at the deputy. "Thanks, Rollo."

"No problem." He nodded as he left. "Let me know what the boyfriend got you."

"It's not your birthday," Griffin said as they walked to her desk. "Valentine's Day is coming soon, though. You think Eamon sent you something?"

"Maybe. Not sure who else would send me an unaddressed package." She picked up the small brown box and undid the tape, but when she peeled back the lid, she froze, the blood solidifying in her veins until she couldn't move.

"What's wrong?" Griffin asked, but Bel couldn't find her voice. She didn't want to believe her eyes, so she merely tilted the package for the sheriff to see, praying he would prove she was imagining things.

Except the color drained from his face when he saw what rested inside the delivery, and she knew she wasn't hallucinating. Her eyes weren't playing tricks on her. They recognized what lay inside, and Bel wanted to throw up at the sight. For in her hands sat a tiny white gift box tied with a crimson red bow… just like the one found at Gwen Rossa's crime scene.

Autopsy Report

CERBERUS

Chapter Ten

BEL RACED FOR THE STATION'S RECEPTION, BARELY STOPPING AS she shouted at the on-duty officers. "Who delivered the package for me?"

"I don't know," the deputy said.

"It wasn't the mailman?" she asked.

"No."

"What did they look like?"

"I don't know."

"What do you mean, you don't know?" She gawked at him. It was his job to address and observe those who approached the station's front desk.

"A giant group of fans was just here trying to get information," he said. "By the time we got them and their social media filming outside, the package was there. We didn't see who slipped it onto the counter."

"Check the security footage!" Bel bolted out the front door, the icy wind punching her face as she skidded to a stop to avoid a pedestrian passing on the sidewalk.

"Geez, watch where you're—sorry, officer," the stranger fumbled.

"Did you see them?" She ignored his comment. "The group that just left the station. Did you see where they went?"

"Um..." the man scanned the now sparsely populated street. "No."

Bel cursed as she jogged out into the road, but whoever had delivered the package was long gone. A horn honked behind her, and she glared at the driver, who had the decency to look embarrassed when he realized she was a cop. The car slowed to allow her to retreat, and she sprinted back into the station and up the stairs to her desk.

"I couldn't find who left this," she said when Griffin raised his eyebrows in question.

"It has no prints," he said. "We got photos before dusting it, but we found nothing."

"Thanks." Her gloved hands grabbed the tiny white box and untied the red ribbon. "You know this means there's another body?"

"I do," he said as Olivia and the other officers present gathered around.

Bel pulled off the lid and withdrew the single sheet of paper. She unfolded it and shoved it into an evidence bag before laying it flat on her desk. "It's a game of hangman, and there's one turn left." She pointed to the stick figure body hanging from the noose. It had a head, torso, and two arms, but only one leg. Some letters were written on the answer lines, but most of the phrase remained blank. It didn't matter, though. She recognized the pattern and the message. The hangman would be complete with only one more wrong letter. They'd lost the game, and a very real victim had lost their life.

"Another riddle," Griffin said. "Five words. Just like the first clue... what did that one say again?"

"What big eyes you have," Bel answered.

"Some of the phrase is filled out." Griffin pointed to the letters. "It isn't hard to guess four of the words."

"What big blank you have," Bel said. "Big what, though? No vowels have been used yet."

"It's a four-letter word... What big legs? Or arms? Lips?"

"Not legs," Bel said. "There's a G in big, but it doesn't repeat in the blank word. And I doubt it's arms. The first riddle led us to contact lenses, so unless the killer stuck a clue in a victim's biceps, it's a body part with a natural cavity."

"Okay, lips work then. You can put something in someone's mouth. Nose and ears too."

"I'm sure we'll find out when we discover the body. The only question is, where is it?"

"In the woods somewhere, I imagine," he said. "I'll check today's filming schedule for an outdoor shoot."

"Detective Emerson," the deputy from the front desk called as he jogged for her. "The security footage is of no use. Everyone wore coats, hats, and gloves, and no one looked up at the cameras. They swarmed the counter, so it's impossible to see who put the package down." He handed her his tablet, and Bel watched the video to confirm his words.

"This was on purpose." She cursed under her breath. "Whoever dropped this off probably encouraged these fans to come in and demand answers for their social media followers. With the weather, he took advantage of everyone being bundled up, making it easy to hide a small box inside a coat."

"Sorry." The deputy turned red. "They all had their cameras out, and I was trying to get them to stop filming. I didn't expect someone to drop off evidence."

"It's not your fault," she said. "Whoever did this predicted we'd remove fans who were recording the station. He played us... have we received any calls to report something odd?"

"No, not yet."

"Well, hopefully, we locate the body first. If fans discover it, they'll destroy the evidence and post the scene all over the internet—"

"You can't be here," Olivia's agitation interrupted her, and Bel glanced across the station to find her partner blocking Ewan from entering the precinct. "This is my place of work, and cornering me won't make me talk to you."

Bel cringed at the hostile interaction. Olivia and Ewan's breakup wasn't public knowledge yet, but it was about to be if she didn't lower her voice.

"Liv..." Ewan glanced over her blonde head and met Bel's gaze. "I'm not here to talk to you."

"Bel?" Olivia gawked at him, clearly offended that he hadn't come to grovel at her feet.

"Yeah." He sidestepped her as if it physically hurt him to leave and gripped Bel's elbow. "Can I speak to you?" he whispered as Olivia glared at their closeness.

"Now's not a good time." Bel backed up, forcing his fingers to fall from her arm. She figured he wanted help with winning Eamon's or Olivia's favor back, but the station with a second murder looming over her head was not the appropriate place.

"Detective, I need to talk to you now." He stared at her with meaning, the bear peering through his irises with predatory urgency, and her skin flushed cold. This wasn't about Olivia or Eamon, and dread settled like a rock on her chest.

"Sure." She gestured for him to follow her to the breakroom so no one would overhear.

"With everything going on, I let *Him* out to relieve stress," he said. "I run on Eamon's property since his presence shields mine, but with how much Olivia hates me, I don't expect him to welcome me here much longer. I won't have Eamon's protection once I leave, so I've been taking advantage of what time I have. I hiked the trails this morning until it was safe to shift into my true form, and that's when I smelled the blood."

"Blood?" Bel stepped closer to him. "Human?"

"Definitely."

"Fresh?"

"Within the past few hours."

Bel cursed. "And it's on the Reale Estate?"

"Yes, but the scent is far from the mansion, so the killer probably assumed it was the state park. But there's definitely a bloody body in the woods."

"Did you see it?"

"No. My senses are stronger when I shift, but the last thing I wanted was to leave bear tracks at a crime scene. As soon as I scented the blood, I shifted back and found you. I wasn't sure how you'd want to handle this tip."

"We'll just tell Griffin you were hiking," Bel said as she led him out of the break room. "Everyone knows you're an enthusiast. You construct half of your designs from materials you find in the woods."

Ewan worked with Violet Lennon at Lumen's Customs. Brett Lumen had been a famous furniture designer before his murder, and he'd left his entire business to his assistant, Violet. She was one of Bel's closest friends, but she was no designer. She'd been at a loss for how to keep the company alive until Ewan moved to town. His style was far more rustic than Lumen's luxury pieces, but the bear shifter with the sexy lumberjack vibe had the skill to turn furniture into art. He often used the recycled or natural materials he found in the woods, so convincing Griffin he'd been merely exercising was probably the easiest task Bel would face that day.

"Sheriff." She cornered her boss and tried to ignore the way Olivia hovered from a distance. "Ewan was hiking this morning."

Griffin's eyes shot to the man clad in outdoor gear beside her with an expression that warned he knew what was coming.

"He thinks he found the body."

"I was hiking here," Ewan said as he led the police through the snowy woods. Bel had texted Eamon to warn him there was another body on his estate before positioning herself between Ewan and Olivia to help keep the hike professional, and she hated every second of it. Her physical position felt uncomfortably similar to the emotional one Ewan's lies had placed her in, but while the trek through the cold was unpleasant, the end of their trip was what she dreaded most. She didn't want to find another woman ripped apart to stain Eamon's land. It seemed hell refused to let him go. He'd abandoned his ways of bloodshed, and in return, his property soaked up the spilled blood of those who murdered in his stead.

"I noticed something strange in the trees here," Ewan lied as he left the trail and ventured into the woods. "I think there's a body if you follow these footprints." He gestured at the sea of endless white.

"I don't see anything." Griffin studied Ewan, and Bel could see the wheels in his head turning. The solitary tracks leading away from the path were human, but if she didn't intervene, her boss might realize Eamon wasn't the only Bajka man to be wary of.

"There." She pointed as she moved through the trees, glancing at Ewan for guidance. He nodded, and she surged forward, an army of officers in tow. "There, I see it…" She froze, her little white lie suddenly true, and she instinctively reached out and grabbed Griffin's hand for support.

"Good lord," he muttered as he squeezed her gloved fingers in return. For a moment, no one spoke, and then Griffin cursed, the words ugly as they echoed through the emptiness. For before them was another dead woman wearing a hooded cloak, only this one wasn't face down in the snow. This crimson victim hung like a crucifix from the tree branches, her body completely naked save for the red fabric and her frozen blood. Just like Gwen Rossa, her abdomen had been ripped apart, the jagged wounds flayed open and horrifying to witness. Her torso and spread arms were pale and bloodless, but her soaked legs had stained the deep drifts below her, and Bel felt instantly light-headed at the brutality of her death.

"The same M.O.," she whispered before venturing closer. "The same wounds. The same box. The same phrase. The same red cloak."

"Don't say it," Griffin said.

"It's the same killer." Bel ignored him. "Two deaths by the same killer. One more makes it a serial."

Griffin cursed again. "Thum, you'll be able to confirm, but she doesn't seem to have defensive wounds. Her feet are soaked in blood, but I'm willing to bet her soles aren't damaged from running in the snow."

"I would have to agree." The medical examiner joined them before the corpse. "I thought Gwen Rossa's scene was terrifying... but this. Hanging from the tree to bleed out like this, her entire bare and brutalized body on display. This was such a violent and hateful death. Whoever killed her did so in a fit of rage."

"You think so?" Bel asked.

"Like with Rossa, he had to face her to kill her." Lina pointed at her mangled abdomen. "The killer inflicted these wounds standing up close and personal. He looked into her eyes when he ripped her apart, and then he laced her arms through those branches while she bled out. I think she was still alive when he strung her up. There's so much rage in these deaths. To be torn to shreds and then left face down in the snow. To be posed like the crucified Jesus of Nazareth. I might be wrong, but this reeks of rage."

"Like a man seeking revenge for an accident that sent him to jail." Bel met Griffin's gaze.

"Thum, can you remove the hood?" the sheriff asked. "Do we have another dead crew member on our hands?"

"Sure." Lina rose onto her toes and pushed the draped fabric away from the victim's face. Sunlight bathed the woman's bloodless cheeks, and Bel lunged forward, her recognition dragging her closer to the disturbing scene.

"Griffin," she whispered, her boss' alarm crowding her back. "It's her. It's the costume designer."

"Ellery Roja," he spoke her name. "We just saw her yesterday."

"Yeah." Bel met the sheriff's eyes with an overwhelming churning pulsing inside her. "When she warned us about Orion Chayce."

"So time of death was probably in the middle of the night like Rossa's," Lina said. "Lividity and rigor mortis confirm that estimate."

"And like with Rossa, I doubt we'll find anything of value," Griffin said. "The elements always compromise outdoor crime scenes. We have footprints this time, but they belong to one, maybe two people. They're mottled, so we won't get any boot prints, and they stretch between the trail and the body. Little good that does us. We already know she was chased here, and the trails are too trodden to track the killer's retreat. No blood drops lead away from the scene, though, which is strange."

"The killer probably cleans the weapon before he leaves the bodies," Olivia said.

"But a kill this violent and personal?" Lina said. "The blood spatter and cast off would've coated his body."

"Except I've seen the designers spray painting the set pieces," Olivia said. "They wear masks and protective suits. White protective suits. The killer would've disappeared out here wearing one, and when he was done with his kills, he could've stripped it off at the scene so the dripping blood would join the rest. He left clean, and even if he was dirty, he could've scrubbed himself with snow and then tossed it below her body. Her warm blood would've destroyed what he used to wash. We won't find anything."

"We might get lucky," Bel said, not believing her own words. Whoever killed Rossa and now Roja had been deliberate in their attacks. These weren't the sloppy murders she'd dealt with while on the NYPD force. This killer was telling a story, and stray evidence wasn't a part of his narrative.

"Story," she whispered to herself as the unsolved hangman puzzle flashed through her memory. A hanged man for a hanged girl. "Lina, the first body's clue read, *'What big eyes you have'*."

"And we found the contacts," the M.E. said as she worked.

"A white box was delivered to the station this morning with a similar style clue," Bel said. "We recognized the words *'what big'* and *'you have'*, but we don't know what four-letter word sits in the middle. Our guess is lips, nose, or ears. Maybe arms?"

"Arms might be right since she's posed like a crucifix," Lina said. "This hanging definitely draws attention to them."

"I didn't think arms would work, but you have a point." Bel stepped closer without disturbing the frozen blood.

"I'll check them, but we'll probably have to wait until the autopsy to locate anything embedded subdermally," Lina said. She took her time examining Ellery, both her skin and the crimson cloak, but after five minutes, it was clear her arms were free of evidence. "Okay, there's nothing here, so my guess is nose, ears, or lips." She stepped back to study the corpse. "I'll perform the autopsy tomorrow, and we'll look for whatever he hid in her body."

"Lina?" Olivia interrupted as she shifted into their peripheral view. "When you examined Miss Roja's arms, you knocked the hood off her right ear." She pointed to the side of the victim's head. "I think the clue is *'What big ears you have'*."

"Oh my god, you're right," Lina said as she rounded the bloody snow and leaned toward Roja's ear. "It looks like a hearing aid. Did she wear hearing aids?"

"Not that we saw when we spoke to her yesterday," Bel said.

"Contact lenses. Hearing aids. It fits," Lina said. "Can someone get a picture of this before I pull it out?"

A tech jumped to oblige her, and when he finished, she withdrew the object. "Okay, not exactly a hearing aid, but it's some sort of earpiece." She dropped it into an evidence bag and handed it to Bel. "I know film crews use earpieces to communicate. Could this be one?"

"Maybe," Bel said. "I've seen people walking around set with them, but this one's different. It looks custom."

"The contact lenses were custom," Griffin said. "It makes sense this is too."

"Another hidden message." Bel retreated a few paces and pulled out her phone to snap a few wide shots before returning to the sheriff's side. "But the first clue isn't this crime scene." She showed her boss the photos. "We'd wondered if the forest etched into the contacts was his next murder site, but nothing about these trees matches the ones in the image. Everything's wrong."

"So if the lenses weren't warning of his next victim, what do they mean?" Olivia asked.

"I don't know." Bel studied Ellery Roja's almost biblical visage. "If this is about exacting revenge for the accident that sent Orion Chayce to jail, I have no idea what a photo of the woods has to do with anything."

"WHAT'S THAT?" Bel's eyes scanned the room for the sound's origin.

"This." The tech held up the earpiece found on Ellery Roja's body.

"It makes noise?" Bel asked as she moved closer. As expected, they'd recovered little at the scene, and the forensics team was currently pouring over the physical evidence. It seemed this earpiece was more than just a plastic mold.

"What did you do?" Bel asked without giving him time to answer.

"I noticed screws in the larger end," he answered. "I took it apart and found this." He pointed to the smallest USB flash drive Bel had ever seen. He'd plugged it into his laptop, and it was playing a sound clip of a man speaking.

"Turn it up and play it from the beginning," she demanded, but the tech was already increasing the volume.

"It is a cold one this January morning, so don't forget to bundle up," the recording began. "Right now, we're looking at a temperature of twenty-two degrees Fahrenheit, but by mid-day, we'll see a high of twenty-nine degrees before it falls back down to the low twenties tonight. Wind speed will be around ten miles per hour, which is a relatively mild breeze, but with these January temperatures, it'll make everything colder. Skies are mostly sunny with only a ten percent chance of rain, so at least we'll have beautiful sunshine to make up for the chill."

"A weather report?" Bel and the tech asked in unison.

"A January weather report," she repeated. "No date. No location. Just a winter forecast. That's even more random than the contact lenses."

"What if that's the point?" the tech said. "To make us chase our tails with nonsense."

"Maybe," Bel agreed. "But let's not dismiss anything yet."

"Right... well, it's January and cold in the report, so it's obviously from a northern state."

"Based on the snow in the contact lenses photos, that's a given. Can you play it again? There might be a hidden meaning."

"Want me to email the recording to you too?" he asked.

"Please."

The tech replayed the clip, emailing Bel a copy when it finished, but nothing stood out. It was a generic winter weather update. An undisclosed day in an unmentioned year in an undetermined location in January. A cold month and a photo of snow in the woods. Maybe this was a witch hunt meant to confuse them while the killer escaped justice.

"I didn't hear anything," the tech said. "Just that it was cold and January. But as you said, the contact lenses already implied it was winter."

"Wait..." Bel whirled on him, something clicking in her brain at his words. "A cold place and a month."

"Yeah?" The word sounded like a question.

"I have an idea." She charged out of the room, leaving a confused man in her wake as she climbed the stairs to knock on the sheriff's door.

"Come in!" he called, but she was already opening it.

"Listen to this." She opened her email and played the recording for her boss.

"What was that?" he asked.

"We found a flash drive inside Roja's earpiece," she explained. "Its only file was a weather report, though."

"Well, that's... random."

"I thought so too," Bel said, a spark flickering in her eyes as her brain assembled the puzzle pieces. "But we wondered if the contact lenses photo was the scene of his next murder. It wasn't, but it's still a location. Then this weather report is for somewhere cold, which matches the image, but it adds another piece of information. The month."

"Okay?" he said, clearly not following her.

"What five questions do detectives always ask themselves when solving a crime?" Bel leaned over his desk before answering her own question. "Who, what, where, when, and why?"

"Right." Griffin squinted as if it might help him see where her train of thought was going.

"The contact lenses had a photo of a location. The where,"

she explained. "The news report mentions a month. Both are vague and unhelpful, but it doesn't change that January is still a measurement of time."

"Which would be when," Griffin said, catching on.

"What if these clues are part of a bigger puzzle? What if the snowy woods are the where and January is the when? The killer is trying to paint us a picture."

"There are five W questions." The color drained from Griffin's face. "If you're right, we only have two answered."

"Which means we still need Who, What, and Why to solve his riddles," Bel said. "He isn't done killing. There are three more murders to go."

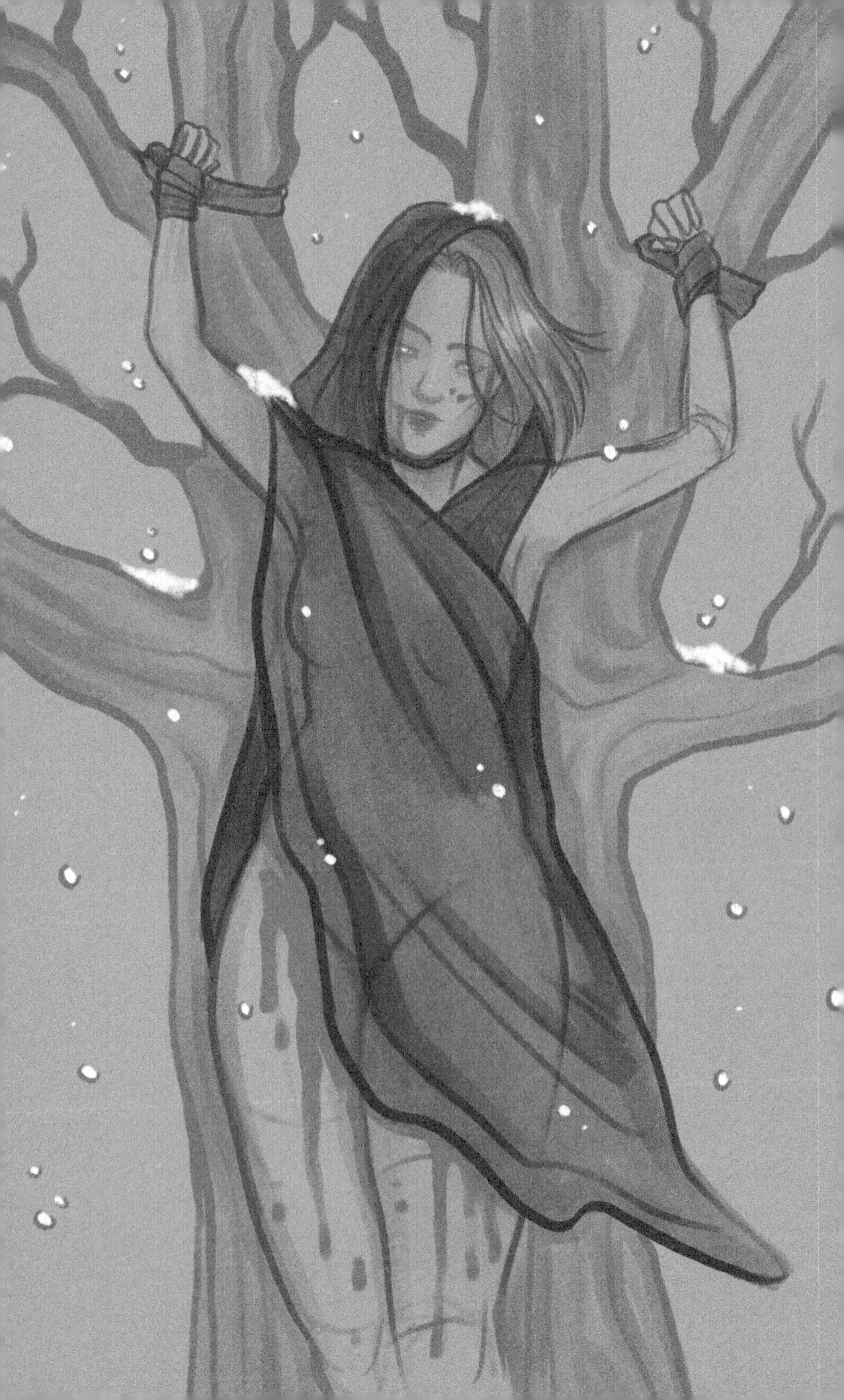

Chapter Eleven

"I don't know what I can tell you about Mr. Chayce that you haven't already learned," Evelyn Pierce said.

Griffin had gathered the precinct to brief them on Bel's suspicions before questioning the producers yet again. He didn't normally share her theories without concrete evidence, but with victims this prolific, her boss had no intention of letting this case turn into a serial killing. One more body, and the murders of Aesop's Files crew members transformed from disturbing crimes to the work of a sadistic serial killer. Humanity's obsession with true crime would spread news of these homicides like wildfire, and if discussing half-baked speculations about disgruntled ex-cons lit a fire in the department to find Chayce, he'd share every theory Bel dreamed up. Especially because she had a sixth sense about her when it came to death, and if she believed three more had to die before their killer left Bajka in his wake, he promised to hunt down her every lead, no matter how absurd.

After the briefing, Bel and Griffin had cornered the producers with the hope they'd have more information on Orion Chayce than Ellery Roja did, but Miss Pierce's tone told Bel all she needed to know. Nothing productive would come from this conversation... again.

"He was overseeing the props on set that day, and he wasn't paying attention," Evelyn said. "His carelessness resulted in another crew member's death, and the police ruled the accident a byproduct of his negligence. He was charged with involuntary manslaughter and sentenced to a few years in prison. It's a fairly straightforward if not unfortunate story."

"Were you aware Mr. Chayce was out on parole?" Bel asked, watching both producers for their response.

"Yes, we'd heard," Alistair Rot said.

"Did you know he'd broken parole?" Bel asked. "He's missing."

"No." An odd flicker disrupted Evelyn's expression. "We hadn't heard."

And there it was.

"We believe he might be in town," Bel pushed, secretly smug that both Pierce and Rot reacted exactly how she'd hoped.

"If he was, I'm sure your people would've already found him," Alistair Rot said. "I doubt he's here."

"Of course, it could just be a rumor," Bel continued. "Or he could be stalking the show. It would be best to shut down production until we find him."

"That's out of the question," Alistair said. "And if our former employee is in town, it's your job to arrest him for breaking parole. He's no longer our responsibility."

"And you're sure nothing happened that day that would drive Mr. Chayce to seek revenge?"

"We've told you all we can," Evelyn stood, signaling Bel had struck more than one nerve. "Now, if you'll excuse us, we need to get back to work. If you have any further questions, please direct them to our assistants."

"You saw that, right?" Bel asked when the door to the producers' trailer shut behind them.

"There's something about that day they don't want anyone figuring out," Griffin said.

"I doubt Orion Chayce caused that accident," Bel said. "I think something else happened. Something bad, and he's who they chose to take the fall."

"That would explain why he's killing crew members… if he's the murderer," Griffin said. "But it still doesn't make sense why Gwen Rossa was his first victim. How is a writer connected to a prop malfunction? And Ellery Roja? She was the one who alerted us to him."

"He's going after anyone from the show he can gain access to?" Bel said. "Or Roja warned us in the hopes we would catch him before he came for her? Or the accident was far more involved than we realize, and the entire crew is guilty? Take your pick."

"I realize we're hung up on the idea that Chayce is the guilty party, but I don't want this consuming us. We'll miss something," Griffin said. "I'll head back to the station and dig into Chayce's life and known associates. He's our best suspect, but I don't need to tell you how focusing on the obvious often turns investigations into cold cases."

"I know. I won't miss anything."

"You rarely do."

"It just frustrates me that two women died horribly, yet they refuse to so much as pause filming. Can't we force the issue?" she asked.

"If the murders took place on set, yes," he said. "But they were killed on the Reale Estate. It has nothing to do with the show's production, and the producers argue that what their employees do overnight when not at work is their own business. They aren't responsible for the crew's personal time or Stone's private property. We have no cause to shut filming down because it's not the problem. If anything, Stone is the one in trouble since both deaths occurred on his land."

Bel raised her eyebrows at her boss.

"Don't worry, I don't consider him a suspect... yet. The studio might go after him, but somehow, I doubt that would end well for them. What concerns me is that we found both women on his property. Was that on purpose or by accident? Rossa was killed close to a filming location, but Roja wasn't."

"She was attacked closer to the trails Ewan and morning exercisers frequent, though," Bel said. "She was bound to be discovered quickly."

"So, are we looking for someone familiar with Bajka?" Griffin asked.

"Another reason we shouldn't solely focus on Chayce."

"It would stop us from asking these questions... but why would a Bajka resident be hunting these women?"

"It might not be someone who lives here," Bel said. "Shows have location scouts. It's how they found our town. Maybe they wrote up a detailed report along with photos when pitching Bajka to the director and producers, and the killer is using that data."

"And we've circled back to Chayce," Griffin said. "As a former crew member, he could've gotten his hands on that information."

"Maybe," Bel said as The Espresso Shot came into view. "I'm going to stop for coffee and then drive to the bed-and-breakfast. Hopefully, someone saw Roja—or Rossa—leave the nights of their murders."

"Sounds good." Griffin angled toward where he'd parked his truck. Bajka's largest hotel was located off the highway, but the cast and crew had rented out the entire bed-and-breakfast so fans couldn't search the halls and harass the actors' accommodations in the middle of the night. The hotel hosted the meet-and-greets, and the attendees were staying in the surrounding motels and rooms for rent, but the bed-and-breakfast was smack dab in the center of town. Someone had to have seen something.

Bel pulled out her phone as she waited in the almost too-long line for her coffee and asked Olivia to meet her. She also asked if her partner wanted a drink, but Olivia ignored the question, only responding to confirm she'd be there in fifteen minutes.

"Detective," David's voice interrupted her self-pity, and she looked up to find The Espresso Shot's owner carrying a large to-go cup. "Here." He handed it to her, and she instantly smelled the vanilla. "You shouldn't have to wait in line."

"You didn't have to, but thanks," Bel said. "What do I owe you?"

"On the house."

"I can't just take your coffee," she protested.

"Leave a big tip next time." He leaned closer so he could lower his voice. "Officer Rollo mentioned you found another body. I don't want to waste your time by making you stand in line." He nodded to the corner where Rollo and Violet were chatting... or flirting, depending on how well you knew them, and Bel knew Violet pretty well.

"Thanks, David," Bel said.

"No problem. Besides, it's been hectic. Beau Draven came in earlier, and a fight almost broke out. Thankfully, Officer Rollo was close by, so he stopped in for some crowd control."

"Just what we need with two bodies in the morgue." Bel shook her head. "Being spread thin because fans feel the urge to fight over an actor."

"Hence the coffee to stop you from waiting in line." David patted her back.

"I appreciate it. I'll pay extra next time." She left the line and crossed the room to where Violet and the deputy stood, and she didn't miss the way her pretty friend turned bright red when she realized she'd been caught flirting.

"Hey." Bel pretended not to notice for her dignity's sake. "David told me there was a fight."

"Kind of," Rollo said. "For him, it probably felt like a fight, but it was mostly just loud."

"So, no one got hurt?"

"No, thankfully."

"Good," Bel said. "We don't need another crime happening here."

"It's why I rushed over when I heard Mr. Draven was involved."

"Every life is important, but if something happens to the stars, it would ruin Bajka's reputation," Bel said. "Thanks for stopping by so quickly. And I just wanted to say hi. Violet, I feel like I haven't seen you in forever."

"Because you haven't." Violet hugged her. "You died, then you were with your family, and now this madness. We need to hang out because I still haven't recovered from that news report."

"News report?" Bel asked.

"The one that reported on your accident and death." Violet shuddered, and Bel didn't miss the way Rollo reached out to comfort her.

"I haven't watched it," she said. "I don't want to."

"You don't," Violet agreed.

"Eamon saw it though," she said, and Violet's expression fell.

"I know. He picked up Cerberus from me. I've never seen someone behave the way he did. It scared me. I knew you were dating, but I didn't realize how much that man loved you."

"The feeling's mutual."

"It is?" Violet lit up.

"It is." Bel hugged her friend goodbye. "We'll hang out soon, but I have to go. I need to stop by the bed-and-breakfast to ask some questions."

"Okay." Violet refused to release her. "I'm so freaked out

Evidence of a Folktale

that women are being murdered in our town. I won't survive you dying again. Are you okay to be doing this?"

"Yeah..." she trailed off because sometimes she was, but then her body would grow cold.

"Want me to head over with you?" Rollo asked.

"Thanks, but Olivia's meeting me." Bel smiled at the handsome officer. It was kind that he offered, but asking some questions didn't require three cops. Besides, Olivia's matchmaking seemed to be paying off. She hated interrupting what might be a budding romance.

"Okay, well, if you need me," Rollo said.

"I know where to find you." She winked as she squeezed Violet's hand one last time before leaving the coffee shop.

"Have you or your staff seen this man?" Bel slid her phone across the front desk so the owner of Bajka Bed-and-Breakfast could view Orion Chayce's mug shot.

"I can't say I have," the woman responded. She was a silver-haired grandmother who looked perfectly at home inside the adorable inn, and Bel felt odd asking her about her guests' murders. The bed-and-breakfast seemed too cozy with its cheery fireplace, grand dining room, and vintage bar for such topics.

"Do you mind if I take a photo?" the woman asked, pulling out her own phone. "I don't think he's been here, but perhaps housekeeping or the kitchen staff saw him. I can ask around."

"Go for it." Bel withdrew her hands so she could get a clear picture of the mugshot. She'd met Olivia outside the inn a few minutes ago, but her partner suggested they split up to cover more ground. She volunteered to visit both the hotel and the motel by the highway's exit to inquire about Orion Chayce while Bel dealt with the bed-and-breakfast. She claimed it was to save time, but Bel saw through her attempt at efficiency. She didn't want to be around her, and Bel almost cried watching her drive off. After everything she'd been through, she needed her friend, but Olivia wanted nothing to do with her.

"Okay, here you go." The inn's owner slid Bel's phone back to her. "I'll ask around, but don't get your hopes up. I grew up in this bed-and-breakfast, and I live in the basement apartment. Nothing happens here without me knowing, so I doubt this man has stepped through my doors. But I'll still ask. Who knows, perhaps he stopped by when I was out."

"I appreciate it. And as for these women." She showed the innkeeper the photos of Gwen Rossa and Ellery Roja. "They were staying here."

"Yes, I recognize them. Those poor girls. It's terrifying what happened to them."

"It is," Bel agreed. "Do you recall seeing those two involved in anything unusual? Did someone come to meet them, or did they get into fights with anyone? Did they behave oddly at any point?"

"Can't say that they did," the woman said. "Everyone staying here is too busy for anything besides work. The studio booked my entire bed-and-breakfast for security purposes, so we've been working hard to keep the fans out of the inn. It's an exciting contract." She grinned. "Although I would prefer it didn't include murdered guests."

"We all would," Bel said. "So, nothing strange happened to them?"

"Nothing," the woman confirmed.

"When was the last time you saw these women?"

"This one." The innkeeper swiped through Bel's phone to find the first victim's photo.

"Gwen Rossa," Bel said. "She was the show's head writer."

"Yes, her. I don't remember seeing her return to the inn the night before she died, but I figured it was only a matter of time before the police stopped by. I have the security footage ready.

It's a simple in-house system, so you can look now if you'd like."

"Yes, please," Bel said.

"I'll show you in my office." The woman led her into a cozy back room where monitors lined one wall. Live feeds played across the screens, and a quick survey told Bel they covered the main desk, lobby, entrances and exits, and parking lot.

"That second woman you showed me," the owner continued.

"Ellery Roja, the costume designer."

"Yes, she returned last night and went straight to her room."

"What time was that?"

"Hmmm, let me rewind..." The woman fell silent as she scrolled through the footage, and Bel was relieved that she was remarkably tech-savvy for her age.

"Wait, there." Bel pointed to the rewinding footage.

"Oh, good catch." She paused the recording. "You got those young eyes."

"More like I spend a lot of time watching rewinding surveillance."

"True... and those young blue eyes. Your boyfriend must love them... you do have a boyfriend, don't you?"

"I do." Bel smiled. Women in this town loved to inquire about her love life.

"I thought so. A pretty girl like you. Is he anyone I know?"

"The man who bought the Reale Estate."

"A rich man. Good for you." The woman beamed at her. "Can't say I've seen him, though. I heard he's a recluse.... And wasn't he a murder suspect at one point? Oh dear, here I go running my mouth. I guess if a detective is dating him, he isn't a murder suspect."

"Oh, he was," Bel laughed. "But he was cleared... obviously."

"Obviously. One more question, and I'll stop being nosy. Is he handsome?"

"Very."

"More handsome than that dreamy Beau Draven. You can be honest, it's just us girls."

"Yes, he is. Taller too. By a lot."

"Oooo, I could forgive a man's reclusiveness if he was tall and handsome."

"It does work in his favor."

"You love him," the woman said. "I see it on your face. You light up talking about him... okay, I'll stop grilling you about your love life. Sorry, it's a side effect of running this inn. Everyone loves to chat with granny about their lives, and it's turned me into a busybody."

"It's fine," Bel said, remembering Vera when she first moved to Bajka. Alcina, the witch murdering the townsfolk, had masqueraded as her elderly neighbor, but before Bel knew the truth, she'd enjoyed the grandmotherly affection. "I don't mind."

"Of course you don't. No one ever minds talking about beautiful men." The innkeeper turned back to the monitors. "Okay, Miss Roja returned from the shoot last night at 9:38 p.m. She'd been gone for over twelve hours."

"What floor was she staying on?" Bel asked.

"The third."

"So she couldn't have jumped out the window to avoid being seen?"

"Not unless she wanted a broken ankle. It's a straight drop."

"Can you fast-forward the footage? She ended up in the woods, so she must've left the inn at some point."

"Sure, let me know if you spot her...is that her? Oh, no... um... wait. There. That's her, right?" The innkeeper pointed to a woman exiting the front door at 11:54 p.m. The figure was bundled up, but the build looked familiar.

"Do you ever see her face?"

"Not with the indoor cameras. She had her hood up, and she's on the phone."

"What about the parking lot's view?"

The innkeeper switched the footage, and they watched the woman pause to speak to the squad car stationed outside and then disappear down the street. She never looked at the camera, but as she vacated the property, she twisted sideways long enough for Bel to confirm that it was indeed Miss Roja leaving alone in the middle of the night.

"I can't tell if that's her," the innkeeper said.

"It's her... do you mind?" Bel gestured for the controls, and the woman relinquished them. "There. You can see her profile for a few seconds. That's her. She leaves just before midnight, and based on her time of death, I don't think she ever comes back." Bel fast-forwarded to confirm, but her guess was right. Ellery Roja never returned.

"Oh, I feel awful," the innkeeper whispered. "This is the last time she was alive, and I just let her walk out of my inn."

"This isn't on you," Bel said. "I wonder why she left so late, though?" She rewound the tape. "She doesn't look nervous or under duress. And she waves at the officer before chatting with him... who's in that squad car?" She paused the video and leaned closer to the monitor, Rollo's handsome features barely visible through the darkness. "Right. I think that's all I need from last night. Can I get a copy?"

"Sure. I'll email it to you."

"Awesome. Here's my contact information." Bel slid her card across the desk. "Before I go, can you rewind to the night Rossa died?" She gave her the date.

"Sure." The woman obliged her, but Gwen Rossa never returned to the bed-and-breakfast before her death, making it significantly harder to trace the writer's final hours. At least they could track most of Roja's movements. She'd been alone in her room until something forced her to leave. She'd been on the phone when she departed the inn, so maybe the killer lured her out with either friendship or a threat.

"Could I see Rossa's and Roja's rooms?" Bel asked as the women exited the office.

"Of course." The innkeeper gestured for her to follow, and they climbed the carpeted stairs together. Bel examined Roja's room before moving on to Rossa's, but there was little to see besides luggage and script pages. The victim's computers had already been turned over to the police by their assistants, so the dirty undergarments and half-used toothpaste tubed held no earth-shattering secrets.

"Thank you so much for your help," Bel said when the women returned to the first floor.

"Of course. I'll let you know if any of my staff saw that man."

"Thank you. Have a good one." Bel waved over her shoulder, holding the front door open as Taron Monroe blew into the lobby. The show's main actress was somehow even prettier up close, but it wasn't her beauty that struck Bel. It was her scowl. She glared at her as they passed, and Bel reeled back to avoid the disdain. What had she done to deserve such disgust?

She watched Miss Monroe disappear up the stairs with her assistant, and shaking off the encounter, she dialed her boss. "Sheriff, can you do me a favor and request a warrant for the victims' phone records?" she asked when he picked up. "Ellery Roja left the bed-and-breakfast last night a few minutes before midnight, and she was on the phone. What if the killer called to lure her outside?"

"Sure," he said. "Any luck finding Chayce? Gold called right before you. Neither the hotel nor the motel has a record of him staying with them. They're sending over their security footage for us to review, though, just in case."

"That sucks," Bel said. "And no. No luck finding Chayce here."

Griffin cursed. "All right, I'll get you those phone records."

"Thanks." She hung up and dialed Officer Rollo.

Evidence of a Folktale

"Detective?" he answered on the third ring.

"I have a question," she said. "You were stationed outside Bajka Bed-and-Breakfast last night."

"I was."

"What did Ellery Roja say to you?"

"What do you mean?" he asked.

"Last night, she left at 11:54 p.m., paused at your squad car, and then walked down the street."

"Wait…" he trailed off. "That was the victim? That woman was so bundled up, I didn't recognize her. I assumed it was someone's assistant because she yelled something about chips at me."

"Chips?"

"I think that's what she said. She was on the phone, so I figured an actor had sent their assistant out for a midnight snack."

"Chips…" Bel faced the street Roja had walked down before she disappeared from the camera's view. "The twenty-four-hour mini-mart," she said, understanding dawning on her. "It's a short walking distance from the B and B, so she bundled up to buy snacks. She probably saw your squad car and figured she should explain herself."

"I should've offered to drive her, but I wasn't supposed to leave the parking lot. My shift ended at midnight, but I chatted with Yates when he relieved me for a bit. When I left, I didn't see her walking back, but I admit, after working a double, I was just trying to stay awake to drive home. Was I the last person to see her alive?"

"Maybe. Unless she made it to the mini-mart."

"Do you want me to stop by and check?"

"Thanks, but I'm already halfway there. At least we have a map of Roja's movements before she died."

"I feel bad didn't recognize her."

"Don't be," Bel said. "I only knew who she was because

183

Griffin and I just interviewed her. We can't follow everyone everywhere. We're already stretched too thin."

"You can say that again. Well, if you need my help, just call."

"Will do. I'll talk to you later." She hung up and wrapped her arms around herself to ward off the cold as she jogged the rest of the way to the store. It was a quick walk, and the shop's owner was in his office when she arrived. He confirmed that Ellery Roja had indeed stopped by, and like the bed-and-breakfast, the mart had an in-house security system. The owner played her midnight shopping spree for Bel, but it offered little insight into the designer's last movements. A few minutes after she left Bajka's Bed-and-Breakfast, Roja walked into the mini-mart, still on the phone. She didn't seem under duress or upset as she grabbed an armful of chips, soda, and miscellaneous snacks, and then she hung up her call to pay with cash. She then left the building, having been there for all of six minutes, and vanished from the surveillance's sight, not to be seen again until the following morning, naked and gutted on Eamon's property.

"When the judge learned who the victims were, we received the warrants and records so fast that I almost suffered whiplash," Griffin said when Bel arrived at the station. "We reviewed Rossa's and Roja's calls for their last few days. We also had both victim's assistants confirm phone numbers, but we found nothing."

"What do you mean?" Bel asked. She'd finally returned from the mini-mart to update her boss, and it seemed they both had much yet so little to share.

"No random numbers called or texted either victim. So, I think it's safe to say, the killer didn't use a phone call to lure them into the woods," Griffin said. "The records confirmed Roja was on the phone at midnight, but it was business. Something about last-minute fabric requests. I don't understand the technicalities, but we verified with the caller. They're her supplier, so it wasn't a threat. Seems she really left the bed-and-breakfast for snacks. I don't know, could we be looking at crimes of opportunity? What if Rossa and Roja weren't the targets? They were just the only crew members the killer found unattended?"

Bel cursed. "That's possible. She had her phone with her at the mart. I saw it on the security footage, but all her belongings, cell included, were missing from the crime scene. The killer probably dumped them... or maybe he was stupid enough to keep it."

"One can hope."

"Can the phone company tell us where their phones last pinged the cell towers?"

"In town," Griffin said. "Nowhere near the Reale Estate, though. The phone company believes both devices have been powered down."

Bel cursed again. "I doubt the killer kept them then. If he knew to turn them off far away from his killing grounds, he knew not to keep evidence. He probably dumped them, and my guess is far from both the crime scenes and their last cell pings. Those locations would be too obvious."

"I'll still have deputies search the areas," Griffin said. "The killer might be smart, but accidents happen."

"And all we need is one."

GWEN ROSSA and Ellery Roja's phones were still missing when Bel finally left the station for the night. She'd hoped the killer dumped the victims' belongings either in a drain or a dumpster, giving them an idea where the women were taken, but it seemed their killer was not only smart enough to remove the batteries but also had the foresight to keep their phones far from the police's reach. It wouldn't surprise her if he'd destroyed the devices so they could never be traced back to him. Killers loved keeping souvenirs, but it's also what got the guilty caught, and something warned her their guy wasn't ready to be uncovered just yet.

A short drive later, Bel pulled onto her dark street and parked on the gravel before her cabin. Her single-room home sat on the outskirts of Bajka, her backyard the woods that eventually led to the Reale Estate. A few rental cabins lined the lonely road, making for a private existence, especially since the unit across the yard from her had stood empty ever since a witch murdered its owner. It was normally a peaceful neighborhood, and the dimly lit road never bothered her, but the minute Bel stepped out of her SUV, she felt it. She was being watched, and it wasn't Eamon's presence. She recognized the way his eyes caressed her skin. He'd stalked her from the darkness long enough for her to grow accustomed to the weight of his gaze, but this was a stranger's presence.

Bel inched closer to the front door, her hand slipping to her holster. She silently undid the strap as she scanned the snowy yard, but before she could reach the stoop, a dark shape emerged from the street's shadows and raced for her.

Autopsy Report

CERBERUS

CINEMA TICKET
ADMIT ONE
9891102

CINEMA TICKET
ADMIT ONE
9891102

PROD.NO. | TAKE | SOUND
SCENE | |
DIRECTOR | CAMERAMAN | EXT. | INT.

Chapter Twelve

"Hands in the air and don't move!" Bel snatched her gun from its holster and aimed it at her stalker, thumbing off the safety with deadly ease.

"Oh god!" a feminine voice shrieked, and Bel watched in disbelief as the stranger slid to a stop, slipped on the snow, and plummeted to her backside. "Ow!"

"Miss Monroe?" Bel leaned forward to get a better look, but there was no mistaking the actress. "I almost shot you! What on earth are you doing here at my home?"

"I'm sorry," Taron Monroe moaned as she rubbed her tailbone. "Can you put your gun away?"

Bel glanced from her weapon to the pretty woman and then held her aim steady. "Why are you here? Are you following me?"

"Kind of," the actress admitted.

"What is wrong with you?" Bel asked. "Stalking a police officer? I realize you only play one, but you should know better than that."

"I'm sorry. I figured you would recognize me. Please, can you put the gun away? I just want to talk."

"How do you know where I live?" Bel flicked the safety on and slipped her gun back into its holster before pulling out her phone. She didn't know why Taron Monroe had followed her home, but she wasn't taking any chances. She'd learned her lesson about innocent encounters turning deadly, so she thumbed open her text thread with Eamon and typed two words.

BEL

Cabin. Now.

"I waited until you left the station and then followed you," Taron said, still lying on the snow. "Can you help me up?" She extended her hand, but Bel had half a mind to leave her where she sat.

"Following a police officer home is extremely inappropriate, if not illegal," Bel said without moving to help her. "If you wish to speak to me, please stop by the station."

"I wanted to talk to you in private."

"We could've done so there."

"Clearly you don't pay attention to my show."

"Not really."

"Aesop's Files is one of the most watched shows on television right now," Taron said, finally realizing Bel wasn't going to help her. "I can't go anywhere without being photographed and plastered all over social media." She stood to her feet, still rubbing her backside. "If I went into the station during business hours, it would end up on the internet within five minutes. It's quiet here. No fans followed me, so that's why I came… can I come in? It's freezing out here."

Bel stared at the actress, taking stock of the woman's form. She was athletic in a Hollywood way. She looked great on screen, but necessity hadn't forged her muscles as it did Bel's. Ever since Abel had locked her in his basement, she'd made a point to strength train and hone her hand-to-hand combat skills. It had served her well when Dr. Blaubart kidnapped her. She'd been handcuffed, yet still fought him off. Pretty Taron Monroe had nothing on her... but then again, Bel's elderly neighbor had turned out to be a witch so powerful she could control Eamon. Size didn't matter when magic was involved.

"I swear I'm not here to hurt you." Taron glanced behind her as if she expected the paparazzi to suddenly materialize from the snowplow's dirty mounds. "I just want to talk."

"Fine." Bel beckoned her visitor toward her door. She had her sidearm and her pitbull... and Eamon. As long as the actress was human, Bel was the dangerous one.

"I have a dog," she warned as she unlocked the front door. "He's—"

"Oooooo a baby!" Taron bent over and shoved her hands out for Cerberus' exuberant greeting, and Bel couldn't tell whose tail wagged harder, her dog's or the actress' metaphorical one. Cerberus instantly took to her, so maybe she wasn't a threat after all.

"Wow! Okay, big boy, woah." Taron toppled backward... again, falling to the snow as Cerberus blew past her and into the yard. He lifted his leg to pee and then bolted for the darkness. For a split second, Bel's heart lodged in her throat until she heard the low rumble of a man greeting his favorite animal.

"Your dog is so cute," Taron said as Bel helped her to her feet this time. "I can't have a pet since I'm so busy, and I hate it."

"You like pitbulls?" Bel asked as she led the woman into the warm kitchen, and after they removed their coats and shoes, she gestured for her visitor to make herself comfortable.

"I'm not really a breed or species person," Taron said, settling at the table. "I'm more of a *'I would pet a crocodile if it wouldn't kill me'* kinda person."

"You sound like me," Bel laughed. "But I'm partial to pitbulls now that I have one."

"I don't blame you. His meaty head is ridiculous."

"Tea?" Bel held up the teapot as Eamon blew through the front door, Cerberus tucked under his arm as if he were a chihuahua and not a seventy-pound bundle of muscles.

"Yes, please..." Taron trailed off as he stormed past her, her entire body recoiling in fear at the pulsing aggression wafting off his towering form.

"You okay?" He ignored the actress as he settled beside Bel at the kitchen stove.

"Yeah," she whispered. "She scared the crap out of me, though. She followed me home, and I almost shot her. I almost shot Taron Monroe."

Eamon's glare flicked to their visitor, but Bel grabbed his forearm to rein him in.

"She wants to talk to me in private," she said.

"Couldn't she do that at the station?"

"She doesn't want the public finding out."

"Why?"

"We haven't got that far yet. It's why I texted you. She's probably harmless, but she also followed me home."

"You did the right thing texting me." Eamon kissed her forehead before setting Cerberus down on the kitchen floor.

"Thanks for coming so fast. Tea?" She squeezed his arm again, and when he nodded, she filled the kettle with enough water for the three mugs. "Miss Monroe, this is Eamon Stone," she said as she set her collection of teas on the table for the actress to pick from. "He occasionally helps the Bajka police, and he's discreet. You can trust him," she half lied. She wouldn't play all her cards until she learned what game she was involved in.

"Mhhmmm." Taron nodded, and Bel couldn't tell if her expression was because she was terrified of Eamon or wildly attracted to him. Or perhaps it was both.

"So, you want to talk to me?" Bel pulled her attention back

to their conversation, and Eamon settled out of sight on the couch with the dog.

"Right... yes... um." Taron glanced at the imposing millionaire one more time before focusing on Bel. "And call me Taron, if you don't mind. I'm in your cabin drinking tea. Miss Monroe seems so formal."

"Okay." Now that her alarm had subsided, it dawned on Bel just who sat at her kitchen table. Taron Monroe. America's sweetheart detective, and she curled her fingers around the quirky teacup as if she were Bel's friend... her very pretty and famous friend. Maybe she shouldn't have invited Eamon to hang out with one of the most beautiful women in the world.

She handed him his mug before returning to the kitchen table, and while her visitor was busy sweetening her tea, Eamon's hands shot out and lightly slapped her ass. It was subtle and intimate and unbearably sweet, and Bel rolled her eyes at herself. Eamon didn't care that Taron Monroe sat four feet away from him. He saw only one woman in this cabin, and she was the exhausted one wearing the clearance rack jeans.

"So, what's wrong that you couldn't visit me at the station?" Bel asked as she slipped into the seat across from the actress.

"I heard through the grapevine that you talked to the producers about possible suspects and obsessed fans who might have killed Gwen and Ellery," Taron started, and Bel sat to attention. This was not the direction she'd expected this conversation to take. "Evelyn probably gave you... oh, what's his name? Tony Rays?"

"Tony Royce," Bel corrected.

"Yes, him."

"Your producers did give us Royce's name. We already looked into him and ruled him out. Royce feels passionately about Willow Moon's departure from the show, but he isn't a murderer."

"I know. He was just the easy answer. A way to help you without actually helping you."

"What do you mean?" Bel leaned forward again, extremely thankful she hadn't shot Miss Monroe.

"They needed to appease you with plausible information, so they purposely helped you in the least helpful way," Taron explained. "They know that kid is harmless, all talk and no bite. We all know it. He's obsessed with the show, and no matter how much grief he gives us about me replacing Willow Moon, he still watches every episode. He's irritating at best, but he's no threat. It's obvious to everyone, but they needed to give you a suspect, so they gave you someone who'd get you nowhere."

"Why would they do that?" Bel asked.

"Because if a serious threat linked directly to the show, they'd have to shut down. It would lose them a lot of money, and the studio doesn't want that if they can avoid it. The murders didn't occur on set, so they won't halt production. And on the one hand, I understand. I think Gwen and Ellery would've wanted their legacy to live on. Aesop's Files is so much bigger than one person, and as long as the show isn't at fault, there's no reason to stop filming. But if it's proven that a crazed stalker is killing crew members, and the studio knew about it, there'd be trouble. It's why they gave you a patsy."

"I understand the pressures of running a multimillion-dollar business, but why is the studio so resistant to pausing their schedule when faced with a double homicide?" Eamon asked from the couch, and Taron flinched as if she'd forgotten he was there.

"Have you heard of syndication?" she asked, the look of fear and attraction flooding her features again.

"I have," he answered.

"I haven't," Bel said.

"Syndication happens when a show reaches one hundred episodes, and they can license it out," Taron explained. "Normally when a show first airs, it remains on its home network or platform, but once it hits one hundred episodes, it can start airing on multiple streaming platforms and networks. We're almost at episode one hundred, and the minute Aesop's Files crosses that threshold, we're looking at a massive payday."

"Why one hundred episodes?" Bel asked.

"Because it allows networks to work it into their regular yearly rotation without having repeats," the actress said. "One hundred episodes give them months to air every season before they have to start over with episode one, therefore increasing watch time on the network that licenses it. The more episodes, the better. They can schedule multiples per week, and constantly have viewers because nothing was being repeated."

"Got it," Bel said. "So halting production would ruin that. How close to number one hundred are you?"

"They're the episodes we're filming in your town."

"Right... so they really don't want murderers or crazy fans stopping anything." Bel dropped her head into her hands. The more she learned about this studio and its famous show, the more she hated it... except for Taron Monroe. The pretty woman liked her pitbull and was risking the company's wrath to be here. Hopefully, she was exempt from the toxicity.

"That certainly explains a lot, so thank you," Bel continued. "But unfortunately, we already realized Tony Royce wasn't a threat. I appreciate you being honest with us. It's the first time anyone from the show has been, but there's little I can do with this information."

"I'm not here because of him," Taron said, suddenly too serious, and a pit yawned wide in Bel's stomach. "I'm here because I'm terrified. Because all the women working on Aesop's Files are terrified. Two of us are dead, and we're afraid of who's next. So I asked around when I learned you were on Gwen and Ellery's case. Everyone says you're the person to talk to if you want something done... especially the guy at that cute coffee shop. He believes you're to be trusted."

"I am," Bel said. "I solved his wife's murder."

"She was murdered?" Taron leaned back in her chair. "That's terrible. I figured by his statements that she'd died, but he didn't say how. Although speaking highly of you should've clued me in."

"It was a difficult case."

"So I can trust you, right?" Taron stared so deeply into Bel's blue eyes that she felt her gaze in her soul. "And you too?" She threw a glance at Eamon.

"You can," Bel said. "I realize you don't know me, and I did just try to shoot you, but I take my job seriously. I don't care who you are. If you need help, I help, but if you're guilty, I'll take you down no matter the cost."

"Good." Taron nodded and gripped her mug tighter. "Because I have a real suspect for you."

Autopsy Report

CERBERUS

PROD.NO.
SCENE TAKE SOUND
DIRECTOR
CAMERAMAN EXT. INT.

CINEMA TICKET 9891102
ADMIT ONE

CINEMA TICKET 9891102
ADMIT ONE

Chapter Thirteen

"His letters initially seemed harmless," Taron said. "Someone goes through my fan mail to assess the safety before it ever gets to me. Is something harmful in the package? Would it be damaging to my mental health? Does it include content that warrants dialing 911? If she doesn't find anything concerning, she passes the mail on to me, and this fan seemed innocent, if not a little nonsensical. Written in beautiful prose, his letters read like the ramblings of a well-spoken poet, but then I noticed this." She slid her phone across the table. "They look like normal hand-written correspondence." She pointed at the photograph. "But see how some words are penned darker than others. It's not instantly noticeable, but when you keep getting flowery letters delivered to you repeatedly without rhyme or reason, you start searching for meaning. At first, I wondered if it was just the pen running dry, and the author needed to press harder, but for curiosity's sake, I wrote those words down on a separate piece of paper, and his messages suddenly made sense."

Bel grabbed the expensive phone and pulled it closer, her eyes trailing over the darker words on the written page. "*You wore that red scarf I love,*" she read the hidden message out loud, her stomach clenching at the fan's mention of red clothing. *"It fluttered behind you, and I wondered what would happen if the wind blew too hard. Would it choke you? Would you die? You would be so pretty sprawled out on the sidewalk with crimson around your throat. It would be like a scene from your show. I watch every episode. I love them all. You would be so pretty if you died, but I would miss you. The. W. O. L. F...* the wolf?" Bel's eyes shot up to Taron's before flicking to Eamon. "Do you know who sent this?"

"No," Taron said. "All I know is that he always traces the letters W, O, L, and F darker after the word The, so I think he calls himself The Wolf. There's never a return address on the envelopes, and because his mail is whimsical yet meaningless, they make it through the screening process."

"He did that on purpose," Bel said. "If he wrote that line about the sidewalk outright, the letters would've been delivered to the police."

"I know," Taron said. "But the dead on the sidewalk isn't the scariest part."

"What is?" Eamon asked.

"The red scarf," Taron said. "The paparazzi and random social media users post photos of me all the time, so it's easy to reference what I wear, but every letter The Wolf sends mentions something he shouldn't know. Like the scarf fluttering in the wind. Before I received this one, I'd gone out for coffee alone, so that day stuck in my memory. I felt safe going by myself because it was freezing, and I was bundled up. No one recognized me, but there was this massive gust of wind that almost ripped my favorite red scarf off my throat."

"He was watching you," Bel said.

"I think so. Everything he says is always slightly off-color and personal. Like the letter where he mentioned he didn't like when I cursed when my heel got stuck in a crack. I remember muttering it under my breath because people were taking photos of me. The last thing I wanted was a video of me cursing like a sailor going viral, which means he had to have been extremely close when that happened."

"Have you brought this to anyone's attention?" Bel asked. "Or taken it to the police."

"I showed the letters to the studio executives, but they dismissed it. The slightly darker words aren't exactly hard evidence."

"But when you read them together, they make sense," Bel said. "Anyone can see they're threats against you."

"But if there's a stalker, the show might have to pause production, so the executives view The Wolf as merely a fan who writes nonsense. So you can understand why I didn't want to visit you publicly. I need help. I need someone who believes me. Listen, I love my job. And yes, I'm shallow. I love being famous and pretty, and I love all the clothes and handsome men, but I'm self-aware enough to recognize it. I'm not cruel. I'm never mean to my fans, and I'm not delusional. I appreciate that I live a life of privilege, but I'm a decent person. I don't deserve someone stalking me only to have the studio ignore my fear, and now with these murders, I'm worried I'm next."

"Well, I don't dismiss concerns like this," Bel said. "Not when two other women have already died horribly. Tell me, how well did you know Orion Chayce?"

"Who?" Taron asked.

"The crew member who worked on the set design. His malfunctioning prop killed a lighting technician."

"Oh, that guy. Sorry, I never met him. He was arrested before I joined the cast, so I couldn't tell you anything about it."

"Wait... so you don't know Chayce?"

"Not in the least."

"Hmmm," Bel grunted, her theory hitting a snag. If Taron wasn't part of the show when Chayce's accident occurred, he'd have no reason to kill her.

"Why did you ask about that guy?" the actress asked. "Did he kill Gwen and Ellery?"

"We don't know. Right now, we're just looking for possible suspects. His accident led to jail time, so he could be seeking revenge."

"Okay… that makes sense, but I doubt he'd be after me. I'm more afraid of whoever this Wolf is."

"Do you still have his letters?" Bel asked. "I'd like to test them for prints and DNA."

"Not here, no," Taron said. "I turned most over to the producers. I should've gone to the police instead, but they want us to bring things to them first so they can prep their lawyers if needed."

"Have you received any since you arrived in Bajka?"

"No, thankfully."

"Okay, well if you do—"

"You'll be the first person I show them to," Taron said.

"And talk to your mail assistant. See if she can get me the originals of those older letters."

"Will do."

"And Taron, thank you for being honest. We keep getting roundabout answers, and it's making it difficult to work this case."

"Yeah, well, I don't want to die, or anyone else for that matter. I'm not a detective like you, so I don't do death and dismemberment unless it's a prop. I enjoy acting, and pretending to be a tough cop is fun, but I'm not the real deal, nor do I wish to be. These deaths are freaking me out, and I don't want to be next."

"I won't let that happen," Bel said. "We're taking every precaution to protect the cast and crew while you're in town, but for the love of God, do me a favor, please. Don't leave the bed-and-breakfast alone at night again. I mean it. We don't know how he got Rossa, but we believe the killer took Roja when she made a midnight snack run. Don't do that. Go to work. Go home and stay there. If you need to leave, get a police escort."

"Or call me," Eamon said. "I have the money to ensure your safety, and I would prefer no more women die on my property."

"Thanks," Taron said, and Bel realized he was trying to help, but Miss Monroe seemed to take his invitation a little too personally. Bel understood. It was hard not to grow intoxicated by her millionaire, and the brief flicker of green in her chest proved how much she loved him. It also betrayed how much of his dark past she'd forgiven. She couldn't bear the thought of losing him to another woman, but her dog lying across his lap was convincing proof that the Impaler no longer belonged to the devil but to her.

"It's getting late," she said, gathering the empty teacups and placing them in the sink. "And we all have early mornings. Was there anything else you wished to share?"

"No, that was it." The actress returned her focus to Bel. "And thank you for listening. You have no idea how relieved I feel now that someone is taking this seriously."

"Of course." Bel shook the woman's hand. "If you remember anything else, find me... not in the dark where I might shoot you, though."

"I will, and I'm sorry about earlier. Thanks for not shooting me." Taron moved for the door and donned her outerwear. "I'll see you soon."

"Wait." Bel grabbed her coat and gestured for Eamon to join her. "A deputy is posted outside the bed-and-breakfast, but remember what I said about not wandering alone at night. That means even in a car, so we'll follow you back."

"CAUSE OF DEATH was exsanguination just like Rossa's," Lina said the next morning as she and Bel conducted Ellery Roja's autopsy. Olivia was, once again, conveniently absent. She'd declined to attend the exam in favor of tracking down Gwen Rossa's final movements. Roja had returned to the bed-and-breakfast the night before she died, leaving at midnight to walk to the mini-mart alone, but Rossa's last hours were still unaccounted for. Splitting up to tackle the mountain of work was smart when the department was spread so thin, but her partner's absence was eating Bel alive. Was this how it would be for the rest of their careers? Was her best friend destined to become a stranger?

"Roja has no defensive wounds on her arms, and her feet aren't badly damaged," Lina continued, oblivious to Bel's distress. "It's identical to Rossa's body."

"No sexual assault?" Bel asked.

"No sexual activity at all," Lina answered. "Doesn't mean she wasn't expecting to hook up with someone, though."

"I don't know," Bel said. "She was seen at a twenty-four-hour mini-mart buying chips in the middle of the night before she went missing. That doesn't scream torrid affair to me."

"The killer could be tailoring the way he lures them into the woods to each victim," Lina said as she leaned over Roja's butchered abdomen. "But Rossa wasn't drugged, so I suspect neither was Roja. The lack of defensive wounds suggests both women knew their killer, or at least trusted him enough to go willingly."

"Or he threatened them from the start," Bel said. "Aim a gun at a woman walking alone in the dark, and she'd probably obey. If Orion Chayce is the perpetrator, both Rossa and Roja were aware he'd been sent to prison for manslaughter. I doubt they would've gone with him willingly."

"Either way, their end was horrible," Lina said. "I can't even imagine being chased through the snowy woods in nothing but a cloak..." she trailed off as she remembered who she was talking to. "I'm so sorry, Bel."

Evidence of a Folktale

"At least I made it out of the trees alive. I got away."

"And thank God for that. It's bad enough examining strange women on my table. Seeing you was hell."

"Was the likeness really that close?"

"It was exact," Lina said. "It even fooled your father. The only one who noticed was Mr. Stone, but that makes sense. You're a couple. I don't want to assume anything, but he's probably seen a lot more of you than we have. The body's lower half was ripped apart, much like this woman's. That surgeon saw you on vacation in a bathing suit, but he didn't see everything, so he was obviously trying to conceal what he couldn't recreate. Thank god Mr. Stone spotted the discrepancies. But the time the doctor must've spent altering your doppelgänger. He must have been planning on taking you ever since he met you at Wendy Darling's wedding. How else did he find time to perform all those surgeries on Jane Doe?"

"He must have," Bel lied. Lina was oblivious to the evil that roamed the earth, and she had no intention of enlightening her. She already had one friend and coworker angry at her. She didn't need another. "And yes, Eamon said the body wasn't right," she half lied this time. There was something wrong with Jane Doe, just not the appearance. It was her blood. "We'd just returned from a tropical and romantic vacation. He knows what I look like."

"Thank goodness. I'll never forget what that man sounded like before he realized Jane Doe wasn't you. His cries still give me nightmares. He didn't sound human."

Bel froze at her comment.

"And neither is this." Lina leaned down to examine the severed flesh. "This is different." She used tweezers to pluck something from the wound and held it up to the light. "It's fur."

"Fur?" Bel shifted closer, but the M.E. was right. It was a long strand of fur.

"There's not a lot, but there's fur stuck in the wounds," Lina said. "I can't tell if it's animal or synthetic until I run some tests, though. Wounds that look like claws inflicted them and then fur trapped in the blood." She met Bel's gaze. "If I didn't know better, I'd say a creature from Aesop's Files came to life and killed Ellery Roja."

"Hey, Violet, is Ewan here?" Bel asked as she entered Lumen's Customs.

"Yeah," her friend answered. "In the workshop."

"Thanks." Bel stormed out of the office to find the studio's new furniture designer. The minute she spotted him, she grabbed his biceps and hauled his formidable mass into the back room.

"Is everything okay?" he asked when they were far from Violet's ears. "Is it Olivia?"

"I hate to ask you this, but I have to," Bel hissed. "Did you kill those girls in the woods?"

"What?" Ewan reared away from her, but she held his arm tight. He was significantly stronger than her, but she belonged to the beast. If he valued his life, which he did, he wouldn't so much as raise his voice around her.

"Both women were killed with claw-like weapons, and the latest victim had fur stuck in her wounds… like that of a bear's. You killed someone in the woods before, so I'll ask you again, did you murder those women?"

"Absolutely not, and I can't believe you would ask me that," Ewan hissed. "You know full well I killed that hunter because he was trying to wipe out my entire pack. It was self-defense of both me and my family. I don't kill innocent people, and I'm not a monster despite what Olivia thinks."

"I had to ask," she said.

"And would you feel the same urge if it was your beloved millionaire?" he spat. She could tell her suspicion wounded him,

Evidence of a Folktale

but better damaged pride than more dead women. She didn't believe he was a cold-blooded murderer, but he'd killed for a good reason before. The presence of claw marks and fur had her wondering if he had reason again.

"I was always the first person to assume his guilt," Bel said. "Not even he's allowed to get away with murder in my town, so I had to ask. The deaths remind me so much of your bear, and you were the one to find Ellery Roja."

"I can't believe you think I could do that," Ewan growled as he leaned forward until he was at eye level with her. "I'm not a monster, and if you believe I could do something that heinous, you're not the woman I believed you were."

"Well, you're the man who lied to my best friend and made her hate me," Bel said, not backing down. "And I've experienced the repercussions of mistakenly assuming someone was harmless."

"I know. I was there alongside Eamon, searching for you. I saw the accident where you supposedly died, and I held Olivia as she sobbed. You've faced unspeakable darkness, but I'm not it. I'm trying to win Olivia back. Do you think murdering women would help my cause?"

"No," Bel conceded. "It wouldn't. Could there be another shifter in town?"

"I don't know," Ewan said. "New people flood Bajka every day, and I keep detecting inhuman scents. Nothing crazy, just your garden variety supernaturals, which is to be expected with this kind of show, so it's possible. Eamon would be the better man to ask since his senses are superior to mine."

"So you haven't encountered other bears?" she asked.

"Not that I've detected."

"I'm sorry, Ewan." She finally released his arm. "I am, but life has been chaos lately. Every time I step into the cold, I'm back on that mountain being shot at by Blaubart. Olivia won't talk to me. I just learned the truth about Eamon's past. And now women are being ripped apart on my boyfriend's property. So, I apologize for not behaving with more decorum, but I needed to prove it wasn't you. To look you in the eyes and see your breakup hasn't driven you mad."

"Oh, it's driving me mad, but not to murder," Ewan said. "And have you ever stopped to consider the fur wasn't an accident?"

"What do you mean?" Bel asked.

"A paranormal detective drama where creatures of all kinds live among humans comes to our town, and suddenly women start dying in theatrical ways with supernatural undertones. Now there's animal fur stuck in a victim's wounds. It seems alarmingly like an episode of Aesop's Files. We're living the show, and what if that's what the killer wants? Clues, oddities, riddles. Girls in red, dead in the snow, clawed apart by a monster. What if this isn't a supernatural killing at all? Have you considered that? What if the killer's playing too close to the show, and everything you've found is merely part of the act?"

Autopsy Report

CERBERUS

CINEMA TICKET 9891102 ADMIT ONE

CINEMA TICKET 9891102 ADMIT ONE

PROD.NO. TAKE SOUND
SCENE
DIRECTOR
CAMERAMAN EXT. INT.

Chapter Fourteen

"I SWEAR TO GOD, I FEEL LIKE I'M THE ONE ON A TV SHOW," Griffin said when Bel relayed Lina's autopsy findings and Taron Monroe's late-night visit. "And the studio knew about this Wolf guy?"

"Miss Monroe claims they do," Bel said.

"But they refused to tell us because we might shut down production." Griffin cursed. "Are we being pranked? Women are dying, yet they're making us chase our tails so we don't cost them their fortune."

"I saw a photo of one of The Wolf's letters. I was convinced, but then again, we've seen things. A letter with words printed darker than others isn't exactly a smoking gun. I doubt most would take it as seriously as us."

"Maybe before, but now? We found two women left half naked and torn apart, and they don't at least warn us that a man calling himself The Wolf might be stalking Miss Monroe. The letter mentioned her death by a red scarf. Rossa and Roja were killed wearing a red cloak. It was signed by The Wolf, and fur was embedded in Ellery Roja's wounds. These letters should've been the first thing we learned about."

"I agree." Bel sank to the couch and stared blankly at her boss.

"I don't know. What do you think?" Griffin asked. "Orion Chayce seemed like our man, but now I'm not convinced."

"Honestly, you could argue cases for both men. They might even be the same person. Or they could be two separate crimes. The only thing confusing me is the victims. Chayce might have cause to kill Roja since he worked on the set design, and she was the costume designer. Their paths probably crossed, but the writer doesn't fit unless she was physically present during the accident. Then there's Miss Monroe. She joined the show after Chayce was sentenced, so he has no reason to punish her... unless The Wolf is just a stalker and Chayce is the killer."

"The red scarf and his signed name keep bringing me back to this The Wolf, though," Griffin said. "But why would he go after the writer and costume designer? If he's stalking Miss Monroe, what do the crew members have to do with it? Are they friends?"

"I don't think so." Bel leaned against the couch cushion, sinking deep into its softness in the hopes it would swallow her whole so she'd no longer have to theorize why men were hunting women through the Reale Estate. "The letters," she finally said, her brain putting the puzzle pieces together. "It was threatening without being a threat. The Wolf is smart, at least with how he composes sentences. The prose is lyrical and meaningless until you read the darkened words. Then it's aggressive, but only to Miss Monroe. He wants her afraid, but he's careful with how he inflicts fear. He doesn't want to get caught, so he hides his meaning, creating more and more terror as time passes. No one believes her, so she's alone and terrified someone's stalking her.

"But words eventually aren't enough." Bel leaned forward with purpose as the final jigsaw pieces snapped together in her brain. "For almost every criminal, the status quo eventually no longer satisfies their cravings. They need more, a larger dose to experience the same high. Following her and then writing his death fantasies lost their spark. He has to act them out now, and because he's obsessed with her and the show and his wolf persona—"

"He became the wolf," Griffin finished for her.

"He became the wolf," Bel agreed. "Taron Monroe is a detective in a paranormal crime drama. He's killing people similar to how the show's monsters murder their victims. Perhaps he believes that if he creates crimes worthy of Monroe's character, she'll arrive to work the scenes, and he can swoop in as the love interest. Or maybe he's taken his stalking to the extreme. He wants her terrified, and what better way to scare someone than to kill women like the wolf you claim you are?"

"So his victims mean nothing except they share the same gender as his intended victim?"

"Yes? No? I don't know. Chayce is still a good suspect, but a man getting revenge for serving time doesn't strike me as someone who'd replicate episode scenes. Granted, we've seen weirder, but it makes more sense if The Wolf is the one imitating the show's crimes."

"I have this pit in my stomach." Griffin pushed his chair away from his desk and doubled over. "I hate when you make sense. It scares me."

"The idea of a stalker calling himself The Wolf scares me."

"I don't mean to be insensitive, but while Rossa's and Roja's deaths are tragic, they aren't national news. If Miss Monroe is murdered..." He shuddered. "I don't want to think about that. One of the most popular actresses on a beloved show dies in our town because we let some stalker gut her like a pig. This won't end well, will it?"

"Not if the producers keep jerking us around." Bel sank back into the couch. "What do we do from here? We have very little evidence, and too many theories."

"I think we can agree that no matter the theory, the women of this show aren't safe," Griffin said. "Two are dead, and Miss

Monroe feels she's being threatened. The killer's M.O. is consistent on victim choice, at least."

"Women who work on Aesop's Files."

"We're already stretched so thin. How are we supposed to protect every female cast and crew member when we have two murders to solve and a town bursting at the seams?"

"Miss Monroe is the priority," Bel said. "And not because she's a famous actress. Realistically, how long can the killer keep murdering women before something interrupts him? He's gotten away with it twice, but now that we're increasing our efforts, it'll be harder for him to kill. I think Miss Monroe is his next target."

"That makes sense," Griffin said. "We'll focus on her, but if we visibly increase security, The Wolf might panic. He'll feel like a cornered animal, and predators get nasty when trapped. If he suspects we're on to him, he could start killing anyone he gets his hands on."

"I'll do it," Bel said. "I'll work Monroe's protection detail in plain clothes, and we'll sell my presence to the public as a police consultant. Shows use them often, and we can feed the fans that narrative. That Taron Monroe wants to perfect her role on Aesop's Files, so she hired a real-life detective to accompany her on set. Yes, I'm still the police, but as a woman, I'll hopefully fuel The Wolf's fantasy, especially if I play up my femininity. If I come across as more friend than protector, he won't view me as a threat, but as another female to satisfy his delusions. Instead of threatening him with an increased police presence, I'll become bait, and hopefully, he'll target me when he makes a play for Monroe."

"Absolutely not!" Griffin practically shouted at her. "What's wrong with you? I am not putting you in the line of fire, especially not after Blaubart. That's not happening."

"Where's Olivia?" Bel asked, ignoring his outburst, even though she secretly loved that he cared so deeply.

"Still trying to track down Gwen Rossa's final hours."

"Well, if she were here, she'd agree. She can handle the investigation, and I'll play the consultant to Miss Monroe. If we can draw The Wolf out, we won't have to worry about searching for evidence that isn't there."

"Did you not hear what I just said?" Griffin gawked at her. "The answer is no. An absolute, resounding, and definite no. We aren't using you as bait. I don't care who's in danger. Your life is more important to me. If that makes me a terrible sheriff, so be it, but you always come first."

"I know." Bel stood up and leaned forward, kissing her boss' forehead. "I come first to Eamon too, and he's mastered walking through the shadows. He can be invisible when he chooses to be, a fact that was made clear when I interviewed the bed-and-breakfast owner. She has no clue what he looks like. All she knows is he's reclusive."

"Ha," Griffin snorted. "I wish he would be a recluse instead of bothering me all the time."

"You love it." She reached for her boss' hand, and he took it, his larger fingers swallowing hers whole. "So, Olivia will take over the case, I'll protect Miss Monroe, and Eamon will protect me. He'll have no problem getting onto the sets. His... skills or money will guarantee he can follow me around."

"I don't know."

"You said it yourself; we're stretched too thin. We need help, and we need someone we can trust. Eamon didn't kill those girls, and he won't let anyone harm me. It's the best plan we have."

"Would he even agree to it?" Griffin asked, and Bel glared at him with raised eyebrows. "Right, of course he would. Do you just bat your eyes and get everything you want?"

"Pretty much," she teased. "It works on you too, though." She batted her eyes at him, and he rolled his in response.

"All right, all right." He swatted her away. "Fine, we'll try your idea if, and only if, Eamon can be on set with you at all times. And I mean it, Emerson. I want him glued to your metaphorical hip."

"I HAVE an idea to sell our story," Taron Monroe said as she and Bel entered the building. They were scheduled to film inside Bajka's picturesque courthouse, and both Eamon and Taron had readily agreed to help Bel pose as Miss Monroe's personal consultant.

"We should do a live," the actress continued.

"A live?" Bel asked, and as they passed through the courthouse's secondary doors, a hand shot out and grabbed her fingers. She didn't react as the cool skin caressed hers. Her gaze remained on Taron as the grip held her until the distance forced them apart, and without glancing over her shoulder to see who hovered in the crowd, she smiled to herself. She loved having Eamon work alongside her again. She was a braver cop with the devil guarding her back, and facing the bitter outdoor shoots was suddenly less daunting with him by her side.

"Yes, a social media broadcast where people can watch me live," Taron explained. "I'll introduce you as my new consultant and explain how a real female homicide detective will guide my character. The fans will eat it up, and it'll help portray you less like a guard and more like a set piece."

"You want to show my face?" Bel stopped walking, catching sight of Eamon leaning against a wall just beyond the set's commotion.

"I mean…"

"No," Bel said. "I don't have social media, and I don't want my face online. It's bad enough when I end up on the news."

"Oh… Okay," Taron paused. "I just thought it would sell our charade since you believe The Wolf might be more inclined to take the bait if you weren't a threat."

Evidence of a Folktale

"No, it's smart, but can you do it without me?"

"What about a compromise?" the actress asked. "Go talk to Beau and offer to help him when I don't need you. I'll film the live here, and it'll capture his face and the back of your head. It'll add to the legitimacy because it'll appear that I'm catching you hard at work. Besides, Beau loves the attention, so he'll position himself to be in the shot instead of you."

"You promise not to reveal my face or name?"

"Absolutely. You're the only person taking my concerns seriously, and I cried when you promised to help. I've been so freaked out by this wolf character, and I'd never post you online without your consent. I realize as an actual cop, you want to keep a low profile."

"I appreciate that," Bel said. "Mr. Draven doesn't know about our arrangement, so I'll stick to the act when I offer him my help."

"Sounds good. I'll wait till your back is turned before I start filming."

"Thanks." Bel twisted on her heels and approached the lead actor, smirking as she felt Eamon's eyes track her. Perhaps this was the real reason he agreed to her scheme. To keep Hollywood's sexiest actor from stealing her away from him. "Mr. Draven." She extended a hand. "I'm sure you heard, but for the next few days, I'll be acting as Miss Monroe's consultant, but if you need clarification on anything, I'd be happy to offer my expertise."

"Thanks." He dismissed her as if he couldn't possibly learn anything from a woman so attractive. He didn't care about her brain, just the curves of her body, and Bel had to hide another smirk. Eamon had nothing to worry about. She preferred men who saw her as a human being, not a body. But Beau? He'd have something to worry about if he didn't stop glancing at her legs.

"But what about the murders?" he asked.

"My partner and the sheriff are heading up the investigation," she answered. "Trust me, the case is in capable hands."

"Oh okay, cool." He smiled, dialing up the charm, and Bel understood why so many women obsessed over Aesop's Files. His smile was intoxicating... or at least it would've been if he hadn't just lewdly scanned her head to toe. "So, is that a New York accent I detect?" he asked.

"Yes. Born and raised. My dad was the chief of police." She wondered if that would deter his flirting.

"What's a big city girl doing in a town like this?"

"Solving murders." She deadpanned.

"You're funny. I like—"

"Hello Mon-hoes!" Taron Monroe blurted behind them as her live began, and Bel instinctively ducked despite her turned back. "I'm here on location, and we're shooting an explosive episode for all our fans, so make sure you catch up on the previous seasons if you haven't binged them already. Before I announce my fun news, I'd like to observe a moment of silence for our fallen crew members. May they rest in peace." She fell silent, and Bel didn't miss how Beau shifted to get further into the shot.

"Gwen and Ellery will be greatly missed, but we'll honor them by making this season the best yet," Taron continued after a few seconds. "And now for my news. You can see her behind me helping Beau walk through his scene, but I have my very own homicide detective on set with me today. She'll be consulting for the next few days, and honestly, how cool is this? A real-life female homicide detective. Women like her are why I play such a badass character, so I should probably steal her back from Beau. Us girls got to stick together. Sorry, what?" She faked being interrupted. "Sure, I'll be right there... All right, Mon-hoes! Love you all. Wish me and my new detective bff luck. Hugs and kisses!" She ended the live. "How was that?"

"Good." Bel rejoined her, thankful to escape Beau's unoriginal flirting. "Definitely played up the girl power and not the protection aspect. Hopefully, The Wolf was watching and doesn't consider me a threat."

"I get why you're saying that, but that freaks me out," Taron said. "You're literally hoping my stalker isn't afraid of you so that he attacks you."

"It's part of the job." Bel shrugged.

"I'm glad I only play a cop because I never want that to be... *part of the job*," she threw her voice to mimic Bel's.

"That was pretty good."

"You sound surprised. You don't watch the show?"

"No, sorry. My life is endless death and crime already, so I normally just read. I also have my dog, who keeps me busy."

"Makes sense," Taron said. "Well, I am a decent actress, so while you're here to protect me, maybe I can pick your brain. I could learn a lot."

"Absolutely. As long as it doesn't become distracting. It's smart, though. It'll help sell the lie about why I'm hovering."

"Okay, now I'm excited... well, not about being stalked, but we've never had a female officer consult before. We've had male cops on the show, but never women. It feels very girl-power. Especially since you have a female partner. I love it."

Bel loved it too until Olivia decided she couldn't forgive the lies.

"Speaking of girl power, can I ask you about him?" Taron nodded to where Eamon leaned against the far wall. "Why is he here?"

"You've been shooting on his property," Bel half lied. "The producers are letting him watch as a thank you."

"That gorgeous estate?" Taron asked. "Wow, rich and hot. My type... are you two a thing, though?" She glanced at Bel as if she just realized that Eamon hadn't arrived at the cabin and sat on the couch with Cerberus because he consulted on cases as they'd claimed. "He kissed your forehead when I followed you to your house, but friends do things like that. Are you friends, or are you dating? Because he's sexy, but I don't hook up with guys who belong to other women."

Bel bit her tongue to keep from laughing at Eamon's reaction to the actress' words. He could hear them despite the distance, and he didn't bother to hide the amusement from his features. It seemed they both had the same response to Taron's belief that he'd absolutely hook up with her despite possibly being in a relationship.

"We're friends," Bel said. She couldn't help herself. She wouldn't mess with Taron—or Eamon—for long, but this woman had followed her home, witnessed Eamon arrive to protect her, and still assumed she had a shot. Bel liked the actress. She seemed fun and adorable, if not slightly out of touch, and it was understandable that Eamon's unnatural attractiveness had gotten the better of her.

"Best friends," Bel continued when he quirked his eyebrows at her answer.

"Oh okay, so you aren't dating?" Taron asked. "That's good to know."

"Oh no. We are very much dating," she clarified. It was silly, but she enjoyed teasing both the actress and her boyfriend. It felt so normal, so trivial and ridiculous, and Taron's cluelessness and Eamon's mock annoyance brightened the unending death and destruction clouding her path. "But he's also my best friend. He makes me laugh if you can believe that. It's why we work. We started as friends."

"He makes you laugh? But he's so... well, that's nice," Taron said, trying to hide her disappointment. "So, are you two serious?"

Eamon leaned forward, staring Bel down as he waited for her answer.

"He keeps asking me to move in with him, so I guess so." She winked at him, and he rolled his eyes.

Evidence of a Folktale

"But you have your own place?" Taron looked genuinely confused. "A rich man that looks like that wants you to live with him, yet you still live alone. Girl, you have more willpower than I do."

"I'll move in with him eventually," Bel said. "But I like keeping him on his toes."

"Is that why he's really here?" Taron glanced between the couple as she saw their relationship in a fresh light. "Because you keep him on his toes so much that he's nervous about The Wolf coming after you?"

"That can't be public knowledge," Bel said. "We want The Wolf to target me, but if he suspects I'm being protected, he won't make a move. But yes. I watch your back, and Eamon guards mine."

"My god, that's disgusting," Taron laughed. "That's too romantic this early in the morning. Girl, you won the jackpot."

"I like to think so," Bel said, loving that eavesdropping on them brightened Eamon's black eyes so beautifully that his predator disappeared for a fleeting moment. Life had certainly not been a lottery winning lately, but in her choice of partner, she'd won. She'd found someone who put her first, who actively communicated rather than bulldozing her emotions to get his way, and who trusted her enough to be vulnerable about the worst parts of his nature. As much as she wanted to smack him for his reaction at the hospital, it was a valid concern. One he thankfully cast aside long enough to listen to her, and now, here he stood guarding her back instead of inflicting irreparable damage on their relationship. Instead of leaving her unprotected before the wolves. Yes, she'd hit the jackpot.

"And on a work note," Bel said, "this is good. Girl talk will help solidify that I'm not a threat or a bodyguard. That I'm just another... what did you call them? Mon-hoe."

"My fans made that up," Taron laughed. "I hated it at first, but I decided to embrace it."

"Pick your battles."

"Exactly," Taron said. "Okay. Hopefully, girl talk works... even though I don't really want it to. I don't want The Wolf coming after us like he did Gwen and Ellery."

"THANKS FOR TODAY," Taron said as Bel dropped her off at the Bajka Bed-and-Breakfast. They'd spent the entire day filming at the courthouse, and what started as an act had turned into Bel genuinely helping the actress. Miss Monroe had her celebrity flaws, but she was a sponge when it came to learning. She absorbed every tip Bel offered, and by the end of the shoot, they looked almost identical standing side by side.

"You're welcome. It was fun."

"It was," Taron said.

"I'll stay until you get inside, and a squad car will be stationed in the parking lot all night," Bel said. "Don't leave the inn. If you need to go somewhere, ask an officer to escort you. And I mean it. Don't even walk outside to smoke or make a call or cool down."

"I don't smoke."

"Great. You have no excuse to leave then."

"I vow to lock myself in my room." Taron crossed her heart in a promise.

"Thank you. I'll see you tomorrow."

"See you." The actress fled the car and raced through the cold to the front door. The moment she locked herself inside the inn, an expensive truck rolled up beside Bel's SUV, the direction facing the opposite way so the drivers could speak.

"Did you notice anything?" Bel asked.

"Other than Beau Draven staring at your legs in ways that begged me to gouge out his eyes?" Eamon asked. "No."

Bel cursed. "We'll find something. We have to... right?"

"I hope so. Even though I'm there, I still hate using you as bait." He reached across the divide, and she took his hand.

"I'll be fine. I can fight." She winked at him. "But seriously, thanks for being there. I love having you around on cases. I feel invincible."

"Well, you aren't, so don't get cocky," Eamon laughed. "But I agree. I like being with you, and not just to keep you safe. I love watching you work. I never loved any of my jobs. Well… I enjoyed the first one, but that's because I was born for bloodshed. Everything else has been about making money, but you live and breathe your job. Seeing you help the cast today reminded me why I can never ask you to stop being a cop, even if it puts you in danger. You were brilliant to watch."

"I love you," Bel blurted, unable to keep the words inside her after that speech. "I really love you."

"Am I actually your best friend, or was that a tease for Monroe's sake?" he asked.

"Of course you are. Why would you question that?"

"Well, you have Violet and Olivia."

"I do, but you're more than just my boyfriend. Disturbing past aside, I don't just love you. I like you. I have great friends, but you're the best of them."

"So, I really make you laugh?" he asked.

"Surprising, I know."

"Making people laugh is not something I've ever been guilty of."

"Yet we have fun. Like when you threw me on your back and raced through the jungle."

"So we could find a black market surgery." Eamon smirked.

"Exactly. Fun."

"Thank you for talking sense into me."

"What do you mean?" she asked.

"Your death turned me irrational. I couldn't function, but seeing you work today made it clear. I belong wherever you are."

"Hey." She rubbed his hand with her gloved fingers. "It's cold. How about you take me home, and we pretend we live together?"

"I'd like that."

"And while you're at it, forgive yourself for that hospital conversation. You were trying to take care of me. Plus, you thought I died. Trust me, if you died, I'd be worse. I'm serious. Nothing is allowed to ever happen to you because if you die, I'll lose it. You at the hospital would be downright sane compared to me."

"Well, I'm not dying on you, nor am I leaving. I also plan to keep asking you to live with me."

"Hey." She withdrew her hand back into her car. "I said we could pretend. Don't push your luck."

"Fine. It was worth a—"

"Detective!" Taron's voice ripped through the air as she launched herself out of the inn's front door and bolted across the parking lot, Bel barely able to get out of her SUV before the actress skidded to a halt.

"Detective," she sobbed, her voice shaking and muscles rigid, and that's when Bel saw the paper clutched in her hands. "It was left at the front desk for me. No name, no stamp, no return address."

"So it didn't come in the mail." Bel stole the letter from the terrified woman and opened it, a pit widening in her stomach. "Which means someone personally dropped it off." She unfolded the note, and her eyes caught on the signature even though she already knew who'd penned it. The Wolf was in Bajka.

Autopsy Report

CERBERUS

PROD.NO. TAKE SOUND
SCENE
DIRECTOR
CAMERAMAN EXT. INT.

CINEMA TICKET 9891102 ADMIT ONE
CINEMA TICKET 9891102 ADMIT ONE

Chapter Fifteen

"So, there's been no further contact since the letter?" Griffin asked. It had been a few days since Taron received The Wolf's newest message. Like its predecessors, the note was lyrical yet pointless until they read the darker traced words.

"Nothing," Bel said. The sheriff had called a meeting in his office to catch everyone up on the different aspects of the case, and Bel and Olivia currently sat on opposite sides of the couch as they briefed their boss, the divide ripping Bel's heart in half.

"The letter's secret didn't divulge much, either," she continued. "Just, *'I'm glad you found a friend as passionate as you are.'* We assume he means me, but that's not exactly damning evidence since she posted that on social media. But the letter had no return address or postage, so he physically dropped it off."

"Could someone have delivered it for The Wolf?" Griffin asked.

"Maybe, but I doubt it," Bel said. "Taron says his letters often illustrate how close he gets. He likes being near her. I don't think he has access to the sets, but he's in town. He delivered the letter."

"Security cameras?" he asked.

"I checked the inn's. Nothing incriminating. He either waited until a car blocked the mailbox from view, or he employed a similar diversion to the killer when he left the box at the station."

"Storm the front desk with fans," Griffin said.

"There was no DNA on the letter," Bel continued. "The envelope was a peel and seal, and even though it was handwritten, there were no prints. Techs are running a handwriting analysis, but without something to compare it to, we won't get an ID."

The sheriff cursed. "So, we have nothing."

"So far? No. But the killer attacked Rossa and Roja at night," she continued. "Miss Monroe hasn't left the bed-and-breakfast after work since she visited me, so we need to change tactics. We need to bait him at night."

"That's out of the question."

"But—"

"I said no, Emerson. I'm not letting you or Miss Monroe die on my watch. Having you shadow her on set is one thing. Feeding you to the wolves will never happen."

"But we're getting nowhere," Bel said. "Thankfully, we've had no more deaths, but we're at a standstill."

"Maybe not," Olivia interrupted for the first time since she'd entered the office. "Lina called. She ran tests on the fur found during Ellery Roja's autopsy. It was canine."

"Canine?" Griffin repeated. "So we're looking for someone with a dog."

"Probably not," Bel said. "The bodies were clean. No prints, no defensive wounds, no trace evidence. The killer left nothing but blood, the red cloak, and those little boxes, yet suddenly there's dog fur present? The Wolf," she said, and the office fell quiet as the realization sank in. "It was The Wolf. I think he's telling us he's responsible."

"No new letter. No new murders. Do you think The Wolf's gone?" Taron asked as she mimicked how Bel drew her weapon. "Or are there too many cops on set?"

"He's still here," Bel said. The case had grown cold over the past few days, and The Wolf had returned to his silence. "The murders were leading to something. He isn't done. He just hasn't found a way to reach you yet."

"Because I don't leave the bed-and-breakfast?" Taron asked, making a big show of practicing her gun draw before they started shooting the next scene. "Gwen and Ellery died because they were alone in the middle of the night. We should try walking around in the dark."

"Trust me, I presented that idea already, but my boss shot it down," Bel laughed.

"Oh well. I just feel useless. We're doing all of this for nothing."

"You're still alive. I wouldn't call that nothing."

"True. I just meant—" Taron screamed as Officer Rollo appeared out of nowhere and yanked her violently against his chest. She beat against him, her fists pounding his torso as she fought to free herself, and Bel's fingers instinctively twitched closer to her sidearm when an earsplitting crash shattered the silence.

"Oh my god!" Bel leaped backward as a light crashed to the ground right where Taron had been standing. If Rollo hadn't pulled her out of the way…

"Are you okay?" Bel sidestepped the debris as the entire cast and crew turned their alarm towards the trio.

"Yeah," Taron's voice shook as she clung to the handsome deputy. "That light almost killed me. You saved my life." She flung her arms around Rollo's neck.

"Just doing my job, ma'am," Rollo said as he peered at Bel over the top of the actress' head. Bel nodded her thanks, and the man shrugged as if he hadn't heroically rescued THE Taron Monroe from being crushed to death.

"It's him," Taron sobbed as she released the officer to grab Bel's hands. "It was The Wolf."

"The Wolf?" Bel scanned the set for Eamon, but she couldn't find him. Thank goodness Rollo had been close instead. "But how did he sneak onto set and tamper with the lights without anyone noticing?"

"It was him," Taron insisted. "He tried to kill me."

"With a light?" Bel asked. "I doubt it."

"He can't kill me like Gwen and Ellery because I never leave the bed-and-breakfast, so he did this." Taron gestured to where Rollo was helping clean up the crash. He was certainly the man of the hour. He'd saved the actress and was knowledgeable enough to handle the set lights. And he was gorgeous. Bel needed to steer Taron away from him before she started trying to date Violet's man.

"This was just a careless accident," Bel said, Orion Chayce suddenly popping into her mind. His mishap landed him in prison, and while he might not be the guilty party, the only people who could've killed that technician were crew members. Similarly, if this falling light wasn't an accident, the only way The Wolf could've gained access to it was if he belonged on set.

"Oh my god, my dear!" The director Warren Rouge rushed for Taron, ushering everyone to the far wall while the crew handled the mess, and the lighting technicians banished the helpful Rollo back to his guard post. Seemed they didn't want to accept responsibility for any more accidents his lack of expertise might cause despite the fact that he apparently knew what he was doing. He obliged the techs, though, and with a nod at Bel and another checkup on the actress, he left to resume his post at the outside perimeter. He must have come inside to use the restroom and noticed the light's precarious position. Eamon was unexpectedly absent, so without Rollo's heroics, more than glass would need to be cleaned up. Unless...

Bel backed away from the swarming crowd, a horrifying idea growing roots in her brain.

"What happened?" Eamon's hand slid against her back, halting her retreat from the swarm around Miss Monroe, and she flinched at his sudden closeness. She hadn't seen him re-enter the set.

"That falling light almost killed Taron," she answered, and Eamon cursed low and savage in her ear.

"Are you okay?"

"I'm fine. It didn't fall near me, and Rollo saved her," she said, that nagging thought worming its way deeper. "Where were you? Did you see anyone tampering with the lights? I didn't, but I wasn't paying close attention."

"I got an urgent call from one of my overseas investors. It was too loud in here to hear him, so I stepped outside. It's been a while since I've had to hold a conversation in Japanese, so I needed the quiet. I checked the set before I left, though. There were no threats."

"You speak Japanese?" She squinted at him.

"I speak many languages," he answered. "And I didn't see anyone tampering with the lights. I watched the tech setting them up, but he was just doing his job. Maybe he didn't secure it properly... What are you thinking?"

"Could Taron be the killer?"

"What do you mean?"

"She's convinced The Wolf broke onto set and tried to kill her, but what if she asked the technician to loosen the clamp on purpose? Rollo snatched her out of the way, but if she'd known it was coming, she could've dodged it herself. Plus, with security this tight, no one's here that shouldn't be," she said. "If the killer's present, he's supposed to be here. He's someone people wouldn't bat an eye at. Someone women would climb into a car at night with... like a famous actress."

"And the letters?" Eamon asked.

"She sent them to herself," Bel said. "If you tell a female cop that a man's stalking you and the studio executives don't care, you'll have said cop eating out of your hand because victims aren't usually the killers. What if the producers aren't worried about the letters because they aren't real? She sends them to herself to throw off suspicion the same as the falling light."

"But why kill those women? And why draw your attention to her stalker if the letters are her own creations?"

"Not sure. To solidify herself as a victim in our minds? Beau Draven is a flirt, and Taron loves male attention. Maybe Gwen Rossa and Ellery Roja were romantically involved with him, and she grew jealous."

Eamon cursed, and his grip on her back tightened. "There haven't been any deaths since you joined Miss Monroe on set. She has access to props and costumes, and you're right. Luring women into a car at night without force points to someone they weren't afraid of, and there's nothing scary about Taron Monroe."

"She doesn't seem the type to hunt down and butcher girls in the woods, though." Bel sagged against his chest.

"She's an actress," Eamon said. "A good one, from what I've seen. This nice guy act could be just that."

"It's just a theory, but are we protecting a murderer?"

"It's possible," Eamon said. "There's someone here who isn't human."

"Who? And why didn't you mention it earlier?" Bel's eyes flicked around the chaotic room. "It can't be Taron. She was at my house, and you didn't scent anything."

"Because everywhere I turn lately, there's an unfamiliar scent. When I was outside just now, a girl in her twenties was trying to sneak onto set for a photo. She realized I was the alpha of the area when I caught her and gave me this tiny bow before practically breaking into a terrified run. She was merely a lesser witch, but I could only tell because she stood so close, and there was no one else nearby to muddle her scent. Most of the time, though, there are too many people clumped together for me to distinguish. Plus…" he gestured to the actors dressed in full creature makeup. "I can't tell who any of them are. One of them could be a supernatural playing a supernatural for the irony. The costumes and synthetic makeup distort scents with their chemicals."

"Maybe you should hang back," Bel said.

"What? No." He leaned around her torso until his glare forced her to meet his disapproving gaze.

"Not leave me. Just hang back." She shoved him, but the wall of muscle didn't budge. He resisted her strength for a defiant moment before shoving forward to kiss her scarred throat. The room was preoccupied with Taron's brush with death, granting the couple anonymity amidst the crowd.

"Taron was asking about you the other day," Bel laughed as his lips tickled her skin, and she nudged him with her hip until he stood up. "I thought it was because she genuinely wanted to learn if you were single, but what if she was gauging how closely you're monitoring me? If you stay out of sight, she might assume she's free to act. Let's see if it tempts her to move against me… and if she isn't The Wolf, the killer might emerge from hiding without you hovering."

"Your phone." Eamon slipped it from her back pocket and shoved it into her hand for emphasis. "I can track your location as long as it's on. Keep this charged and on your person at all times, do you understand? Otherwise, I'm throwing you over my shoulder and taking you home."

"How barbaric."

"You didn't complain the last time I did that," he said with a dangerous pitch to his deep voice, and Bel elbowed him in the ribs... hard. He didn't so much as flinch.

"Of course, I'll leave my phone on," she said. "If anything happens and you don't come for me, I'll make you mortal and kill you myself. I'm not running down snowy mountains alone anymore. Next time that happens, I expect you to toss me over your shoulder and carry me down instead."

"Don't say that. You're never ending up alone on a snowing mountain again."

"You're right." She reached behind her and pinched his thigh before peeling herself off his chest to rejoin Taron. "Because I'll have my phone on, and you'll find me."

"Bᴇʟ!" Violet called as the detective walked toward her car. "Do you have a second?"

"What's up?" Bel asked.

"I realize you're busy with the case, but I wanted to ask you for a favor."

"Sure."

"Would you get drinks with me and Ethan?"

"Who?"

"Sorry, Rollo," Violet laughed.

"Oh, right." Bel fake smacked her forehead. "We all go by our last names so often that I forgot his first."

"Meanwhile, you all say Rollo, and I'm like who?"

"I'm sure." Bel winked at her friend.

"Oh, stop." Violet swatted her biceps. "But seriously, would you and Eamon come for a drink with us?"

"When?"

"Right now."

"I guess I can ask Eamon." Bel scanned the cars for her boyfriend. She'd spend the day at war with herself. On the one hand, Taron was the perfect suspect, but on the other, the pretty, slightly clueless, good-natured actress was the furthest thing from a monster. Bel's brain hurt from the incessant back and forth, and a drink with her friend was exactly the medicine her overthinking needed.

"Thanks... I realize you're busy. It's just I like Ethan, and you guys work with him."

"And you want to know if I approve?" Bel asked.

"Pretty much."

"I mean, he seems nice at the station."

"Yeah, but that's work," Violet said. "I want to know what you think of him as a man, not a deputy."

"A very hot man." Bel winked, and her friend shoved her again.

"Stop that."

"Hey, you teased me about Eamon. It's only fair. But yes, I'll ask him. Nothing's happening with this case, and it's stressing me out. I could use a drink."

"Thank you." Violet hugged her. "We're going to walk to the bar. Join us when you find Eamon."

"Will do." Bel smiled at her friend's back. If only Olivia were here to witness her matchmaking paying off.

"There you are." Eamon stood from where he leaned against his truck when he spotted her. "You ready?"

"Violet invited us to get drinks with her and Rollo," she said. "She wants our opinion before she agrees to a date with him."

"Smart girl." He caught Bel's waist and yanked her against his chest. "When does she want to go?"

"Now."

"Oh..." His face fell. "I'd love to double date with your friends, but I've spent so much time with you on set that I'm falling behind on my work. I have stuff that has to get done tonight. I'm sorry."

235

"Don't be. You've gone out of your way for me and this case. We'll reschedule."

"Just because I can't go doesn't mean you shouldn't," he said. "Go get dinner and drinks with your friend and interrogate her potential boyfriend. Cerberus can hang out with me, so don't worry about him being alone. It's the perfect night since I'll be locked in my office for the next few hours."

"You sure?" Bel wrapped her arms around his neck. "I could use a drink."

"Yes, have fun. Cerberus will keep me company, and you can crash at my place… since I'll have your dog."

"That's the real reason you always want to hang out with him." Bel kissed him full on the mouth in a shameless display of public affection. "Forces me to sleep over all the time so that we live together without living together."

"Alas, I've been discovered." Eamon buried his face in her throat until she laughed at the tickle of his lips against her scars. "The struggles of dating a detective."

"Okay, okay." She kissed his temple before shoving him off her. "I won't be late."

"Take your time."

"Fine, I won't be too late."

"Better." Eamon climbed into his truck. "See you later, Detective."

Bel blew him a kiss as he pulled away, and then, drawing her coat closer around her body, she jogged through the throng to locate her ward. She escorted Taron to the bed-and-breakfast, and when the actress was safe, she rushed through the town to the bar.

"Hey!" Violet waved from where she was waiting by the entrance. "Thanks for coming. Where's Eamon?"

"He has to work," Bel said as she peeled off her coat, noticing that her friend looked suspicious. Maybe Rollo didn't realize he was about to be interrogated, but then she noticed blonde hair hiding in the background.

"I'm sorry." Violet grimaced. "I don't know what's bothering you and Olivia, but I work with Ewan, remember? Something is going on between you three, and while I won't insert myself into a romantic relationship, we're friends. If I'm here, hopefully, you two can smooth over whatever happened."

"I doubt it." Bel glared at her friend. She wasn't the one unwilling to talk it out. "Was this a trick to get us in the same room? Is Rollo even here?"

"Of course he is," Violet said. "I like him and want your opinion. I just figured putting you and Olivia in a neutral setting might help whatever's bothering you two."

"Fine." Bel relented. "I could use a drink, anyway."

"Thank you." Violet slipped an arm through hers and escorted her to their booth.

"Detective." Rollo stood as they approached and shook Bel's hand. "Nice to see you out of work."

"Agreed." She smiled at him and then Olivia, but her partner merely threw a questioning glare at Violet.

"Can I get you a drink?" Rollo asked, oblivious to the arguing partners. "I have a beer, but Violet and Olivia have martinis. Would you like one?"

"No...." Bel trailed off. If she was going to survive sitting next to her hostile partner, she'd need something stronger. "Actually, yes, thank you."

"Sure thing." Rollo started toward the bar. "Sweet or strong?"

"Dirty," Bel said.

"Coming right up."

"Wait." Bel dug for her wallet. "Let me give you my card."

"Don't even think about it. It's on me."

"Well, that's a step in the right direction to impressing me."

Bel winked at Violet. "Do you think his desire to impress could result in a basket of fries or wings?"

"He's one step ahead of you," Violet said. "He already ordered appetizers for the table."

"Even better." Bel settled into her seat and smiled at her partner. "How are you?"

"Fine," Olivia said, and out of the corner of her eye, Bel caught Violet giving them an encouraging smile.

"Has anything new come up since I've been on set?" Bel pushed.

"No. But I don't want to discuss the case. I'm so over this show."

"Right." Bel glanced at Violet and shrugged. The three of them used to laugh nonstop, their voices tripping over each other as they fought to be heard, but now they felt like strangers.

"One dirty martini for you." Rollo saved the trio by slipping the drink onto the table. "Wasn't your boyfriend supposed to come too?"

"He unfortunately has to work," Bel said.

"What does he do?" he asked. "Doesn't he own like half of the town?"

"Something in finance, and yes, he does," she answered. "He works with companies, which is like speaking Greek to me, but whatever he does, he's good at it."

"I'll say. He'd have to be to own the Reale Estate."

The four dissolved into small talk, the awkwardness growing as the night progressed. Olivia made it extremely clear she wanted nothing to do with Bel, and after the initial nerves wore off between Violet and Rollo, the couple's flirting doubled with every round of drinks. Drinks that Bel shouldn't indulge in, but did anyway. Between Olivia's cold shoulder and Violet's heart-eyes, vodka was her best friend.

"I didn't know you had a tattoo," Bel said when the food was finally gone. Between the fried carbs and alcohol, the foursome had grown sweaty, and Rollo had shed his flannel to reveal a tee shirt stretched over a sculpted frame.

"Oh, yeah." He rolled up his sleeve to expose the inked image of a woman reading a book to the child leaning against her. "I got it for my grandmother. She raised me after my parents passed."

"That's so sweet," Bel said, her brain suddenly fuzzy. She should've opted for something weaker than vodka because the clear liquid had gone right to her head. "I bet she's proud of you."

"I like to think she is." He released his sleeve as he draped an arm around Violet's shoulders… which was Bel's clue to leave. She was drunk… too drunk, and Violet and Rollo were minutes away from forgetting they had an audience.

"It's getting late." She stood, her fuzzy brain making her want to trip and giggle at the same time. She thankfully did neither. "I should head home. We have another signing event tomorrow, and I'm meeting Miss Monroe early."

"No, stay," Violet crooned. Seemed she'd drunk a lot as well.

"Would you like me to drive you?" Rollo asked, and despite being drunk, Bel could tell that while her intoxication worried him, he didn't revel in the idea of leaving just yet.

"That's sweet, but don't worry about me."

"Detective, I don't…" he paused. "You shouldn't drive."

"Good man." She patted his hand where it rested on Violet's shoulder. "But I'm not driving. I'll make Eamon pick me up."

"Oh okay, great." He smiled, and Bel knew Violet was in trouble. He was way too gorgeous when he smiled.

"Make sure these lovely ladies get home safe, though," she said as she hugged Violet goodbye. She leaned for Olivia when she was done, but the stiffness in her partner's back warned her not to follow through.

"Yes, Detective," Rollo said.

"Night, guys!" Bel waved at the table as she aimed for the

bathroom. She texted Eamon, undoubtedly riddling her message with typos, and then used the restroom.

"Hey!" Violet ambushed her when she emerged, and Bel smirked at her friend. She felt good… for now. When the haze wore off, her head would ache from both dehydration and depression over Olivia, but right now, her mood was blissful.

"You okay?" she asked.

"I'm fine," Violet said. "Well?"

"Well, what?"

"What do you think of Ethan?"

"He paid for dinner and drinks. He wouldn't let me drive intoxicated, and he clearly loves his grandmother," Bel said. "Plus, he's hot."

"I know, right?" Violet giggled.

"I say go for it. He has a good job, and he's well-liked at the station. I don't see any reason not to give him a chance."

"Yeah?"

"Yeah." Bel pulled her into a hug. "Love you."

"Love you too. Get home safe." Violet returned to her table, and Bel watched with an ache in her heart as Olivia aimed for the exit.

"Olivia." She chased after her and grabbed her arm before she could leave the bar. The vodka's courage made her do it, and she might as well act while it offered its aid. "I know you don't want to talk to me, but I'm sorry. I did what I did for a reason, and I stand by it, but I still love you."

"Bel…" Olivia trailed off.

"I know, I know." Bel let go of her. "I love you, that's all."

Olivia fled, and the dismissal should've wounded Bel, but her brain was too hazy to get the memo.

"Hey, Detective, anyone ever tell you how gorgeous you are?" a male voice growled as a dark truck parked before the front door. "Hurry and get in the car before your boyfriend arrives."

Evidence of a Folktale

"I would be careful, sir," Bel said as she hopped into the passenger seat. "My boyfriend's the jealous type. He'd kill you if he found out you were hitting on me."

"Then we can't let him find out." Eamon slid a hand behind her neck and pulled her across the center console, kissing her deeply. "How drunk are you?"

"Sober enough to remember I hated that Olivia wouldn't look at me, but drunk enough to get in a stranger's car because he's hot." She traced her fingers suggestively over his thigh as he pulled out of the parking lot.

"I'm sorry things are rough between you two." Eamon peeled her hand off his leg and brought it to his mouth. "But this hot guy is glad you got in the truck with him." He kissed her knuckles.

"Oh yeah?" Bel leaned across the divide and kissed his cheek, sliding her free palm up his thigh.

"I'm driving, Detective," he laughed. "And the roads are still a mess from the storm."

"You could drive blindfolded and handcuffed, and still be the safest driver on the road," she said as she grabbed his jaw and pulled his lips to hers. "Are you telling me that the man who can survive an IED blast can't steer while kissing?"

"Are you challenging me?" he growled, returning her kiss with more force than she'd expected.

"What's the fun of dating an ancient immortal if you can't do this?" Bel undid her seatbelt, her vodka courage inspiring her for the second time that night.

"Isobel," he warned.

"Eamon," she moaned, her body suddenly burning with need, and all her insatiable longing craved was him.

"You asked for it." Eamon jerked the steering wheel and slammed on the brakes. The truck skidded to a halt on the side of the dark and empty road, and without giving her a chance to register their surroundings, he dragged her onto his lap.

Bel gasped as he expertly ripped her clothes free of her body, and she lost all control of her inhibitions. It didn't matter that anyone could drive by and see. Eamon's skin against hers was all she cared about. Something about this setting. About the idea that they might be caught, the reality that they needed each other so desperately that they couldn't wait to get home drove them to madness, and the windshield fogged as they moaned and gasped and writhed. It was wild and messy, her handprints left all over the windows. It was raw and honest, his handprints left all over her body. It was ravenous and filthy, filled with dirty words spoken in her ear and confessions of devotion whispered against her mouth. The encounter was not a quick affair. It lasted and lasted and lasted until Bel couldn't breathe, until her muscles grew sore, until even Eamon was out of breath, and then with a roared confession of absolute adoration, they collapsed in the driver's seat. They remained locked together for so long that she fell asleep atop his chest, and the next thing she knew, it was morning. Eamon had somehow gotten her into bed without waking her, and surprisingly, she didn't have a hangover. He must have given her something before tucking her in.

"Good morning," she said as she joined him in his kitchen after she showered.

"Here." He handed her a cup of coffee fixed exactly how she liked it. The perks of dating a man who could hear her coming down the stairs. Coffee was waiting the second she set foot on the kitchen tiles.

"Hi, handsome." Bel stooped and kissed Cerberus, who was chewing on a massive toy in his dog bed beside the stove. "Did you eat?"

"He ate and went for a walk," Eamon said.

"Wow, busy morning. How long have you been up?"

"I couldn't sleep," he answered as he popped bread into the toaster.

"I'm sorry." She sagged against the counter to study his

profile. "My behavior last night was... not what you needed. I didn't mean to upset you."

"Upset me?" He squinted at her as if he had no clue what she was talking about.

"You couldn't sleep," she said. "I was intense and sloppy after all that vodka, but it wasn't my intention to make you uncomfortable."

"Oh, Isobel." Eamon leaned over and kissed her so fiercely that she almost dropped her coffee in favor of repeating last night's excitement on the kitchen table. "I couldn't sleep because I was wired. You were... amazing."

"My being drunk and needy didn't bother you?"

"Detective, if I'm the first thing you want when you're tipsy, I'm truly a lucky man." Eamon grabbed her waist and pulled her into his arms. "Inhibitions are lower when humans drink, which often leads to cheating. But you? You got drunk and wanted me... a lot. I was honestly so happy. That's why I had trouble sleeping. We've worked through some difficult conversations these past few weeks, so knowing I'm still your choice when nothing's holding you back felt amazing."

"I really wanted you, didn't I?" she laughed into his chest. "I can't believe we did that on the side of the road. What if someone saw us?"

"We were closer to home than you realized." Eamon kissed her hair. "The minute your hand grabbed my leg, I knew how the night would end, so I drove fast. I thought we'd make it here first, but we were on the winding road on my estate. Only people driving to my house use it, so no one was there."

"Oh thank god." She laughed again. "I wasn't embarrassed in the least, though. I should've been, but I wasn't."

"It's because you trust me enough not to put you in a weird position."

"What are you talking about? You had me in a lot of weird positions last night?"

"Oh my god." Eamon playfully spanked her.

"Okay, okay, I'm done." Bel snagged the toast from the toaster and shoved it into her mouth. "I guess that's why I was so free last night. I always feel safe and cared for with you. Speaking of taking care of me, why don't I have a hangover?"

"It's a little witch's trick," Eamon said. "It's basically Advil with an extra kick. I made you take one with an entire bottle of water before I put you to bed."

"Thank you. For all of it. For picking me up, for being happy that my drunk self is obsessed with you, for not letting me go to today's signing with a headache. All those screaming fans." She shuddered. "I would've been miserable. I hate that I drank so much, but Olivia's indifference was depressing. It was like sitting next to a wall of ice."

"I wish I could fix that for you. You did nothing wrong, but we have a different worldview. Everything blew up for her in a matter of seconds while she was mourning your death. I don't think she hates you. She's just hurt and scared."

"I know, but I'm afraid we'll never be the friends we were."

"I'm sure you will." Eamon put two more slices into the toaster since she'd helped herself to his. "At least I hope you do. I realize it isn't the same, but even if she doesn't forgive you, you have me. I'll always be here for you."

"I know, and I appreciate it." She cupped his jaw, wanting to drown in the adoration coloring his death-black eyes. "But sometimes a girl needs her girlfriends. Especially when it concerns romantic advice... but I guess I have my sisters for that."

"And Violet."

"And Violet," she agreed.

"I'm sorry I can't be that for you, though."

"Don't be. I love you, and you truly are my best friend." Bel seized his fresh toast and shoved it into her mouth, enjoying the way he frowned at her. She was starving, and around her, the man had a wonderful sense of humor that she enjoyed goading.

"We're going to fight. We'll get mad and endure painful periods, but I want that. I'm glad we had our first argument. It proves we emerge together. Plus, I love making up."

"Me too." Eamon put yet another two pieces of bread into his toaster. "But can I please get some of this breakfast, or were you looking to have our second fight be over toast?"

"Hmmm, you can eat." Bel raised onto her toes and kissed him, her heart light and her smile wide. They were happy. They were the couple who would make it until death parted them. "But only because I'm late and don't have time to argue about bread." She took off running, coffee clutched in her fist as she climbed the stairs. Romantic bliss had to wait. She needed to arrive at the hotel for the signing long before the fans started crowding Miss Monroe, and today was the day they'd put her plan to the test. Eamon had promised to hang back in the hopes it would prove Taron was the killer.

BEL'S romantic bliss was long gone by the time their lunch break arrived. The screaming fans, the crying women, the demanding ticket holders, the constant noise, the constant barrage of people hovering and shoving and complaining had her ready to lock herself in her cabin and never emerge. She'd lost count of how many times a fan had plowed into her to get to Taron, and Bel was thankful she'd asked Eamon to hang back. He was tracking her via her phone, so he hadn't witnessed the horde trample her. One man had bumped into her so hard that she'd smacked the table and could already feel the bruise blooming on her hip. The discoloration would anger Eamon enough when he saw it later. It was better that his anger didn't rear its head in the middle of this sardine-packed conference room.

Some fans were sweet. Some even asked if they could photograph her. They'd figured out she was the female detective Taron mentioned on social media, but Bel politely declined. She wasn't stupid, though. She realized people had snapped photos of her from a distance, but one of Eamon's contacts owed him a favor. A quick call, and he employed an algorithm to blur her face from any image that found its way onto the internet.

"I'll be right back." Taron stood abruptly, yanking Bel out of her thoughts. "Bathroom." She pointed to the exit to her left.

"Want me to come with you?" The bathroom down that hall was reserved for the cast and crew, but off-limits meant nothing to obsessed fans.

"I'll be fine," Taron said. "I just have to pee quick before we leave for lunch, so stay here and watch my seat."

"Okay." Bel nodded, understanding the woman's need for solitude after their morning. "I'll give you five minutes before I come looking for you." She was half joking, but Taron flashed her a pale-faced expression before fleeing the conference room. With pinched eyebrows, Bel traced her movements until she disappeared down the private hallway. What was so unsavory about her comment? She'd be a lousy bodyguard if she let the actress disappear without so much as knocking on the bathroom door to check on her.

Bel planted her hands on the table and collapsed forward, not caring if the stragglers witnessed her exhaustion. Her feet ached, her back ached, her neck ached, and she wondered if Taron would mind if she snagged a few minutes of rest in her chair. She'd asked her to watch her seat. What better way to guard it than sit in it?

"Watch my seat," Bel whispered, suddenly registering Miss Monroe's odd request. Why did she ask her to babysit her chair? Had a fan ducked under the tablecloth to hide? Bel leaned down, readying to rip the cloth aside and catch the perpetrator red-handed when she spotted it. A simple piece of paper sat folded on the chair's cushion, and she understood. Taron didn't want her to guard her seat. She wanted her to look at it.

Evidence of a Folktale

With an unwelcome bolt of adrenaline coursing through her, Bel snatched up the paper and unfolded it. The note was only two sentences long, but she recognized the handwriting. Fear clogged her throat, but not because she knew who'd penned this. Unlike his letters, this hadn't been written with flowery prose or poetic text. It was straightforward and to the point, its message unmistakably clear.

THERE'S A BATHROOM DOWN THE HALLWAY TO YOUR LEFT. USE ITS WINDOW TO CLIMB OUTSIDE, OR I'LL BLOW UP EVERYONE IN THIS HOTEL.

Autopsy Report

CERBERUS

PROD.NO.
SCENE TAKE SOUND
DIRECTOR
CAMERAMAN EXT. INT.

CINEMA TICKET 9891102 ADMIT ONE
CINEMA TICKET 9891102 ADMIT ONE

Chapter Sixteen

BEL CURSED, DROPPING THE NOTE ON THE TABLE FOR GRIFFIN TO find when the police swept the room and bolted for the hallway. She couldn't afford to wait for backup. Taron had a two, maybe three-minute head start. If Bel was fast, she might catch up with her before The Wolf whisked her into the woods. Was this how he'd killed Rossa and Roja? She'd assumed they knew their killer, but maybe they hadn't. What if he'd threatened them with a bomb?

BEL

Explosives. Taron's table? Call bomb squad.

She texted Griffin, not bothering to check for typos as she raced down the hallway. The distance was short, yet it felt like miles, the monotone carpet stretching endlessly before her feet.

"Taron!" She burst through the bathroom door, but she felt the emptiness the minute she stepped inside. The restroom was freezing, the back window leading outside wide open. The actress was gone.

Bel cursed under her breath and rushed to the window, thrusting her torso out into the winter air, but only the dirt-streaked snow covering the hotel's property greeted her. Taron had vanished, and she cursed again, readying to call Griffin and lock the entire town down when movement caught her eye. She squinted at a solitary couple rushing for the sidewalk, and the stiffness in the woman's body suggested she wasn't aiming for the parked vehicle willingly. Her haste was born of duress, and her familiar clothing warned that if Taron Monroe got into that car, the next time they'd see her would be in the woods with her intestines spilling from her shredded gut.

Bel glanced down at her phone. She had seconds to decide. Seconds before Taron vanished from sight, and she decided. Bel vaulted out of the window, her feet sliding on the ice, and then she was running, unsure how she'd kept her balance. Her footfalls were silent as she raced toward the car, and just as the man escorting his prisoner eased out of his parking spot, Taron twisted her terrified gaze to meet Bel's.

"Unlock the door," Bel mouthed, pressing an imaginary lock button with her finger, but Taron had already arrived at that idea. She reached down and unlocked the doors, and as the kidnapper pulled into traffic, Bel flung the rear door open and dove into the backseat.

"What the—" the driver glanced back at her as the vehicle's speed increased. "You're that cop!"

Bel slammed the door behind her, the insignificant act binding her fate to Taron's.

"What are you doing here?" he asked.

"Taron, are you hurt?" Bel ignored him as she met the actress' gaze in the rearview mirror.

"No—"

"Shut up!" the man shouted, his rage silencing Taron as she flinched. He was younger than Bel expected. Better looking too, in a slightly unnerving way. Like he'd never left the house as a child, so he'd spent his entire adulthood yearning to fit in, yet always missing the mark.

Evidence of a Folktale

"Shut up, both of you!" he ordered. "What are you doing here? You're ruining this."

"You are kidnapping a world-famous actress and a police officer." Bel withdrew her sidearm. "You're the one ruining things, so pull over."

"I don't think so," he said.

"I said, pull over!" Bel aimed the gun at their captor's skull, but the man jerked his fist into the air to reveal an old flip phone.

"Hand it over," he demanded as he thumbed the device open and poised a finger over the call button. "Or I'll blow that entire hotel to hell."

Bel's finger shifted to the trigger. If he didn't have a thumb, he couldn't dial the number to detonate the bomb.

"Don't think about it," the driver yanked his fist out of sight, stealing her only hope of emerging from this encounter unscathed. "I mean it, cop. Hand over the gun, or you'll get to watch the hotel go up in flames through the rear window. I'm sure you have friends inside the building. Do you want them all to die?"

"Do it," Taron begged, fear engulfing her like a death shroud. "Please, listen to him."

"I don't want to kill all those people, but I will," he continued. "Give me the gun, or I'll hit the call button."

"Okay, okay." Bel flicked on the safety. She hadn't considered this outcome. She assumed she could force him to obey, but what good was a gun when faced with a bomb? "Here." She handed it over, praying he didn't shoot her with it, but he thankfully tucked it out of her reach.

"You shouldn't have done this," he spat. "You're ruining everything." He stepped on the gas, and the vehicle picked up speed. What was she ruining? What did he have planned? And could she stop it unarmed in the back seat of a car that belonged to the kidnapper with her weapon and an explosive at his disposal?

"What am I ruining?" she asked.

"Shut Up." The man swerved to avoid a pedestrian, and both women flinched at the near collision. If he didn't slow down, he'd kill someone, and Bel couldn't bear the prospect of being part of a hit and run, of hearing a body crack upon impact before they left it mangled on the asphalt. She also didn't want to leave town, which, based on his directions, was their abductor's plan. Chances of survival dropped drastically when victims were moved to a second location...

But Eamon was tracking her phone.

Careful not to make any sudden moves and alert their kidnapper to her betrayal, Bel slipped her cell from her pocket and laid it on the seat beside her. She turned the volume down instead of muting it. She needed him to hear her, not the other way around, and then she dialed Eamon's contact.

"Isobel?" Eamon practically shouted into the phone when her number lit up his screen. Cops swarmed the hotel as they evacuated the hundreds of occupants, but he hadn't been able to find her. He'd hung back during the signing to give Taron a chance to act, if she was the guilty party, and he cursed himself for his stupidity. Bel was missing, and Bajka didn't have a bomb squad. They'd have to wait for experts to arrive from out of town unless he handled the explosive himself, but he refused to risk setting off the explosion while she was unaccounted for. She'd stepped on an IED once, and the sound of that pressure plate still haunted his nightmares. He was the son of the devil. Monsters like him never dreamed, yet when the darkness swallowed him, his mind forced him to watch Bel explode into nothing but tissue and fat until the terror woke him. One IED was enough. He wouldn't risk blowing her to shrapnel ever again.

"Where are you?" he demanded into the phone, nausea

curdling his stomach. He couldn't scent her amidst the horde of sweating bodies exuding their fear. He couldn't see her. He couldn't hear her, and the overwhelming panic threatened to render him unconscious. He wouldn't survive her second death. He refused to pick up her splintered bones until he had enough to fill a coffin.

"Isobel, where are you?" he repeated when she didn't answer. "Are you okay? Are you safe?"

"Where are you taking me and Miss Monroe?" Bel asked, her words distorted as if she'd dropped her phone onto the floor after dialing.

"Isobel? What's going on?" He charged toward Griffin.

"Are you The Wolf?" Bel asked, but a muted male voice shouted for silence.

"He has her," Eamon growled as he seized the sheriff's biceps. "The Wolf has Isobel and Miss Monroe." He tapped the speaker button so Griffin could hear Bel's inconspicuous communication.

"Are you The Wolf?" her muffled voice repeated. "Are you the one who wrote all those beautiful letters?"

A car horn drowned out the man's response, and at the sound, Eamon clicked on Bel's location. A map loaded, and the moving blue dot was all the confirmation he needed. "They're in a car, and he's leaving town… fast." He tugged Griffin toward the exit.

"What?" The sheriff dug in his heels, forcing them to a halt. "There's an active bomb threat in this hotel. I can't leave,"

"There's no bomb," Eamon said. "The Wolf knew Isobel was watching Miss Monroe, and he needed a distraction to isolate the actress. Only now he has my girl too, so move."

"Despite your convictions, I abide by the law," Griffin protested. "A bomb threat is not something I can abandon."

"And I can't let Isobel get gutted in the woods." Eamon dragged the sheriff outside, and this time, the mortal couldn't resist his ancient strength. "Gold, you take over," he shouted at

Olivia, and she scowled at him, readying to bite his head off for ordering her around when she saw Griffin's face.

"Yes, sir," she aimed the answer at her boss, and then Eamon shoved Griffin into the driver's seat of his sheriff's truck.

"Drive." Eamon jumped into the passenger side. "I'm tracking Bel's phone, so I'll guide you."

"BOMB THREATS AND KIDNAPPINGS," Bel said, praying that the more damning her sentences were, the faster Eamon would understand her meaning. "This won't end well for you."

"Shut up," The Wolf shouted. "I said shut up!"

"Bel, please," Taron sobbed, recoiling against the car door to get as far from their kidnapper as possible.

"Listen to her," The Wolf said. "And I'm so sorry, Taron. She's ruining it. *Ruining it, ruining it.*" He repeated the phrase over and over, and Bel crossed her metaphorical fingers. He hadn't planned for two victims, and she was digging her way under his skin. Aggravated criminals often got sloppy... or started pulling the trigger.

"You're ruining it!" The Wolf exploded, slamming his palm against the steering wheel. At that exact moment, another car swerved in front of them, and he slammed on the brakes to avoid a collision. Bel flew forward, the seatbelt choking her as it jerked her to a halt, and she watched with horror as her phone catapulted off the seat.

"What was that?" he asked, straining his neck to see what had wedged between the seats. Bel lunged to recapture her device, but their kidnapper aimed her own weapon at her.

"Hand it over," he demanded, and Bel wondered if she was fast enough to unbuckle her seatbelt and attack before he figured out that he needed to switch off the gun's safety.

"I said hand it over." The Wolf thumbed off the safety, and

she sagged in her seat. So much for that idea. "Now, cop, or I will shoot you."

Bel handed him her phone, the call disconnected from the fall. It didn't matter, though. Eamon had excellent hearing. He knew she needed him, and he could track her cell regardless of who's hands held the device—

"No!" Bel shouted, but her alarm was too late. The Wolf rolled down the window the second she placed her phone in his palm and launched it into the snowbanks. He increased his speed to a reckless pace, leaving her phone behind in his proverbial dust. And for the first time since she climbed out of the bathroom window, Bel felt the sharp claws of terror fist her gut. Eamon wouldn't know where to search, and the cops were too busy with the bomb threat to care about a speeding car. No one was coming for them, and if Bel didn't find an escape, she and Taron might end the day wearing red cloaks.

"She stopped." Eamon grabbed the steering wheel to steady the car before holding the GPS up for Griffin to see. "She's close. Turn here."

Griffin expertly guided the truck around the bend before accelerating through the empty town.

"Make this right," Eamon said, impressed with how the mortal sheriff handled the vehicle.

"Where to now?" Griffin asked as he followed his directions.

"There." Eamon pointed to the side of the road. "Up ahead."

"Why is the GPS taking you to the snow?" Griffin's voice sounded how Eamon's chest felt.

"Maybe she escaped" Eamon leaped out of the truck before it even skidded to a stop and raced over the deep snow, nausea fighting for control of his body, especially when he saw the rectangle hole in the drifts. "No." He snatched Bel's cell from the white, but there was no mistaking it was hers. He'd bought this model, and Cerberus's meaty face grinned up at him from the lock screen. The Wolf must have tossed it so the police couldn't track her, but there was one silver lining. The phone's location had only just stopped moving, meaning they were close, but with every passing second, Bel slipped further and further from his grasp.

"Get out." Eamon seized the sheriff and hauled him out of the driver's seat. "I'm driving."

"This is my truck," Griffin protested.

"And Isobel just angered The Wolf." Eamon slid behind the steering wheel, barely pausing long enough for Griffin to scramble to the passenger side. "He threw her phone out of the car, which means I can't track her. We're close, though, so the only way we'll find them is if I drive. You don't have the reflexes for this." He hit the gas pedal, and Griffin's head bounced off the headrest before smacking the window.

"Put on your seatbelt," Eamon ordered as their speed increased to a dangerous acceleration. "It's only going to get worse."

BEL GLANCED out the rearview mirror as they left Bajka behind in favor of the lonely tree-lined roads that wound through the surrounding forests. Between the multitude of side streets and the highway entrance, Eamon wouldn't be able to predict which route they'd taken. He couldn't scent them locked away inside the vehicle. He couldn't track them without her phone. But he'd answered her call, so he'd heard her pointed questions. He was coming for them. She just needed to delay their trip long enough to allow him time to catch up.

Bel scanned the back seat, but there was nothing she could use as a weapon besides herself... and a crash. The Wolf was armed with both her gun and a bomb, but he was also preoccupied. As the car sped through the snowy woods, his focus was divided between his captives and the poorly plowed roads. Driving at this speed took concentration, and he'd be slow going for the gun. His distraction was the only advantage she had, and she'd lose it the minute they parked.

Bel slid her fingers between the door and the front seat to hide her movement and tapped Taron's arm.

"Seatbelt," she mouthed when the actress met her gaze in the rearview mirror, and Taron nonchalantly buckled the strap into place. The moment she was locked in, Bel lunged sideways, curled her legs against her chest, and kicked. Her heel connected with the driver's skull, the car swerving wildly as he lost his grip on the steering wheel, and she dove forward. The pitching vehicle almost knocked her to the floor, but with a growl birthed from a primal need to survive, she jammed her fingers against his seatbelt's release button. The lock gave way, and she seized the loose belt like a garrote, wrapping it around The Wolf's throat as he fought to regain control of their speed.

"What the—?" he shouted as the seatbelt cut off his oxygen supply. Bel threw herself into the back seat, planted her heels against his chair, and heaved. He choked as the belt strangled him, and instinct forced him to release the steering wheel in favor of freeing himself. Bel grinned at her good luck and opened her mouth to order Taron to steady the swerving car, but they hit an ice patch before she uttered a single syllable. The vehicle veered sideways as The Wolf clawed at his throat for air, tilting dangerously, and Taron screamed. As if she read Bel's mind, she lunged across the center console to grab the wheel, but she miscalculated. She over-corrected in her panic, and the car slid for the snow bank at an alarming speed.

It happened so fast, yet Bel witnessed every second as if time had stopped just for her horror. She saw the car aim for the sky. She saw the world outside invert as they flipped with nauseating speed, and she braced for the impact. She wasn't wearing a seatbelt, but she refused to let go of the belt choking The Wolf. He wasn't getting away on her watch. If he survived the crash, he'd shoot them both. So she wedged her legs against the front seat, praying the position would save her neck from snapping, and then waited for the pain.

The vehicle hit the ground with a cacophony of violence. Glass shattered. Metal groaned. Asphalt shrieked, and the mangled wreck skidded onto the cushion of unblemished snow. The world was alive with chaos, and then Bel was on the car's roof, the past few seconds erased from her memory as the air fell eerily silent.

"Bel!" Taron was screaming, and Bel blinked at the upside-down woman. They weren't dead. Not yet, at least. They'd survived her suicide of a plan.

"Bel, wake up!" the actress shouted from where she hung, and Bel realized she must have blacked out.

"Can you undo your seatbelt?" she asked, her head thundering an uncomfortable rhythm.

"Oh thank god." Taron started sobbing.

"Can you?" she repeated.

"I think so."

"Brace yourself first so you don't fall."

"Okay." Taron wedged her arms and legs against the dashboard and undid her belt. She plummeted to the roof despite her efforts, and Bel finally got a clear look at her. Besides the scrapes on her face from the broken glass, she wasn't seriously injured. Bel, on the other hand? She couldn't tell if it was merely an impact bruise or something worse.

The Wolf groaned as he woke, and Bel cursed. Her fear over her aching ribs would have to wait.

"Where's my gun?" She scanned the wreckage for her weapon, but it was nowhere to be seen. "Taron, do you see my gun?"

Evidence of a Folktale

"Um..." Taron's eyes flitted about, an unhinged edge glazing her sight. "It probably flew outside when we crashed."

"Can you climb out of that window?" Bel asked. She needed the actress out of the car before her panic escalated their already dangerous situation.

"I think so."

"Go. Get out and find help."

"No, I can't," she protested.

"Go, now!" Bel ordered. "Run back the way we came. Get Eamon."

The Wolf groaned again as he fumbled to sit up.

"Run, Taron!" Bel screamed, and the actress finally obeyed. She crawled out of the broken window, their captor clawing at her heels, but she was too fast. She wriggled free of the crash and took off running, and Bel prayed Eamon was driving with the windows down. Taron was barely bleeding, but it was enough to alert the Impaler. He'd find her. She'd be safe. Bel just hoped he picked up the scent in time to help her too.

"I'm gonna kill you," The Wolf coughed as he turned his rage on Bel, and she took that as her cue. The back window had shattered, and its frame had collapsed in on itself. Crawling out would prove difficult, but she refused to remain locked in this metal cage with a predator. Flattening her body, she slid over the glass shards until her head slipped out into the snow. The Wolf captured her ankle, but his grip was weak. He'd suffered the most in their crash thanks to her, and she kicked his hand off with ease.

The broken glass stung as her stomach grated over it, but then her shoulders were free of the car, then her chest, and then her hips. As soon as her thighs hit the snow, she curled her legs below her and started crawling. Her every muscle ached, but she refused to stop. The news had falsely reported her death thanks to a car crash once before. She wasn't about to make that a reality.

"You're going to pay for ruining everything," The Wolf shouted behind her, and before she could register the closeness of his voice, his body crashed into hers. She collapsed face-first into the snow as his weight crushed her. Her world blurred white, and she was instantly back on that mountain. Blaubart's gunshots echoed so harshly through her memory that her ears rang. She sputtered into the cold, the snow flooding her tongue, her eyes, her sanity, and terror vaulted through her limbs. She dug her bare and freezing palms into the razor-sharp cushion below her and shoved onto her back. The Wolf rolled with her, but she only landed one decent punch before his fists found her throat. And then he squeezed. Bel choked as he strangled her, the force crushing her windpipes. She flailed below him. Her nails clawed at his fingers like a wild animal, but her will to live was nothing compared to his grip. It tightened mercilessly as he straddled her waist.

"You'll pay for this," he snarled, smiling at how her face changed color. She couldn't breathe. She couldn't fight back. Everything hurt. She flailed and sobbed and choked, but it was no use. She had seconds before his fists crushed the life out of her.

"I'm going to—uff!" The Wolf flew sideways as something hard connected with his skull, and he crashed to the snow unconscious, blood dripping from his forehead.

"Oh my god!" Taron screamed, throwing the bloody tree branch to the ground as if it was on fire. "I killed him... Bel? Oh god, Bel, please be alive."

Bel could barely move, her voice useless, but she managed to offer Taron a weak thumbs up. The woman heaved a dramatic sigh at the proof of life before collapsing into a heap of tears beside her, and Bel felt guilty for ever suspecting the actress. She wasn't the killer, nor had she lied about The Wolf's letters. And for all her talk about not wanting to be a real cop, she'd just saved Bel's life.

Evidence of a Folktale

"I can't believe I killed a man," Taron sobbed, and Bel slid her hand over the freezing ground to grab the woman's leg. She hadn't killed The Wolf. His chest still moved, but Bel couldn't find her voice, so she gripped the actress's knee. Clearly needing the reassurance, Taron captured her fingers in a death grip, and the women lay side by side in the snow until the melody of skidding tires filled the air.

"Isobel!" Eamon's fear ripped through the cold, and Bel burst into tears, the dam in her chest finally breaking free at the safety that whiskey-rough sound heralded. "Isobel!" He collapsed to his knees and slid his arms beneath her, yanking her against his chest, and compared to the freezing snow, his cool skin was a welcomed fire.

"She's alive," Taron sobbed. "She crashed the car so I could escape. He tried to choke her to death, but I killed him. Oh god, I killed a man. I'm a murderer." She dissolved into tears again, throwing herself against Eamon for support, and he stiffened. It hurt to laugh, but Bel's spirit chuckled at the interaction. He terrified most people, yet here Taron was hugging him like a little kid. Eamon awkwardly patted her back, and the rattle of handcuffs told Bel Griffin had wisely heeded her boyfriend's warnings.

"He isn't dead, Miss Monroe," Griffin said as he locked The Wolf's hands together. "You just knocked him out, and good thing you did. Seems you saved our detective here."

"I didn't kill him?" Taron jerked off of Eamon's shoulder. "Oh thank god. She stayed behind to save me, but then I saw him choking her. She wasn't getting up, so I found that branch and hit him. I didn't know I could hit anyone that hard."

"Thank you," Eamon said. "You saved the woman I love. I'm forever in your debt."

"She told me to find you when we crashed." Taron glanced between the couple and the sheriff. "Not the cops."

"The Bajka Police Department is a little preoccupied at the

moment. Plus, Emerson knows if there's one person who'll drop everything and drive like a lunatic, it's this guy." Griffin thumped Eamon's back. "Yes, Eamon drove my truck," he added when a string of questions flooded Bel's eyes. "And no, I never want to get in a car with him again."

"Thank you," she mouthed, and the sheriff reached down to cup her cheek before dragging the barely conscious driver off the ground.

"You have the right to remain silent," he started as an ambulance siren filled the air.

"And thank you," she whispered, meeting Eamon's gaze.

"Don't thank me," he growled. "I was too late... again. Taron saved you."

"After she saved me first," the actress said. "I never want to be a cop. Playing one is fine, but don't ever make me get a real badge. Your girl here is something else. She literally dove into a kidnapper's car to save me and then beat him up so he'd crash. We need to write an episode like this into the show... if you'd be okay with it?"

Bel smiled weakly to give her approval before wrapping her arms around Eamon's neck so he could carry her to the waiting EMTs. "Don't feel guilty," she whispered with a raw throat, praying this incident didn't trigger the guilt he'd felt at the hospital. "We caught the guy. I'm just annoyed at myself that I let him take my phone."

"Calling me was smart, and your phone's fine. It's in my pocket, but you shouldn't be talking right now," Eamon said. "Let's get you to the hospital first."

"I love you," she said as he loaded her into the ambulance.

"I love you too, Detective. More than you know." He lifted her knuckles to his lips before threading his larger fingers through hers. Their intertwined hands fit together like a key sliding into its lock, and by the expression he wore while staring at them, the sight had a profound impact on him. "But please stop talking. I don't want you to damage your throat." He kissed her forehead before moving out of the EMTs' way. "Don't worry. I'll be with you the entire time." He tightened his grip on her fingers. "I'm not going anywhere, remember?"

Bel grimaced as she sank into the stretcher. Everything hurt without the adrenaline pumping through her veins, and its absence signaled her body to crash… or maybe it was because Eamon was with her, and if Eamon was here, she was safe. He wouldn't let the wolves near her.

Autopsy Report

CERBERUS

PROD.NO. TAKE SOUND
SCENE
DIRECTOR
CAMERAMAN EXT. INT.

CINEMA TICKET ADMIT ONE 9891102
CINEMA TICKET ADMIT ONE 9891102

Chapter Seventeen

"OH MY GOD!" VIOLET WAS A TORNADO OF EMOTIONS AS SHE burst through the cabin's front door. She kicked off her heels, still wearing the towering stilettos despite the snow, and shoved the overflowing grocery bags on the table before launching herself at the couch. She landed gently on top of the reclining Bel and started sobbing as she hugged her friend.

"When I learned about the accident, I got the most horrible déjà vu," she cried. "I almost threw up…. How is she?" She glanced over her shoulder to where Eamon stood watching them from the kitchen.

"Surprisingly okay, considering she survived a choking and a car crash," he answered. "The snow's so deep, it cushioned the car's impact, so she escaped without any broken bones or stitches. She's banged up, and her throat will hurt for a while, but she's all right."

"Oh, thank goodness." Violet lay back down on Bel, and the detective chuckled despite the pain.

"What's with the groceries?" she whispered in a voice almost as rough as Eamon's.

"After I heard about the crash, I had a full-blown panic attack and had to sit on my kitchen floor. I never sit on the floor. My cats were freaked out, but my brain kept replaying that news report about your faked death. Thankfully, Eamon found your phone, and he answered when I called you." Violet shifted on top of her, and Bel couldn't figure out what her friend was doing until a palm pressed against her chest. She was searching for a heartbeat, and that simple touch broke Bel's heart.

"He told me you were at the hospital, but they expected you to come home tonight," Violet continued. "I asked if you needed anything, and he texted me a grocery list for soup."

"I have soup in the pantry," Bel whispered. With her ears so close to her mouth, Violet could hear her low words, and Eamon's senses could pick up even her faintest sounds. It was an inconvenience when she muttered under her breath in annoyance at him, but it came in handy now since speaking set her throat on fire.

"I'm not feeding you canned soup," Eamon said as he dug through the groceries. He hadn't relaxed until they arrived at her cabin, but his muscles still hadn't fully released their tension. Much like Violet, the accident had resurrected his crippling despair and anxiety. He was trying to hide it, and to anyone else, he seemed unbothered, but Bel knew him. He was fighting not to fall apart, and now that she was safe on her couch, she felt horrible about crashing the car. In the heat of the moment, it was all she could think to do, and while Eamon and Griffin agreed her actions were the reason she and Taron were alive, the scene sliced open the wound Blaubart had inflicted when he faked her death.

"And I wasn't about to leave you alone, so I asked Violet to shop for me," he continued.

"It was no trouble. I needed to see you anyway." Violet finally pulled herself off Bel's chest and settled beside her on the couch, clutching her hand as Cerberus debated whether to join the women for snuggles or beg Eamon for scraps.

"Do you want to stay for dinner?" Eamon asked. "I'll cook the meat in a separate pan."

"I don't want to intrude," Violet said. "I just needed to prove Bel is alive."

Eamon stiffened almost imperceptibly at her words. "It's no intrusion," he said. "You bought the groceries. At least stay until the soup is done so I can send you home with a container."

"You sure?" Violet glanced at Bel, who nodded her agreement. It was comforting to have someone hold her hand while Eamon cooked, plus he needed another person to help him bear the burden. He was struggling after the crash, and having Violet present to watch over his girlfriend while his back was turned clearly brought him comfort.

After Griffin arrested The Wolf, Olivia called with an update on the bomb threat. They'd successfully evacuated the hotel, and a neighboring SWAT team had arrived to take over. They found no evidence of explosives, which proved Eamon's theory that The Wolf never intended to blow up the building. He merely used the threat to control Taron, and ultimately Bel. The SWAT team still planned to conduct a thorough investigation, but they didn't expect to find anything. The bomb was a ploy. One everyone fell for.

Griffin had then visited the hospital to get Bel's statement, knowing she needed an update as badly as he needed to see her exam results. It seemed everyone refused to believe she was alive until they witnessed her breathing themselves. Griffin had gone so far as to press his fingers against her throat when they hugged goodbye so her heartbeat could echo against his skin, and after the doctors discharged her to Eamon's care, her boyfriend drove the entire way home with his grip wrapped around the pulse in her wrist. They'd opted to stay at her cabin for the night, the familiar setting cozier for her recovery, and he hadn't left her side since.

Violet remained with Bel as Eamon cooked, the women

holding hands as they watched sitcom reruns. Before long, the kitchen turned aromatic, and the trio ate on the couch together. It hurt Bel's throat to swallow despite the pain pills, but she managed most of her soup. It made both her friend and boyfriend happy that she'd eaten, but the minute the meal hit her stomach, fatigue assumed control of her body. She sagged against Eamon, drifting between consciousness and oblivion, and the last thing she remembered was Violet creeping for the front door in an attempt not to wake her.

A WEIRD GRUNTING shoved through her dreams, and Bel opened her mouth to ask what was making such a peculiar sound so ungodly early, but only a groan escaped her lips, pain igniting her body like a live wire as she rolled onto her side. She breathed through the sharpness, and when her nerves settled, she peeled her eyelids open. Eamon sat at her kitchen table, working on his laptop with one hand while gripping a toy rope in the other. His incredible strength made for an ideal playmate, and Bel realized it was Cerberus' grunts and growls as he fought an epic game of tug-of-war that woke her. She also realized it wasn't morning, for the red clock on her microwave read thirteen minutes past noon.

"What happened to my alarm?" she whispered, her voice achingly hoarse, but Eamon heard her despite Cerberus' piggish grunting.

"I turned it off." He released the toy, and her dog bolted for the bed, assuming he'd triumphed in the war. He climbed onto the mattress and plopped across her thighs to chew his hard-won prize.

"Why?"

"You need the sleep." Eamon filled a glass with filtered water and brought it and her painkillers to the bed. "Besides,

Evidence of a Folktale

Griffin made me promise. He swore he'd arrest me if he saw you so much as drive by the station. He'll call once he has news, so if you can't go to work, what's the point of waking you?"

"Thanks." She popped the painkiller into her mouth and swallowed it, grimacing as the cold water burned her throat.

"How do you feel?" Eamon settled on the mattress beside her.

"Like I was in a car crash and then choked." She reclined on the pillows as she folded her fingers into his grip. "Oh... what was that pill?"

"Not your painkillers. They're stronger versions of what I gave you for your hangover. I could barely sleep because you kept groaning... and then your neck. Don't look at yourself in the mirror if you can help it."

"It's that bad?" Bel fingered her throat.

"I can't bear the sight." Eamon wrapped both his hands around hers and collapsed forward until their foreheads kissed. "I can't give you something that'll heal you. Your throat is too visible, and the sudden absence of bruising would raise questions, but I put in a call to my witch contact. She overnighted these pain pills. They're significantly stronger than pharmaceuticals, so at least you won't suffer."

"I already feel better." She sighed as she settled deeper into the pillows. "Thank you."

"Of course." He lifted her fingers to his lips and kissed her knuckles. "It was selfish, really. I can barely look at you. I'm a coward, but it's why I wasn't facing you in the kitchen. I couldn't get to you in time, and you almost died."

"You aren't a coward."

"I am." Self-loathing curled through his menacing voice. "You are the love of my life, yet I can't look at you."

"Hey." Bel tugged her hands free of his grip and cupped his jaw. His self-hatred hurt worse than her bruised ribs and purple throat, and she couldn't bear the sight of him crumbling before her. He was Eamon Stone, the devil made flesh. He was the strongest person she knew, and nothing terrified her more than watching fear eat his power alive. "You aren't a coward." She pulled his lips to hers, kissing him softly until his rigidness thawed. God, how she loved this man. "Don't do this. Don't punish yourself."

"I shouldn't be this weak," he argued. "I've never been weak before."

"You're half human." She trailed her lips across his cheek. "Weakness defines us. We either live by it or overcome it."

"You certainly overcome it."

"Because I'm special like that." She winked, the absence of pain returning her sense of humor.

"You're something, that's for sure." Eamon rolled his eyes as he pulled her into his arms. "God, I love you. You told Taron that I'm your best friend. Well, Isobel, you're mine, and your accident is no joking matter, yet here you are teasing me to help me feel better. I rarely smiled until I met you. You know I care, but for the record, you're my best friend, too."

"Stop, I don't want to cry." She shoved the heels of her palms against his chest, but he wouldn't let her go, so she surrendered to his embrace, kissing his throat until the tickle drove him to release her.

"I don't want you to either." He traced her smile with his thumb, satisfied with himself that his forced hug stopped her tears, but she didn't miss the way he avoided looking at her neck.

"I must look awful." She tried to touch her throat again, but he captured her hands and pulled them into his lap.

"I'm glad Miss Monroe was the one to save you, and not me."

"Why?"

"Because I wouldn't have hit him with a tree branch like she did. I would've ripped his head clean off, which is why I have a gift for you."

Evidence of a Folktale

"If you say The Wolf's head, I'll puke," Bel teased, and Eamon rolled his eyes.

"Here." He handed her a book charm necklace, and her fingers instinctively flew to her throat.

"My necklace." She lowered her hand from her empty neck and took her jewelry from him. "Did it fall off in the snow?"

"No, I removed it while you slept," he said. "I called more than one contact last night because while it's best for everyone involved that I didn't find that man's hands around your throat, I won't ever be too late again."

"I know." Bel squeezed his hand. "But what does that have to do with my necklace?"

"You're not exactly an easy woman to keep track of. I appreciate that you called me after you jumped headfirst into a kidnapper's vehicle, but phones can be thrown out of windows or destroyed. I lose a scent's trail when cars are involved, and I can't read minds. Every time you've been taken, your attackers removed your phone, your car, and sometimes even your clothes, but you know what they never took?"

"My necklace." Bel stared down at the simple book charm. After the cursed Eamon had attacked her in New York City, he'd left this necklace in her hospital room. She hadn't known who the gift was from then, but at his request, a witch had charmed it to keep her safe. She often wondered if that's why she'd been unnervingly lucky since her move to Bajka. She always escaped. She always survived.

"They never take your necklace." Eamon trailed a finger over the chain. "Blaubart would've eventually since he's planned to transform you surgically into his wife, but my point is, he didn't. Not right away, at least, and that's all the head start I need. I was tracking your phone yesterday, but when The Wolf threw it into the snow, we thought you'd stopped. If Griffin hadn't pulled over to check, we would've arrived before he choked you. Maybe even before the crash. When it comes to mortal life and death,

271

seconds make the difference, and tracking your phone isn't enough. So I sent a car for one of my contacts last night. I gave him your necklace, and he took it back to my place to work. He finished it this morning."

"What did he do?" Bel twisted the charm in her fingers, but it looked the same as it had yesterday.

"He outfitted it with a military-grade tracker," Eamon said. "It's not even on the market, so no, you can't ask how he got it because we'd both be branded enemies of the state. It's undetectable and doesn't require a battery source. I'm not sure how it works. All I know is this tracker's technology is a highly guarded government secret. No matter where you go, as long as you're wearing this, I'll find you. And if your necklace is ever removed, I'll already know where you're headed, especially because of this." He flipped the charm over to show her the back of the book. "It's an invisible panic button. No need for phone calls or clues or breadcrumbs. Just swipe your thumb over it, and it'll alert me."

"Can I test it?" she asked.

"Sure."

Bel brushed her thumb over the panic button, and Eamon's phone and laptop exploded with a deafening alarm. "Oh my god." She flinched with a squawk before bursting into a fit of laughter. "There's no way you'd miss that call for help. I think all of Bajka heard it."

"I have no intentions of missing it," Eamon said. "All my devices are linked to your tracker. It's coded for your fingerprints only, so your skin or a stranger won't set it off. If you like, I can program the alarm to alert others, like your father or Griffin. I'm the default, but backup is always smart."

"I agree," Bel said. "If you're away for business, Griffin and Dad need it."

"I'll give them access. I hope you never have a use for it, but it's safer than a phone call."

"This would've come in handy yesterday," Bel said.

"So you like it?"

"Of course. I don't enjoy being choked... or flipping a car. If this helps you find me faster, I'll gladly wear it. Will it track me at all times, or just when I hit the panic button?"

"All the time, but it's no different from tracking your phone."

"Gotcha, so take it off when I visit my other boyfriends?"

"Exactly." Eamon chuckled as Bel handed him the necklace.

"I play with this sometimes. What happens if I accidentally trigger the alarm?" She leaned forward so he could fasten the clasp around her neck, loving that her stupid jokes made him laugh.

"I come for you." Eamon shrugged.

"Just like that?"

"Just like that." He traced the chain, his fingers dancing over her collarbones. "I'm glad this didn't freak you out. We've talked a lot about how to navigate our relationship and the dangers I present by staying. Calling me was smart, but it's not enough. We need a faster, more efficient way of communicating when you're in danger, and yesterday made that painfully obvious. I figured a tracker in your necklace wasn't invasive. It's similar to using your phone's location, and I didn't want to embed a subdermal tracker before asking."

"The necklace is smart, but a subdermal tracker? That's definitely what I'd call invasive," Bel said.

"So, that's a hard no?" Eamon raised his eyebrows in a mostly teasing gesture.

"Obviously." She shoved him, and he good-naturedly faked losing his balance. "I believe The Wolf is human, but he was a very real reminder of the dangers out there... and that I also dive headfirst into trouble. I like this solution. The necklace is blessed by magic and technology, so if I'm ever trapped in some lunatic's car again, you'll find me before I have to flip the vehicle. And I can take it off, so it gives me autonomy."

"To see your other boyfriends," he teased.

"Exactly." Bel wrapped her arms around his waist, her head falling against the thundering heart that always brought her peace. "I was so scared," she whispered. "If Taron hadn't come back for me... So, yeah. You need to find me faster."

"I will. I promise." Eamon kissed her head, but as his lips slipped lower to her mouth, her stomach let out an unladylike growl. "Are you hungry?" he asked as she burst into laughter. "You mostly ate broth last night, so I'll make you breakfast. Eating will be easier after those pills."

"Maybe something soft, like hot cereal?" she said. "No oatmeal, though. And some tea." She hadn't been able to bring herself to eat oatmeal since Abel kidnapped her, but grits always graced her pantry.

"Okay." He kissed her forehead before venturing into the kitchen. "I'll work from here today, so I can help you out. I don't want you doing much."

"Sounds good, but please face me."

Her trilling phone drowned out the reply he uttered from inside the pantry, and she snatched it off the bedside table to find Griffin's name plastered across the screen.

"Emerson," he said when she answered. "I won't hurt you by making you talk, but I wanted to call with an update. Just listen because I already warned Mr. Stone what would happen if he let you do any work."

"So I heard," she whispered.

"I'll start with the good news," Griffin said. "Swat concluded their search. There was no bomb. It was just a plot to force Taron away from you."

"Thank God."

"And the rest isn't exactly bad news, but it's not what we were hoping for. The Wolf's legal name is Alaric Randall, and until a few days ago, he worked as a cell phone repair tech. He has no criminal record or relationship with anyone on Aesop's

Files. We ran a handwriting analysis, which is a positive match for the letter Monroe received at the bed-and-breakfast, but the search of his hotel room revealed nothing. He's either hiding his murder weapons elsewhere, or he's not the killer. He's refusing to talk, and we're still digging into his life, but we learned he attended an event a while back and met Miss Monroe. Despite their interaction and his letters, she didn't remember him when he came to our town, so he used the threat of a non-existent bomb to lure her outside. He just hadn't expected you to be crazy enough to launch yourself into the backseat of his car."

"I said the same thing," Eamon shouted from the stove, and the sheriff chuckled.

"This is what I get for not having kids," Griffin said. "The lord saw fit to give me you and your urges to make up for all my years of missed panic attacks."

"Sorry," Bel whispered. "But Taron Monroe did not die, so that's a win."

"I guess. It's hard to think things are a win when you're the price."

"It's a win," Bel said.

"Whatever you say, Emerson," he chuckled. "All right, I'll let you go. Please get some sleep. I'll call if I have another update."

GRIFFIN DIDN'T CALL, so the couple spent a peaceful day together. Bel barely stepped foot off the mattress, and if she pretended her throat wasn't mottled with black and blue fingerprints, she almost enjoyed the bedrest. She binged one TV show after another, skipping the Aesop's Files episodes, and Eamon kept his word. He worked with his face turned toward her until he closed his laptop to make dinner. Then he held her in his arms until sleep stole her from him.

"Hey, welcome back," Officer Rollo said as he passed Bel's desk the next afternoon. She'd overslept again at Griffin's insistence. He promised she could return for a few hours of paperwork if she slept without an alarm interrupting her rest, and after another one of the witch's pills, she felt strong enough to work. Eamon reasoned she needed food first, though, so she hadn't arrived at the station until well past midday.

"How are you feeling?" Rollo asked, and Bel wanted to cry that it wasn't Olivia welcoming her back. Granted, Violet was probably behind half of his concern. She'd doubtlessly ordered her new date to keep an eye on her friend.

"Not as bad as yesterday," she said.

"You are one badass woman," Rollo chuckled. "Jumping into a car with a kidnapper and then crashing it. I don't think I'm that brave."

"Safer for your health and Violet's sanity," Bel laughed. This was why she'd donned a turtleneck to hide the gruesome shades of purple. Better the officers' admiration than their horrified pity.

"True. You worried everyone, though. I was working here in Bajka when the news reported you died in a car crash, so when I heard over the radio that you were in a real one, my stomach dropped."

"It's nice to know I work with people who care about me." Bel smiled at the handsome deputy. Gorgeous and caring with a stable job... yes, Violet was in trouble.

"All right, I got to go. It's been insane ever since the bomb threat," Rollo said. "It doesn't matter that it was proved a lie. Everyone's using it as clickbait, which is only making things worse."

"Ugh, I don't envy you."

"Milk the desk work, Detective." He winked at her. "See you later."

"Bye." Bel waved as Griffin exited his office and pulled a chair next to hers.

Evidence of a Folktale

"You okay to be here?" he asked.

"I can sit at a desk just fine... at least until the pain meds wear off."

"Well, let me know when that happens. How's your..." he pointed to her throat.

"The color's worse than it feels." She tugged on her turtleneck so he could see the fingerprints.

"Good lord." Griffin pulled her hand away, keeping her fingers tucked in his fist as her sweater bounced back into place. "You should be home."

"The painkillers are strong," Bel said. "I can be useful for a few hours."

"You sure?"

"I am. So, do we have any updates on Alaric Randall?"

"Yeah, and he isn't our killer."

"Between his hidden messages, the kidnapping, and attempted murder, I really thought we had our guy."

"Me too," Griffin said. "We dug deeper into his life. He works as a cell phone repair technician, and Miss Monroe's assistant just ID'd him. Right before the letters started, Miss Monroe dropped her phone while they were shooting. The screen shattered, but there was a repair shop down the street. Her assistant ran it over and had a replacement installed, and Randall was her tech. As a fan of the show, he recognized her, so he slipped a tracker below the replaced screen, which is why his letters were always so personal."

"That's unnerving," Bel said. "But jumping from tracking her location and writing letters to choking me to death is a drastic escalation. You mentioned she met him once before, but didn't remember him. Could that have triggered him that severely?"

"Randall was the middle child of a large family. His grades were high, but his parents couldn't afford to send him to college after spending so much on his siblings. So he paid for community college himself and became a cell phone tech where he rarely got raises and never received promotions."

"So, he lived his life in constant mediocrity without recognition from his family, his school, or his job, and then he meets Taron's assistant," Bel said. "He's a fan of Aesop's Files, and he had this fantasy that if he could connect with her, she'd fall for him. He wrote her letters, assuming she'd enjoy the hidden clues because his delusions confused her with her character. The detective loves the hunt, not Taron, but he became obsessed with his idea of her, so when she didn't recognize him, he snapped."

"He'd always been the forgotten one," Griffin said as he mulled over her words. "Then the woman he'd convinced himself he loved forgets him. It made him desperate, but it didn't give him a motive for murdering Rossa or Roja. He wanted Taron to fall in love with him. He wasn't trying to scare her, was he?"

"So, we're back at square one with the murders." Bel sagged in her chair. "Two different crimes. Two different perpetrators."

"And a show that still won't shut down."

"Seriously? Even after a bomb threat?"

"It wasn't a genuine threat, so they don't see it as an issue."

"Good God, these people. The bomb wasn't real, but I have handprints on my throat." Bel rubbed her temples as she tried to exhale her aggravation. "When the murders stopped, I assumed The Wolf was the killer, but now it seems Orion Chayce is our best bet again. Any word on his whereabouts?"

"Nothing. No one's seen him… which reminds me, I meant to call his patrol officer. Maybe he has insights into his character that will help us locate him." Griffin used Bel's computer to search for the man's number. Unfortunately, he reached the officer's voicemail, so he left a message and hung up in defeat. "Can you revisit the evidence and crime scene photos since you're staying at your desk?" he asked. "Maybe we missed something.

Bajka is overrun, but we aren't a huge town. If Chayce is here, how has he gone undetected for so long?"

"I'll recheck everything," Bel said. "I never got out of bed yesterday, so hopefully my rested brain will spot something."

HER RESTED brain embarrassingly spotted nothing, and by the time darkness fell, the irritation in her throat had grown violent to match the frustration headache galloping through her skull.

"Griffin." Bel poked her head into his office. "I'm sore and struggling with fatigue. Would you mind if I—"

"Go home, please," he finished for her. "I'm surprised you lasted this long. Anything for me?"

"Nope. I dug into Rossa, Roja, and Chayce's backgrounds, but nothing jumped out. The women have no connection to him beyond the Aesop's Files. Then, to play devil's advocate, I searched for a link between just Rossa and Roja that might point to a killer other than Chayce. Still nothing. This show seems to be their only connection. That and they're women."

Griffin cursed. "Well, thanks for double-checking and for helping with the paperwork. That was a huge weight off mine and Gold's shoulders."

"No problem. Goodnight." Bel returned to her desk and grabbed her coat as Olivia walked by her for the first time that day.

"Hey," Bel said, desperate for her friend to even look at her.

"Hi," Olivia said, and the softness in her voice gave Bel hope. "How are you feeling?"

"Achy. It's why I'm going home."

"I hope you feel better soon."

"Thanks." She smiled at her partner. Had almost dying reminded Olivia that they loved each other?

"It was brave what you did," she blurted before Bel could leave.

"Thank you."

"You're welcome." Olivia glanced at her desk as if searching for an escape route. "Well, drive safe."

"Thanks." Bel didn't want the conversation to end, but a few kind words were better than nothing. "Have a good night."

Olivia didn't answer, but Bel still counted it as a win. It was sad she had to almost die in a car accident again to get her partner to acknowledge her, but if a brush with death brought them back together, the crash was worth it... maybe. At least that's what she'd tell herself when she woke up sweating after a nightmare. Which thankfully hadn't happened yet. She knew it was thanks to Eamon sleeping beside her and her magic-laced painkiller high, but the bad dreams were coming. There was a nightmare in her future with fists meant for her throat.

But it was not tonight. Eamon had returned to the Reale Estate to work on the renovations while she'd been at the station, but he promised to return to her cabin afterward. The attack made her crave the security of her own home, and despite being one large room, the cabin fit the trio nicely. In the short term, at least.

Bel pulled into her parking spot. The single light illuminating the living room told her she'd beat Eamon home. She always left that lamp on for Cerberus so he could find his toys and water, but it was dim, meaning her pup was the only one inside. Shoving her key into the door's lock, she smiled at his welcoming bark, but before she twisted the key, something by her foot caught her eye.

Bel froze, the blood in her veins colder than the wind gnawing at the world. The sky was dark, the yard covered with white snow, but there was no mistaking the red curling around her toes. The killer had been here, and he'd left her another box.

Autopsy Report

CERBERUS

PROD.NO. TAKE SOUND
SCENE
DIRECTOR
CAMERAMAN EXT. INT.

CINEMA TICKET ADMIT ONE 9891102
CINEMA TICKET ADMIT ONE 9891102

Chapter Eighteen

Bel withdrew her sidearm from its holster so fast that she didn't even realize she'd moved until the black metal reflected the moonlight into her eyes. There was a white box with a red ribbon on her doorstep. Was she the next hooded girl? The forest flanked her cabin. Was she about to be chased into its darkness and gutted?

Bel scanned her yard, gun aimed and safety off. Alcina had tried to kill her in these woods. Blaubart had hunted her through the snow. If the killer expected her to run, he had another thing coming. She would stay and fight. She would make this messy... for both of them because she had no intention of dying tonight. But if Griffin had to find her body, she'd take as much evidence to the grave as she could.

When no one jumped out of the darkness at her, Bel stepped off the front stoop and shifted through the crunching snow. The first two victims had died in the woods. It made sense that the trees behind her home were the next crime scene. The forest was pitch black, the moon playing tricks with its shadows, and Bel wished she had Eamon's eyes. She couldn't see anything in the blackness. She heard nothing but the wind rustling the branches, and she reached for her phone when her gaze landed on the garden bench Eamon had installed for her.

"Oh god." She choked on her words. The killer had been here, but not for her. Not in the way she'd feared, at least. She wasn't the next red-hooded victim. The show's producer, Alistair Rot, was, and he was still bleeding. Thick blood pumped from his abdomen. It dripped down his legs to stain the snow, and a crippling fear tightened its hold around Bel's chest. She didn't need Lina Thum to predict time of death. Alistair Rot had died only minutes before she arrived home, which meant the assailant was probably still here, watching her from the woods, but it was impossible to guess which direction he'd fled. The snow was disheveled from Cerberus' playtimes and long walks, so tightening her grip on her gun, Bel pressed the necklace's panic button.

EAMON TURNED off the water and yanked a towel off the hook. He'd started a new project at the rear of the mansion, one he was anxious to complete. That section of his expansive home held the most decay, so when Bel texted she was leaving the station, he was more dirt than man. He didn't want to leave her alone, but he'd ruin his car if he drove that filthy. Bel would also probably lock him outside if he tried to enter her cabin that disgusting, so he'd opted for a quick shower first. Not bothering to wait for the water to heat, he jumped under the spray, the steam only just starting to fill the bathroom by the time he finished. He toweled off and grabbed his boxer briefs, but before he could slip them on, the air exploded. A violent and desperate alarm ripped through the house, shattering the silence and his sanity with it. Bel's panic button.

Shoving his legs into his boxers, he abandoned the rest of his clothes and raced down the stairs and out into the snow. He glanced at his phone, the tracker telling him she'd made it home, so he ignored his car and took off barefoot through the woods. It was a straight shot to her cabin if he cut through the trees, and he leaned into his speed. He pushed his legs to their breaking point, and the closer he drew to her property, the stronger the scent grew. Blood, and a lot of it. Someone had died, and his only consolation was that the blood wasn't hers.

"Isobel!" He collided with her, wrapping her body protectively in his embrace and dragging her with him as he skidded to a stop in the deep snow.

"My house." She shook against his chest. "He killed him outside my house. Oh god, Cerberus. Is he okay?"

Bel ripped free of his grip and bolted for the cabin, fingers shaking as she tried to unlock the front door. It took her two tries and then she flung herself inside, catching the very alive pitbull in her arms.

"Oh my god." She collapsed to the floor with her pup firmly cemented against her chest. "My baby. You're okay." She kissed his head over and over before throwing her gaze up at Eamon. "The killer? Is he gone?"

"Yes." He squatted beside them. There was no evidence to suggest the dog had been in danger, but panic was never reasonable. A fact he'd recently become well acquainted with. "It's just us and the body."

"He killed Alistair Rot." She reached for him, and he wrapped the duo in his arms. "But when I saw the box on the front stoop, I thought I was next."

Eamon unconsciously tightened his hold on her and her dog.

"He was here. At my house!" she shouted, his chest absorbing her rage. "He murdered a man on that bench you gave me. He wanted me to find Rot still bleeding. He wants us to know we're chasing our tails. That all our theories are wrong and we won't catch him, even though he's right under our noses."

"I should've been here."

"How could you have known? At least the panic button works... your hair's still wet." She reached up and slipped her fingers through his blond locks. "And you're naked."

"I told you I would come no matter what." Eamon leaned into her touch, fully aware that he and Cerberus had that in common. "I managed to pull my boxers up, but that's because they were already half on. Plus, I don't love the prospect of fighting someone with everything swinging out in the open."

Bel smirked, the smile not quite reaching her eyes as she pictured that mental image, and he was glad the humiliating scene humored her. He'd say just about anything to erase her fear.

"I have some of your clothes here." She offered him her hands so he could pull her to her feet. "I can't believe you ran all this way in the snow naked." She brushed a hand over his freezing abs before fishing a pair of his sweats from her dresser.

"I don't feel cold like you," he said as he slipped them on. "I do feel panic."

"I'm sorry for using the necklace." She fished one of his shirts out from her pajama drawer. "I was worried the killer was still here, so I didn't want the phone distracting me."

"That's why I gave it to you. Don't censor yourself because the minute you do, you'll start making mistakes. I'd rather show up unnecessarily than not at all."

"And you're sure the killer isn't out there?" she asked.

"All I smelled was blood and your fear," he said. "But I'll double-check now that I'm not worried about you."

"I'll come with you."

"You don't have to."

"I do. A homicide occurred on my property. I'm a witness, and now that you're here, I'm safe to take a closer look. I just needed to check on Cerberus first."

"He's okay." Eamon slipped his feet into a pair of sneakers he'd thankfully been too lazy to take home, and he wrapped an

Evidence of a Folktale

arm around her shoulders before guiding her back outside. "The killer didn't want to hurt you. He wanted your attention."

"He's taunting us." She pointed at the box still on her front porch. Neither of them wore gloves, so they left it alone as they moved for the victim.

"Just like at the station," Bel continued. "The killer sent me a box, and then we found a second body on your property. Now there's one on mine. Is he targeting us?"

"I don't think so," Eamon said as he observed the scene before them. Alistair Rot sat on the beautiful bench he'd gifted Bel, completely naked save for a red hooded cloak. Just like Rossa and Roja, his abdomen had been eviscerated, his corpse posed in the woods... almost.

"I think the killer wants his victims to be found," he continued. "So he's putting them in places we'll notice. My property by the shooting location. On the trails where people hike regularly. In your backyard, which I am furious about, and if I catch him before you, he'll regret this decision."

"Eamon..."

"I won't kill him," he relented. "But I gave you this bench to prove I care for you. So that you could always look outside and see me, and he violated your home by murdering someone on it."

"You can build me a new bench." Bel patted his chest, which reminded him to breathe. "Maybe a second one in your flower garden too."

"Yeah?" He grabbed her fingers and pinned them over his heart.

"Yeah." She withdrew her phone with her free hand, the palm plastered against him absentmindedly rubbing his skin as she texted her boss a 911 message. "I need to alert Griffin, but you have time to inspect the scene before everyone arrives."

"Okay." He kissed her forehead before turning back to Rot's body. "And to answer your question, no, I don't think he's targeting us directly. These deaths don't mimic my kills, and neither of us is connected to the show. He's telling a story, and you represent his perfect audience. He just wants the bodies found quickly on properties that won't shut filming down."

"If the show goes, so do his victims," Bel said. "All of them have worked for Aesop's Files, and we officially have a serial killer on our hands. I thought he was targeting women, but Rot changes the M.O.. A writer, a costume designer, and now the producer. This body's fresh, so can you smell it for me before we have an audience? Are we dealing with a human or something else?"

Eamon leaned forward and inhaled a deep breath. "Rot definitely came into contact with something unnatural."

"Can you tell what?" she asked, but sirens lit up the air, putting an end to their conversation.

"HE WAS STILL BLEEDING when you got home?" Lina asked.

"Yes," Bel confirmed.

"That at least makes time of death easy to pinpoint," the medical examiner said.

"Unfortunately, the killer left before I noticed the body," Bel said as her yard churned with officers. Griffin must have called the entire department because she'd never seen so many people at one crime scene. With this level of chaos, she wondered how long it would take for the news to arrive and brand her cabin a murder house.

"Do you have a security system?" Griffin asked.

"No. The cabin's a rental, and I'm secluded here," she answered. "I never expected to need one."

"Even after Alcina Magus almost killed you here?" The sheriff glared at her with fatherly disapproval, and she gave him a tiny shrug. What could she say? She had a security system, albeit an unconventional one. Her pitbull had proved himself

Evidence of a Folktale

vicious when her life was in danger, and the devil with death-black eyes used to stalk these woods at night before she invited him to sleep in her bed. What were cameras compared to an overprotective Dhampir?

"I can install some for her," Eamon said.

"Good, but that doesn't help us now," her boss said. "Did you see any cars while driving home?"

"Yeah, but none stuck out," Bel said. "And the snow on my lawn and surrounding trails is destroyed from walking Cerberus. Finding the killer's tracks will be impossible."

"How did he know where you live?" Griffin asked. "Have you noticed anyone following you?"

"Just Taron," Bel said. "She followed me home to warn me about The Wolf's letters."

"Bajka is overflowing with people. You can barely walk two feet without a fan shoving a phone in your face," Eamon said. "Unless they were obnoxious about it, Isobel wouldn't notice someone stalking her. And killing the show's producer on a detective's property seconds before she arrives doesn't point to someone stupid enough to get caught following a cop."

"Are you sure you're okay?" Griffin placed a comforting hand on Bel's arm.

"Just freaked out."

"Me too." Griffin turned his questioning on Eamon. "You've been staying with her. Have you caught anyone hanging around the property? Or maybe innocently jogging by on a morning run?"

"No. There are a few cabins down the road, so we see the neighbors, but most people don't have a reason to drive this street. Granted, I can't attest to what happens when we're at work. If someone wanted to find her house, it wouldn't be that hard. The actress did it."

"Until we catch this guy, I don't want you here alone," Griffin said.

"Oh, she won't be," Eamon answered before she could open her mouth.

"Big surprise here. The box has another puzzle," Olivia said, joining them before the desecrated bench.

"What kind?" Bel asked.

"Word search." She held it out.

"I bet What, Big, You, and Have are hidden in here." Bel plucked the solitary paper out with gloved fingers. "So, we're probably looking for another body part... yup, there's big... and have."

"There's what and you," Eamon pointed to the short words.

"Nose." Bel jabbed her blue finger against the four letters. "*What a big nose you have.* Lina, can you check his nostrils?"

"Sure thing." The M.E. grabbed her tweezers and crouched before Rot's face. "Good god, that's wedged in there." It took a few tries, but she finally eased a long roll out of his nostril and dropped it into an evidence bag.

"It looks like a newspaper article." Bel took it from her and unrolled the coil. It was indeed a newspaper clipping wrapped in plastic to save it from disintegrating in the snot and blood. "There's not much information here, though," she said after scanning the text. "It's from a few years ago, and it mentions Aesop's Files' renewal for another season. Talks about how the show achieved sudden viral success despite its near cancelation."

"We already know this case revolves around the show, so why leave this in Rot's nose?" Olivia asked.

"A negative of trees, a weather report, and a news article," Griffin said. "Why any of them?"

"Why," Bel whispered. "It's the why. The trees were where, the weather report's date was the when, and this show's renewal is the why. Cryptic? Very, but that's because the killer doesn't want us solving his riddle yet. He's not done. Two more have to die before he makes his point, and he's preventing us from arriving at the finale before he can lead us there. That's why he keeps killing crew members away from the sets, but on properties we'll find." She repeated Eamon's conclusion. "He's taking us on a journey so we understand why he started this, but his explanations are vague to ensure he finishes."

"Which fits our Orion Chayce theory," Griffin said. "He's getting revenge, and he wants us to know why, but only after he's done."

"I'm sure once we figure it out, it'll be obvious," Bel said.

"We keep circling back to Chayce, but could it be someone from Bajka?" Olivia chimed in. "Rossa was killed on the Reale Estate, which belongs to Mr. Stone, who's dating Bel. Granted, that one's easy to explain since it was close to the shoot. But then Roja was discovered on the hiking trails where Mr. Orso often hikes, and lastly, Rot is in Bel's backyard. Three locations connected to the police and easily found."

Bel tried not to flinch at her partner's use of Ewan and Eamon's last names. At least she'd called her by her first. She had a point, though. She and Ewan hadn't broadcast their breakup, so unless the killer was in their close circle, he would've assumed they were still a couple. The first two bodies were found on land associated with their boyfriends. The third in Bel's backyard. Was Olivia's apartment the next site?

"The show has location scouts," Griffin said. "People whose job requires them to traipse all over, taking pictures and discussing shooting angles. It wouldn't be hard for them to pinpoint ideal locations. Plus, Taron Monroe found Emerson by simply following her home. Our town is packed with phone-obsessed crime junkies. How difficult would it be for someone to follow us through the throng? We're so busy trying to protect a show that refuses to shut down that we forget to look over our own shoulders."

"Besides, the death on my property was connected to the shoot," Eamon said. "Traveling to a bathroom would take time, so I guarantee the killer predicted a crew member would wander into the woods to urinate instead of trekking down the trails. As for the second body, it was near a trail. Bajka is crawling with newcomers, and someone is undoubtedly either a hiker or a fitness enthusiast. The cold would've preserved Roja until someone ventured up there, so I doubt the killer expected Ewan specifically. Isobel's cabin is the only one he explicitly targeted."

"And with her stunt in The Wolf's car, everyone's been talking about her," Griffin said. "Makes sense why the body was posed in her backyard. A little ballsy, though. Killing Rot minutes before Emerson got home."

"It gets dark early this time of year," Olivia said. "It's possibly more about waiting until dark than scaring Bel. She's been working late because of the case. We didn't release that Randall tried choking her to death to the press. The public doesn't know she's still recovering, so the killer probably assumed she'd arrive home long after he left Mr. Rot on this bench."

"I agree with that assessment," Lina said. "Rot's wounds are slightly more haphazard than the women's. The killer was in a rush."

"If I'd only been a few minutes earlier," Bel said. "I would've caught him."

"Thank god you weren't," Eamon and Griffin said simultaneously.

"I could've stopped this," Bel argued.

"Or you could be sitting here beside Rot," Griffin said.

"I have a gun."

"And it was dark. You didn't notice anything was amiss until you kicked the box. He could've attacked while your back was turned."

"Give me some credit," she said. "I did just survive a car crash."

"Oh, sweetheart." Lina patted her back. "We give you plenty of credit, but that's why we're thankful you weren't here. None

Evidence of a Folktale

of us want you going up against another psycho... again. You've gotten lucky, and we don't want to tempt whatever guardian angel is protecting you. You in my morgue was one time too many. And on that note, let's load the body. I'll see either you or Olivia at the autopsy."

IT WAS WELL past midnight by the time both the press and police vacated Bel's bloodstained property. Griffin was the last to leave, but before he climbed into his truck, he grabbed Eamon's arm.

"I don't want her staying here. Not tonight at least." He kept his voice low, but Bel heard him all the same. "Take her home with you."

Eamon nodded, not that he needed Griffin's orders. Bel had no intention of sleeping in her own bed until the bloody snow melted from her backyard.

"Would you clean that up?" she asked when they finally retreated inside her cabin to pack her an overnight bag. She didn't need to gather Cerberus' things since Eamon's mansion had morphed into a pet store.

"Won't forensics need it?" he asked.

"They took what they needed, and the elements have compromised the blood," she said. "If this were a building, we'd eventually approve a biohazard cleaning crew to sanitize the floor, but since this is my backyard..."

"You want the vampire hybrid to handle your dirty work?" He winked at her.

"Don't make me sound like I'm in that show." She aimed a warning finger at him. "But yes. You aren't exactly squeamish."

"Neither are you." He took her bag from her and threw it over his shoulder, playfully nudging her jaw before grabbing Cerberus' leash. "I've heard stories from your own mouth about some of your autopsies." He waited for her to exit the cabin, and

293

after locking up, he helped her dog into her car. "But of course, I'll handle it. Do you want the bench cleaned or replaced?"

"Replaced. Even if you scrub the blood off, I'll still see him sitting there every time I look out my window." She collapsed in the passenger side of the SUV. It was her car, but all her adrenaline had been burned away, leaving her empty and sore. She was overdue for her next dose of painkillers, and everything within her longed to curl up and cease to exist.

"Consider it gone." Eamon backed out of her parking spot and slid his hand onto her thigh as he sped off down the street. Another reason Bel wanted him to drive. They'd get home faster.

"We got interrupted earlier," she said to keep herself awake. "You scented something. Is the killer like you?"

"I think so, but I can't be certain. The scent was strong, but he could've come into contact with something before his death."

"Come in contact? How?"

"Ewan and I aren't the only beings of power in town, remember? But don't worry." He squeezed her thigh to keep her from interrupting. "Fantasy conventions draw everything from your garden variety witch to shifters to those in between."

"How many people with unnatural powers are here?" she asked.

"I can't give you a number, but it's enough for me to catch scents of them everywhere. Some I recognize and some I don't. And before you ask why, my kind survives by hiding. We don't exactly have support groups or chat rooms, and everyone hides from me. I mean death for humans and monsters alike, so I haven't met everything out there. It's whyEwan hid in Bajka when that hunter was after his pack. My scent shielded him. But most here are harmless. They enjoy settings like this because they don't have to hide, and a family of witches taking their kids to meet an actor who plays a werewolf isn't concerning."

"Except one of these harmless visitors might be killing

people, so it's become concerning." Bel straightened in her seat, fully awake now.

"The number of supernaturals who attend events like this almost outnumber mortals. You probably met a lot of shifters you assumed were humans in costume, especially if you worked those big conventions in New York." Eamon said as he parked before his front door.

"Are you serious?"

"Not people like Ewan. He's incredibly powerful. It's why his bear is so massive. He's an alpha predator, but most shifters are weak imitations of what they used to be because of their decades of interbreeding with humans. Some makeup, and they look like every other cosplaying mortal."

"So when Olivia freaked out over that kid in a mask, she might've had cause?" Bel waited for Eamon to open the door, and then the trio climbed the grand staircase to the master bedroom.

"Maybe."

"But could something powerful be in town? If they can sense you, they know you can scent them. What if they're hanging on the outskirts so the lesser powers mask them?"

"It's entirely possible. I had trouble tracking down Ewan when he first moved here because he avoided me and kept to his human form."

"You didn't find him until we arrested him."

"Because his scent was all over somewhere you frequent." Eamon dropped her bags at the foot of his bed.

"What about me? Have I come into contact with anything?"

"A lot. Especially after you work the signings. So, to answer your question, I can't tell if someone of power murdered the producer. If only the cast and crew were here, I could give you a definitive answer, but hundreds of conflicting scents are transferring between bodies because everyone's touching and hugging and crowding and shoving. I can't be certain. A creature could've killed Rot. Or he might have hugged one for a photo or knocked into them while ordering coffee or had a one-night stand with a supernatural. He wasn't ugly, and he was a rich man. I'm sure plenty of women tried to get him into bed, and that would cause a massive scent transfer."

"So does that mean..." Bel paused with her pants halfway down her legs.

"It does." Eamon kissed her cheek before collapsing to the mattress.

"Oh god." She blushed a deep pink.

"If it makes you feel better, I always smell like you now, too. Maybe that's why that young witch fled from me the other day. She realized I was a very taken man." He leaned forward and captured her waist, pulling her half-clothed body into bed with him. "But it's a good thing. Every supernatural being you've encountered these past weeks knows you belong to someone powerful. Unless they have a death wish, most will give you a wide birth."

"Except that doesn't always work. Crazies still come for me... although, most have been human lately," she said as she wiggled out of her clothes and slid below the sheets. "I guess the shield your scent offers makes up for people smelling who I sleep with."

"It's not foolproof, but it's one more layer of protection," Eamon wrapped her in his arms. "Especially if this killer is like me or Ewan."

"It didn't stop him from killing outside my home, though."

"But he hasn't come for you."

"True." Bel buried her face in Eamon's chest as Cerberus circled five times before laying across their legs. "What do I do? This show refuses to halt filming or cancel its events. Something's off about Aesop's Files, and if a predator is hunting in this town, what good are the police? They couldn't help in the Darling case, and Pann was just a mortal with a magic-laced tattoo. Do I let Griffin walk around blind, or do I give him a heads up?"

"That's up to you," Eamon said. "He knows there's something different about me, but he doesn't care to learn any truth beyond that. If he was notified, though, Ewan and I could help monitor things."

"But you aren't God. You can't be everywhere at once."

"So, it sounds like you have your answer."

"Do you have a second?" Bel asked.

"Sure." Griffin gestured for her to come into his office. "Learn anything new at the autopsy?"

"No." She collapsed onto the couch. Olivia had graciously attended the morning's postmortem to let her rest, and the two had exchanged notes by their desks before Bel knocked on her boss' door. "Same cause of death as Rossa and Roja. Same wounds, same red cloak, same box, and no evidence, no fingerprints, no defensive wounds, no fur. This guy is good. He knows what we're looking for and makes sure we never find it."

"Mimicking the cop show a little too closely," Griffin said. "A lot of shows have consultants. If the killer is Chayce searching for revenge, he had plenty of opportunities to question them."

"About that," Bel said. Now was as good a time as any to sound crazy. "You know our theory about a set prop creating the claw wounds?"

"Yeah..." he nodded.

"What if they weren't?"

Griffin stared at her, his understanding not catching her meaning.

"What if the claws weren't props?" she repeated. "What if they're real?"

"Real?" He pinched his eyebrows to ask if she was okay to be back at work, and she had to fight the urge not to cringe.

"Yeah." The word was painful to speak.

"Um..." He shook his head. "Is that even possible?"

"How do you want me to answer that?" she asked.

"I think you just did." Griffin cursed as he finally caught her drift, and with a frustrated breath, he leaned back in his chair. "I obviously can't share this... possibility."

"No, but I felt uncomfortable leaving you in the dark. And it's just a *'what if'* question right now. Eamon said—"

"I don't want to hear it." Griffin cut her off with a wave of his hand. "Knowing real claws might be to blame is enough." He cursed again. "And you know what pisses me off about that? It makes sense. The nature of the crimes and the lack of evidence. Humans aren't that clean..." he paused, staring at her as if he remembered something, and Bel knew he was picturing Alcina Magus' crime scenes. She'd built her victims into furniture, yet she hadn't left so much as a speck of sawdust behind.

"Anyway, we need to halt production," he continued. "It's bad enough that someone is murdering crew members, but if we have some sort of *'thing'* after us, that'll get messy fast."

"Both Evelyn Pierce and Alistair Rot were adamant about not shutting down, but she might be more receptive now that her partner is dead," Bel said.

"I hope so." He grabbed his phone. "And if they refuse, I'll call the mayor. Maybe he can help our cause."

But before he could dial, his cell blared to life, startling both of them. "Sheriff Griffin..." he answered on the first ring. "Yes, thank you for calling me back. Let me put you on speaker." He glanced at Bel and mouthed, *"Orion Chayce's parole officer."*

She nodded, and he tapped the speaker button.

"All right, go ahead."

"As I was saying, Sheriff, sorry I missed your last call," the

Evidence of a Folktale

parole officer said. "We've had a hectic twenty-four hours. We found Orion Chayce."

"You did?" Griffin asked, his hopes rising. "Where?"

"In the hospital."

"The hospital?" Bel and Griffin asked in unison.

"Yes, it was an unfortunate accident," the officer said. "He didn't violate his parole. Mr. Chayce was out for a jog when a car hit him. He was running in the park by his residence, so he didn't think to carry his phone or ID. The driver ran over a nail which popped a tire. He lost control and crashed into Chayce while he was crossing the street. He was rushed to the hospital after hitting his head and suffered severe brain swelling. The doctors put him in a medically induced coma to help reduce the inflammation. We couldn't find him because they'd listed him as a John Doe. He woke after a few days, but with the brain injury, his recovery has been slow. He didn't remember who he was until yesterday."

"And he's been in the hospital this entire time?" Griffin asked.

"He has."

"And he's still there?"

"He is. Now that he's remembered his name, the doctors believe he'll go home soon, but they want to keep him for a few more days."

"I'm glad he recovered." Griffin shifted to stare at Bel, their only suspect vanishing into nothingness.

"Us too," the officer said. "And even though I wouldn't wish an accident like this on anyone, I'm thankful he didn't violate parole. Chayce is a good man. He's been working hard since he got out, and I didn't want to see him go back inside."

"That's great," Griffin said. "Before I go, can I ask one more question?"

"Shoot."

"What's your opinion of him? Did Chayce do what he was accused of?"

"It was an accident," the man said.

"I realize that, but I'm sure you've seen the news about our Aesop's Files case. Chayce's name has surfaced more than once as well as doubt surrounding his guilt."

"I've heard rumors of doubt too, but he was found guilty. I'll never know what happened on set, but Orion Chayce isn't irresponsible or cruel. It's why his disappearance was so alarming. He isn't the type to jeopardize his future."

Bel and Griffin shared a silent exchange that was more conversation than most could convey with an entire dictionary.

"I see," the sheriff said. "Thank you for returning my call."

"No problem. Have a good day." The man hung up, and both officers sagged in their seats.

"I'm glad the guy's okay, but that leaves us with nothing," Bel said. "We've ruled out Alaric Randall and Orion Chayce. We have no other suspects."

"Where do we look now?" Griffin crumbled the junk papers on his desk and launched them into the trash with a little too much force.

"It would help us narrow our suspect pool down if fans weren't flooding our town for these events," Bel said.

"Or it could take the killer with them if they leave."

"It wouldn't. He's not done. If the killer's a fan, he'd find a way to stay behind, but now I wonder if he's a current show employee. We believe the killer is trusted among the cast and crew, and he's someone who knows enough police procedure to keep us guessing. The first victim was the head writer, and they research forensics and law enforcement for the scripts. Multiple police consultants have worked on Aesop's Files over the years, so I'm sure their writers know far too much about how to stage a clean murder scene. I might have even helped. I was there protecting Taron, but to sell the act, I acted as a

Evidence of a Folktale

consultant. Everyone asked me questions. I thought I was helping, but what if I was feeding the killer all the info that he needed to trick us?"

"With Chayce and Randall eliminated, that's the next most logical place to start. I'll have Gold look into the show's writers and consultants." Griffin stood and shrugged into his coat. "I'm going to talk to Miss Pierce. I suspect she'll be more receptive to our request now that our killer is targeting producers."

"I can help Olivia."

"No." He grabbed his keys and aimed for the door. "This is only your second day back after the accident, and you just found a dead man in your backyard. You're working from the station."

"Sheriff—"

"This isn't up for debate, Emerson. Give me at least one more day before I have to start worrying about you again." And before she could protest further, he exited his office.

"How did it go?" Bel asked instead of saying hello.

"Better than I expected and worse than I wanted," Griffin answered through the connection, and she pinned her phone between her shoulder and ear to free up her hands.

"I got the mayor involved, and thankfully the studio listened to reason," he said. "Evelyn Pierce is to thank for that. Alistair Rot's death proved she isn't safe, so they agreed to cancel the fan events."

"That's good," Bel said. "Not that there are many left."

"No, but it'll reduce our town's population. Not everyone will leave, but we're putting out a request that they do. The fewer people, the more the killer will stand out... I hope."

"I'm guessing that's what went better than expected," she said. "What's the part that didn't?"

"They refuse to halt filming," he said. "Moving locations

would require massive reshoots. It would cost them too much, so they'll stay and finish the episodes."

"I'm glad I'm not a fan of this show because their behavior would've ruined it for me. They've had three brutal deaths, and their bottom line is still worth more than their crew's lives."

"Let's just hope the reduced population will help us find the killer before he finishes his five *W's*."

"Speaking of the *W's*, I found the full article that Rot's nose clue came from," Bel said. "It was published five years ago in an entertainment journal, but it's nothing groundbreaking. It just detailed how Aesop's Files aired for a few short seasons with abysmal viewership and was on the verge of cancellation when it suddenly became one of the most streamed shows. It did so well that it was renewed instead of being canceled, and here we are with a show so popular, they unconventionally turn their location shoots into conventions."

"And you still believe that's the why?" he asked.

"I do. I'm just not sure how it fits," she answered. "This article is dated five years ago, so I'd wondered if the weather report was from the same year. The contact lens image is of generic snowy trees. That eliminates the southern states, but that still leaves half the country. Plus, even if something happened five years ago in January that drove someone to kill crew members, that's thirty-one days and multiple states to search."

"Are there other articles about the show's renewal?" Griffin asked.

"Tons."

"Did you read any?"

"Some, but they all say the same thing. Nothing details what made the show popular."

"Did you search for January and red cloaks?" he asked.

"Yes," she answered. "I tried multiple variations, but I didn't find anything. It was a long shot, anyway. There are an average of twenty thousand reported homicides in the United States every year. Robberies, burglaries, assaults, and violent crimes number in the millions. Trying to uncover what happened in January five years ago—if that's even the right year—is almost impossible, especially if the riddles aren't referencing a crime. We won't find police or news reports about personal issues. I don't know what to search for, but something about this show's renewal is worth killing over."

"Well, keep looking," Griffin said. "And in the meantime, let's pray Gold has luck with the writers' consultants."

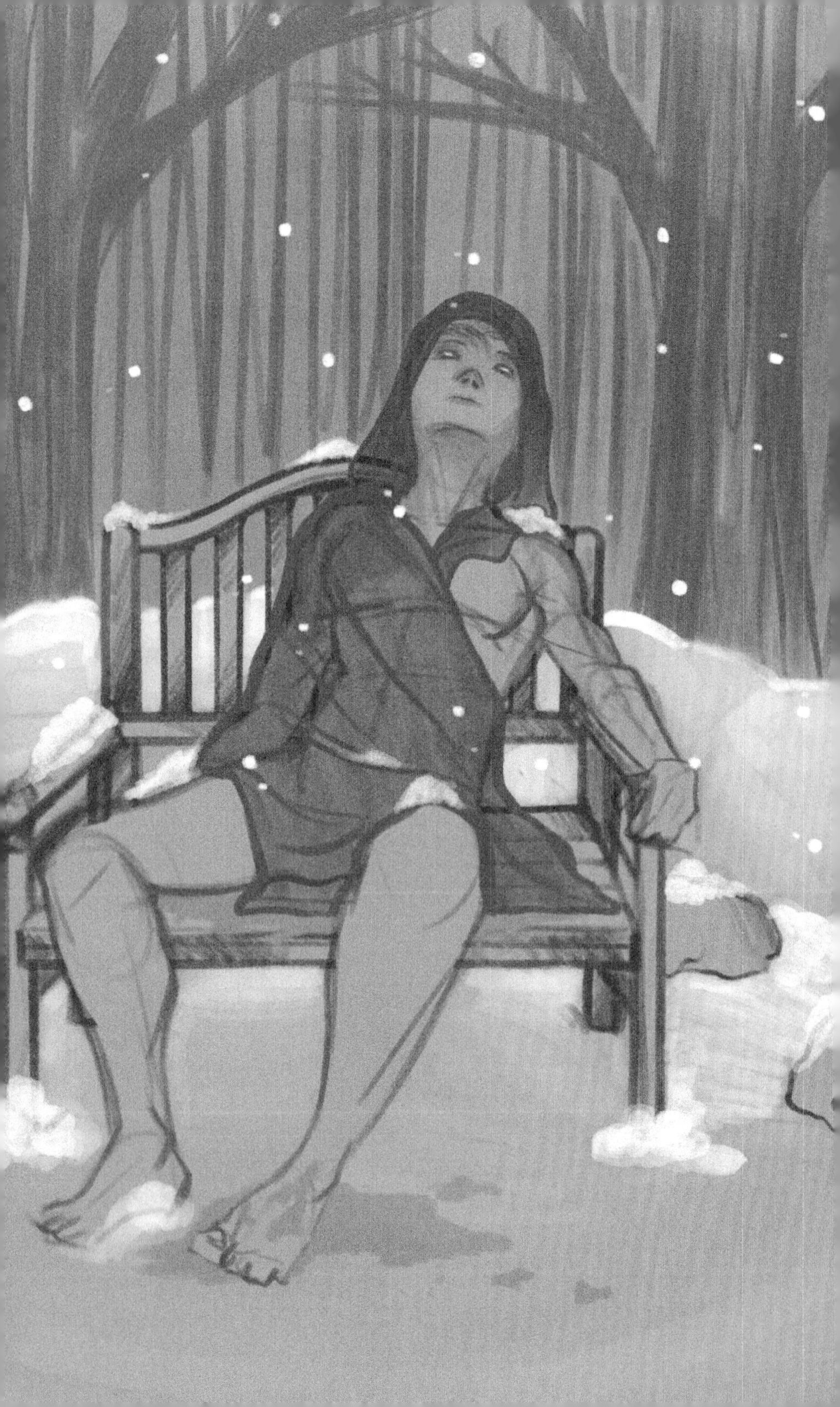

Chapter Nineteen

EXCEPT FOR THE RANDOM FILM SET BEING CONSTRUCTED, AND the occasional fan refusing to vacate the hotel rooms they paid for, Bajka regained a semblance of her former self over the next few days. The peace was a welcomed relief, but with it arrived a mountain of dead ends. There were, thankfully, no more murders, but there were also no new leads, evidence, or suspects. The police were no closer to solving the murders of Rossa, Roja, and Rot than they were a few weeks ago, and they'd become the laughingstock of the national news outlets. The backward town that let three of Aesop's File's crew members die and the detectives too stupid to figure anything out. Bel was surprised a task force hadn't been sent to seize control of the case, but then again, that would halt filming, and the studio seemed keen never to let that happen.

"Are you becoming a secret fan on me?" she whispered as she curled against Eamon's side, the sounds of Aesop's Files playing on the television waking her. It had taken a few days for her to work up the courage to sleep at home, even though Eamon had replaced the bloody bench, and this was their first night back in her cabin.

"No." He wrapped an arm around her as his eyes remained glued to the episode, and Bel reached across his stomach to scratch Cerberus' head. Her mattress was significantly smaller than Eamon's, but he was a good sport about her and her dog sandwiching him until he could barely move.

"Your comment has been bothering me," he said, as if that explained why he was binging the show in the middle of the night.

"What comment?" she asked. They hadn't talked about anything serious over the past few days. Had she said something hurtful or concerning by accident?

"About why a show with no viewership went viral overnight," he answered, and Bel sagged in relief. That comment. She'd given up trying to hide case details from him. She never shared her work with civilians, but was an ancient evil really a civilian?

"I was curious about the season that transformed an almost canceled show into a success," he continued. "Aesop's Files aired for a few years with a minimal budget and short seasons, but its fame was nonexistent, and then suddenly it became a cult classic. I figured something must've happened. You're too busy to watch multiple seasons, so I decided to help you. I started with season one and have been working my way through every episode, hunting for what transformed its viewership. I was interested to see if it was different writers, a new hot actor, or maybe steamier sex scenes."

"Have you found anything?" Bel asked, suddenly wide awake.

"Not a single thing." Eamon sagged against her. "This show was bad. Like I'm immortal, and it's still a waste of my time bad."

"Seriously? I've seen a few episodes. I don't love it, but I didn't think it was that awful."

"I only just started the newer seasons, and I'll admit those are entertaining. The writing and production value improves as it goes on, but I'm talking specifically about the season that went viral," he said. "It sucks. I was alive when the cinema was invented. I saw the classics before they became classics, so I think I'm a decent judge of film quality, and Aesop's File's original episodes are painful to watch. I had to force myself to keep going because I kept thinking surely something must've happened in that transition season to change the studio's mind, but no. It was as boring as the others. It eventually improved, but based on the material available at the time, it should've been canceled."

"It's really that bad?" Bel asked. "So why wasn't it?"

"I looked into that," Eamon said. "Some people enjoy garbage television. I figured a celebrity watched it and became a fan, therefore influencing their fans. I also considered a scandal. Something so controversial it made viewers tune it. I found nothing. When they said this show blew up overnight, they literally meant overnight, and there's only one force I can think of that's strong enough to accomplish that."

"Someone involved has connections?"

"No. A deal... much like the one Charles Blaubart struck to get his scalpel."

"Black magic," Bel whispered.

"Yes. Black magic can grant you your wildest dreams, but the price is always devastating. Alcina Magus used black magic to bind me to her servitude, and you were the sacrifice needed to complete the curse. We were strangers, but you became the only person I've ever truly loved. If Alcina's curse had succeeded, her deal would've robbed me of my future." He twisted to kiss her head before continuing.

"Alcina consumed the hearts of her victims to steal your neighbor's face. Charles Blaubart's scalpel cost him his wife, and then all the women he tried to replace her with. Black magic always comes at a price, and you rarely understand the gravity of what you'll sacrifice until it's too late."

"You think someone made a deal to stop Aesop's Files from being canceled?" Bel asked. "The victims? Are they the ones who struck the deal? Are their deaths after they achieved success the price that they didn't know they'd pay?"

"It would explain the scent on the producer's body," Eamon said. "I can't be certain, but their refusal to pause filming despite the murders. The show's fame despite its mediocrity. It makes sense."

"Then why the red cloaks and the claw wounds?"

"Who knows? Maybe it means something to the entity. Maybe I'm wrong and the deaths aren't the price. It just feels a little too coincidental."

"I agree. This entire case has been bothering me. I couldn't understand why they refused to pause filming. Three brutal deaths are more important than an episode, but not to a deal, right?"

"Black magic is all-consuming. Even those who aren't involved suffer the effects, for as they say, the show must go on."

"My theory predicts there will be two more murders," Bel said. "Is that a useless idea now?"

"No. Based on the clues, it's a sound conclusion, but you need to be careful, Detective." Eamon sat up, gently shifting Cerberus's drooling head off his abdomen so he could study her in the darkness. "If an entity made a deal with this show, it won't stop until its debt is settled, and it won't care who's standing in its way. You included. I know you want to find the killer, but you've encountered people who've struck deals before. You barely survived."

"I have a panic button now," she said. "You'll be there."

"I always promise I will, yet I'm always too late."

"Not next time." She smiled as she peeled his hand off her cheek and pressed it against her chest. "I can feel it, but I'll try not to jump into the back seats of any more cars. Filming is almost over, and I think the killer chose Bajka as his hunting ground because of its miles of undeveloped land. It's a lot easier to kill celebrities undetected here. I obviously don't want people to die, but once the cast and crew leave town, my job of protecting them is over. Once they return home, they are another department's responsibility, and probably one much larger than ours. So, all I have to do is keep them alive until shooting ends."

"DO YOU WANT MORE COFFEE?" Bel asked as they sat in the kitchen eating breakfast. "Or can I finish—"

"Quiet." Eamon silenced her with a hand pressed against her mouth, and for a split second, she gawked at his rudeness before realizing what it meant.

"It's a woman," he said after listening to the stillness. "She's screaming." He launched to his feet, and the urgency in his tone took her with him. The couple rushed for the door, shoving boots and coats over their pajamas, and pausing for Bel to grab her badge and gun, they bolted from the house.

"Down there." Eamon caught her hand and dragged her down the street. Bel had driven the entire length of this road when she moved to Bajka. The neighborhood lined a dead end with expansive stretches of trees between each home, making for a private existence, but she'd ultimately chosen the empty cabin across from Vera's. They were the first two on the lane, and being closer to town was best in the event of police emergencies. It was also the cheapest model since it was a single room.

An inconsolable scream ripped through the frigid air, and she finally heard what Eamon's senses had detected at the breakfast table.

"Is it him?" She aimed the gun out before her because that unnerving wail was pure fear. It was the sound of a woman being chased through the snow by a predator who wanted to flay her open and bleed her dry.

Eamon tugged her faster, and she had her answer. Their red hood killer was here... on her street once again. He'd waited for her to grow brave enough to return home, and then he reared his bloodthirsty head.

"Help!" a woman screamed. "Help me!"

The couple rounded a bend in the road, and a storm of white and red barreled for them.

"Help! Oh my god, please!" A woman aimed for them, a bed sheet fluttering in the wind behind her, and Bel realized what she was seeing. The hysterical stranger was naked and barefoot, her only protection against the cold a white sheet stained with blood. Had their killer tried to force her into a red cloak? Had they finally found a victim who'd fought back?

"Ma'am!" Bel shouted over her hysterics. "I'm with the Bajka Police. Are you hurt?"

"Oh my god!" the woman screamed, deaf to her question. "Oh my god, please. Please help me!"

"Ma'am, where are you hurt?" Bel shoved her gun into Eamon's hands before capturing the woman's biceps in gentle fists, but her neighbor continued to scream as if she couldn't see the couple.

"Where are you hurt?" Bel repeated

"It's not her blood," Eamon interrupted, and Bel discreetly grabbed the sheet and pulled it away from the stranger's stomach. Smooth skin met her eyes. Her neighbor wasn't the victim, but she wasn't from Aesop's Files, either. So whose blood did she wear?

"The man who did this?" Bel asked. "Is he still here? Is he in the house?"

"Oh god!" Her neighbor stumbled, almost toppling to the pavement, but Bel held her tight.

"Is he still in the house?" she repeated.

"Yes!" the woman screamed, and Bel released her, seizing her gun from Eamon as she bolted for the cabin's front door.

He chased wordlessly after her, slipping protectively before her as they crossed the threshold, and moving as if they were one body, they followed the trail of bloody footprints.

"Is he here?" Bel whispered as they slipped silently down the hall to the bedrooms. Unlike her single-room cabin, this model resembled a traditional home with the living room, dining room, and kitchen at the front and a hallway that led to the solitary bathroom and bedroom at the rear.

"The house is still," he answered. "He probably fled when your neighbor escaped. Is she married?"

"I don't know. I've never met her."

Eamon paused before the bedroom door, listening for any signs of life, and then he pushed it open to follow the bloody footprints.

"Eamon," Bel gasped as she froze in the middle of the room. "It was him. He was here, and he was waiting for me to move back home." She patted her pockets. "I forgot my phone. Do you have yours?"

"No, but there's a landline in the kitchen," he said. "I'll call Griffin, but why the change of location? Why kill inside this time?"

"He didn't." Bel walked to the floor-length curtains. "You don't feel cold like I do, but it's freezing in here." She grabbed the fabric and yanked it wide to reveal a sliding glass door that led directly into the woods. It was open, letting the outdoors rush in, and with the morning sunlight pouring into the room, the horrifying bloodbath burned to life in vibrant color.

For there, on her neighbor's bed, lay a naked and eviscerated Warren Rouge, his only covering a blood-soaked red hooded cloak.

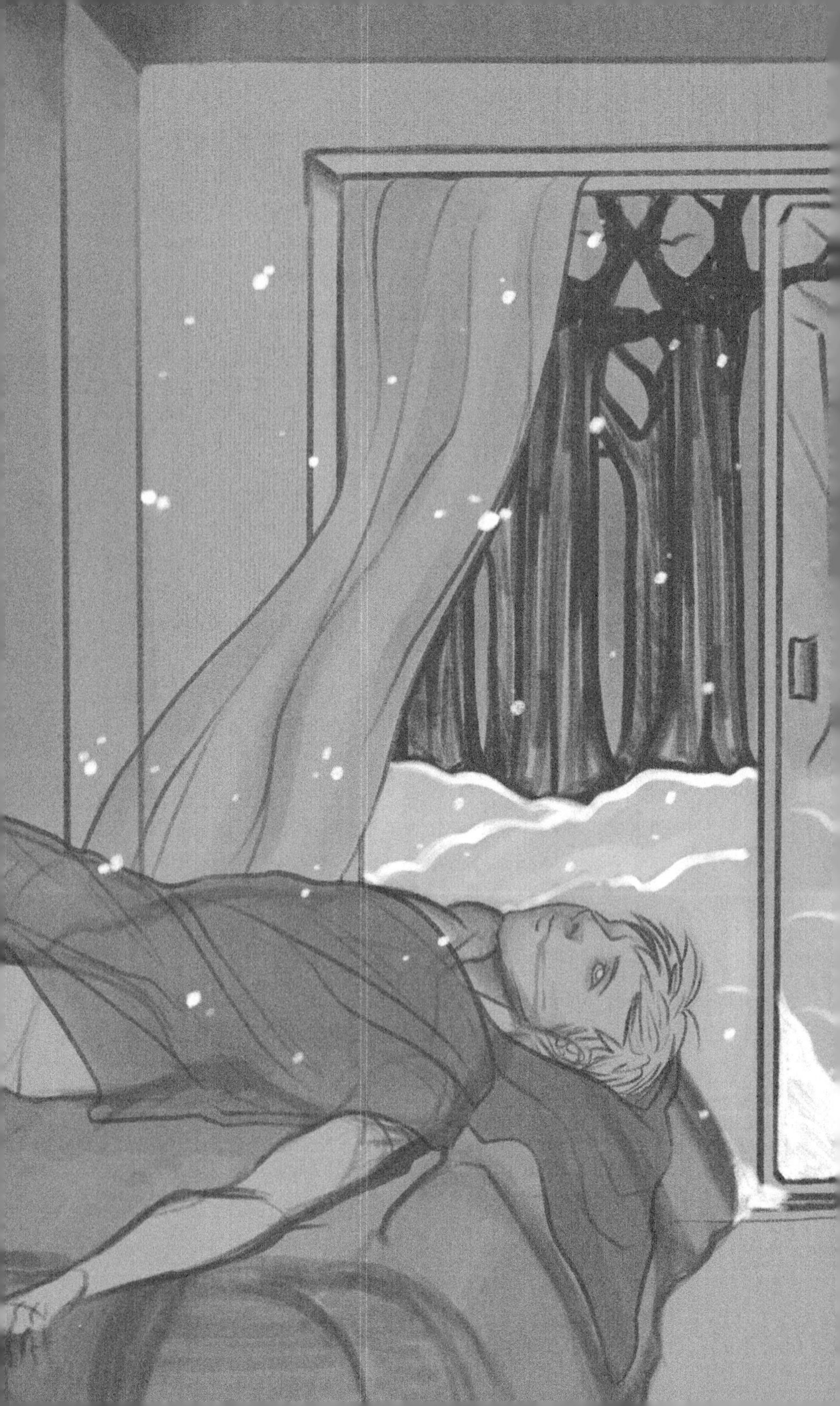

Chapter Twenty

"WARREN ROUGE," GRIFFIN SAID AS HE STARED AT THE AESOP'S Files' director. "This isn't good."

"No, it isn't," Bel whispered. "He's escalating. A writer, a costume designer, a producer, and now the director."

"All that remains is an actor," Eamon said, and the sheriff looked like he might pass out at that prospect.

"What's Rouge doing here, though?" Olivia asked. "The cast and crew know not to leave the bed-and-breakfast after filming."

"I think the naked woman wearing a sheet is the answer to that question," Griffin said. "But how did he get past our patrol units?"

"Gwen Rossa never returned to the inn," Bel said. "Rouge could've done the same."

"Only Gwen Rossa didn't know crew members were being hunted at night. Our director here did." Griffin cursed as he ran his fingers through his hair. "That poor woman. He killed Rouge right next to her while she slept. There are no footprints in the snow leading to the sliding door, so our killer probably entered from the front walkway. The couple was already naked, so he only needed to drape the cloak over him and wait for her to wake up."

"How on earth did they sleep through this?" Olivia answered.

"One-night stands are usually preceded by alcohol," Eamon said, and while his observation was common sense, Bel guessed it was because he smelled the liquor wafting off the body. "They were probably too drunk to hear an intruder."

"If this was a one-night stand, I'll talk to my neighbor," Bel said. "She might feel more comfortable giving her statement to a woman."

"Sounds good," Griffin said. "Is there a box?" He scanned the room for the white and red gift.

"Yeah. Kitchen counter," Bel said. "I spotted it when I used the landline to call you, but I left it to be photographed. I'll go grab it." She retreated down the hall just as Lina Thum stepped into the cabin.

"Is it true?" she asked. "Is it the director?"

"Yes." Bel grabbed the tiny box.

"Good god. How is this happening?" She looked around. "And inside? Why did he change M.O.s for this one?"

"He didn't," Bel said. "The bed's before an open glass door that leads into the woods."

"I saw your neighbor outside. They're saying she woke up to find him dead beside her."

"She did."

"That poor woman," Lina gasped as she confronted the sight of Warren Rouge's brutalized body. "I don't know if I'd ever recover from that."

"It's odd that he attacked with a witness," Olivia said. "But then again, with our security so tight, this was probably our killer's only shot at taking out Rouge. I guess our director didn't think leaving the bed-and-breakfast for a hookup was dangerous."

Evidence of a Folktale

"He should've," Bel said. "Ellery Roja left to get chips, and it killed her."

"It's impossible to protect people who won't halt production or follow the rules," Griffin sighed, his chest deflating like a punctured balloon.

"They refuse to listen, yet we're the ones who will be blamed," Lina said. "All this could've been prevented if they'd just shut down after Gwen Rossa's death."

"No point in descending that rabbit hole," Griffin said. "What's in the box?"

With gloved fingers, Bel untied the bow and tugged the lid off. "Oh... god." Her lips recoiled at the sight. "It's a tooth."

"A tooth?" Griffin leaned over, and she aimed the box's contents at him. "That's a canine, and it looks like it was just pulled."

"It's probably Rouge's," Lina said. "But where's the riddle? All the other boxes came with riddles."

"No," Bel said. "All the boxes came with body parts. Eyes, ears, and nose. This is the same. What big teeth you have."

"So, the clue's in his mouth." The medical examiner stepped to the head of the bed and pried Rouge's lips apart. "It's his tooth," she confirmed, angling his face so everyone could see the missing canine. "And there is definitely something in here." She withdrew a plastic-wrapped square of folded paper. "Here. My hands are dirty." She placed it on Bel's waiting palm.

Bel peeled off the wrapping and dropped it into the evidence bag Olivia held open for her. Changing her gloves to a fresh pair, she pulled the paper back out and unfolded it. "It's a piece of an autopsy report." She showed it to Lina. "It's incomplete, though."

"It's just the body diagram where we denote wound locations." The medical examiner leaned closer, and Bel watched her face go from studious to horrified. "If this is a real autopsy

315

report, it depicts a victim who was stabbed five times in the abdomen."

The entire room's attention snapped to Warren Rouge's disemboweled belly.

"It's the what," Olivia's southern accent broke the heavy silence. "Where? In the snowy trees. When? January. Why? Because the show was renewed. What? Five stabbings to the abdomen."

"I'll see if I can find what autopsy this belongs to," Lina said. "Don't get your hopes up, though. There are thousands of fatal stabbings every year, and all we know is January. We don't know city or year."

"Wouldn't it be five years ago when that article was published?" Olivia asked.

"Maybe, maybe not," the M.E. said. "These clues have been incredibly vague. I bet this is no different."

"There's one more victim to go," Bel said. "He doesn't want us figuring out who his last target is before he kills them."

"But we will. We have to." Griffin broke free of the trance this destructive death had placed all of them under. "All right, Mr. Stone. I have to ask you to leave so the techs have room to work. Emerson, you aren't exactly dressed for a crime scene, so can you go outside and talk to your neighbor about last night? Also, the press is arriving, but I don't want anyone talking yet. Make sure no one does anything stupid."

"Will do." She grabbed Eamon's arm and pushed him before her, following in his footsteps so they wouldn't step in the blood on the carpet.

"I'm sorry that we have to meet this way, but I'm Detective Isobel Emerson," Bel said when they rejoined her neighbor and the deputies outside. "I live in the cabin down the road." She gestured toward her home.

"You're where they found the producer's body, right?" the woman asked. She was no longer hysterical, and she now wore

Evidence of a Folktale

proper winter attire, but the look in her eyes matched the same expression Bel had worn the night Alistair Rot bled out in her backyard.

"I am," Bel answered, and the woman's gaze flicked to Eamon as she waited for him to introduce himself, and it wasn't lost on Bel that she didn't recoil from his presence. She just stared at him as if she were resolved to accept whatever fate he inflicted on her. She'd already survived a monster. She had no fear left for the devil.

"Eamon Stone." He extended a hand, and she shook it.

"Chloe Rider," she said.

"Miss Rider, I understand this morning has been incredibly difficult for you, but if it's okay, can I ask you some questions?" Bel asked.

"How did he get into my house?" Chloe stared through Bel as if she were invisible, the violated cabin the only thing her eyes could focus on.

"There were no footprints in the snow or signs of forced entry, so I suspect he picked the front door lock," Bel said.

"I..." Chloe started. "I actually don't remember if I locked the front door. Oh god. Did I let him inside?"

"Don't feel guilty. He would've gotten inside, regardless. I know it doesn't feel like it, but you are very lucky. The man we're looking for is extremely dangerous." Bel waved down a passing tech and asked him to grab Olivia and check for signs of lock tampering.

"You're right. It doesn't feel like it." Chloe finally focused on Bel's face.

"I'm sorry. Is there someone we can call for you?"

"No. My sister lives a couple of neighborhoods over. I'll go stay with her."

"We'll have a deputy escort you, but if you're up to it, I need to ask you some questions."

"All right." Chloe sighed, resigned to her fate.

"Thank you." Bel shifted sideways to block Miss Rider from the news crews hoping to capture the winning shot, and catching her meaning, Eamon blocked both women with his size. "The Bajka Police Department advised the cast and crew of Aesop's Files to stay at the bed-and-breakfast when they weren't shooting. How did Warren Rouge end up here?"

"Most find Beau Draven sexy, but he's too pretty for me." Chloe shrugged. "I prefer men in their forties." She tossed her eyes up at Eamon to illustrate her point. "Warren was hot, and we're consenting adults. It's not a crime."

"Your date is not my concern," Bel assured her. "I'm worried about how he slipped past our deputies at the inn."

"I might have helped him with that," Chloe said.

"I see… What happened last night? If you remember, can you recount your movements from the time you met him until you woke this morning?"

"I was at the signing with the bomb threat," Chloe said. "Warren and I had instant chemistry when I got his autograph. I wanted to give him my number, but people were staring, so I left. Later on, I got a little tipsy at the bar and started talking about my regrets. Another fan overheard and told me I was Warren's type. He said the bed-and-breakfast had a wine-tasting menu, and he thought I should go and shoot my shot with Warren."

"This fan?" Bel asked. "What did he look like?"

"Couldn't tell you, other than he was a man wearing wolf makeup. It was after the signing, so everyone was still in costume."

Bel met Eamon's gaze, a wordless understanding passing between the couple. Had the killer dressed as a wolf to encourage Miss Rider to lure Rouge away from their protection, or was this simply star-struck fans excited about the idea of a famous one-night stand?

"Did you go to the inn?" she asked.

"No, I chickened out," Chloe said. "But I ran into him at The

Espresso Shot the other day. We had the same chemistry, and I was brave enough to write my number on his cup. He called last night and invited me over. The bed-and-breakfast upped their bar service to accommodate the cast and crew's curfews. He told me everyone was tipsy, so no one would notice if I showed up. I was thrilled he called, so we met up. We hit it off and drank a lot... probably too much." She fell silent as the gravity of her overconsumption struck her. "Then he asked if I wanted to get out of there. He didn't want to go to his room since the inn was packed. He wanted privacy. So I helped him sneak out, and we caught a cab here. He was hot, and it was fun until..." she trailed off.

"Did you notice anyone following you last night?" Bel asked. "Did anything unusual happen when you got home?"

"I was with Warren Rouge," Chloe emphasized. "I wasn't thinking about anything else."

"Right." Bel nodded, trying to keep the disappointment from reaching her face. Chloe Rider was the first witness their killer had left alive, but a drunk, star-struck woman was little help. "Do you remember what time you arrived home last night?"

"I don't know. Late?"

"Late as in after midnight or almost dawn?"

"Um..." Chloe kicked at the dirty snow with her toes. "Somewhere in between? Maybe two-ish? It was still dark."

"Do you have a security system?" Bel asked.

"No. But after this, I plan to get one... not for this cabin, though. I can't live here after this."

"I don't blame you. It took me days to face my house after Alistair Rot died in my backyard."

"I wish Warren died in my yard and not next to me." Chloe started sobbing, and Bel placed a comforting hand on her arm. "I liked him. How could anyone do this? How come you haven't arrested the murderer yet?"

Bel opened her mouth to answer, but what could she say? That she was failing at her job? That the killer might be a deal that wouldn't stop until the debt was paid? That every time she stood in the snow, she was transported back to that mountain with Charles Blaubart hunting her just like this killer hunted its hooded victims?

"We're doing everything we can," Bel settled on her standard answer despite its hollowness. "If you think of anything else, call me at the station, but you're free to go. I'll have a deputy escort you to your sister's." She waved an officer down and asked him to deliver Miss Rider to her family.

"Don't let what she said bother you." Eamon massaged her shoulders as Chloe ducked into the squad car. "This production has been uncooperative, and our town might be playing host to black magic. Neither of those bode well for justice."

"I know." Bel sagged against him, shutting her eyes as his thumbs worked out her knots. "But he killed Rouge next to her, and she woke up covered in his blood. He forced her to sleep beside a dead man. I can't even imagine that."

"So don't." Eamon kissed her cheek. "You've been through worse. Don't add more to your... plate." He bristled, and Bel scanned their surroundings in search of his annoyance.

"It's just Jerry." She reached behind her and patted his thigh. Jerry was the middle-aged cameraman from the news station that had aggressively chased her down during The Matchstick Girl case. Eamon feared his hyper focus on Bel was because he was the killer, but it turned out he was merely an eager father who followed his dream later in life.

Bel gave a small wave, and the cameraman jogged over to greet her, stumbling over his own feet when he saw the hulking man glowering at him.

"Hi, Jerry. How are the kids?" she asked.

"What?" he gawked at Eamon.

"The kids, Jerry," Bel repeated.

"Oh right, yeah." His excitable speech pattern returned as he collected himself... for the most part. "Everyone's good. Sorry about all this. I'll try to keep you out of the shots."

"Thank you."

"Me too," Eamon said, and Jerry looked like he'd swallowed his tongue.

"Right... sure. Who are you?"

"Hers." Eamon's evasiveness sent a thrill through Bel's chest, and she leaned her head back against him with a stifled grin.

"Clearly." Jerry fixated on his massive hands gripping her shoulders. "You guys make a good couple, though. I can see it."

"Thank you," Bel said. "We haven't released anything yet, so even if you hear any names—"

"I didn't," he finished for her. "Sure thing."

"Thanks, Jer—" His name died on her tongue when she registered who stood beyond the police tape... and what he was doing. She cursed, her skin flushing hot despite the morning's bitter chill, and without a goodbye, she ducked under the yellow tape and stormed through the squad cars for Beau Draven.

"But Warren's death won't be in vain," the actor said into his phone's camera. "His commitment to our show will never be forgotten, and I intend to honor his memory by taking up the director's mantel. Aesop's Files was our dream years ago, but now the show belongs to everyone. Warren wouldn't want us to give up."

Bel picked up her pace. He couldn't be saying those things, especially not on a live stream before an active crime scene. She wanted to strangle him for his flagrant lack of respect and common sense, but attacking a beloved actor while thousands of his fans watched was the worst idea, so she lunged behind his camera and seized the phone, using her hand to block the view.

"What's wrong with you?" she spat after she ended the livestream. "This is an active crime scene. Someone was murdered here. Violently. Have you no decency?"

"Give me back my phone," Beau demanded.

"No." Bel shoved it into her pocket. "We haven't released the victim's name or done the death notice yet, and you just broadcasted Rouge's murder to the entire world. His family doesn't deserve to find out that way, plastered across social media like trivial entertainment. Someone's killing members of your crew, and you're going live like this is some scene in your show. Well, it's not. This is real. This is a tragedy."

"All right, all right, point taken." Beau raised his hands in surrender. "I'll stay off the internet like a good boy. So, can I have my phone back?"

"Fine," she growled. "But if I see you on it—"

"Yeah, yeah, you'll be the bad cop," he said. "This is my big break."

"Big break?" Bel pinched her eyebrows at the sudden shift in conversation.

"Yes. If I direct the rest of the episodes while we're here, the studio will have to recognize my talent. This is the next step in my career."

"Are you serious?" She couldn't be hearing him right. A man had been brutally murdered, and all the actor could think of was progressing his career. "A killer is targeting your show. This needs to stop. You need to shut down production."

"Why would we do that?" Beau asked. "Warren would want us to continue. The fans want us to continue."

"Because continuing could get you killed!"

"So protect me."

"I am not a bodyguard," she hissed. "I'm a homicide detective, and these murders are escalating. Enough is enough. Filming needs to stop."

"The show must go on, you know? This could change everything for me."

Bel's mouth fell open, but no words came out. How was this happening? Why did no one care about the four dead crew members? Eamon believed a deal was to blame, and staring at Beau Draven, she knew her millionaire was right.

"What did you do?" She grabbed the actor's arm and pulled him to the snowy trees lining the road. "I know what this is about. I know you did something."

Beau's handsome face paled, and for a moment, he stood more frozen than the ice-coated branches. "I have no clue what you're talking about."

"What did you do?" Bel repeated, pulling the taller man closer. The actor might play a cop, but he was no match for the scowling reality that stood a foot shorter than him.

"Nothing." His voice was unconvincing as his eyes flicked to something over her head. Cameramen were starting to take note of their conversation, and while Jerry graciously tried to force their focus to the investigation, the gorgeous actor being harassed by a detective was a treat they couldn't resist.

"Your phone stays in your pocket." She released his arm and stepped away. "If I see you filming again, you won't get it back."

Before he could respond, she stalked to Eamon's side, her rage boiling so forcefully that she slipped her hand around her boyfriend's and squeezed hard enough to break a human's bones. "I don't know if it's a deal, but something won't let this show shut down," she hissed at him. "Something wants this crew dead, and we need to find it before these deaths ruin our town."

"I don't think the deal is in Bajka." He dragged her closer. An inch of air separated them, but his strength radiated off his body to steady her. "If he's the killer, he only steps inside town limits to kill and then retreats, otherwise I'd scent someone powerful enough to wield black magic."

"Did you smell something in the cabin?" Bel jerked her head at the crime scene.

"Yes." He nodded. "But the doors were open and hours had passed, so it dissipated."

"But it's not black magic?"

"No."

"So, the killer isn't the deal."

"Not necessarily," he explained. "If a deal was made, it was struck years ago, so no magic transferred between bodies during the killings. He left enough of a trace to warn he isn't human, but that's it."

"Regardless, he has one more debt to collect," Bel said, setting her sights on Beau Draven. "And I can guess who the last man standing is."

Autopsy Report

CERBERUS

Chapter Twenty One

"Detective, can I talk to you?" Deputy Rollo asked when Bel walked through the station doors later that afternoon.

"Of course." She gestured for the visibly upset officer to sit at her desk, and she prayed his distress wasn't bad news about Violet.

"I'm worried it's my fault the director is dead," he said, and Bel sank to her chair. That wasn't the direction she'd expected this conversation to take.

"What do you mean?" she asked, forcing her features to remain neutral.

"I was on patrol at the bed-and-breakfast last night, and I remember your neighbor," he said. "The inn started serving drinks because the cast and crew were nervous to leave once it got dark, so it's common for dates to show up. Your neighbor stopped by, and hours later, at around 1:45 a.m., she stumbled out into the cold. She was drunk, and I panicked. I didn't want an intoxicated woman getting into an accident or freezing to death, so I called her a cab. I stayed by her side until the driver arrived and then packed her into the car myself. I thought I was helping, but now I think it was a ploy to keep me from noticing the director's escape."

"I swear to god, these people want me to strangle them." Bel rubbed the exasperation from her face and then reached out to grip his forearm. "Don't blame yourself. This isn't your fault. It was freezing, and you did the right thing by helping my drunk neighbor. I agree it was a distraction, though. Rouge probably snuck out while you kept Chloe from passing out in the parking lot. The cab most likely picked him up down the street."

"Logically, I know you're right. It's not my fault the costume designer left for snacks or that a drunk woman took advantage of my concern to sneak the director out, but I still feel responsible."

"And two women were murdered on my boyfriend's property. The producer was killed on mine, and the director down the street from my house," Bel said. "It's easy to assume responsibility, but this isn't on us. We're cops, not bodyguards. You couldn't have known she was lying. Besides, my neighbor admitted to being drunk last night, so while she was exaggerating for your benefit, it wasn't far from the truth."

"I just feel awful," Rollo said.

"I know. Me too." Bel released his arm.

"Hey," Olivia interrupted them. "We checked the front door's lock."

"You're busy." The deputy stood. "I'll let you get back to work. Thanks, Detective."

"Of course." Bel smiled at him, earning a criminally attractive grin in return, and she hated that Olivia and Ewan might never rejoin their friend group. She'd been looking forward to a future of couples' dates.

"Chloe Rider's house showed no signs of forced entry." Olivia sat in Rollo's vacated seat. "There aren't even scratches on the lock to suggest someone picked it."

"So, she left the door unlocked," Bel said. "She was drunk

Evidence of a Folktale

and hooking up with her celebrity crush. She admitted locking up was the last thing on her mind."

"I'm so sick of this case." Olivia collapsed forward, her elbows digging into her thighs to support her head's weight, but Bel didn't move. She didn't want to jinx this moment of comradery and spook her partner into another stretch of unbearable avoidance.

"We have no evidence, no leads, no suspects, but we finally have a slight change in the M.O.," Olivia continued. "He opened the sliding glass door to *'put'* Warren Rouge in the woods, but he killed the director inside and left your neighbor alive. She's a potential witness, and unlike the snow that washes away everything, Miss Rider's cabin preserved the scene... but she left the door unlocked. She practically invited him in."

"She didn't know Rouge was a target," Bel said. "And we've all forgotten things while drunk."

"I know. It's just frustrating. Your neighbor could've provided us with something worthwhile."

"If she remembered anything about last night, she'd be dead, too. It's better this way."

"I guess. But how does someone butcher four people without leaving so much as a blood trail?"

"The snow," Bel said. "He probably wiped the blades off by the bodies because the corpses' heat and pumping blood would hide his mess in the melting snow."

"That's why the house is so frustrating. No elements to degrade the scene, yet we still learned nothing. It's like our killer is a ghost " She swallowed as if she could un-speak that word.

"He may have used the tub to clean the weapon," Bel said. "We should check the sinks."

"I'll get on that," Olivia said. "Not that it'll help us find him unless he washed something useful down the drain and it got stuck. You still think there's one more murder?"

"We need the who," Bel said.

"What happens if he kills his fifth victim? Does he vanish into the wind, never to kill again? Does he pick a new town and start over? Will he turn himself in and confess?"

"It depends on his motive, I guess. If he's killing for revenge, he'll probably stop. If that's the case, he'll take care to disappear, though, and we'll never find him. If his riddles and clues are a ritual, he'll eventually select another five to sacrifice. As for confessing? He'd have to feel guilty, and I don't think our killer does. The violence. The premeditation. The theatrics. He isn't suffering from guilt."

"So, no option ends well for us." Olivia sagged in her chair, and Bel had to fight her hands to stop them from reaching out and taking her partner's. "I realize I'm not part of Aesop's Files' cast or crew, but it still makes me nervous to be alone at night. I keep seeing their gutted bodies and imagining what it's like to die like that. Is that what that hiker we found months ago endured because of Ewan?"

"That hiker was trying to wipe out an entire pack," Bel said. "That's different."

"So you say."

"Because it's true," Bel said. "Ewan loves you, and he'd die before he let anyone hurt you. What's happening in our town isn't normal, but he would keep you safe."

"I'm not getting back together with him." Olivia stood, signaling the end of the discussion, and Bel clenched her fists so hard, her nails dug into her palms. Olivia had initiated a conversation, and she'd gone and ruined it by bringing up her ex.

"You don't have to," Bel said, desperate to make her stay. "But he'd do anything for you."

"Except tell me the truth," Olivia said, and it was Bel's turn to sag deeper into her chair.

"I know you want me to forgive him," her partner continued. "I don't understand how you're okay with this, but at least you knew. You fell in love with Eamon knowing the truth, but what if he'd lied? What if he'd pretended to be normal and only revealed he was a monster after you loved him? Could you love him like that? Would you forgive him, then?"

The Impaler flashed through Bel's mind, and she had her answer. When he told her about his past, she'd fled the house with her dog, choosing to sit out in the cold rather than be near him while she processed his reality. And she'd been expecting a horrible truth. How would she have reacted if she thought Eamon was human, only to learn that history remembered him as the man who guarded his castle with the corpses of his staked enemies?

"So, you see," Olivia said, reading Bel's answer in her eyes. "I can't forgive him."

She left, signaling the end of their ceasefire, and Bel rubbed her chest as if the friction could stop the aching. Her partner's words promised she wouldn't forgive Ewan, but there was an underlying message to her frustration. She couldn't forgive any of them, Bel included.

"Olivia, wait!" Bel chased after her partner. She might not forgive them, but Bel would be damned if she let Olivia ignore her. If she intended to hold a grudge, she'd have to do so up close and personal.

"I'm going to stop by the bed-and-breakfast," Bel continued when she caught up. "Come on, I'll drive."

Olivia tried to protest, but Bel strode for the front door and held it open expectantly. At a loss for how to refuse, Olivia caved, and the women climbed into the SUV. It was the first time they'd been in the same vehicle since Bel's resurrection. They didn't talk as they drove, though, but Bel hoped that if she forced Olivia to endure enough awkward moments, her friend might cave and agree to a genuine conversation that didn't involve her storming off.

"What's going on?" Olivia asked, jerking Bel out of her thoughts as they pulled into the bed-and-breakfast's parking lot.

The pavement was alive with activity, and she dared to hold her breath. Had the cast and crew finally seen reason? Had they agreed to halt filming and leave town?

"Taron?" Bel rolled down the window as the actress rushed by. "What's going on?"

"Beau talked to the studio and received their blessing to direct what remains of the episodes," she said. "We're heading to the location."

"You're shooting today?" Bel had to order her mouth not to gape.

"I know." Taron hugged her arms around her chest as she sagged in on herself. "Warren's dead. TV shows always have multiple directors per season, but Warren has directed the most Aesop's Files episodes. His vision is the show, but we're returning to set as if he's simply out with a cold. I'd refuse, but if I don't show up, Beau will be pissed. I'd rather not start drama with the guy I'm supposed to be in love with on screen."

"I get that," Bel said.

"It feels so wrong," Taron said. "Plus, I'm freaking out. First Gwen and Ellery are murdered. Then I get kidnapped. Now Alistair and Warren are dead. How many more of us need to die before the studio admits they're risking our lives?"

"None if I can help it."

"Beau said you'll be on set with him as protection. Is that true?"

"He misspoke."

"Oh." Taron's features faltered. "It's just I feel safer around you."

"We'll work something out." Bel hated the disappointment on the actress' face. She felt like a parent unable to deny their child, and while Taron was too old to be Bel's daughter, she was woefully unprepared for the demands of an actual case. She played a convincing cop, but she was no Isobel Emerson.

"Okay, well, I have to go," Taron said.

"Be safe!" Bel called after her as she parked the car.

"Detectives," the inn's owner greeted over the bustle when they walked through the front door. "Are you guys here for my security footage?"

"We are," Bel confirmed.

"I figured. When I heard about that poor man, I knew you'd be stopping by. Come on, I have the tapes ready for you." The woman gestured for the detectives to follow her into the office.

A little after the 9 p.m. timestamp, Chloe Rider arrived at the inn, and the parking lot stood empty except for the patrol unit until 1:39 a.m. Just as Rollo said, Chloe stumbled out of the bed-and-breakfast, and Bel understood why her theatrics had distracted the handsome deputy. It was freezing last night, and the poor girl tripped down the porch steps to collapse on the sidewalk, her head using a pile of shoveled snow as a pillow. Seconds later, Rollo raced to her side where he spent the next ten minutes keeping her upright. Miss Rider was an exemplary example of what not to do after midnight in the dead of winter, and true to his word, Rollo practically carried her to the cab. He waited for the vehicle to drive off before returning to his squad car, but right before he closed himself inside, his head snapped to attention. For a moment, he didn't move, and then he slid behind the steering wheel and drove off camera. A few minutes later, the front few feet of the car's hood inched back into the camera's sights, where it remained until Rollo's shift was over, which was when Bel ran into him at the station.

"He acted like he heard something," Olivia said. "Are there any other exits?"

"The back door." The owner switched the footage on the screen to the rear-facing cameras. "But as you can see, no one used it at 2 a.m. I checked already. That door stayed locked all night."

"So how did Rouge leave?" Olivia asked.

"Are the windows bolted shut?" Bel asked.

"No," the elderly woman said. "This is only a three-story inn, so there's no need to seal them. In the spring, we often open them for a nice breeze."

"Some of the first-floor windows are out of the cameras' range," Bel said. "Rouge could've opened one and jumped out."

"The man was certainly young enough," the woman said. "Do you think that's what your officer heard? Mr. Rouge slamming a window behind him?"

"Probably," Bel said. "Rollo didn't mention seeing anyone climbing out of the windows, though."

"He parks almost out of the camera's reach after he checked the perimeter." Olivia pointed to his barely visible squad car hovering on the monitor's edge. "From that corner of the parking lot, you can see most of the building. He was worried he'd missed something."

"Poor Rollo. He felt so guilty this morning."

"I understand why, but Rouge should've known better than to climb out a window with a killer on the loose," Olivia said.

"Yes, but pretty girls make men dumb," the inn's owner said, and Olivia grunted her agreement.

"Have you noticed anyone hanging around outside?" Bel asked, Rollo's position at the corner of the camera's view giving her an idea. She suspected the killer was the one who encouraged her neighbor to flirt with Rouge, but unless he knew Chloe Rider, he wouldn't know where she lived. Maybe Rollo hadn't heard a window slam. Maybe he heard someone watching from the shadows or another car start as it readied to follow Rouge to Bel's normally peaceful street.

"Tons," the woman said. "It's slowed since the fans left, but it was a madhouse. Lots of girls hoping to make Beau Draven fall in love with them."

"So it would've been easy for someone to stalk the inn," Olivia said. "Except last night, Rollo almost caught him. He didn't see anything, otherwise he would've told you, but you know who might've noticed something? The cab driver."

Thirty minutes later, the detectives followed the cab company's manager through the garage to find last night's driver.

"Yeah, I remember them," he said when they asked about Chloe.

"Them?" Bel repeated.

"The girl and the show's director," the man confirmed. "I was called to the bed-and-breakfast last night around 2 a.m. by a police officer waiting with a drunk woman. He loaded her into my cab, and I remember hoping she wouldn't throw up in my back seat. So it surprised me when she started acting normal when we got down the street."

Bel and Olivia shared a glance at his words. Rollo's guess had been correct. Chloe had been exaggerating her intoxication to distract him.

"Then she asked me to pull over," the driver continued. "She wasn't as wasted as she'd led that cop to believe, but she was drunk, and I wasn't comfortable leaving her out in the cold. Thankfully, she didn't get out. She just wanted to pick up the director who was waiting around the corner."

"So after you picked him up, you dropped them off at Miss Rider's residence, correct?" Bel asked.

"That's right."

"Did you make any other stop?"

"No, Ma'am."

"Did you notice anyone following you?"

"No." His features twisted, and Bel realized there was more to his answer.

"Are you sure?" she pushed.

"No." He sagged against the cab's trunk. "Someone could've followed us, but I wasn't paying attention. The minute the director got in my cab, they started going at it. I was no longer worried about her vomiting on my seats but instead about them making a baby right then and there. Those two were very... attracted to each other and seemed to forget I was in the front. If I'd checked my rear-view mirror or looked behind me, I would've gotten an eyeful of things not intended for me, so I drove with my gaze forward until they got out of my car. The only good thing about that humiliating experience was the director left a massive tip."

"So someone could've followed you, but you wouldn't have noticed," Olivia asked.

"Correct."

"If someone were following Rouge, they would've turned off their lights, anyway," Bel said.

"That's true," the driver said. "I would've noticed headlights behind me. It's pretty dark at 2 a.m."

"One last question," Bel said. "When you dropped Miss Rider and Mr. Rouge off at her cabin, did you notice anything odd? Any idling cars? Anyone lurking?"

"Not that I remember. It's secluded out that way. Sorry I can't be of more help. If I'd known the director was a target, I would've paid more attention."

"Thank you for your time," Bel said, and after exchanging pleasantries, the detectives left.

"Another unhelpful witness," Olivia muttered as they climbed into Bel's SUV. "I'm so frustrated, I could spit. The killer was probably following them, yet he was oblivious."

"Can you blame him?" Bel turned the key in the ignition and shifted the car into drive. "I wouldn't look behind me if my passengers were making a baby, as he put it."

"True," Olivia said. "But a killer's picking off crew members, yet no one's seen anything. None of the victims struggled. Who doesn't fight back?"

"Driving around in the middle of the night..." A thought popped into Bel's head, and she slammed on the brakes so hard that their seat belts gagged them as they surged forward. "Who's

Evidence of a Folktale

someone strangers willingly get into cars with, especially after dark?"

"Cabs," Olivia said, catching her drift. "People give them their addresses too. A cab driver makes the perfect suspect."

"It's certainly worth looking into," Bel said.

"Right... but what's his motive?"

"I don't know." Bel shrugged as she eased back into a drive. "Why kill regular passengers when you can murder famous ones?"

"EMERSON!" Griffin called, leaning out of his office door as Bel returned to her desk. "Can I talk to you?"

Bel dropped her stuff and crossed the station to join her boss.

"You can probably guess what I'm going to say," he said. "And you won't like it either, but Evelyn Pierce informed me that filming won't halt despite Warren Rouge's death. Beau Draven is taking over as director for the remainder of the shoot."

"Unbelievable." Bel collapsed onto his couch, the cushions hissing as they released their air as if they too were pissed at this announcement.

"They want you on set to watch over Mr. Draven," Griffin continued. "But they hope your presence will protect the rest of the cast and crew."

"It won't help them if they insist on sneaking out to hook up with our town's residence," Bel muttered. "Why me, though? I'm a homicide detective who's needed on this case. Deputies are already monitoring the sets and the bed-and-breakfast."

"Why you?" Griffin scoffed. "Why the officer who threw herself into the back seat of a kidnapper's car and then crashed it to save Miss Monroe?" He laughed. "I hate dangling you in front of a serial killer, but could Eamon watch over you like he did with Miss Monroe? I don't want to ask this of him. He isn't the police, and it's inappropriate to keep involving a civilian, but he's the only person besides myself that I trust to protect you."

"I'll talk to him," Bel said. "But the days aren't dangerous. It's after midnight. I can't help the cast or crew if they escape our surveillance after dark. Neither can Eamon."

"I know. But four people have died on our watch. We can't let that number become five. Filming is almost done. We just have to keep them alive long enough to leave town because if things get worse, I'm afraid the studio will try suing us for negligence."

"And my protection is the price we must pay to avoid that."

"I'm sorry, Emerson." Griffin leaned forward. "Spend time on set. Show everyone we're taking their safety seriously. Don't jump into any more cars, and it'll be an easy assignment for you. We can't afford to lose you on this case, but we can't afford to let another crew member die. And the way Mr. Draven is panicking, he believes he's next."

"I'll do it," Bel said. "Of course, I'll do it. I just wish it would actually help."

"Who knows?" Griffin stood and patted her on the back. "The last time you followed an actor around on set, you saved them from a kidnapper. Maybe this time you'll save them from the killer."

"Let's pray we're so lucky. Although it would be safer for them to halt filming."

"A fact I've repeated until I was blue in the face."

Bel stood, an idea taking root. "Maybe I can help."

"What?" Griffin smirked at her. "You gonna let Mr. Stone loose on them?"

"That would be the quickest way," she laughed, wishing that was an option, but she wasn't trying to out her boyfriend's secret to people who made their living filming others.

"I'd pay to see that." The sheriff escorted her out of his

Evidence of a Folktale

office. "I told them you'll start tomorrow, so get as much work done today as you can."

"I'll try my best to solve the case before then."

Griffin gave her a humorous eye roll, and then she dialed the only person besides her ancient evil of a boyfriend who might be able to help her.

"Detective, how are you?" Agent Jameson Barry answered on the second ring, and while they weren't close, Bel almost sobbed at the sound of his voice. He'd been the first familiar face she'd seen after she helped carry Dr. Charles Blaubart's wife down that snowing mountain, and she would never forget the way he hugged her when he found her alive.

"I need your help," she said as she crossed the station floor to her desk.

"Sure. Are you okay?"

"Yes, I'm fine," she answered by launching into an explanation of their situation. "They won't halt filming for the police," she said in closing. "But they might for the FBI."

"You want me to shut them down?" Barry asked.

"Can you?"

"None of the murders occurred on set, correct?"

"Correct," she confirmed.

"Have any accidents happened on the set? Any threats? Have you found any evidence on set or in the production trailers?"

"No."

"Have any cast or crew members been named a suspect or person of interest?"

"No."

"So, Aesop's Files isn't to blame? It's Bajka."

"Basically."

Barry sighed, and Bel already knew what he was going to say. "The crimes occurred far from the sets and production trailers. They also happen away from the fan events and the cast and crew hotels," he explained. "The show isn't the problem. Your

339

town is. You wouldn't close a coffee shop because its employees died after hours at another location, would you?"

"No," Bel conceded.

"And you wouldn't force a bank to halt all business because its tellers were murdered in the woods, would you?"

"No."

"The same goes for this show," Barry said. "I don't see how I can shut filming down because their cast and crew members leave their hotels to grab snacks or hookup with strangers and cross paths with a killer. Nothing happened during production, so they have every right to work. Is it considerate or smart to keep filming? Probably not, but their sets are safe and void of evidence."

Bel fell forward, her head bouncing off her desk as she groaned.

"What I can do is send an agent to assist with the case," Barry said, clearly hearing the aggravation in her sigh. "I'm too busy to come, but perhaps an FBI agent's presence will speed things along."

"Yeah, maybe," Bel said. It was a smart idea, but it wasn't the answer she'd hoped for. She'd hoped Barry would ride into town like a knight in a black sedan, but he was right. The studio valued their bottom line more than their cast and crew, but the act of filming the episodes wasn't the issue. It was people leaving their hotels when they shouldn't, and that's when the studio lost all responsibility. They were liable for what happened on their set, or in their trailers or accommodations. They weren't responsible for drunk men who snuck out to sleep with strangers who purposely tricked the cops or women who craved chips. That wasn't the show's fault. It was Bajka's for not having safe streets and homes.

"Say the word, and I'll send someone to help you," Barry said.

"Thanks. I'll let you know."

"Sorry it's not what you wanted to hear," he said, his voice more sympathetic than his words.

"It's okay," Bel said. "Nothing about this case is what I want."

BEL PULLED into her parking spot and jumped out of her car, the night late and her mood irritable. Maybe she should accept Barry's offer and let an FBI agent relieve her of this case. She was tired of chasing theories that turned out to be figments of her imagination, and she couldn't bear hunting evil through the snow. Her fingers were eternally cold, and her exhaustion fought to convince her it would've been better if she lost them on the mountain so she wouldn't have to feel the frost stiffen her joints.

Bel dug her aching fingers into her pocket and pulled out her house keys. She needed to eat and hug her dog before her downward spiral dragged her any further, but before she made it halfway down the walkway, a black luxury SUV burst from the shadows and skidded to a halt behind her car, blocking any vehicular escape. Its rear door shoved open the instant the wheels stopped spinning, but Bel had her sidearm in her hand before the Italian leather shoe crunched down on the snow.

"There's no need for that, Detective," the stranger said as he settled before her, and the already frigid air burned colder in his presence. He was handsome and dressed in a suit that cost more than her car, which was saying a lot since her SUV originally belonged to Eamon. But it was his eyes that stole the breath from her lungs. They were more snake than human.

"I'm simply here to talk." He raised his hands in surrender, yet somehow, the gesture was a threat. "You've been making a lot of..." he paused as if trying to convey his insult diplomatically. "Noise," he settled on. "Reports of your concern have reached even my ears, and it's becoming a problem. You want

Aesop's Files to halt filming, but I'm here to tell you that cannot happen. Too much is at stake to approve any delays."

"And too many lives have been lost," Bel spat, tightening her grip on the gun. "Human beings are more important than a TV show, regardless of its popularity. This needs to stop before the death toll becomes a burden we'll never recover from."

"Humans can be replaced," the man said, and Bel's stomach cramped at the way he spoke the word, as if mankind was a swarm of ants that he was contemplating grinding to a pulp below his heel. "New directors and writers can be hired. New designers can be found. Actors can be recast, but if production shuts down, it'll ruin the season. Ratings cannot be replicated as easily as producers can. I won't risk our show's standing."

"I won't be bullied by ratings," Bel said, her hands gripping her gun so tightly that her knuckles strained under the pressure. "I won't—"

The stranger lunged forward, shoving his face into hers, and Bel flinched, his aggression almost as forceful as a slap. Gooseflesh pricked her already icy skin, and he had her wrist in his fist before she could even think to pull the trigger.

"Don't get in my way," the man whispered, his mouth so close that his breath hit her lips, and tears unconsciously ran down her cheeks. How could she be so stupid? Why had she provoked him? She knew who this was. This was the deal, the reason the show had grown so popular overnight, and he'd traveled to Bajka to collect his debts.

"I have no issue with you, Detective," he continued, pushing his face closer to hers until his lips practically brushed against her recoiling cheek. "I have no desire to hurt you. I don't care about your existence at all, but the moment you stand in my way, you become my problem. I can't have that, Detective. The show must go on."

"Get your hands off me," she demanded, her tears freezing to her cheeks, and as if he understood the danger she was in,

Evidence of a Folktale

Cerberus loosed an earth-shattering growl. She could tell by the rattle of her front door that he was slamming his body against the wood, his violence so profound that even the deal hesitated to toss a wary glance at the cabin.

"Let go of me," Bel repeated, reaching for her necklace with her free hand, but her movement caught his attention.

"Don't fight me, Detective." The man grabbed her wrist, stopping her from pressing the panic button, and despite the defiance in her voice, her tears still came. This stranger had eviscerated four people. She didn't want to be the fifth.

"If you get in my way, I'll be compelled to deal with you," he said over Cerberus' rage. "I will ruin you. Do you understand me?"

"I know who you are," Bel whispered, ignoring his question as she forced herself to be brave. "The question is, do you know who you're threatening?"

The deal threw his head back and laughed, his grip loosening slightly on her wrists, but the second she tried to wiggle free, his fists choked her skin. "Oh, Detective," he sighed as his laughter dissipated. "I am not afraid of some small-town cop."

"I'm not the one you should be afraid of," she growled. "It's who I belong to that you should be terrified of."

"Belong to?" He stared at her as if he didn't understand her words, and then he leaned closer and inhaled.

"I see." He released her as if she was a live wire. "I apologize, Detective. I didn't scent it at first, but it seems you do belong to someone." He lunged backward until his hand found the door handle. "You of all people should know there's more than one way to ruin a life, though. You may be under this force's protection, but what about your family? What about the friends you love? They don't belong to your protector." The deal slid into the car, the darkness swallowing all but his eyes. "Stay out of our way. Getting involved won't be worth the price."

He slammed the door without waiting for a response, and the

SUV reversed down the street, its blackness disappearing into the night as if it too wasn't entirely of this world. The moment it vanished into the shadows, Bel raced for her front door, fingers shaking as she tried to unlock it. It took her two tries before it swung wide, and Cerberus leaped into her arms with a desperate cry.

"Oh baby," Bel choked as she slammed the door behind them and bolted for her car. She didn't bother grabbing anything but her favorite boy, and throwing his stocky body into the SUV, she slid into the driver's seat and careened down the road.

Her speed was reckless, too fast for such dark and icy roads, but she couldn't bring herself to slow down. She pushed the car to its limit, and then she was in Eamon's gravel driveway, all memory of her trip wiped from her mind.

"Eamon!" she screamed as she practically tumbled from her car. "Eamon!" She and Cerberus bolted for the front door, and the duo exploded into the mansion's foyer with a resounding bang.

"Isobel?" He rounded the corner, panic etched with excruciating detail into his tense muscles, and Bel flung herself at him. He caught her, and in one fluid motion, he slammed the door behind them. He locked it without breaking his hold on her waist and then retreated into the house until the warmth of his home signaled that she was safe.

"You were right," she murmured into his chest, her heart beating against her ribs like a caged animal. "Aesop's Files made a deal with black magic for their success, and he's collecting his payment here in our town."

"What happened?" Eamon stilled against her, his body stone below her touch.

"I saw him." Bel leaned back so he could see the terror in her eyes. "He came for me."

Autopsy Report

CERBERUS

PROD.NO.
SCENE TAKE SOUND
DIRECTOR
CAMERAMAN EXT. INT.

CINEMA TICKET ADMIT ONE 9891102
CINEMA TICKET ADMIT ONE 9891102

Chapter Twenty Two

"He stopped you from pressing the panic button?" Eamon asked as Bel stole the whiskey from his fist. "He shouldn't have known it was there."

"My gun was in my other hand." She grimaced as she gulped the amber liquid. Eamon bought expensive whiskey, and as much as she loved the way his voice sounded like the alcohol, she didn't enjoy the taste. He'd poured her a glass of wine to calm her nerves while she recounted what happened, but the wine wasn't strong enough. It was one thing to face off with a serial killer. It was another to confront a serial killer in possession of black magic. A witch who possessed the dark arts had the strength to control the likes of Eamon. She hated remembering what that kind of power could do to her.

"So, he didn't know you were aiming for the necklace?" he asked as he reclaimed his almost empty glass.

"I don't think so," she said. "He was probably trying to stop me from shooting him."

Eamon's fingers slid through her hair as he pulled her against his chest.

"He had his hands on me, and I could feel the power." She

tried not to cry as she breathed in the fragrance of the laundry detergent woven into his shirt. It was such a normal scent for someone never meant to walk the earth, and she let the familiarity settle her. "It wasn't like your power. It was... I don't know. And the way he cornered me. If Cerberus hadn't started barking, who knows what I would've let happen? I was paralyzed."

"Black magic isn't an art to be taken lightly."

"I know, but I couldn't get to my necklace."

"And that was his first mistake." Eamon released her to check that their dinner wasn't burning. "His touch left a scent on your skin. I know what he smells like now, and if he ever crosses my path, I'll kill him for putting his hands on you. But do me a favor. Next time, go for the panic button before the gun."

"As soon as he scented you, he backed up," Bel said. "I don't think he'll come for me again. My family..." she trailed off. She'd already repeated his threat to Eamon, and she didn't care to recount the fear for a second time.

"At least he had some sense. But Isobel, listen to me. This deal. It has nothing to do with you, but he's made it very clear. If you don't leave it alone, he'll come for you too. I'm not saying that you shouldn't do your job, but if the killer isn't human, then you need to stay out of the show's business... even if it costs the final victim his life."

"I can't do that."

"I'm serious, Detective." His towering frame loomed over where she sat at the kitchen island, the gravity of his tone making him impossibly large. "Someone's metaphorical deal with a devil isn't your price to pay. You were already the sacrifice needed in my unwanted deal, and you barely escaped with your life. If the crew of this show bargained away their souls for fame, I won't let you take the fall for them. Swear to me that if it comes down to it, you'll get out of the deal's way when he comes to collect. Let the victims sacrifice for their own desires."

Evidence of a Folktale

"You want me to stand aside while an innocent person is gutted before me?" Bel glared at the man she loved. Did he even know her?

"People who make deals with devils aren't innocent." Eamon refused to back down. "Alcina murdered six people just to get to you. Blaubart killed five wives after his deal cost Anne hers. I don't know what sins this cast and crew have committed, but I can assure you, they deserve to die more than you."

"I—"

"God, Isobel." He swore as he slammed his palm on the island's counter. If Bel were anyone else, she would've flinched at the force, and she did slightly, but not in fear. The sound surprised her, but not his aggression. Most wouldn't understand his true meaning, but she did. He loved her, and he was fighting for his humanity to remain in control.

"Just let me be selfish," he continued, seizing her face in his hands. "You want me to stay in Bajka with you and never leave? Then listen when I tell you to get out of the way. You can fight me about anything you like, but do not fight me on this because when it comes to your survival, I don't care who else dies in this world."

"Eamon…"

"No. I don't care who dies as long as it isn't you," he cut her off. "I'll kill them myself if it saves you. Even the innocent. Let that sink in. You fight for innocence, but I would murder them in a heartbeat to keep you alive. To stay in your good graces, I would rather not, though. So please, if the deal is the one killing these crew members, and he threatens you with dark magic, step aside and let him have his final payment. Let the guilty pay because a TV show isn't worth so much as a single drop of your blood."

"Are you done?" Bel smiled as she slid her hands up his chest. She shouldn't smile. The man was terrifying as he hovered over her, and she didn't doubt his oath. He would kill even the

349

innocent if it bought her survival, but she couldn't stop the girlish grin from curving her lips.

"Yes..." He squinted down at her. "What's so funny?"

"You."

"I'm being serious, Isobel." He looked like he might blow steam out of his ears.

"I know. You're just so intense." She slid her fingers up his neck to brush over his clenched jaw. "You really love me, don't you?"

"Of course, I love you." He gawked at her as if she was dense. "You're all I love... well, the dog too, but he's basically part of you. I like your family and friends, but you and Cerberus are my entire world." He lowered his forehead to hers, unconsciously inhaling her scent as their skin collided.

"I do want you to stay," she whispered, their mouths so close, her words feathered his lips like a kiss. "So, I promise. If the deal comes for his final victim, I'll step out of the way. I'll do everything in my power to stop him first, though."

"I'd expect nothing less." Eamon leaned closer until his mouth pressed against hers. Bel surged forward, kissing him deeply as she hugged his neck, and he pulled her off her chair to deposit her on the counter.

"I shouldn't like it when you get aggressive about my safety." She wrapped her legs around his waist, the alcohol and fear and his intense devotion winding through her like a haze of drugs. "But I'm learning your tells, and when you're cranky, it's your way of saying I love you."

"I'm not cranky," Eamon growled against her mouth as he yanked her further against his chest.

"You are," Bel teased, her fear from her earlier encounter evaporating as he held her against his thundering heart. Let that suited man come for her now. He'd learn what it meant to pay the price.

Evidence of a Folktale

"Quiet." Eamon gripped her hair and pulled her head back, stealing her moans like a man possessed.

"Cranky," she whispered, sliding her hands below his shirt, but as her fingertips traced the contours of his muscles, she jerked backward. "What's burning?"

Eamon cursed, leaping away from her to shove the pot off the stove, and Bel burst into laughter.

"How did I smell that before you?"

"You were distracting me." He ran his hand through his hair, his features still dazed by their kiss. "I was trying to have a serious conversation, but then you laughed at me and pressed your perfect body all over mine, and all rational thought went…" He made a throwing gesture at the kitchen window.

"I wasn't laughing at you." Bel hopped off the counter to help him salvage their meal. "I was terrified earlier. That man restrained both my wrists. I couldn't shoot. I couldn't call you. Then I get here, and you're not known for keeping your cool when it involves me. It would scare other people, but your intensity betrays how much you love me. I don't know what it says about me, but I find it unreasonably attractive."

"What a pair we are." Eamon wrapped his arm around her neck and fake pinned her against his chest like they were wrestling teenagers, and she played along, shoving him until he finally let go. "But before all my whiskey goes to your head, swear to me you'll stay safe. If I can't get to you, step out of the way because your death won't stop the deal. He'll still need to sacrifice his last victim. Don't die in vain."

"I won't," Bel promised. "I'll be stubborn about it, but I won't."

"Yeah, well, we've already proven you enjoy keeping me in a constant state of cardiac arrest." Eamon kissed her scars before grabbing a new pan to start dinner over. "But I like a girl who can hold her own against me. I sometimes worry my strength will hurt those around me, but you? Not so much."

"Cause you're afraid of me?" She winked.

"Yup," he said so fast that she couldn't help but laugh at the seriousness in his tone.

"Good, Mr. Stone. You should be afraid of me." She pinched his waist hard, wondering if she would ever make him flinch, but he caught her wrist and yanked her into his arms. Her laughter doubled at the playfulness, and while the teasing seemed wrong after what occurred on her front lawn, it was exactly what she needed. Eamon was her best friend. He was the man who made her laugh. The man who kept her safe, who made her strong, who loved her so violently that he'd willingly become a monster to keep her breathing. This was where she belonged. Bothering the Beast of Bajka until he smiled.

"The deal isn't here, so you should be fine," Eamon said after sweeping the set. He couldn't afford to abandon his work any more than he already had, but he agreed to stop by and examine the sets every morning before filming. Aesop's Files was shooting at the Bajka Library for the next few days, so the locked building would be easy for the deputies to defend from the straggler fans without him. Bel wasn't worried, though. Death reared its gluttonous head only at night, so her presence was more performance than practical.

"Thank you." She grabbed his hand and squeezed his fingers. "But no one's going to attack Mr. Draven in front of dozens of crew members and cops." She gestured to the swarming library.

"Call me if you need me for anything." Eamon scanned the crowd, and finding no one watching, he stole a kiss.

"I will." She cupped his cheek as he trailed a finger over her necklace. "I love you, Mr. Stone."

"Thank God for that... your phone is vibrating." He tapped her pocket and then he was gone, a ghost who'd never existed.

Evidence of a Folktale

"Bel," Olivia said when she answered the call. "I just left the morgue."

"And?"

"What do you think?"

"Death by exsanguination. No evidence. No defensive wounds. No fingerprints," Bel said.

"Ding, ding, ding, we have a winner," Olivia groaned. "I don't understand. That much blood and none of it splattered onto the killer. How did he not track it around the house? He could've used the snow to wash up in the woods, and the bleeding body would've covered his mess. But inside? Plus, Rouge was sleeping next to your neighbor. How is there no evidence? Unless there's something you're not telling me? Is something in our town?"

Bel froze, unsure how much she should reveal, and that was all the answer her partner needed.

"Great," Olivia said. "So, you're lying to me again."

"We aren't certain of anything," she protested. "They're just theories."

"Theories that you don't think I'm entitled to."

"Olivia…"

"It's fine. Whatever. I'm going to look into your cab driver idea. It's a decent theory."

"It is." Bel sagged against the wall. They'd been making progress, but this omission had murdered it.

"I'll keep you updated." Olivia hung up before Bel could answer, and she shoved her phone into her pocket to rub her face. If she rubbed hard enough, perhaps she'd wake up and learn this chaos and turmoil had been nothing but a nightmare.

"Detective?" Taron's voice slipped through Bel's fingers. "Are you all right?"

"Yeah." Bel peeled herself off the wall. "It's just been a long month."

353

"You can say that again. But we're almost done here... will the deaths stop when we leave town?"

"I don't know."

"Yes, you do," Taron pushed.

"He won't stop until he completes his mission," Bel answered. She liked Taron. They were nothing alike, but the actress deserved safety at work.

"Gotcha. Am I in danger?"

"I don't think so," Bel said. The show had gotten popular before her addition to the cast. If a deal had been struck, it had been made long before Miss Monroe morphed into a fictional detective. "Nevertheless, I wouldn't wander alone at night until we catch this killer."

"My character might be reckless enough to leave after dark. You're definitely brave enough to try something like that." Taron patted her shoulder with a laugh. "But thankfully, I'm no cop."

"What did you think, Detective?" Beau settled entirely too close to Bel, and she had to grip her thigh to keep from shoving him a few inches back.

"What do I think?" she silently repeated to herself. *"That you're obnoxious and selfish for not shutting down production, and you overcompensate around me because I'm the only woman you've met who hasn't begged you to bed them."*

"It was great," she said instead. "I love this library. It'll make a beautiful scene."

"Me too." Beau shifted closer, and she regretted telling Eamon she wouldn't need him. She could use a protective boyfriend at the moment.

"I bet it's pretty exciting for you to be here on set," he continued. "Small town like this. Not much ever happens."

Bel forced her features to remain neutral. Not much ever

Evidence of a Folktale

happens? It seemed that finding over forty women in a freezer and being shot at by their murderer was nothing to write home about. Plus, she and Eamon weren't exactly subtle. How had Beau missed the obvious signs that she wasn't on the market?

"I used to work for the NYPD," she said instead. "I'm also working this case. I've seen enough for a lifetime."

"NYPD?" he repeated. "That's sexy."

Bel wondered if it would be inappropriate to smack him upside the head. Maybe she should just press her necklace's panic button.

"My father was the chief of police." She stared pointedly at the actor. Other women might kill to be in her shoes, but she was too frustrated with this case and her aching feet to be swept up by Hollywood's favorite boyfriend.

"We should add that backstory to Taron's character," he said. "Make her father her inspiration. Good idea." He shifted to face her. "Are you hungry? How about you and I—"

"Reds," a writer interrupted before he finished asking her out. "Can I run tomorrow's scenes by you? They don't work anymore because of the changes we made today."

"Sure, give me a second." Beau returned his attention to her.

"Reds?" Bel asked before he could resume his line of questioning.

"It's a nickname," he said. "Well, not exactly. It was my birth name, but Reds doesn't scream movie star. I changed it to Draven, but the nickname stuck."

"Reds." Bel nodded, not entirely sure why that felt significant.

"Yeah, so anyway. Since we both have to eat, and you're here for my protection, we should—"

"Hey, I wasn't sure how late you'd be, so I figured I'd stop by to ask if you were coming home for dinner or if I should eat on my own?" a calculated voice asked, cutting Beau off as a massive hand slid against her spine.

"We're done here, right, Mr. Draven?" Bel said, loving how his eyes almost popped out of their sockets at the sight of Eamon suddenly hovering over him. It seemed Mr. Stone was better at hiding in the shadows than she'd realized. She hadn't even noticed him enter the library.

"Filming?" he asked. "For today, yes."

"Then I'll be home for dinner unless Griffin needs me," she answered Eamon's deliberate question. "I just have to escort Mr. Draven to the bed-and-breakfast first."

"Excellent." Eamon didn't kiss her, but by the look in his eyes, he should've. It would've been less erotic if he'd just pressed his lips to hers, and Bel gave up trying to hide her blush. Seemed she didn't need to press her panic button. Eamon had arrived to stake his claim, and he'd done so without a puffed chest or aggression. He'd simply asked about food, and everyone present knew who she belonged to. Or should she say who he belonged to because the adoration in his death-black eyes swore his allegiance to her?

"I'll wait for you to discuss the script, and then I'll escort you to the inn," Bel said, and with a nod, Beau retreated, clearly not interested in going toe to toe with a man who, unlike the characters in this show, could beat him in a fight.

"What are you doing here?" She asked as the actor joined the writer across the library. "I thought you had to work."

"And leave you alone with Beau Draven?" Eamon said. "I'm not that stupid."

Bel rolled her eyes.

"No, I stopped by the hardware store, so I was down the street," Eamon explained as he took her hand and pulled her toward the front door. "I'm trying to restore the dumbwaiter I found."

"You found a dumbwaiter?"

"Of course I did. All old estates had them."

"Please say it's salvageable because I need to live in a house with one."

"Live?" Eamon's eyes brightened until his black irises looked almost grey.

"Yeah, yeah." Bel waved a dismissive hand. "Can you fix it?"

"I'm trying. I was working on it between calls and realized I was missing parts. It's late, and since Cerberus is at my place, I wanted to check on your plans. Glad I did." He winked at her. "If I hadn't, I might have lost you to another man."

"You ruined my shot." She shook her head in mock disappointment.

"Oh well." Eamon unlocked his truck and slipped into the driver's seat. "Guess you're stuck with me."

"Oh, the horror." Bel leaned forward and planted a kiss on his lips. "But seriously, perfect timing. Thanks."

"Always, Detective." He brushed her hair back, and his expression from earlier returned. How was it possible to hold so much love in soulless black eyes?

"I'll stay at your house since you have the baby," she said, cupping his jaw in her hands, and over his shoulder, she noticed Rollo jump out of his idling patrol car at the edge of the set's perimeter to slide into Violet's vehicle. Unlike Eamon, who'd greeted her with a palm to the back, Rollo greeted Violet with a kiss most couples saved for the bedroom.

"Remember when we were young and in love like that?" she teased, and Eamon glanced over his shoulder to see what she meant.

"I guess we were that cute once." He played along. "Too bad our honeymoon stage is over, and we never kiss like that."

"Go home, and I'll kiss you like that later." She shut the door on him, smirking at his expression while trying to ignore Violet and Rollo across the street. She was glad her friend had found someone, but she didn't want to watch her find him so publicly.

If only Olivia and Ewan could mend their fences. It would bring Bel much-needed joy to see all three of them happily in love. Unfortunately, she kept putting her foot in her mouth, and she feared reconciliation wasn't in their cards.

"Do you have a minute?" Olivia asked when Bel answered the phone.

"Sure." She grabbed her coffee from the craft service table and moved to the rear of the library. Eamon had returned with her to set that morning, a little too smug with himself when Beau Draven avoided him, but as they suspected, nothing dangerous hid within the walls. So he'd left Bel with little to do save watch Mr. Draven enthusiastically enjoy the benefits of Warren Rouge's death.

"I looked into the cab company," Olivia said, and Bel was thankful she'd called instead of passing information through Griffin. Perhaps their relationship wasn't as hopeless as she feared.

"That theory is dead in the water," she continued. "The cast and crew have cars or personal drivers, so the only record of anyone using the service was Warren Rouge when he was with your neighbor. Obviously, they could've driven the victims without logging the trip, but there are no records of Rossa, Roja, or Rot ever taking a cab.

"The driver's alibis are all over the place, too. Some have alibis for all the murders. Others only have provable alibis for some, but they alternate. Driver A has an alibi for murder one and two, while driver B has an alibi for one and three, and so on. Unless they're all in on it and took turns killing, no driver sticks out. None of them fit the profile, either. Most drive around all day and have the physique to prove it. I don't see them chasing people through the woods to slash them to death. Plus, what's

Evidence of a Folktale

their motive? And where's the evidence? The owner let me examine the cabs. If you violently murder four people, you're bound to leave behind trace evidence, but the taxis I examined were filthy, not bloody."

"It was a long shot anyway," Bel said.

"Cab drivers make the perfect killer," Olivia said. "People get into their cars willingly, especially when it's cold and dark, and they never pay attention to who's in the front seat. I just don't think Bajka's drivers are to blame because why would they leave clues about January or the show's renewal… is the killer doing this to make us chase our tails?" she asked, and Bel practically saw her eyes blinking with the sudden idea. "We've been so focused on why he's targeting the crew, and his riddles reinforce our suspicions, but what if that's the point? What if this is all one big misdirect so we don't figure out his plan?"

"Anything's possible," Bel conceded. "I think the clues mean something, but there's a chance they don't. The national news is painting us as idiots, so maybe that's his intention. We're hunting the wrong clues."

"I'm headed back to the station to look into the victim's pasts," Olivia said. "We've been so focused on Aesop's Files that we might have missed something. Perhaps these four weren't the actual targets. Some killers attack multiple victims to hide their true purpose."

"It's worth a shot," Bel said, even though it wouldn't produce the answers her partner hoped for. She knew in her gut that the suited businessman who cornered her was involved. She had nothing tangible other than her memory of his threats, but they wouldn't hold up in court… if the legal system could even contain a man like that. Eamon was their best hope at stopping the bloodshed, but she still needed proof. Without evidence to convince the public, the fans and lawyers of Aesop's Files would crucify Bajka. It was smart that Olivia was thinking outside the box. Maybe she'd stumble on something they could use against the deal.

"I'll keep you updated," Olivia said.

"Thanks." Bel hung up and waved at Griffin, who'd just slipped into the library.

"Figured I'd check on you," he said when he joined her. "How's it going?"

"There's no reason for me to be here," she said. "The killer won't attack with this many witnesses present."

"No, but the killer might be watching."

"I considered that, but only the cast, crew, and police are here. Someone on set could be the guilty party, but they're impossible to detect when everyone's supposed to be here. We're all watching Mr. Draven at this point."

"Is there anyone purposely not observing him?"

"I thought of that, but no." She grabbed her boss's arm and pulled him deeper into the shelves so no one could read their lips. "What if we baited the killer?"

"Excuse me?"

"He's too smart to get caught stalking his next victim," Bel said. "He's been exceedingly patient, biding his time over the past month until he cornered his victims alone. He won't break that pattern now and kill in broad daylight."

"But he could be growing desperate," Griffin said. "Aesop's File's time here is coming to a rapid end. If he doesn't move quickly, his fifth victim will slip beyond his grasp."

"He has a plan. I'm sure of it. Somehow, he'll isolate number five, and by then it'll be too late, so what if we gave him what he wanted? Let's give him Draven alone in the middle of the night."

"Like the studio would go for that."

"Not Draven in the flesh," Bel said. "There's enough makeup here to transform humans into monsters. We could utilize it to dress a deputy like Draven and use him to lure the killer out. By the time he realizes he's been tricked, we'll have him."

"Or we'll get an officer killed."

"I would offer Eamon's help, but he's too big to play the actor."

"I feel uncomfortable using a civilian as bait, anyway," Griffin said. "It doesn't matter that he's unusual. I can't do with the law what I will. It's one thing when it might save your life. It's another when we're running an operation that I have to file reports on."

"I just don't know how else to catch this guy," Bel said.

"I'll think about it, okay?" He patted her back as they emerged from the shelves. "Gold has an idea she wants to investigate. Thum is trying to track down the autopsy report that clipping belongs to. We might yet find our smoking gun, and if not, I'll consider your way. For now, keep Draven alive... and yourself," he added.

"I know, no jumping into kidnapper's cars." Bel rolled her eyes. "Trust me, the only danger I'm in here is boredom."

"Really?" Griffin stared at her as if her neck was sprouting a second head. "I think this is pretty cool. You don't enjoy the filming process?"

"It's fine." She shrugged.

"But you aren't happy unless you're giving everyone in your life a heart attack." He cradled her head and pulled her in for a forehead kiss. "Well, I like you here. It means I don't have to worry."

"But Eamon does." Bel squeezed her boss' hand before pulling her vibrating phone out of her jeans pocket. "Draven keeps asking me to eat with him."

"See." Griffin's head fell back as he laughed. "Not happy unless you're giving us heart attacks."

"Blame my dad. He raised me." She tapped on the notification, her teasing falling aside as she read Olivia's text.

361

> **OLIVIA**
> Why is Ewan following me?

> **BEL**
> I don't know.

Her partner's response came so fast that Bel heard her escalating voice through the words on the screen.

> I told you I can't trust him.

> And I didn't tell him to follow you.

"Eamon," she whispered to herself, the realization hitting as soon as she hit send. He probably warned Ewan about Bel's late-night visitor, and worried that Olivia would receive a similar visit, Mr. Orso was hovering too close.

> Well, tell your boyfriend that we're not getting back together, so he can order Ewan to stop following me.

> That's not why he's following you.

> Then tell him I can take care of myself.

> Tell him yourself.

Bel's phone went silent, and she ground her teeth at the exchange.

"You all right?" Griffin asked as he watched Taron Monroe move across the set as if she were Bel herself. She'd clearly been studying the detective.

"Yeah." Bel shrugged off the conversation. Despite her hopes, it looked like she and Olivia were destined to forever remain only partners.

Evidence of a Folktale

"HAVE YOU HEARD FROM OLIVIA?" Bel asked her boss when he answered her call. It had been two days since she spoke to her partner, and while she no longer expected them to chat like they used to, she fully expected case updates.

"Yes, she left town this morning."

"Left town?" Bel repeated. Ewan's presence had upset her, but she hadn't predicted it would force her partner to flee. "Is she okay?"

"She's fine, sorry," Griffin said. "She found someone who knew the victims, so she drove out to speak with them. She didn't tell you?"

"No."

"Well, you've been busy, and this conversation is a long shot," he said. "I doubt she'll get anything from her contact, but there's no harm in her taking a meeting."

"We can't let this become a cold case," Bel said as she sank to the chair in the corner of Bajka's quaint vintage thrift store. They'd finished the library shoots and had moved to the thrift store, its eclectic vibe perfect for a fictional vampire, but because filming was running behind schedule, shooting days had grown unbearably long. Bel had barely seen her own bed, and the snow had returned to Bajka. It was already sticking to the roads, and the only upside to the storm threatening to bury the coated town was she wouldn't get stuck working until after midnight again.

"I know." Griffin's tired voice slipped through their phone connection, and Bel hated how he didn't assure her that wouldn't happen. Seemed even the sheriff believed solving these homicides was as much a fantasy as Aesop's Files.

"Well, let me know if she finds anything," Bel said. "I called her earlier, but she didn't answer, so I was just trying to figure out where she was... hold on, I'm getting another call." She

363

checked the screen before pressing the phone back to her ear. "It's Thum."

"I'll let you go," Griffin said, and she hung up with her boss before answering the medical examiner.

"Detective, can you stop by the morgue today?" Lina asked. "I realize you're busy, but since Olivia's out of town, I need to show you something."

"Um..." Bel rose from the chair and crossed the floor to the window to watch the fat snowflakes hide the street behind their fluffy curtain. "The weather will force us to halt shooting for the day soon, so maybe I can stop by before the storm gets bad."

"I don't want to make you drive in a blizzard," Lina said. "But you need to see this. Is there any way you can come now?"

"I'll check if another officer can escort Mr. Draven to the bed-and-breakfast for me." Bel scanned the thrift shop and spotted a deputy's head behind a vintage wardrobe.

"Sounds good. Let me know if you can't make it. I don't want to get stuck here."

"I'll text you in a few minutes." Bel hung up and jogged over to the officer, realizing it was Rollo when she tapped him on the shoulder.

"Can I ask for a favor?" she asked.

"Sure." He smiled. "What's up?"

"Lina needs me at the morgue," she said, "but I'm supposed to escort Mr. Draven back to the bed-and-breakfast after they wrap. Would you drive him for me?"

"Um..." Rollo shifted his weight, a conflict of interest wrestling on his features. "I'm technically past the end of my shift, and I've already put in overtime today. I planned to head over to Violet's before we get snowed in. I promised to spend the storm with her so I could shovel her out."

"Right." Bel rubbed the back of her neck as she tried to formulate a Plan B. "Okay, I'll see if I can find someone else."

"No, don't do that." Rollo sighed, his body sagging with the same weariness her muscles ached with. "I'll help."

"Are you sure?" she asked. "Is Griffin going to yell at me for how many hours I'm about to add to your overtime check?"

"Probably," he laughed.

"Okay. I'll ask someone else." She tried to leave, but the deputy captured her wrist before she made it two feet.

"No, Detective, I'll help," he insisted. "The snow's getting bad. I don't want you to have an accident because I wasted your time. I'll escort him back to the inn. It's no trouble."

"Thank you." Bel squeezed his biceps. "And you can blame Violet having to shovel her car out on me."

"Oh, I intend to!" Rollo shouted after her. "But maybe if I put in a good word, she'll forgive you."

"Let's hope!" She crossed her fingers over her head and then pulled Draven aside to warn him about her departure. The dusted streets slowed her trip to the morgue to a snail's pace despite her SUV's all-wheel drive, but she eventually made it, white flakes coating every inch of her just from racing from her car to the front door.

"How bad is it?" Lina asked as Bel stomped the snow off her boots.

"Getting there," she answered. "Thank god I have an SUV."

"I saw the new wheels," Lina said as she led the detective to her office. "It's nice." She raised her eyebrows to punctuate her words.

"Perks of coming back from the dead." Bel smirked. "It was Eamon's. He pulled it out of storage for me."

"Can you imagine having a car like that and keeping it in storage?" The M.E. shook her head. "Does he have any other cars he's looking to unload?" She gestured for the laughing Bel to take a seat and then slid behind her desk to wake up her computer.

"So, it took a lot of digging, but I finally located a cold case that matches the torn autopsy report in Warren Rouge's mouth," she continued, turning suddenly solemn, and such intensity filled her gaze that Bel's stomach clenched in anticipation. "This is it. This is why he's killing." She twisted her monitor so they could review the records together. "Six years ago, one year before the show became a viral sensation, a Jane Doe approximately in her seventies was found murdered in the snowy woods of the parks that line the Palisades Interstate Parkway just north of New York City." Lina clicked on the crime scene photos, and Bel almost threw up at the sight.

"What big eyes you have," she whispered as she traced the image of the snow-dusted pine trees. The same pine trees that were printed on the contact lenses inserted into Gwen Rossa's eyes.

"They line up exactly." Lina held up a print of Rossa's negatives, and the landscape from the police report matched it with beautiful uniformity. "There's no official time of death. Her body was discovered in January, but they don't know when she was killed. It was particularly cold that year, and with the freezing temperatures, she could've been there for days or even weeks."

"What big ears you have," Bel said. "That's why the weather report didn't mention a date just a month."

"I think so," Lina agreed. "Jane Doe was found stabbed five times in the abdomen, each wound made with the same weapon, but driven into her body with different force and angles. The medical examiner on the case questioned if that meant more than one assailant."

"What big teeth you have," Bel said, referencing the torn autopsy report in Rouge's mouth. "Five stab wounds. Five killers. Five murders here in Bajka."

"Well, technically four."

"But the fifth is coming. The killer isn't done, but he isn't targeting the show. He's getting revenge."

"That was my first thought," Lina agreed. "But I can't

imagine why members of the cast and crew, especially powerful players like the producer and director, would murder a woman."

"For a deal," she whispered to herself. What a big nose you have. The show's renewal article shoved into Rot's nostrils. It was this case's why, and Jane Doe was the who. A deal had been made to save Aesop's Files, but the victim's lives weren't the price. Jane Doe was. Five members of the show sacrificed an innocent woman to launch them into the limelight, and the man who'd threatened her outside her home had accepted this poor woman's death as his offering. He granted their wish in exchange for staining their souls with murder, and someone was picking them off one by one in a morbid display of revenge. The only question was who? Was the killer connected to the victim, or was it the deal himself? Dark magic almost always exacted payment in the cruelest ways. It had tried to steal Bel from Eamon. It had taken Anne from Blaubart. Had the Aesop's Files victims not read the fine print, and were they paying for that mistake now?

"That's not all," Lina said, interrupting her thoughts, and Bel froze in her seat. She didn't like the expression on the M.E.'s face.

"Jane Doe was found wearing one of those long and puffy winter jackets. The kind with hoods that reach mid-thigh. It was a white coat, so the police on the case figured the killers had tossed it over her body to hide her in the snow. They forgot to consider the blood, though, and that's how witnesses spotted the corpse. The blood seeped into the fabric, turning it completely red, and passersby noticed it.

"A red hooded cloak." Bel felt sick. "Stab wounds to the abdomen and a red cloak covering the bodies… he's replicating Jane Doe's death."

"Theatrically, but yes," Lina said.

"Because he's also mimicking the show with the claw marks and the pageantry. He wants us to understand that Jane Doe and

Aesop's Files are connected. Did the show shoot in New York six years ago? Were Rossa, Roja, Rot, and Rouge in the City? Could they have murdered Jane Doe?"

"I'm not sure," Lina said. "That'll be easy to confirm, though."

"I'll ask someone when I get back to set," Bel said.

"So it seems we found our who, but I thought he wouldn't reveal that until the final kill."

"He hasn't, though," Bel said. "We have no idea who Jane Doe is, and without an ID, we can't pinpoint who wants revenge. We still have to wait for the last death."

"We're so close," Lina sagged in her seat. "We practically have him, yet we have nothing. The detectives investigating Jane Doe's murder never even had a lead on her identity."

"It's why the killer gave this to us." Bel gestured to the digital report. "He knew that even if we found the cold case, we wouldn't figure it out. He's smart. He won't give us anything that can stop him."

"It makes you wonder who we're dealing with," Lina said.

"Yeah." But Bel didn't have to imagine. She knew. He'd threatened her. Only she had no way of learning his identity. He was as much of a mystery as Jane Doe.

"Doctor?" Lina's assistant leaned into her office. "The weather has taken a turn for the worse. If we don't leave now, we'll get stuck here. The news is warning people to go home and stay there."

"That bad already?" Lina asked. "Wow, okay. Thank you. And make sure everyone leaves."

"Will do," the man said as he disappeared down the hall.

"Well, thanks for coming." Lina stood to gather her things. "I hope you don't get stuck driving home. You have a longer trip than I do."

"I should return to set first and make sure everyone gets to

Evidence of a Folktale

the bed-and-breakfast safely," Bel said. "At this rate, I'll probably be sleeping there. Hopefully, they have an empty room."

"On the bright side, no one will leave the inn in this nasty weather. We shouldn't have to worry about anyone getting killed."

"Gwen Rossa's murder took place during a snowstorm," Bel reminded her. "Hence why I'm going back to check on everyone. I don't want to take any chances."

"Right... but this storm is shaping up to be worse than that one. Please be careful. No more car crashes, okay?"

"I'll try my best." Bel hugged the examiner goodbye but froze when her eyes landed on the computer screen. "Lina, what's that?" She released the M.E. and stepped back toward the desk, jabbing her finger at a wide-shot photograph of the Jane Doe evidence.

"Oh... um..." Lina leaned closer to the photo. "The detectives found that necklace at the scene, but they weren't convinced it belonged to the victim because of its location to the body."

"Close, but not that close?" she asked.

"Something like that. It's why the jewelry was never released to the public in case it alerted the killers that they'd been discovered."

"Do you know what the pendant is?" Bel strained to make out the carving.

"There's a closeup somewhere." Lina leaned down and scrolled through the images. "I looked it up, though, and it's a depiction of Saint Anne — oh, here's the photo. Saint Anne is the patron saint of different types of women," she continued, oblivious to Bel's sudden distress. "But most notable is that of grandmothers."

Bel studied the enlarged engraving, and her stomach plummeted through her body when she saw the image. The alarm-

369

ingly familiar image of a saint reading a book to the child leaning against her lap. She'd seen this saint before, but it hadn't been on a medallion. It had been a tattoo, and she'd just handed the actor they believed to be the next victim over to its owner.

Autopsy Report

CERBERUS

PROD.NO. | TAKE | SOUND
SCENE | |
DIRECTOR
CAMERAMAN | EXT. | INT.

CINEMA TICKET ADMIT ONE 9891102

CINEMA TICKET ADMIT ONE 9891102

Chapter Twenty Three

Bel launched into a run, leaving a baffled Lina in her wake. She slid on the snow as she exploded from the morgue's front door, cracking her knees on the sidewalk as she stumbled, but she was on her feet in seconds, tumbling with bruises and all into her SUV. She knew who the killer was, and she'd handed Beau Draven over to him. This storm was worse than the one that fell the night Gwen Rossa died, but it was a storm all the same—a perfect cover for a murder. No one would notice Beau Draven's or Ethan Rollo's absence until it was too late.

Bel smashed her car's Bluetooth button, sending Eamon a silent thank you for gifting her a vehicle with all the bells and whistles, and ordered the automated voice to dial Griffin. Death grip on the steering wheel, she waited for him to answer, but when his cell went to voicemail three times in a row, she radioed dispatch.

"Has anyone seen Griffin?" she asked.

"There was a multi-car accident a few minutes ago, and he's at the scene," the operator said. "There are unconfirmed reports of casualties."

"Oh god."

"It's awful," the operator said. "Be careful out there, Detective. It's getting bad."

Bel gritted her teeth as she took a turn too fast and prayed that no one died in that crash.

"If I hear from him, I'll tell him you called," the woman said. "Do you want me to pass along a message?"

"Yeah..." Bel snapped her mouth shut. What if she was wrong? She couldn't broadcast her theory about Rollo without proof. It would ruin him if she were mistaken. "Actually, no. Just tell him to call me."

"Will do, Detective."

"Thanks." Bel slammed on her brakes, her SUV skidding to a stop outside the thrift store, and she launched herself out into the snow. "Mr. Draven?" she called as she burst through the front door. "Mr. Draven...? Excuse me." She grabbed a production assistant's arm. "Have you seen Beau?"

"You just missed him," the man said. "Filming shut down early, and we're just getting the last of the set packed up."

"Was he with Officer Rollo?" she asked.

"Yeah, but they only left for the bed-and-breakfast a few minutes ago."

"Thanks." Bel raced back to her car, her shoulder slapping on the frame in her haste to jump into the driver's seat. She gritted her teeth to keep from groaning as she threw the SUV into drive and surged down the coated street. She had time. She could still catch them.

Ten minutes later, though, the traffic ground to a halt. The red and blue lights of the squad car painted the snow-laden air, and realizing she wasn't getting anywhere soon, Bel parked and jogged to the deputy directing the cars.

"What's going on?" she asked, wrapping her arms around herself to shield her chest from the piercing wind.

"Accident," the deputy said. "The entire road is closed off. We're rerouting people."

Evidence of a Folktale

"I heard that there might be casualties. Is that true?"

"I don't know. Maybe. It's bad."

Bel cursed as she peered behind the man. She'd never reach the inn using this street. She'd have to take the long way.

"Did you see Officer Rollo pass by here?" she asked.

"Yeah, a bit ago," the deputy said. "He was driving that actor to the bed-and-breakfast."

"Did he take the detour?"

"I think so."

"Thanks." Bel sprinted back to her car and used the Bluetooth to dial the inn. "This is Detective Isobel Emerson. Has Mr. Draven returned yet?" she asked when the owner answered her call.

"Hi, Detective," the woman said. "No, I've yet to see him. Returns are slow with this weather, though. I hope you're staying out of it."

"So you haven't seen him?"

"Not since this morning, no."

Bel cursed under her breath. "Thanks." She hung up and drove recklessly around a smaller car blocking her path. Beau hadn't returned to the inn, but that meant nothing in this blizzard. It was slow going, especially with the accident. They might still be driving. She still might catch them.

Bel honked her horn, and the sedan ahead of her swerved out of the way. The driver flashed her a glare as she passed, only for his expression to turn sheepish when he saw her raised badge. She continued to honk, receiving car after car of dirty looks until the drivers realized she was a cop on a mission, and through the curtain of snow, blue and red flashing lights finally came into view. Sagging into her seat, Bel pulled up beside the squad car, confident she'd found Rollo until she recognized the officer's features. She cursed as she rolled down her window, and Yates leaned down from where he stood guiding traffic.

"You okay, Detective?" he asked.

375

"Officer Rollo and Mr. Draven," she shouted over the commotion of horns and distant sirens. "Have you seen them?"

"Um..." the officer peered behind her. "I'm the only squad car I've seen. Most are at the accident site."

"Do you know if there were casualties?"

The deputy stared down at her with pinched lips, and she had her answer. Someone had died, and her mind flashed to Violet. According to Rollo, she was supposed to be home waiting for him. She prayed that was the truth.

"So, to confirm, Officer Rollo never drove past you?" she asked.

"No. I don't think so."

"Thanks." Bel rolled up her window with a curse. Somewhere between the last officer directing traffic and Deputy Yates, Rollo and Draven had disappeared, and she turned her car around. Creeping through the wall of white, she scanned the streets for a clue where Rollo had taken the actor.

It all made sense now. Why the bodies provided no evidence. Why the victims didn't have defensive wounds. The killer was a cop. He knew what the detectives would search for, so he'd been careful. People trusted police officers. They'd be quick to accept a lift from a handsome officer in the cold. Rollo had been on duty when Ellery Roja left the inn for snacks, but his shift ended only minutes later. Had he driven to the twenty-four-hour mart and offered the costume designer a ride home just beyond the reach of the store's surveillance? Had he promised to protect her and then flirted to distract her from where he was driving? Or had she enjoyed the flirting and agreed to disappear with him? Was that how he'd convinced Gwen Rossa to get into his car? Had he used his beauty to catch her eye and lure her into the woods?

Bel couldn't figure out how he'd tricked Alistair Rot into his car, but being a police officer, she imagined it took little convincing, and with Warren Rouge, Chloe Rider did all the heavy lifting. After Miss Rider left the bed-and-breakfast in the cab, Rollo drove to check out a noise. He'd then parked so only the front feet of his hood were visible on camera, and Bel assumed it was because he wanted a better view of the inn. Only he hadn't been there. The car's lights were merely his alibi. He'd left, killed the director, and returned before the end of his shift, his squad car never moving from the camera's watchful eye.

And now Draven, or as he'd been born, Reds. Bel had handed him to Rollo on a silver platter, a dangerous blizzard and a fatal car crash granting him the perfect night of chaos. With all the snow, Rollo probably excused his deviation from the detour as a way to skirt traffic. Draven was unfamiliar with Bajka. He wouldn't know that Rollo's alternate route was a lie. He wouldn't remember which directions led back to the inn and which led to the tree-concealed hiking trails.

Bel slammed on her brakes, her SUV sliding a few feet before it slowed to a halt. Tire tracks. They were faint, meaning no one else had traversed that side street in a few minutes, but she knew whose car they belonged to. This was where Rollo deviated from the detour because that seemingly inconsequential street led to a road that eventually wound its way to the edge of town… the edge that sat up against the hiking trails and the expansive Reale Estate. He was taking Draven into the woods, and if she didn't catch up with him, Beau would become Bajka's most famous murder victim.

Bel eased through the cars blocking the turn. She could barely see more than a few feet ahead of her, and she thanked God this part of town was abandoned. She pushed her car to a reckless pace and hit the Bluetooth button to dial her boss.

But nothing happened.

She dialed again, but a quick glance told her she had no service. The accident or the storm must've knocked something out, and she glanced at her useless phone as she barreled after a serial killer. Olivia was out of town and the entire force was dealing with the crash. If she didn't catch Rollo, Beau would die, and while he might be guilty in his own right, she couldn't let Hollywood's favorite heartthrob die in Bajka. Rollo was bigger than her, but he wasn't as experienced. He was younger, and he hadn't faced evil like she had. He hadn't survived a witch or two kidnappings. He hadn't fought a man cursed by a drugged tattoo or lived through the Impaler's attack. He was nothing but a young officer with a gun. Bel was the woman who threw herself into kidnappers' cars and choked them until they crashed. As long as she reached Rollo before he murdered Draven, she was the one with the upper hand.

"I'm coming, I'm coming," Eamon called as he jogged down the grand staircase. Cerberus was barking at the front door, signaling he wanted to go outside, and Eamon felt guilty. He'd been so distracted by helping Bel these past few weeks that he needed to play catch-up on his own work. He'd sequestered himself in his office, gifting Bel's pitbull a pile of new toys to keep him busy, but that was hours ago. It seemed the poor animal had to potty so badly that he'd taken to shouting in the foyer so his voice would echo endlessly throughout the mansion.

"I should build you a fence out back and a doggy door," he said as he shoved his feet into his shoes and pulled open the door. "I'll have to install security cameras though, because I don't think your mom would like you hanging outside alone, even with a fence."

Cerberus ignored his musings and leaped off the front stoop, almost disappearing in the deep snow as he landed on the driveway. Eamon burst into laughter as the pup's stocky legs fought the white drifts, and then he froze. He'd been locked in his office all day, and while he'd noticed the snowflakes falling past his window, he'd been on the second floor. He hadn't realized how

Evidence of a Folktale

deep it had gotten, and panic replaced his humor at Cerberus' antics. Bel wasn't home, nor had she called, and he pulled out his phone to click on their text thread.

> EAMON
>
> Just checking in since the storm's getting worse. Are you okay? Do you need me to come get you?

Cerberus barked, and Eamon glanced up, shoving his cell into his pocket when he realized the pitbull was glaring at him.

"Are you stuck, or are you mad I'm not playing?" he asked, and the pup barked again, shifting his weight to tell Eamon his tootsies were cold.

"Big baby." Eamon chuckled as he jumped down into the white. "You can do it. I just saw you walk out there. And I know you don't mind the cold... granted, the snow doesn't usually reach your shoulders." He scooped up the dog and dusted the snow off his chilly body. "Better?" he asked as he strode to the front door, and Cerberus planted a messy kiss on his cheek. "Like I said, big baby." But he kissed the dog's beefy head for good measure before depositing him inside. "Once the storm slows, I'll shovel a section for you, okay?"

Cerberus wagged his tail as if he understood Eamon's promise, and Eamon patted his head before leading the dog into the kitchen. He was up. He should feed them both before he metaphorically chained himself to his desk for the night.

"I hope your mom's okay," he said, checking his silent phone before dumping food into Cerberus' bowl. "I know she's an adult... and a tornado of a woman, but I hate when she doesn't call." He turned on the kitchen TV and scratched the munching pup before turning to the fridge. He always waited to make dinner until Bel returned home so he could eat with her, but these meals he preferred to eat alone. She'd yet to see him feed. He could go for extended periods without blood, but he couldn't quit

379

it. It was one of his only weaknesses. If starved, he would eventually wither into dust. Lucky for him, and unfortunately for his enemies, he was almost impossible to restrain, and human blood was one of the easiest meals to obtain. It was harder to consume when he drank ethically, but it would take him an exceptionally long time to starve. Many had tried starving him, including his own mother. Not one had come even close.

Eamon removed the shelf and unlocked the secret compartment in the back of his fridge. He didn't want Bel stumbling onto his stores while fishing for a snack, so he'd commissioned a custom refrigerator. He funded multiple private medical groups, which made it easy to skim donations off the top. Bel knew blood ensured his survival, and she appreciated the absence of death, but he wasn't sure how she would react if she saw him sucking down prepacked blood as if it were a juice box.

"No, this isn't for you." Eamon pushed the piggy Cerberus aside. The dog had finished his meal, and his curiosity had him chasing Eamon through the kitchen. "You just ate, and your mom would get mad if I overfed you and then the vet yelled at her. I don't get off as easily as you do. She thinks you do no wrong, but she likes to yell at me. She'll blame me if you get tubby." He gave the pit's muscular ribs a loving thump. "So no begging. You don't want me getting into trouble, do you?"

Eamon put the blood into a bottle warmer. Infants drank formula at around ninety-eight degrees Fahrenheit, and human blood was around one hundred degrees when flowing through the body. The bottle warmer was such an innocent thing to purchase, yet its use in his house would shock most mothers, this pitbull's mom included. Or maybe not. Bel loved him even though his crimes had inspired the most feared literary creature. Maybe this setup wouldn't freak her out.

Eamon glanced at his phone again, the dog's mother still ignoring him, and he hated how his stomach roiled at the silence. The weather was atrocious, and her attention was undoubtedly focused on driving, not checking her texts, but the same fears plagued him every time their communications went silent. In reality, both her hands were probably glued to the steering wheel, but in his mind, her lack of response meant she was bleeding out in a ditch.

"Get a grip," he growled at himself as he grabbed the warmed blood and stared at the television to distract himself. She was fine. She was watching an arrogant yet unreasonably handsome actor. Being flirted with was the only danger threatening her, but that didn't bother him. Not because he wasn't jealous, but because Bel was a special breed of woman. She didn't give him reason to doubt her loyalty. She might tease him, but she'd never betray his trust. It was one of the many reasons he loved her so unconditionally. He didn't need to worry about her leaving him for the flattery of a celebrity. He did worry about her leaving him because she'd been reckless... again.

Eamon downed the blood, bored with the television program. It was yet another special on Aesop's Files and the murders plaguing Bajka. He'd watched season after season to help Bel, and he was so sick of the show that the clips on the screen made him want to gag on this dinner, so he grabbed the remote and aimed it to turn off the TV when the camera zoomed in on a behind-the-scene recording from years ago.

Eamon's already cool body flushed as cold as the snow coating the earth outside his mansion, and he hit the pause button, freezing the shot so he could get a better look. But his eyes weren't lying. The footage was of Beau Draven and his original costar Willow Moon speaking to the director, Warren Rouge. The handheld camera shook as it captured the interactions, but it wasn't those familiar faces that rooted Eamon's feet to the ground. It was the man behind the actors. He was young, practically a kid helping to run cables through the set. He was clearly only a production assistant, and while his outfit differed vastly from the uniform he wore now, his face was the same. Ethan Rollo had worked for Aesop's Files before its rise to fame, and Eamon understood. The Bajka Police Department hadn't hired Rollo by accident. He was here on purpose.

Eamon dialed Bel's number so fast that he almost cracked the screen with his force, but the call failed. He tried again, but then he noticed the absence of service. The storm must've damaged a nearby cell tower, so he pulled up the necklace tracker on its app. Its advanced technology didn't rely on conventional networks, and to his relief, the red dot marking her location lit up his screen. His relief was short-lived, though, because Bel wasn't on set. She wasn't at the station or the inn. She wasn't even in town. The location pinged from the woods near his property, and with a jolt of fear so powerful that physical pain lanced his chest, Eamon raced for the door. He didn't bother with a coat. He didn't bother with car keys. He simply ran out into the blizzard, praying he wasn't too late.

BEL PULLED up next to the parked squad car, but even through the thick snow, she could see it stood empty. She cursed, slamming her fist on the steering wheel before scanning the trees. Confronting Rollo by their cars was one thing, but chasing him into the whiteness? That wouldn't end well, and if Rollo had forced Draven into the woods, it would be a matter of minutes before the officer gutted him. Not that she'd be able to find them in this blizzard. Her SUV handled inclement weather well, though. Maybe she should push forward and see—

Bel jumped out of the car and reached for her necklace, the crimson fabric a beacon in the white only a few yards ahead of the parked vehicles. The men hadn't wandered far. Draven was still alive, and he wasn't wearing the red cloak. It still hung from Rollo's clenched fist... his unarmed fist. The deputy didn't even

Evidence of a Folktale

have his service weapon on his person, and Bel withdrew her weapon instead of pressing the panic button.

"Don't do it, Rollo!" she shouted above the winds, and both men flinched at her voice.

"Oh thank god, Detective!" Beau shrieked, but Rollo clocked him in the head, silencing his plea.

"Shut up," he growled.

"Whatever you're thinking about doing, don't!" Bel inched closer, thumbing off her gun's safety. "Drop the cloak and put your hands in the air."

"You shouldn't be here, Detective," Rollo shouted. He wasn't wearing his uniform either. Only a simple white tee shirt and loose hanging sweats protected him from the cold.

"And neither should you, Ethan." Bel switched to his first name, hoping it would give him pause. "You've done nothing yet. We can get in the car and go home."

"Except that's a lie!" he shouted. "I've already killed four people. I can never go home, so I'm going to finish this."

"Please don't do this, Ethan," she begged. "I can't let you kill him, and I don't want to shoot you. I will, though, so don't make me."

"Leave, Detective. I like you... a lot. I don't want to hurt you."

"Then don't!" Bel stepped another foot closer. "Just get back in the car. It's that simple."

"I can't stop now!" he shouted. "You don't understand, but I won't let him get away with what he did."

"I know what he did," she said, changing tactics. Pleading with him wasn't working. Maybe assuring him someone understood his pain would. "Jane Doe, six years ago. Her body was found in the woods with multiple stab wounds. The police surmised a different person inflicted each blow. Five killers. Five victims. Jane Doe was your grandmother, wasn't she?"

"And they slaughtered her like an animal!" Rollo shouted,

383

and the waver in his voice warned Bel he was crying. "I worked for the show then. I was just a production assistant, so I meant nothing to these monsters." He shoved Beau, and the falling stage light that almost hit Taron flashed through Bel's memory. He'd known exactly how to help because he'd worked on a set before. It was how he got his hands on the prop-like clues and weapon. He still had connections from his time with Aesop's Files.

"They were going to cancel the show," he continued, and Bel crept another foot closer. "They were all losing their shot at fame, so the... never mind, you wouldn't understand!" He grabbed Beau by the throat, and Bel lunged forward, her finger ready on the trigger

"Except you know I do!" she argued. "It's why I've never seen you and Eamon in the same room together. You recognize what he is and have been hiding from his power, so of course I understand. I know why the show became famous overnight. These five made a deal, and your grandmother was the price. All black magic is bought with blood and pain, and your grandma was the sacrifice."

Rollo gawked at her, and Bel seized his shock to move yet another foot closer. If he learned she understood the darkness that plagued this world, maybe he'd listen to her.

"They must have selected your grandmother because of you," she continued. "Did the deal demand an offering who meant something to the cast and crew? Did they choose your grandmother because you loved her? They didn't want to sacrifice their own families, so they condemned a nobody. A lowly production assistant."

"Yes" Rollo collapsed in on himself, and Bel let herself exhale. She was getting to him.

"They needed someone loved, otherwise the magic wouldn't be powerful enough," he continued. "I was nothing to them. Just some broke assistant with no family, save an old lady. So they

Evidence of a Folktale

butchered her and became famous while I suffered for six years. Six years!" His aggression swelled, and Bel feared she was losing him.

"I tried to bring my grandmother justice the legal way." Rollo seized Beau's shirt and positioned him as a human shield. Bel's anxiety flinched, but she controlled her expression. Using the actor as a shield didn't bode well for their outcome. Rollo wasn't listening to her. He had no intentions of complying. He was preparing for a fight, and if Bel took him down, he intended Draven to die with him.

"I went to the police and presented proof, but it didn't help," he continued. "I gave them Grandma's name, yet she's still only known as Jane Doe. It was like they couldn't hear me. The deal wouldn't let me undo his work, so I became a cop. I thought if I joined the force, I could influence change from the inside, but it was pointless. The show's fame eclipsed all justice, so I took matters into my own hands. When I learned Bajka needed new deputies, I applied, and after I was hired, I reached out to my old contacts. I put the idea of filming here into their heads. I sent photos and my praises. I recommended holding the fan events here since a smaller town would be safer, and their greed fell for it. I had them eating out of the palms of my hand, and they lowered their guard. Gwen Rossa, Ellery Roja, Alistair Rot, Warren Rouge, and now Beau Reds. The five people who murdered my grandmother. I made them pay for the life they stole. I killed them the same way they heartlessly cut into her because I wanted them to be afraid, to know I was coming for them. I still have one more to punish for his sins."

"Let me go!" Draven fought against Rollo's hold. "Detective, do your job and get this lunatic off me."

"Ethan," Bel begged, irritated by Beau's arrogance in the face of his guilt. "Please don't do this. Let him go, and I'll make sure he pays. You know me. I keep my word."

"I do know you, Detective," he said. "It's why you need to

leave. I don't want to hurt you, but the deal won't let you take Draven down. Any evidence you think you have against these five will never see the light of day. That devil is Aesop's Files now, so death is the only way to make the guilty pay. I'm already going to hell for my crimes. What's one more death on my hands?"

"Detective, get him off me!" Beau screamed.

"Ethan, don't make me shoot you." Bel raised her gun, wondering if she was doing the right thing. Beau Draven had murdered an innocent grandmother for the fickle future of fame. He deserved this fate, didn't he? "You aren't going to hell for your sins," she continued. "These people are monsters. They deserve what they got, but don't add another murder to your list. Let him go, and I'll help you. I promise to do whatever's needed, but you have to let him go."

"Leave, Detective."

"Please, Ethan, don't do this."

"I said leave, Bel!" he screamed, his body vibrating unnaturally.

"I can't let you do this." She aimed her gun.

"But I have to." Rollo met her gaze, and the violence in his eyes made her stumble backward. It wasn't human. "I've had enough talking," he growled, his voice deepening with an unnatural tremor. "It ends tonight, Detective. Don't get in my way. I don't want to hurt you, but I won't let Beau Draven live. I'll die before I let him go free."

And with that, Rollo's body burst apart, his skin splitting in the most gruesome display of gore… one that Bel had witnessed once before, and just like Ewan when he shed his human shell to inhabit the bear, Rollo's flesh mutated into fur and claws until a wolf more monster than animal stood before her.

Autopsy Report

CERBERUS

Chapter Twenty Four

A WEREWOLF.

Ethan Rollo was a werewolf, and for a split second, Bel forgot to be afraid as the magnitude of this revelation settled over her. The claw-like wounds, the dog fur, the unnatural sent Eamon detected, and Bel's memory rewound to the night they found the Matchstick Girls in their freezer. Eamon had slipped unseen onto the property to comfort her, but he'd sensed something inhuman. Bel had assumed it was the killer or Ewan, and then her kidnapping ensured she forgot their conversation, but it all came flooding back. He'd scented Rollo at that crime scene, just as he had on the bodies in the woods. Only she couldn't remember a single moment when the men had crossed paths. Anytime her boyfriend was on set, the deputy had magically been assigned to the outdoor perimeter, and the one time he'd ventured inside to rescue Taron from the falling light, Eamon had been outside speaking Japanese to a client. Rollo clearly recognized the greater power and steered clear of him, and with supernaturals flocking to the events, Eamon's senses were too overwhelmed to detect a distant wolf. What would've happened if Eamon had joined them at the bar? Would Rollo have suddenly grown ill and canceled?

"Holy—!" Beau screamed before a powerful blow silenced him, and Bel's fear came flooding back. Rollo was gone, a seven-foot werewolf in his place, and she no longer had the upper hand. When he was merely a deputy, she held the power. But now?

Rollo spun on her, fangs bared as he reared onto his hind legs. He wasn't a wolf in a natural sense. He didn't stand on all fours, nor did he resemble the ancestors of the household pet. He was a creature from a nightmare—both man and animal—with canines protruding from his snout and claws curving from his fingers, and Bel couldn't tear her eyes away from their savagery. A custom prop weapon hadn't killed his victims. He'd slaughtered them with his own hands, and by the crazed focus in his gaze, he'd set his sights on her for interrupting his final kill.

"Rollo, don't!" she screamed as he charged, and with a prayer for forgiveness on her tongue, she pulled the trigger. The bullet slammed the werewolf in the shoulder, and he flew backward, crashing into the snow so hard that his body almost disappeared under the mountain of white.

"Draven, run!" she shouted as she reached under her coat and jammed the panic button. Why hadn't she pressed it when the cell service went down? Would Eamon even get her alert if the phone didn't work? Not that it mattered if he did. He'd never make it in time. His mansion was too far away, and Rollo was already moving.

"Draven, now!" She held her gun at the ready, their only hope of survival getting back to her car, and as she backed up through the snow, Eamon's words played out in her head. He'd made her promise to step aside if the deal came for his last victim and proved too powerful for her to combat. Their suspected killer had been wrong, but the sentiment was the same. Bel couldn't fight a werewolf, and was a murderer's life worth hers? Could she step aside and let someone die? Could she just stand there watching as Rollo sliced through Beau and then leave him to bleed out?

"Draven!" Mind made up, she lowered her weapon and raced for her SUV. If he reached the car, she'd help, but if the wolf caught him first, she'd allow fate to punish him for his sins.

"What's going on?" Draven screamed as he fumbled through the snow. "What did you give me? Did you drug me? You must have." He stopped to gawk at the werewolf struggling to regain its footing. "You drugged me, and then refuse to help me? You really are a—"

Rollo's roar cut him off as he surged to his feet, and Beau bolted for Bel. She paused, gun aimed as she tracked the creature's movements, but just before he reached her, Rollo coiled his legs below him and leaped.

Bel couldn't stop her scream as the werewolf sailed over their heads, and with a jolt like thunder, he landed behind her, cutting off her escape to the cars. Bel slipped on the snow, her knee collapsing as she struggled not to fall on her face, and then she took off running in the opposite direction, her weapon aimed at the creature. She fired two shots, neither finding their target, and she grabbed Draven by the arm. She should let Rollo have him. Let the wolf exact his revenge, but then the world would view Beau as a martyr and not the murderer he was. Bel wouldn't let him die here to become a legend. He was going to live and stand trial. He would have to face his fans as they learned he was a monster.

"Let him go!" Rollo's voice was so cruelly guttural that tears pricked Bel's eyes involuntarily, and she twisted, firing off a fourth shot. This one found a home in the wolf's shoulder, but instead of slowing him down, Rollo leaned into the blow and leaped for her. Bel screamed as the wind whistled at her back, as the tip of Rollo's claws sliced through the fabric of her coat, and she braced for the pain. She braced for the end, but before his claws dug into her flesh, a shadow with inhuman speed burst through the trees. The figure collided with the wolf with such force that bones audibly snapped, and she tripped over Beau, tumbling to the ground as war broke out.

"What the—?" he started, but Bel slammed his face into the snow.

"Shut up," she snarled, climbing on top of him to handcuff his arms behind his back. "You have the right to remain silent, so shut up!" She'd finish reciting the Miranda Warning when death didn't hang so heavy in the air, and the minute Beau was secured, she rose to her feet and spun toward the violence.

"Oh my god." She clapped a hand over her mouth to hold in her fear. Eamon had come for her. Somehow, he'd arrived in time, and hell had broken loose on earth. Blood and snow and tree splinters flew on the wind as the Dhampir and werewolf fought. Rollo's claws dug into Eamon's side, ripping his shirt clean off his body as they ravaged his flesh, and Bel thought she might vomit at the sight. Blood poured down Eamon's ribs, and he skidded to a stop, testing the gouges' severity with his fingers as he settled his weight between Bel and the werewolf.

"Isobel?" he shouted as the wolf stalked him, hunting for an opening.

"I'm okay!" she assured him, but no sooner did the words leave her mouth than Rollo attacked. Bel had witnessed Eamon fight Ewan in his bear form, but Ewan hadn't wanted to harm them. He was simply searching for Olivia, so he'd retreated the first chance he got, but Rollo had no intention of backing down. He wanted death. Bel's? Eamon's? Beau's? He didn't seem to care, and Bel gripped her stomach as the men turned the snow crimson with their blood. Rollo's bones broke. Eamon's flesh split apart until gruesome slabs hung loose, and tears filled her eyes as her beloved's roar of pain echoed endlessly through the mountains.

"Please," she begged. She didn't know who she was asking.

All she knew was that she couldn't bear the sight of Eamon's skin peeling away from his skeleton.

"Yield," Eamon growled as he rolled through the snow and landed in a predatory crouch.

"Never." Rollo gnashed his fangs. "I won't stop until Draven's dead."

"But you made a mistake. You went after Isobel," Eamon snarled. "This is your last chance to yield, or I'll kill you."

"I told her to leave." The wolf slashed a tree trunk with his claws. "I warned her, but she wouldn't listen."

"You put your hands on her. Yield or I will kill you."

"Then kill me because I would rather die than let Draven live." And with that, Rollo sprang forward, but the Dhampir expected his attack. With movements almost too fast for Bel to see, Eamon lunged sideways and caught the werewolf's throat. With a strangled gag, Rollo clawed at Eamon's fist, but the millionaire held tight, and with a surge of power, Eamon hauled the wolf to his mouth.

Bel increased her palm's pressure over her mouth as Rollo's unnatural screams polluted the air. He writhed and screamed and flailed, but Eamon didn't relent. He trapped him against his mouth, his teeth biting deeper. And then he drank. Blood pumped from the werewolf's veins passed Eamon's tongue, and with every swallow, the wolf struggled less and less. His screams quieted. His resistance waned, and with a nauseating punch to her gut, Bel realized Eamon was killing him. A few more seconds, and Rollo would bleed to death, and by the bloodlust flooding her boyfriend's eyes, he had no intention of stopping until he drained the werewolf dry.

"Eamon, stop!" She raced for him as Rollo's wolf mutated, skin replacing fur. He was dying, his body reverting to its human form, and Bel fought the deep snow drifts as she ran faster.

"Please," she begged. "Don't kill him." She didn't want

Rollo to die. Despite everything, she still cared for the deputy, and she didn't want to witness his ending.

"Eamon, stop!" She grabbed his shoulder, and like a man possessed, he dropped the bleeding but very human Rollo and whirled on her. Bel flinched at the hunger in his gaze and the blood coating his mouth. This was how he'd looked a year ago when the curse drove him to try killing her. The death in his black eyes had given her nightmares, and the hazy craze in his expression now yanked her back to that horrifying night. She stepped backward, her heart thundering at the beast before her, and she got a glimpse of who he'd been in the first ages. This is what humanity knew him for, and he was terrifying.

"Isobel." Eamon grabbed her, and she shrieked at the speed, but before she could register what happened, she was suffocating against his chest.

He cursed, the words ugly and vulgar as they vibrated his ribs against her face, and he wrapped his arms around her head, instinctively burying his nose in her hair.

"Are you okay?" he asked, his concern so at war with his violence that Bel wasn't sure he'd actually spoken.

"Isobel?" he repeated. "Are you hurt?"

"No." His bloody chest and raging heartbeat muffled her answer.

"Oh, thank god." He kissed a path to her cheek as he forced her to meet his gaze. They hovered wordlessly inside the blizzard, and then his lips met hers, hunger flowing through him in an entirely new way. He was still a predator, but he no longer wanted to kill and consume.

Without warning, he cursed against her mouth, and his almost angry departure confused Bel until she felt his fingers brush against her face. "Sorry," he apologized as he wiped Rollo's blood from her lips. "I..." he fumbled over his words, and Bel had the distinct impression he was high. "I'm sorry...

Evidence of a Folktale

I'm just so relieved." He pulled her back into his arms. "I got here in time."

"Are you crying?" she asked, shocked by the tremble in his voice.

"I got here in time," he repeated, and she heard it clearly. He was crying. "Thank you for pressing the button, but Detective, push it sooner. I thankfully realized cell service was down, so I checked your tracker's location. When I saw you were in the woods, I left the house, but please, for the love of God—or me—push the panic button immediately."

"I'm sorry. I made a bad judgment call." She cupped his bloody jaw, not caring that she was now soaked in his blood. It wasn't the first time, and she suspected it wouldn't be the last. "When I got here, Rollo was unarmed. I didn't know he was a wolf, so I didn't expect to need your help. Thank you for coming for me, anyway."

"I made it." He cupped her face in return. "We can do this. We'll make this work... just press the button sooner."

"I told you we're better together." She kissed him softly, despite the blood still staining his lips. She loved this man. No... she loved this Dhampir. Impaler or not, Eamon Stone was hers, and she would never give him up.

"Are you sure you're okay?" he asked when they finally broke apart, and for the first time, Bel registered how little he was wearing. He was barefoot and now shirtless in the snow, and even though she knew he didn't feel cold like her, she wrapped her arms around his healing waist.

"Physically? Yes," she answered "Emotionally? Not in the slightest. I like Rollo. I don't want to arrest him for this. I don't want Violet to learn she was falling for a serial killer."

"It's no different from you loving me," Eamon said.

"But you didn't come into my town to slaughter people."

"No." he traced her scars. "I only tried to harm you."

"It's why I asked you not to kill Rollo," she said. "It reminded me too much of that night."

"I'm sorry."

"And I hate when you're hurt. It makes me sick."

"You know I heal."

"Doesn't matter." She pressed her ear against his thundering heart. "I love you. I can't watch monsters rip you apart. Are you okay?"

"Of course I am."

"Then why do your eyes look like that?" She pinched his jaw and tilted his head so she could study his unfocused eyes. "Are you on something?"

"I almost drank a werewolf to death," he answered. "That's a lot of supernatural blood running through me."

"Will you be okay?" she asked.

"Yeah." He tucked her hair behind her ears. "A little jacked up on the bloodlust, but it'll wear off. Don't worry. I'm not a danger to you. I fed before I came, and then all that blood. I won't need to feed for a while."

"Ok good." She rubbed his chest as he lowered his nose to her neck to inhale her scent, and it didn't surprise her that she wasn't the least bit afraid of his sharp canines so close to her throat.

"You smell incredible, though… sorry." He cursed as he forced himself to step away from her. "The last time I drank like this was when I attacked you, so my instincts are raging. I won't hurt you; I swear it. I just can't get over how your skin smells."

"I'm not afraid of you."

"I see that." He smiled, and the red bathing his mouth made for an unsettling grin. "Thank you for not being afraid of me. For trusting that I can control myself around you." He tapped his forehead against hers. "God, I made a mess of you, though."

"I don't care." She stared down at the unconscious Rollo. "I was more worried about your life than my coat."

Evidence of a Folktale

"I'll buy you a replacement, but for now, what do we do with these two?" he asked before she could protest.

"I know what we should do," she said, gripping his hand for emotional support. "But, god, I don't want to."

BEL DIDN'T CHANGE, nor did she wash the blood from her body. The Bajka Police Department would demand proof that one of their own was to blame for the bloodshed plaguing their town, and the sight of her crimson coat would persuade even the most cynical doubter. Eamon had helped her dress the weak and wounded Rollo back into his uniform since his tee shirt and sweats shredded when he shifted, and then they'd locked both the werewolf and the actor in the rear of the squad car. He'd heal enough to explain the red on her clothes while not alerting anyone to the fact that he'd been shot twice. Eamon then took her SUV and forged a path through the nearly impenetrable blizzard, and she followed him with their prisoners, struggling not to cry during the seemingly endless trip.

One of Bajka's own had betrayed their trust. A man she liked. A man whose arms she'd pushed her friend into. A man she almost didn't blame for his sins. Because what would she have done if someone sacrificed her father so brutally for a reward as shallow as fame? What would she do if someone desecrated her sisters' bodies and got away with it? What would she do if she couldn't legally bring her family's killers to justice, no matter how hard she tried? Would she walk away and move on from the people she loved, or would the tragedy drive her to madness? Could she ever let such a heinous crime go? Would she ever forget the way her sister's mutilated body looked in the snow? Was she going to hell for arresting a man who did what the police had failed to do six years ago?

Darkness had long since fallen by the time Bel and Eamon

pulled into the station's parking lot. Her hands were slick with sweat from gripping the steering wheel so intensely. It had been the most difficult drive of her life, both because the roads were impossible to traverse and because the image of Rollo's claws ripping apart Eamon's body played on repeat through her memory. It didn't matter that he wasn't easily killed. She loved him, and when he bled, her heart bled with him.

"Are you ready?" Eamon asked when she finally stepped out of the squad car.

"No," she whispered, still shocked they'd survive the drive through the storm. "Are we doing the right thing arresting Rollo? His victims made a deal with a devil to ensure their success. They deserve his punishment."

"I agree, but he chose this fate. Rollo could've killed them quietly. He's a wolf. He could've dragged them into the woods and ensured their bodies were never found, but he shoved his murders in your face. He wanted public vengeance for his grandmother, so this is the price he must pay."

"The price we all must pay." Bel gripped Eamon's hand. "Walk inside with me?"

"I'll raise questions." He glanced down at his bare chest and feet.

"Back seat of my car on the floor," she said. "I took a play out of your handbook after that IED almost killed us."

Eamon jogged to her SUV, and after locating the duffle bag, he pulled on a hoodie and a pair of sneakers. Bel had learned the importance of carrying changes of clothes for them after his entire back had been blown off on the Darling Estate. Her foresight proved wise. She couldn't do this walk alone, but he was right. He couldn't emerge from a blizzard and enter the station half-naked.

"Breathe one word of the wolf, and you'll have to answer to me," Eamon whispered to the actor as they pulled the still listless Rollo and the terrified Draven out of the squad car. "Your testimony will forget what you witnessed earlier. Rollo tried to kill you to exact revenge on you for his grandmother, but if you so much as think of revealing the truth, I'll come for you."

Draven didn't speak. He merely leaned as far away from Eamon as his handcuffs allowed. He'd made a deal, which meant he knew that powers beyond humanity dwelled in this world, and it seemed he understood Eamon was not a welcomed enemy. He kept his mouth shut, and as the foursome strode through the front doors, an oppressive heaviness descended upon them, infecting all trapped within the walls of the Bajka Police Department.

Autopsy Report

CERBERUS

PROD.NO.
SCENE   TAKE   SOUND
DIRECTOR
CAMERAMAN   EXT.   INT.

CINEMA TICKET ADMIT ONE 9891102
CINEMA TICKET ADMIT ONE 9891102

Chapter Twenty Five

"She was all I had," Rollo said, his hands chained before him, and it baffled Bel how a man shrunken by such defeat had been a wolf only hours before. "She was the only person in this world who loved me, and they killed her. For six years, she had no peace. Now she does... almost. I came so close, but I failed her in the end."

The interview room fell quiet as Bel and Griffin stared across the table at their friend. Ethan Rollo had confessed to everything, and while he didn't explicitly mention the deal or his nature, the sheriff had enough sense to understand what filled in the blanks of this story, especially since Eamon was involved. Rollo started at the beginning, intentionally speaking in code so only Bel understood his full meaning. He told a tale of an orphan raised by his grandmother, who eventually joined the crew of a little known show named Aesop's Files. As a werewolf, he didn't care that the production was terrible. It was about police officers and supernaturals, and as a boy, he'd always dreamed of joining the force. His grandmother had encouraged his dream, and Aesop's Files felt like destiny until five selfish human beings slaughtered an innocent woman to secure a contract with a devil. Rollo's wolf genes had come from his mother's side of the family, meaning his grandmother was ordinary. Her frailty couldn't fight back, and she'd bled to death alone in the snow. Rollo uncovered the guilty. He scented their sold souls on her corpse, but it didn't matter. No matter how hard he tried, the deal prevented justice from reaching her.

"I'll sign whatever you need me to. Just promise me that my grandmother finds peace," Rollo said.

"We know her name," Griffin said. "She's no longer a Jane Doe. Her murder is no longer a cold case."

"Thank you," Rollo said, and the trio fell silent again. This moment. The arrests, the confessions, the end of the questions normally brought the station relief, but instead, Bel felt hollow, her soul dug out and scraped until it stood empty and sick.

"One thing I can't figure out," the sheriff said. "The blood. How did you walk away through white snow without leaving cast off or drops?"

"The protective suits we use," Rollo answered. "I put them on... after. They trapped any evidence against my skin, and the white let me disappear into the snow." His eyes flicked to Bel as if to confirm she understood. She did. The wolf killed, and then the naked man slipped inside the suit to vanish. The melting snow would've easily cleansed his hands as could her neighbor's sheets before the blood overtook the scene to hide anything he might have left behind.

"Right...I'll get the paperwork started," Griffin said, and without another word, he fled the room. He was a stoic man, a proud and honorable sheriff of undeniable strength, and Bel hated seeing him like this. She wanted to reach across the table and slap Rollo for harming the people she loved. For hurting Griffin... for breaking Violet's heart. Her friend didn't know yet, but when she found out? Bel ached for her already.

"Why Violet?" she asked as she stood. "Why involve her if

this was always the outcome? Did you need to drag her into your sick game?"

"I didn't do that on purpose," Rollo's voice broke. "I... your Dhampir would understand. We aren't good men, but some women break us. We can't resist them even though we're dangerous. Mr. Stone is a monster far worse than me, yet he can't stay away from you."

"How come Eamon never scented you?"

"There were others in town—"

"I know," she interrupted. "But we both know a Dhampir isn't so easily tricked. I can't remember you two ever being in the same room, but you've worked with me for a few months. He scented you once during the Matchstick Girl case, but that's it."

"I was careful to avoid him," he said. "Also, the prolonged exposure helped him acclimate to me, but Ewan hid me."

"Ewan helped you?" She couldn't have heard him right. After all Eamon had done for Ewan, he turned around a protected a murderer.

"He never knew," Rollo explained. "I realized he was a shifter as soon as I detected him on Olivia, but it was who you smelled like that concerned me. I knew I needed to hide from your Mr. Stone, and much like his presence protects us, I used Ewan to cover my scent. You went on vacation immediately after I was hired, and Mr. Stone is fairly reclusive. I kept my distance from his property immediately surrounding the mansion, and for those two weeks you were gone, I learned Ewan's schedule. I stopped by Lumen's Customs to visit Violet when he wasn't around, and I always found an excuse to slip into his shop. His work rags are covered in his scent, and by wiping them on my clothes, it latched onto me. So every time your Dhampir smelled me, he also smelled his friend."

"And he disregarded any anomalies because he assumed it was the bear."

"That day at the freezer was endless. Ewan's scent probably

faded from my clothes. Did you know he runs through our woods in his bear form? His presence is strongest when he shifts, so all I have to do is walk through his tracks to spread his odor onto my shoes. It masks my wolf."

"You used him," Bel felt sick at the confession. "Is that why you went for Violet? Because she could get you easy access to the bear?"

"No... I swear it. I didn't mean to fall for your friend, and I'm sorry for the pain this will cause her. I visit Lumen's Customs with an ulterior motive, but never her. I don't regret my actions, but I regret they harmed her. Please tell her she was honest. I didn't use her to fit in. I just couldn't stay away."

"You should have." Bel grabbed the door handle, tears threatening her eyes. Rollo's confession almost made it worse. It would be easy for Violet to hate a man who used her, but to be betrayed by genuine feelings...?

"I know," he said. "I'm glad my grandmother's murderers are dead, but I am truly sorry for Violet. She is special."

"She is." Bel swiped at her damp cheeks before opening the door. "One more thing." She sealed herself back inside the interview room. "Do you know if Orion Chayce's accident killed that lighting tech? Or was he just the scapegoat?"

"I told the police my grandmother's name multiple times, yet she remained Jane Doe," he said. "The deal allows no harm to come to Aesop's Files."

"You murdered four of her crew members."

"I'm a wolf. My power is greater than most, and I didn't kill them in ways that would shut down production. I found the loophole. The deal had his crime drama, and I had my vengeance."

"So, Chayce didn't kill that tech. He just took the fall, and it's why he kept quiet in prison. He knew, didn't he? There's no fighting black magic."

"Only those that were there that day remember the truth, and half of them are dead now. But as long as Draven lives, the deal owns the show. Men like Chayce mean nothing to him."

"But if you killed Draven, the deal would still be free to strike another," she said.

"True, but he'd have to find someone willing to pay the price. She was my grandmother, so the five didn't love her, but they still had to bloody their own hands. Not every fame hunter is comfortable with murder, but it doesn't matter. Draven lives. His deal is intact. Aesop's Files will continue to destroy lives."

"We know the truth. We can stop him now."

"You can't, and you won't." Rollo sagged lower in his chair, his massive size a child as he shrank in on himself. "You should've let me kill Draven and end this."

"Maybe I should have." Bel twisted the handle. "And I might have if your animal dragged them deep into the woods where we'd never find them. But you didn't do that. You had to antagonize me, so this is the ending we get." She shut the door, her heart unable to endure any more of this conversation, and she left the deputy behind in search of the only person who could undo the knot in her chest.

"He confessed to everything." She leaned against her desk, the fight draining from her muscles as she gazed down at Eamon. He looked unnaturally massive sitting in her chair, and exhaustion begged her to curl up in his lap and forget the past hours.

"He didn't even wait for a lawyer," she said, crossing her arms over her chest to stop herself from reaching for his comfort. The station was unusually busy since half of the deputies had gotten stuck there overnight, she and Eamon included. After they arrived with Rollo and Draven in custody, the already violent blizzard took a turn for the worse. Not even Eamon's skills could combat the snow, their vehicles buried as the town's street plows fought a losing battle. Griffin had rushed to the station after the accident when he realized Bel was missing. Hours later, she'd returned covered in blood, one of their own officers in tow, and everyone understood the pain the next few days would inflict. Beau Draven clammed up after they processed him, refusing to speak until his lawyer arrived, but with the storm raging outside, he was confined to the holding cell until the roads cleared. Ethan Rollo, on the other hand, didn't care to escape his fate.

"Draven isn't talking, but I expected that," she continued. "But Rollo claims he has evidence that'll prove Rossa, Roja, Rot, Rouge, and Reds are guilty of murder. He tried taking it to the police six years ago, but they ignored him."

"That would've been the deal's doing," Eamon said.

"Luckily, someone dangerous protects this town." Bel cupped his cheek. "Hopefully, whatever Rollo has will give us enough to put Draven away."

"Let's hope." He peeled her hand off his face and folded it into his fist. "I'm assuming the wolf wasn't mentioned."

"No, but Griffin knows we're hiding something. He's smart, though. He'll stick to the narrative we lay out for him."

"So, the murder weapon?"

"Lost in the snow?"

"With the feet that fell last night, no one's driving into the woods anytime soon," Eamon said. "I'll have time to drop *'proof'* up there."

"Thank you."

"It's no problem."

"How do you feel?" She gripped his jaw and tilted his gaze up so she could study his eyes.

"Horrible for you."

"That's not what I meant."

"Physically, I'm great, and the temporary high has worn off."

"Good." Bel released his chin and lifted her fingers to her lips, kissing them before pressing them to his mouth. "I love you, you know that? I realize you're hard to kill, but the fear I felt when he ripped into you. I understand what you meant when you said you're always afraid because of me. You are at the top of the food chain, but what happens when you meet your match?"

"Rollo was not my match." Eamon stood up, his frame looming over her, and clearly not caring that a station full of witnesses swarmed about them, he cupped her face. "I made you a promise. I'm staying by your side until one of us dies, and it's going to take a lot more than a wolf to rip me from you."

"Promise?"

"I swear it." He stared at her lips as if he was debating risking it all, but then he pulled away and sank back into her office chair. "How are you holding up?"

"I hope the snow never stops," she said as she glanced at the pale morning light seeping through the frosted windows. "Violet thinks Rollo couldn't make it to her apartment because of the weather, but when the storm slows and the streets clear, I'll have to confess that I let her date a serial killer. I lost Olivia because of Ewan's lies. How many friends is the truth going to cost me?"

It took most of the afternoon to dig Bajka out from below the heavy snow, and as soon as the roads were manageable, Griffin sent Bel and Eamon home. She'd been on the clock for over twenty-four hours, and while she'd changed clothes, her bloody skin had only seen a sink for a shower. She hadn't slept except for the few hours stolen on Griffin's couch, and no one had eaten anything other than vending machine snacks. Exhaustion filled the station, and Griffin wanted everyone to rest while Bajka's focus remained on the storm. The town was emerging from their shelters, and with the temporary disruption to the cell service, news of Rollo and Draven's arrests had yet to spread. For now, Bajka was a sleepy winter wonderland, but it was only a matter of time before it woke to a nightmare. When that happened, Griffin needed all hands on deck, Eamon included. He didn't know the truth about Rollo, but Bel had chased the deputy into the woods alone and emerged with Eamon at her side. He was smart enough to understand what that meant. So Bel and Eamon raced to the Reale Estate to rescue the abandoned Cerberus. Too exhausted to even speak, they cared for the animal before showering and eating cold leftovers. Then they ceased to exist until their early morning alarm dragged them back to the land of the living twelve hours later.

"Thanks for helping," Griffin said when Eamon climbed out of Bel's SUV. The sheriff had been waiting for them outside the station. "I spoke to the district attorney, and we're moving Rollo to a more secure pre-trial detention jail in about an hour. We don't want such a high-profile murder suspect staying in our cells, and with news of Draven's arrest spreading after the bail hearing, I'm worried about our station's safety. I realize it's unorthodox, but it might be safer for all involved if you're present."

"I agree," Eamon said.

"That was fast," Bel said. "When did all this happen?"

"First thing this morning," Griffin answered. "A case involving an actor as famous as Draven is bound to be expedited. I don't like how rushed it is, but my hands are tied. The legal system favors those with big names and even bigger wallets."

"Will Draven make bail?" Bel asked.

"Undoubtedly," Griffin said.

"Even with the murder charges?"

"The public is already spinning things his way," he said. "His fans believe Rollo's accusations are a smear campaign. Rollo claims he has evidence, but the police didn't listen to him six years ago. I have little hope it'll convince them this time around." Griffin escorted the couple through the station's doors. "So, Mr. Stone, if you don't mind staying until Rollo and Draven depart our custody, I'd appreciate it. Just keep a low profile unless we need you."

Evidence of a Folktale

But they thankfully didn't need Eamon's intervention. An hour later, a transport arrived to remove Officer Ethan Rollo from Bajka's town limits. He did not resist as they escorted him from his holding cell to the van. He did not speak. He simply held his head high, purposefully ignoring Eamon as he strode past, and the only words he uttered were his final wishes whispered into Bel's ear as they loaded him into the vehicle.

"Tell her I'm sorry."

"I'll try," Bel promised. "For her sake, not yours."

And then the doors slammed shut around him to an orchestra of reporters and appalled spectators. The air was too cold for such heated voices. It burned her skin and grated through her skull. One of their own had fallen from grace, but monsters bred monsters. He hadn't been born a murderer. This show had made him one.

Bel crossed her arms over her chest as she watched the transport pull away from the station, but as soon as its size rolled out of her view, a lone figure in black consumed her vision. For a moment, the two women stared at each other, and then the younger crept forward, her normal designer stilettos replaced by flats Bel never thought she'd see grace her friend's feet.

"It's true." Violet's voice faltered. "It was him. He killed all those people."

Bel remained silent because what could she say? All words felt inadequate.

"How can you be sure?" Violet asked. "It could be a mistake, right? Just a misunderstanding?"

"Violet…" Bel gripped her slender shoulders.

"But it could be?"

"No." Tears spilled from Bel's eyes, the cold freezing them to her cheeks with icy bites. "There's no mistake."

"How… I don't…" Violet started crying, and to Bel's immense relief, she didn't pull away. Instead, she collapsed against her chest for all the reporters to see, so Bel twisted until

409

she blocked her friend from the cameras' view. She shielded Violet's betrayal from the crowd as she ushered her inside, noticing that Jerry tried his best to keep the reporters from violating their privacy, but it was already too late. Someone would uncover why Violet was so upset, and then they would plaster her friend's name across the news for the entire nation to mock.

It was rare, but sometimes Bel hated this job. This moment was one of them.

"Everything okay?" Eamon asked when a miserable Bel finally returned from comforting Violet, but she didn't answer him. She didn't even stop walking until she collided with his chest, and he instinctively wrapped his arms around her.

"Violet's crushed," she whispered into his shirt. "They didn't date long, but still... to learn you were with a murderer."

"Do you ever feel that way about me?" he asked. "Because I'm far worse than Rollo. He killed four. I've killed thousands."

"Does it make me a bad person if I say no?" Bel pulled away from his chest. "You were brought into this world to end lives, but you consciously choose to defy your nature. Now, if you were murdering people while I slept next to you, that would be different. I could never forgive you if I learned you were the serial killer I was hunting."

"No, that doesn't make you a bad person, and I'd never put you in the position Rollo placed Violet in. Come on." He tucked her hair behind her ear before ushering her toward the break-room. "Let's get you some coffee to warm you up."

They fell silent as they stood side by side at the counter, stirring the cream and sugar into their drinks. Griffin had requested Eamon's presence because he feared Rollo's reaction, but it wasn't Rollo who needed him. It was Bel, and she slipped a hand

Evidence of a Folktale

against his back. She caught him smile out of the corner of his eyes, but before the grin could fully spread across his lips, his entire body stiffened, his muscles coiling below her palm.

"What?" She raised her eyebrows at him, but Eamon silently peeled her hand off his back and led her out of the breakroom in time to catch Beau Draven and his lawyer exiting the cells.

"He made bail." Bel's voice stuck in her throat when she realized who the lawyer was, and she understood why Eamon gripped her fingers so fiercely. "The deal," she whispered, and as if the suited man heard her hushed words from across the station, his attention snapped to her. For a fraction of a second, he glared at her with the air of a victor, but then his gaze shifted to the wall of muscle protecting her. His movements faltered as he recognized a far more powerful predator stalked his client's exit, and then with rushed footsteps, he and Beau Draven vanished into the world.

"Draven won't go down for the murder of Rollo's grandmother, will he?" Bel whispered, Eamon's power so intense that she couldn't find her voice until the deal was long gone.

"If his lawyer is the deal, then no, Draven won't pay for his crimes," Eamon said. "A single thread of their covenant remains, and as long as black magic has a foothold within the show, he won't let harm come to the production."

"It's an endless cycle. A deal begets death begets fame so inexplicable that not even a serial killer can unravel it. He won't stop, will he?"

"No, he'll never stop."

"I should've let Rollo kill Draven," Bel muttered.

"Hey." Eamon tugged her hand until she looked up at him. "Don't do that. You stopped a murder, and no matter how complicated the morality of this situation gets, you have a compass, and you followed it."

"It's just the deal's going to return to his death collecting, and Draven will continue to star in this show, and the world will love

411

him for playing a hero when he's the worst of us." She pulled free from his grip and returned to their forgotten coffee.

"You can't fix everything."

"But I want to." She collapsed forward, capturing her face in her hands. "And having you on my side makes me believe I can."

"If only more people were like you." Eamon rubbed her back as he kissed her head. "But as you often remind me, we aren't God. We can only do so much." He shifted to kiss her neck as a reminder. "And black magic is an art best avoided."

"I know."

"Detective…?"

"I know, I know." She stood up, her stubborn streak struggling not to argue with him, even though he was right.

"I love you, that's all, and I don't need any more black magic trying to steal you from me." He scanned the station, and confident that no one was watching, he slapped her lovingly on the backside. "And on that note, you don't need me here anymore, so I'll go hang out with your dog. After last night, I feel terrible leaving him alone."

"Me too. His face when we left this morning made me want to cry." She rubbed his chest, not ready for him to leave. The storm explained his presence, but if he kept hanging around, officers might ask questions neither she nor Griffin cared to answer. "But with how much time you spend with him compared to me, you'll have to stop calling him my dog."

"No. He's your dog." Eamon kissed her cheek before pulling out his phone to order a cab. "He won't become my dog until you both live with me."

"So, we're back on that topic?" Bel smiled, her heart lighter at the return of his favorite request.

"Yes, we are." He winked at her as he strode through the station. "And just remember, all you gotta do to shut me up is agree."

Evidence of a Folktale

"I CAN'T BELIEVE it was Rollo," Olivia said as she sank into her desk's chair. She'd finally returned to Bajka, conveniently after Bel had almost finished the daunting stack of paperwork. "I worked alongside him for months... I don't understand. Poor Violet. Have you talked to her?"

"I have." Bel glanced up from her work to study her partner. The blonde hair. The soft features. The southern accent spoken in a sweet voice. She loved her friend, and even if Olivia only ever offered her professional comradery, she'd accept it.

"How was she?" Olivia asked. "Should I stop by after work to be with her?"

"That's a good..." Bel's voice stuck in her throat when she caught sight of Griffin over Olivia's shoulder. He was on the phone, but his movements warned something was wrong.

"What?" Olivia followed her line of sight, and as if controlled by one mind, the detectives pushed free of their chairs and rushed into the sheriff's office.

"What happened?" Bel asked when their boss slammed the phone back into its cradle.

"Rollo's transport never arrived," he said, collapsing into his chair with disbelief painted across his features. "They lost contact with the drivers a few hours ago, and they just called to explain why. There was a crash."

"Oh god." Olivia's fingers flew to her lips to catch her surprise. "The roads are still pretty bad. It's why it took me so long to drive home. Is that what happened?"

"They aren't sure," Griffin answered. "They found the vehicle upside down. The disturbance at the scene suggests it rolled through the snow before hitting the trees."

"The officers?" Bel asked.

"Alive. They were transported to the hospital, but they were mostly bruised. Seems the damage was predominantly contained to the rear."

"Thank goodness," Olivia said.

"And Rollo?" Bel asked what they were all thinking.

"Gone," Griffin said. "The back half of the van was ripped apart in the crash, and there's no sign of him or his body. They're organizing a manhunt, but as of right now, they have no leads."

"Oh my god." Olivia crossed the floor and sank to their boss' couch. "He's on foot, and it's freezing. I would guess he's injured as well, so he can't have gone far."

"No." Griffin pinned Bel with his gaze as if to tell her he suspected the next words to fall from his lips were a lie. "No, he couldn't have."

"KITCHEN," Eamon called as she opened the front door, and a second later, seventy pounds of black slid across the floor to plow into her shins. Bel shed her snowy boots and oversized coat and then scooped her squirming pitbull into a hug before carrying him toward Eamon's voice.

"I didn't have it in me to cook," he said, kissing her cheek hello only to get a face full of dog slobber as Cerberus joined in. "So, I ordered pizza."

"Pizza sounds perfect." Bel placed her heavy best friend down on the floor, but when she stood back up, a wary Eamon greeted her.

"What happened?" he asked, clearly reading the emotions on her face.

"Rollo's transport crashed. He's missing." She grabbed one of the complementary paper plates from the pizzeria and loaded it with a few slices as she recounted her day. "They're blaming the accident on the icy roads, but I don't buy it for a second, especially since the officers escaped with only bruises," she said, taking a bite of the still-steaming Margherita slice. "Rollo did this. He caused the crash."

"I'd bet money on it." Eamon filled his plate with the meat lover's slices and then stacked the boxes before grabbing a bottle of wine and two glasses in his fist. "Come on." He nudged her into the living room, and he set the food and alcohol on the coffee table before the roaring fire.

"It's dark now, but they crashed during the day," Bel said as she curled up on the luxurious couch, and realizing he wouldn't get any salty pizza no matter how big his puppy eyes got, Cerberus shoved his face into his toy box and started throwing stuffed animals around the floor. "I thought werewolves needed the moon to shift."

"Just like I can't walk into a church or step into the sunlight or see my reflection in a mirror." Eamon grabbed her legs and pulled them onto his lap before opening the wine. "It's part of the lore they spread to protect themselves, much like the myths my kind perpetuates to hide our truth. If a Dhampir can't set foot inside a church, then humans have no need to fear those sitting beside them."

"And if werewolves only shift below the moon, anyone you meet midday is safe."

"Exactly." He handed her the wine and then turned on the news for soft background noise.

"So Rollo shifted once he escaped your reach and crashed the van." Bel curled closer to Eamon, trapping him below her legs with the sole purpose of watching his black eyes burn. After today's aggravation, this was exactly what she needed. Pizza, wine, a roaring fire, a comically playing dog, and her best friend and confidant. "I don't know how to feel about this," she continued. "He murdered people... brutally. He stripped them down and forced them to run naked save for a hooded cloak through the snow. But he was also a man so broken by his grandmother's death that he felt he had no choice when the legal system failed him. I want his actions to disgust me, but then I picture my dad in the woods because someone made a devil's deal for something as stupid as fame. I think about finding Briar gutted and frozen, and I fear I wouldn't be any better. If I tried over and over again to convince the police, only for them to laugh in my face, what would I do? Would I move on, or would I hunt the guilty down myself?"

"Don't drive yourself crazy thinking like that." Eamon ran a hand over her hair. "Your family isn't dead, and Rollo isn't you."

"I know what you'd do," she said. "You would hunt down their murderers and make sure nothing was left to find."

"Yes, but that's the key difference. You wouldn't find anything if I was avenging your family, therefore, there'd be no crime. No body? No problem. But compared to the things I've done, vigilante justice would be almost heroic."

"If he hadn't shoved the deaths in our face, we would've never known he was the killer. He had the power to drag them deep into the wilderness, and if he'd chosen to kill close to home, we might have classified them as animal attacks, just like with Ewan's victim. He could've gotten away with it."

"But he didn't want to get away with it. He wanted the world to acknowledge what those five did. He wanted to prove their guilt."

"Will that happen, though?" she asked. "If the deal is their lawyer, he'll spin this Draven's way."

"But you know the truth." Eamon brushed his knuckles over her clavicle. "I know the truth. Griffin knows the truth. That's a good start."

"But not good enough for Rollo. He still escaped custody."

"Bars can't hold wolves," Eamon said. "You begged me not to kill him, so I didn't, but the only way to stop a creature like that is to kill it."

"We're never going to catch him, are we?"

"No, you're not. I guarantee you he's in his wolf form, and

the authorities aren't searching for an animal. My guess is he's headed north into the woods. You'll never find him. But I could."

"Yeah?"

"Yes, I could find him..." He paused, his head twitching as his hearing picked up something only his senses could detect. "In fact, I know where he's been. Tracking him from there wouldn't be hard."

Bel stiffened, her eyes scanning the dark windows. Was he here? Had Rollo returned to exact revenge on her for disrupting his plans? But then Eamon leaned forward and snagged the remote off the coffee table, increasing the news to a volume she could hear.

"Tragedy has struck Aesop's Files yet again, and fans worldwide mourn the sudden and unexpected death of the show's lead actor Beau Draven," the evening reporter said, and Bel sat to attention so fast that she choked on her pizza, gagging and coughing until Eamon pounded relief into her back.

"A series of gruesome murders plagued the crew of the beloved TV show while they filmed on location this winter," the reporter continued, as if Bel wasn't actively fighting for her life. "The man allegedly responsible for the killings was taken into custody during the blizzard two days ago, and actor Beau Draven was arrested alongside him. Details haven't been released to the public yet, but Draven's lawyer issued a statement calling the allegations outrageously false and malicious. Mr. Draven was released on bail this morning, but his car was found crashed on the side of the road early this evening." The woman mentioned a two-lane divided highway that Bel was unfamiliar with, and she wondered what the pair was doing so far off course. She returned to New York City often to visit her family, and if Draven was aiming for the Big Apple, he shouldn't have ended up in the snow miles away from the route any GPS would recommend.

"Beau Draven and his lawyer were pronounced dead on the scene," the reporter's voice said as images of the crash displayed across the screen, and Bel recoiled against Eamon at the sight. The mangled metal. The shattered glass. The annihilated trees and obliterated snow. The news didn't need to tell their audience that the occupants of that expensive vehicle were killed upon impact. No human could survive violence like that, and while the deal possessed magic, his body was brittle, just like Alcina Magus' was when Eamon beat her to death to save Bel.

"The authorities have ruled the crash an accident," the reporter said, yanking Bel back to the present. "With the increasingly bad weather plaguing the tri-state area, emergency services have struggled to keep up with the street cleaning demands. The police believe the car hit a stretch of black ice, which caused the driver to lose control. The studio has yet to release a statement about the actor's passing, but the cast and crew of Aesop's Files have taken to social media to express their condolences to the Draven family."

"There wasn't any ice, was there?" Bel asked as the reporter transitioned to the next segment of the nightly news. "It was Rollo. He got his fifth kill."

"That car hit those trees with a massive amount of force," Eamon said. "It didn't end up there by accident. And why were they in the middle of nowhere? I drive to the city often, and I've never ended up there."

"Rollo's wolf probably corralled them somewhere lonely," Bel said. "He didn't want any witnesses. Are werewolves fast?"

"Based on his wolf's size, he's faster than me," Eamon said. "Not stronger, but I would assume faster."

"Would you even be able to catch him?" Bel leaned over and poured herself another glass of wine because one wouldn't be enough after that news report.

"Come, come, Detective. Have a little faith."

"So, where do you think he's going?" She rested her head against his chest. "Will he turn himself in now that his mission is complete, or will he travel as a wolf to cross the border?"

Evidence of a Folktale

"If it were me, I'd flee north. Of course, he might surprise us by turning himself in, but my guess is he'll disappear. So my question is, do I go after him?"

"How long would it take to find him?"

"I can't say. Depends on how good he is at covering his tracks from people like me."

"But you'd be gone for a few days?"

"At least."

"Do you think he'll ever kill again?"

"No. He wanted justice, and his mission is complete."

"And prison bars won't hold a wolf?"

"Not unless he allows it."

"So you'd have to kill him to stop him?"

"Is that what you want?" Eamon twisted below her so he could meet her gaze. "It's up to you. Do you want me to bring him back, or do you want me to kill him?"

"Neither..." Bel paused to let her decision fully sink in. "Beau Draven and the deal died because their car hit the ice." She stared at Eamon with meaning, and understanding flooded his death-black eyes. "It was a tragic accident that's in no way connected to Rollo's prisoner transport. The accidents occurred hundreds of miles from each other. The freezing temperatures and poorly plowed road caused both crashes, and losing track of Deputy Ethan Rollo has nothing to do with me. I did my part. I arrested a murderer. Both of them. I solved the case, and I'll make sure the world knows of their guilt. But as for tonight? There's no need to leave this house because of reckless driving in inclement weather."

She fell silent, but she didn't need words to hear Eamon's question. His eyes held his meaning, and she read his concern as if it were printed letters on a page. He wanted to confirm this was a path she was truly comfortable with.

"I need to be done." She placed her wine on the coffee table and pressed her hands against his solid chest. "I did my job, and judge me all you want, but Draven deserved what he got. I know that isn't something a detective should say, but I can't feel sympathy for men who strike deals with devils. Black magic made you almost kill me in New York. Another recipient of a deal dragged me into the mountains and hunted me through the snow. You know Blaubart threatened to carve apart my face while I was still conscious? He wanted to make me too hideous for you to love."

Eamon flinched as if her confession had slapped him across the face. She'd never divulged that part of her kidnapping, and it was strange to see an alpha predator riddled with pain.

"Maybe it makes me a horrible person, but I cannot forgive men like that." She slid her hands up his chest to cup his jaw, forcing him to meet her gaze.

"You aren't horrible," he whispered. "Cop or not, some people don't deserve mercy."

"And I'm tired. I'm cold. I'm always cold, and I can't take it anymore." She pulled him to her mouth and pressed a kiss to his lips to stop herself from crying. "I miss you. Blaubart kept telling me he'd change my face so that not even you'd recognize me. Running down that mountain, I never expected to see you again, and then this god-forsaken case blew through town to disrupt our lives so thoroughly that we didn't even see each other on Valentine's Day."

"I screwed up our first Christmas, so it killed me that I couldn't make it up to you for our first Valentine's."

"Me too." She kissed him again, this one lingering as if to make up for their stolen date. "So, don't disappear into the wilderness. Stay here and keep me and Cerberus warm. Let's celebrate our missed Valentines. I'm talking a new dress and heels, a five-star restaurant, and a pet-friendly hotel that offers human and doggy room service."

"Hold on." Eamon grabbed her biceps and yanked her off

him with mock concern. "Did you just ask me to buy you expensive clothes?"

"And shoes." She winked as he pressed a palm to her forehead to check for a fever.

"Can I add jewelry?" he asked, his mouth twitching upward in an excited smile.

"Why not... but no rings." She jabbed a finger into his chest. "Not yet, at least. I'll accept simple diamond earrings if you want to splurge, though."

"I'll take it." Eamon lunged for her, wrapping her in his arms as he collapsed to the couch. "Tell me when you have a weekend off, and I'll plan everything."

"I can't—uff," Bel squealed as Cerberus joined in, his pink tongue lathering both of their faces in drool. "I can't wait."

Eamon pulled the pitbull off the floor and into their cuddle pile. "It seems Baby Beast can't either."

Autopsy Report

CERBERUS

PROD.NO. TAKE SOUND
SCENE

DIRECTOR
CAMERAMAN EXT. INT.

CINEMA TICKET 9891102 ADMIT ONE
CINEMA TICKET 9891102 ADMIT ONE

Chapter Twenty Six

"AFTER THE MURDER OF FOUR CREW MEMBERS, AND A CAR accident that killed the lead actor Beau Draven, the studio has announced that this will be Aesop's Files final season," the reporter said, and Bel wiped her hands as she abandoned her half-assembled sandwich to watch the television. An overwhelming week had passed since the accidents, and while she had the day off, Eamon had requested she stay at her cabin. He had a massive amount of work to catch up on, and the mansion renovations he'd scheduled for this weekend came with loud noises and noxious chemicals. He didn't want her or Cerberus near the fumes, but Bel didn't mind. She hadn't left his house in days, and she had to return home sometimes to perpetuate her stance on not living together yet.

"By combining the already filmed footage with re-writes to give fans a satisfactory conclusion, Aesop's Files will finish the season early," the reporter continued. "Viewers worldwide have mixed responses about the series' finale, though. Some are devastated the show is ending, while others feel the cancellation is necessary considering the new murder allegations. Recent evidence pertaining to a six-year-old cold case has surfaced that police confirm implicates Gwen Rossa, Ellery Roja, Alistair Rot, Warren Rouge, and Beau Draven, birth name Reds, as the perpetrators of the homicide."

Bel sagged against the kitchen counter with an exhale. She'd done it. She kept her promise. A letter had arrived for her a few days after Rollo vanished. It provided no name or return address, but she knew who'd sent it. It held simple directions, but what she recovered after following the instructions was anything but. All the evidence Ethan Rollo promised found its way into her hands, and she was ruthless with it, leaving such a bad taste in the studio's mouth that they abandoned all ideas of suing Bajka for negligence. After six long years, Grandma Rollo had her justice. Her tombstone finally bore her name.

"Fans shouldn't be disappointed, though," the reporter continued. "The studio has announced a spin-off starring Aesop's Files leading lady, Taron Monroe. Sources close to the actress have confirmed that this series will follow Miss Monroe's character as she leaves town for a detective position in a new precinct plagued by the paranormal."

Bel smiled at the announcement and snatched her phone off the counter, selecting Taron's number before typing a text message.

BEL

Congrats on the new show. I just saw the news.

She placed her phone down and grabbed a knife to spread the mustard, but her cell vibrated before she could even grab the bottle.

TARON

Oh my god, thank you so much! I just wish winning a lead didn't arrive on the back of a cold case, four murders, and a fatal car accident.

Evidence of a Folktale

> I understand, but you'll be fantastic. I might actually watch this one.

Girlllllll........... you better!

When you have time off, I'll fly you out to consult.

> Sounds fun. Can't wait.

Me either. Aesop's Files was a great opportunity, but the obsession always felt wrong. I guess now we know why, so I'm excited to embark on something new and honest.

> Seriously, congratulations.

Thanks, girl. Welcome to my Mon-hoes!

Bel rolled her eyes.

Did you just roll your eyes?

> How did you guess?

I shadowed you, remember? I roll my eyes when I'm playing a serious cop now, too.

> Maybe you don't need me to consult.

Nonsense! Anyway, g2g. About to run into a meeting. Talk soon!

Bel picked up the mustard bottle for a second time, only to be interrupted yet again by a knock at the front door.

"Dad?" She gawked at the sight of her father standing unex-

425

pectedly on the other side, but before she could hug him, Cerberus barreled between her legs and almost took him out.

"Hey, baby boy." Reese scratched the dog as he regained his footing and then hugged his daughter. "Hi, baby girl."

"Is everything okay?" Bel squeezed him tight. "Why are you here?"

"I called Eamon to ask if you were free," he said. "I should've called you, but I wasn't sure if you were working, so I didn't want to disrupt you. He said you were home, so I jumped in the car."

"But you're okay, right?" She pulled him inside, hating how her heart rate spiked at seeing him so unexpectedly. Was he sick? Had something happened?

"I'm fine." He brushed a thumb over her cheek. "Starving, but totally fine."

"My sisters?"

"Everyone is healthy and happy. And before you ask, Eamon sounded great when I called earlier. Although there was a lot of banging and grunting going on."

"He's renovating the mansion himself. It's why I'm home. He's using chemicals that he doesn't want me breathing in."

"That's considerate."

"I was just making lunch," she said, returning to the cutting board. "Want a sandwich?"

"Sure, sweetheart. Thanks."

"So, what's up?" Bel asked, grabbing two more slices of bread and another plate.

"I've been thinking a lot about what you said on Christmas, and I've finally reached a decision. But this isn't a phone conversation. I needed to see your face."

"So you want to know everything?" she asked over her shoulder.

"No, sweetheart. I don't," he answered. "It would only make me fear for your life more than I already do, and I want to trust that you're okay. That Eamon is treating you right, and he's truly your protector, not your abuser."

"You have no idea how protective of me he is."

"That's why I'm here. I want to know… within reason," Reese said. "I want to learn enough so you don't need to hide your life from your own father, but that's all. Because if you change my perception of reality, I'd never let you out of my sight again. I'd be terrified to let you live on your own, but that isn't fair. Despite all your hardships and terrors, you seem happy living here with Eamon. I just want to make sure your happiness is coming from a healthy and honest place. Then I'll go home."

"I'm happy you're here." Bel slid the plates onto the table and took her father's hand as she sat beside him. "Because I hate hiding things from you. I never have, and I don't wish to start now. I want you to understand me, and not just because my life is unusual, but because I found someone incredible. I need you to love him like I do." She started crying, but these tears were pure happiness. "Because I love him so much, Dad, and when I tell you everything he's done for me, you'll love him too."

"Hey, thanks for coming," Eamon said as Violet and Ewan walked into his disaster of a house. This crumbling section at the rear of his home was the most daunting mess he had to tackle, and he had special plans for this rubble.

"Where's Olivia?" he asked when he noticed the third member he'd invited was missing.

"She still wants nothing to do with me," Ewan said, his normal confidence absent as he mentioned his ex-girlfriend.

"Bel and Olivia are back on amicable working terms, but I don't think Olivia cares to rekindle their friendship," Violet said. "I hope that changes, but whatever happened between all of you upset Olivia. At least she isn't ignoring Bel anymore."

"Thank goodness for that," Eamon said. "I mostly invited her as Bel's friend, but it's you two and Lumen's Customs that I need."

"Speaking of Bel, where is she?" Violet scanned the construction site as if she suddenly realized her friend was missing.

"Home," Eamon answered. "She's with her dad, so she'll be occupied for the weekend, which is why I invited you here today. I don't want her knowing."

"Okay?" The word escaped Violet's lips like a question.

"So, what's up?" Ewan asked.

"Isobel's birthday is this spring, and I have an idea." Eamon gestured to the filth behind him. "But I need help… a lot of very fast and secret help." He turned back to the girl in designer black and the flannel-wearing bear shifter. "So, what do you say? Will you help me?"

THANK YOU FOR READING EVIDENCE OF A FOLKTALE. BEL, EAMON, & CERBERUS WILL RETURN FOR ANOTHER FAIRYTALE INSPIRE CRIME IN *POSTMORTEM OF A POEM*. IF YOU ENJOYED THIS BOOK AND FEEL COMFORTABLE LEAVING A REVIEW, I WOULD GREATLY APPRECIATE IT. REVIEWS GO A LONG WAY IN HELPING AUTHORS LIKE ME.

SIGNUP FOR FOR MY MONTHLY NEWSLETTER TO RECEIVE WRITING UPDATES, A FREE COMPANION EBOOK TO THIS BOOK FILLED WITH EASTER EGGS & FUN FACTS I HID INSIDE THIS STORY, AND MY NOVELLA *'OF MOMS, MUTTS, & MURDER.'*

SUBSCRIBEPAGE.IO/NICOLESCARANONEWSLETTER

Also by Nicole Scarano

AUTOPSY OF A FAIRYTALE
MURDER MYSTERIES INSPIRED BY FAIRYTALES

Autopsy of a Fairytale

Forensics of a Fable

Kidnapping of a Myth

Criminology of a Character

Evidence of a Folktale

Postmortem of a Poem (Coming Fall 2025)

THE SCATTERED BONES
A DARK FANTASY ROMANCE

THE POMEGRANATE SERIES
A GENDER-SWAPPED HADES & PERSEPHONE REIMAGINING

Pomegranate

Pitchfork

Pandora

THE COMPETITION ARCHIVES
A HORROR DYSTOPIAN

There Are Only Four

There Was Only One

There Will Be None

WE ARE NOT BLOOD (APRIL 2025)
A FOUND FAMILY POST APOCALYPTIC

SEASON'S READINGS

HOLIDAY ROMANCES

*AS N.R. SCARANO

Wreck The Halls

X Marks the O's

Tryst or Treat

Happy Hunting (Coming Easter 2025)

Married & Bright

THE EXPANSE BETWEEN US

*AS N.R. SCARANO

AN ENEMIES TO LOVERS SCI-FI ROMANCE

A LOYAL BETRAYAL

*AS N.R. SCARANO

A CAMELOT REIMAGINING AGE GAP ROMANCE

About the Author

Nicole Scarano *The Mood Writer for the Mood Reader* is a Multi Genre Author who writes Romantic Crime Thrillers/Police Procedurals with twists, Fantasy romances, and Sci-Fi romances because it makes her brain happy. She doesn't like to box herself into one genre, but no matter the book, they all have action, true love, found family, a dog when she can fit it into the plot, swoon-worthy men & absolutely feral females. *She occasionally writes steamy fantasy & sci-fi romances as N.R. Scarano*

In her free time, Nicole is a dog mom to her rescued pitbull, a movie/tv show enthusiast, a film score lover, and sunshine obsessive. She loves to write outside, and she adores pole dancing fitness classes.

For more information & to sign up for her newsletter visit: nicolescarano.com

Made in United States
Orlando, FL
05 April 2025